Naira stared at herself.

The other-Naira stood at formal rest, hands clasped behind her back, studying Tarquin as if she thought she couldn't be seen. Love haunted those eyes. And regret, too.

This variant of herself had shorn her hair, and a network of scars crowned her skull. A fine tracery reminiscent of the scars that'd draped her body when they'd taken her pathways to make amarthite serum.

Naira's mouth dried out. That was no memory. No version of herself she'd ever seen. No moment sneaking up on her out of the recesses of her mind. Tarquin tugged gently on her hand. She scarcely noticed.

She wasn't slipping. Naira was perfectly aware of the world around her, and it was shock alone that narrowed her focus to that alternate version of herself.

The other-Naira had been watching Tarquin, and as he turned to her so did those impostor eyes. Something like desperation clawed through the phantom, and she lunged at the interior boundary of the core, reaching, mouth opened wide with a shout.

Praise for
the Devoured Worlds

"I know it's a cliché to say, 'You won't be able to put it down,' but that's exactly the effect *The Blighted Stars* has on you! Riveting adventure at a rocketing pace, with engaging characters thrown in for good measure!"

—Connie Willis, Hugo Award–winning author

"O'Keefe delivers a captivating exploration of identity in this smart, addictive space adventure full of intrigue, visceral danger, and deeply personal stakes. Come for the epic sci-fi action, stay for the charmingly broken characters just doing their best."

—J. S. Dewes, author of *The Last Watch*

"Full of deftly plotted twists and turns, *The Blighted Stars* is a body-hopping, zombie-popping, rock-licking thrill ride."

—Emily Skrutskie, author of *Bonds of Brass*

"*The Blighted Stars* is everything I want in a book: lots of action, lots of character, and lots of heart. Megan E. O'Keefe delights with every page, from her stunning action sequences set on alien planets to her exploration of the twisted pathways taken by the human heart. This is space opera for the ages, wrapped in complicated and delicious layers of family and loyalty and science and love and duty. I couldn't put it down!"

—Karen Osborne, author of *Architects of Memory*

"Emotional arcs and action sequences, vivid worldbuilding, and interesting explorations of body printing and corporate servitude provide an immersive story...O'Keefe's latest has the intrigue, surprises, and high stakes of her previous novels."   —*Library Journal* (starred review)

"*The Blighted Stars* yields enjoyable adventure full of romantic tension and alien mystery."   —*Wall Street Journal*

"O'Keefe is a master world builder, and *The Blighted Stars* has one of the most fascinating sci-fi concepts of the year....If future entries in O'Keefe's Devoured Worlds saga are as exciting as this book, sci-fi fans will be thanking their lucky stars for years to come."   —*BookPage*

"Thrilling, yearning, and paranoid. This book kept me up way too late!"
                —Max Gladstone, Hugo and Nebula Award–winning author

"Brimming with unconventional gender dynamics and shifting identities, *The Blighted Stars* is character-driven science fiction at its best—a taut novel with human questions at its heart."
                —E. J. Beaton, author of *The Councillor*

"Smart, incisive, and utterly gripping. Megan E. O'Keefe's masterful storytelling will draw you into a complex, brutal, yet hope-charged world, break your heart, and leave you begging for more."
                —Rowenna Miller, author of *The Fairy Bargains of Prospect Hill*

"A delightfully twisty space opera filled with unique worldbuilding and deft explorations of humanity, family, and power. Add in a dash of rebellion and a hint of romance, and I'm hooked—I can't wait for the next book!"   —Jessie Mihalik, author of *Hunt the Stars*

By Megan E. O'Keefe

THE DEVOURED WORLDS

The Blighted Stars

The Fractured Dark

The Bound Worlds

THE PROTECTORATE

Velocity Weapon

Chaos Vector

Catalyst Gate

The First Omega (novella)

THE BOUND WORLDS

BOOK THREE OF THE DEVOURED WORLDS

MEGAN E. O'KEEFE

orbit

orbitbooks.net

Copyright © 2024 by Megan E. O'Keefe
Excerpt copyright © 2024 by Megan E. O'Keefe
Excerpt from *These Burning Stars* copyright © 2023 by Bethany Jacobs

Cover design by Lauren Panepinto
Cover illustration by Jaime Jones
Cover copyright © 2024 by Hachette Book Group, Inc.
Author photograph by Joey Hewitt

Orbit
Hachette Book Group
1290 Avenue of the Americas
New York, NY 10104
orbitbooks.net

First Edition: May 2024
Simultaneously published in Great Britain by Orbit

Orbit is an imprint of Hachette Book Group.
The Orbit name and logo are registered trademarks of Little, Brown Book Group Limited.

The publisher is not responsible for websites (or their content) that are not owned by the publisher.

The Hachette Speakers Bureau provides a wide range of authors for speaking events. To find out more, go to hachettespeakersbureau.com or email HachetteSpeakers@hbgusa.com.

Orbit books may be purchased in bulk for business, educational, or promotional use. For information, please contact your local bookseller or the Hachette Book Group Special Markets Department at special.markets@hbgusa.com.

Library of Congress Cataloging-in-Publication Data
Names: O'Keefe, Megan E., 1985– author.
Title: The bound worlds / Megan E. O'Keefe.
Description: First edition. | New York, NY : Orbit, 2024. | Series: The devoured worlds ; book 3
Identifiers: LCCN 2023040764 | ISBN 9780316291576 (trade paperback) | ISBN 9780316291798 (ebook)
Subjects: LCGFT: Science fiction. | Novels.
Classification: LCC PS3615.K437 B68 2024 | DDC 813/.6—dc23/eng/20230913
LC record available at https://lccn.loc.gov/2023040764

ISBNs: 9780316291576 (trade paperback), 9780316291798 (ebook)

Printed in the United States of America

LSC-C

Printing 2, 2024

For those recovering still

ONE

Naira

Seventh Cradle | The Present

Naira rolled up her sleeve and placed the cold nub of an injector against the interior of her arm. The golden glitter of her pathways obscured the dark tracery of her veins, but Dr. Bracken had assured her that she didn't need to hit the vein precisely for the medication to work. She took a breath. It was fine. She'd done this before.

The injector clicked. Heat burned through her veins, diffusing with the speed of her racing heart. Soft cotton swaddled her thoughts. Her vision dithered around the edges.

Naira snapped the cap back on the injector and slipped it into her pocket, then rolled her sleeve down. Her skin was insensate beneath the brush of her fingertips. That was normal. It would pass.

Tarquin cupped her cheek. After the injection, his touch made the world feel real again.

"Okay?" he asked.

"Yeah." Her lips were numb, the words slow. That would fade, too. The side effects were always temporary. "I'm fine. Let's go."

Tarquin kissed her, and she wasn't sure if he was trying to reassure her or himself. Quite probably both.

Cass and Caldweller flanked Tarquin while Diaz and Helms closed around Naira. She let her hand drift to the weapon strapped to her thigh. Despite the fact she wasn't, technically, an exemplar anymore, Naira still attended formal events in her armor. The extra protection couldn't hurt, and it reminded people of what she was. Made them hesitate before they whispered behind their hands that she was cracked.

"They're ready for you, my liege," Caldweller said.

Tarquin nodded. The door slid open, and Naira had never been more grateful for the numbing fog of the memory suppressant.

It wasn't a warpcore. But it was close enough.

The powercore that would provide energy to the first settlement on Seventh Cradle dominated the room beyond. Ribbed in the dull green of amarthite, the sphere punched a hole of emptiness into the center of the room. Those void-mouth globes, whether installed on ships to facilitate warp jumps or used on stations and cities to generate power, always made her skin prickle. Made her feel like she was being watched.

The ceiling loomed above, vanishing into darkness. Naira locked her face down as she followed Helms, focusing on her exemplar. On Tarquin. On the subtle scent of greenery in the air—air that lacked the metallic edge of station recyclers. Grit crunched beneath her boots from dirt tracked in by the spectators who ringed the powercore at a safe distance.

Her vision blurred. The strongest memory she had—walking across a hangar to the decoy ship that was meant to go to Seventh Cradle, the ship she'd blown up with Tarquin, the one she saw in her dreams, because she'd been forced to make that walk over and over again during interrogation—roared to the surface. It threatened to drown her, to rip her back into the past.

On the edge of the crowd, her mother waved. Dr. Sharp hadn't been anywhere near the hangar that day. The stifling blanket of the medication washed over Naira's thoughts, muting the screaming memory that her cracked mind was certain was the genuine moment. When she came back to herself, she'd missed only a single step. No one seemed to have noticed.

She let her gaze wander up the side of the powercore, pretending to admire it, when a twist of inexplicable fear tensed her from within. The shadow of a face emerged on the matte surface of the core. A brown cheek, quickly turned away. Naira blinked, and it was gone.

Wrapped in the warm, numb fog of her memory-suppressant medication, Naira couldn't be sure she'd seen anything at all. A reflection from
the crowd, perhaps.

But the cores weren't reflective. Must have been a trick of her overburdened mind.

While she waited off to the side, Tarquin stood at a podium in front of
the core, explaining in more detail than his audience probably cared for
how useful the powercore would be to Seventh Cradle's first settlement.
He really couldn't help himself.

She skimmed her eyes over the crowd and found someone she didn't
recognize. A tan-skinned man with a scar running down the side of his
face, intense brown eyes fixed on the powercore. Her mind was playing
tricks on her again. There were only a thousand people in the settlement,
and she knew every one of them. There couldn't possibly be a stranger.
Naira pulled up her HUD and ran a facial recognition query. Nothing.

She opened the exemplar chat and tagged his face.

Sharp: I don't know this man, and he's not in the database. Tell me I'm
hallucinating.

Caldweller: You're not.

Cass: Scrambling Merc-Sec.

Helms: Sharp, please assume spear formation.

Naira fell back a step as Helms and Diaz moved in front of her, the
powercore to her right. She gritted her teeth, resisting an urge to step
in front of Tarquin herself as Cass slipped unobtrusively to his side and
angled their body to be prepared to shield Tarquin at a moment's notice.

Tarquin didn't miss a beat in his speech, though a ripple ran through
the crowd. The man looked straight at Naira and winked, tipping his
chin briefly before he wended his way toward one of the side exits.

Caldweller: Merc-Sec is moving to secure that exit.

Naira bit the inside of her cheek. The stranger had seemed amused.
Confident, even. Catching him was important, but that was the look of
someone who'd already accomplished their goal. She scanned the ceiling, the walls, the other exits. There were no more strange faces in the
crowd. Not a hint of anything amiss.

That face swam into focus on the side of the powercore again. It
wasn't warped, like a projection would be. It seemed solid, as if someone

was standing across from her, only that curve of brown cheek visible behind the otherwise opaque surface of the core. As if it were emerging from shadows.

In the corner of her HUD, the exemplar channel filled with reports on the location of the stranger. He'd slipped past the cordon on the door. Merc-Sec was trying to keep their cool, but they were panicking. Tarquin drew toward the end of his speech, not cutting it off, but definitely avoiding the extra flourishes he was prone to.

Naira ignored it all and focused on that face, on the tug at the side of its mouth, as if it was shouting. Those pathways...They were a muted streak of gold, but they seemed familiar.

"E-X?" Diaz whispered, barely moving his lips so that the crowd wouldn't notice.

Right. The way she was staring at the core and ignoring the chat, she probably looked catatonic. She opened her exemplars' chat channel.

Sharp: I'm lucid. Do you see anything in the core?

Diaz: No.

Sharp: Give me a sec.

Naira wiped all channels away and craned her neck, trying to figure out if it was some kind of holo projection. There was no source she could find. She looked back to the core, frustrated, and thought she saw a sand-crusted boot kick toward the bottom from within, at the amarthite rib.

She broke formation and crouched down beside the rib. They'd checked them all, but—there. On the edge facing away from the crowd was a slim black rectangle.

"Explosive device," Naira called out, interrupting what was probably a very nice set of closing remarks from Tarquin.

Diaz tried to pull her aside, but she shook him off. Shouting roared to life all around her, along with the panicked stomp of boots. Naira's thoughts were fuzzy, but she didn't recognize that device. It was smaller than what the Conservators used. Precise. She glanced at the other ribs near her and saw nothing. A small detonation, then. That's all it would take for the powercore to break containment and wipe out the settlement.

"E-X," Diaz said. "We have to evacuate."

"You can't evacuate far enough. Check the other ribs."

"But—"

"That's an order."

Diaz let out a frustrated grunt and sent Helms around to investigate the ribs while Naira examined the device.

"Naira!" Tarquin shouted.

She glanced over her shoulder and found Cass and Caldweller dragging him toward the exit. Naira waved at him to continue. It didn't matter if Naira died violently; she was already cracked. And she knew a thing or two about explosives. She ran her fingers along the side of the device, where it touched the amarthite. Slightly tacky, the glue not yet set.

"Are we clear?" she asked.

"Clear," Helms and Diaz echoed.

Well, then. Whoever had planted this one didn't want to push their luck by planting others. Or maybe they hadn't had the time. Naira could find no seam on the device, no lights, nothing to indicate when it would blow or what it was connected to. She drew her knife and placed the tip against the sticky glue on the top.

Slowly, she levered it free. It was smooth and cool and fit in the palm of her hand. Naira eyed the cavernous ceiling, made a few brief calculations, and decided she didn't have the time to come up with a better plan.

"You two." She pointed at her exemplars with her knife. "Draw your weapons. I'm going to throw this as hard as I can over there." She pointed up to the place where the wall met the ceiling, lost in darkness. The direction away from the fleeing settlers. "Both of you need to fire on it, because I can't trust my aim right now."

Helms's brow furrowed. "That will bring the ceiling down. Maybe even the wall."

"Neither of which will break the powercore containment. We don't know when this thing will blow, so we don't have time for deliberation or to take it somewhere else. Can you do it?"

They drew their weapons and squared off. "On your mark," Diaz said.

"Duck behind the core for cover after you hit." Naira hurled the device with all her pathway-enhanced strength.

Diaz and Helms aimed, the targeting lasers on their weapons painting sketchy lines in the dark. They waited. Waited. Waited until a fraction of a second before the device would strike the ceiling.

"Mark," Naira said.

They fired in tandem. Naira couldn't say which one of them hit, but the results were immediate.

The blast stole her hearing, temporarily overwhelming those pathways until a muted whine filled her head. A flower of twisted metal bloomed outward from the ceiling, letting in the sunlight above. Smoke choked that light. Metal creaked. Chunks of concrete foam struck the ground. The structure sagged inward, the ceiling and wall both leaning drunkenly for the powercore. Adrenaline burned through her medication too quickly.

Naira's cracked mind slipped.

She believed she was in a Mercator warehouse with Jonsun, Kuma, and Kav, shouting as the bomb they'd planted in a sector full of supplies went off too soon. Stinging smoke clogged her nostrils and a searing flash of heat beat against her skin.

Someone grabbed her. Pain burst through the memory, yanking her back into the present. Diaz had kicked out her knees and dropped her to the floor. He flung himself over her and wrapped his body around her as a human shield.

The impact hit, stealing her breath. Diaz jerked, chunks of concrete and metal bouncing off him. His arm tightened around her and he grunted—a short, pained sound.

She wanted to tell him he was an idiot. That she could be crushed to bits and it didn't matter, because her mind was already broken. But it was too late for that, and so all she could do was make herself as small as possible until the chaos faded so that he could make himself small, too.

The impacts slowed. Diaz groaned. Naira twisted onto her back as he lost his balance and collapsed. Dust smeared his face, coated his armor. His eyes were open, but they were bright with pain.

"Diaz, you absolute moron, talk to me. How bad is it?"

He smirked at her, and that eased some of her panic. "Told you I'd get it."

"What?" Oh. The maneuver she'd taught him to shield a charge with the bulk of an exemplar's body. "Real bad time to learn."

A laugh rattled in his chest. "Fuck. Sorry. Broke some ribs. That's all, I think."

Warm blood seeped through her pant leg, proving the lie to his assessment of the damage. Naira eased him off her and onto his back.

The injury wasn't as bad as she'd feared. A piece of metal had sheared through his calf, showing bone beneath. Naira ripped his E-X kit off his belt, rummaging for medical supplies.

Helms extricated herself from a small pile of debris and rubbed her eyes clean before she found them. She locked eyes with Naira over Diaz's bloody leg, and her face slackened with fear. Naira gave her a subtle shake of the head—*don't panic him by panicking yourself.*

Helms took Diaz's hand and kept him talking while Naira examined the wound. He was losing a lot of blood. Amarthite prints didn't heal as well as exemplars were used to, and his health pathways couldn't keep up. Naira packed the wound with gauze and pulled up her HUD. She ignored Tarquin's call request and opened the E-X channel—they'd tell him she was safe. Diaz didn't have time for Naira to soothe Tarquin first.

Sharp: Diaz needs medical, and he needs it yesterday.

Caldweller: The doors are blocked with debris, but we'll get through as quickly as we can.

Cass: The mystery man was killed in the wall collapse. No other potential hostiles sighted.

Naira abandoned pressure on the wound for a tourniquet. Diaz hissed in pain as she pulled the strap tight. Not a good sign. His painkiller pathways weren't keeping up.

"Hang on. Help is coming."

"Thanks, E-X," he said weakly.

Diaz was unconscious by the time medical got through, but he was breathing. Naira rocked back to her heels, letting her bloodied hands dangle between her knees. The emergency team swooped him up onto a gurney and rushed him away with assurances that he'd been fine. He was alive, and even if he lost that leg, he'd been calm before he lost consciousness. Diaz was unlikely to crack if they determined reprinting was the best course of action.

She knew all those things already. It didn't make watching his dust- and blood-smeared body being hauled away any easier. No one should ever have to be injured in her defense.

Tarquin rushed over the debris toward them, despite his exemplars begging him to be careful. He was dirty but unharmed. Naira stood and held her arms out to either side.

"I'm fine, I'm just a mess—" She grunted as he grabbed her and crushed her against him, smearing his expensive clothes with Diaz's blood. Naira gave up on keeping him clean and wrapped her arms around him. The medication dulled her emotions, and the strength of his fear and relief stunned her. "Tarquin, really, it doesn't matter if I die."

He pulled back and took her face in his hands, trying ineffectually to brush dust off her cheeks. "It matters to me. I thought—" He swallowed. Shook his head. "What happened?"

"Diaz shielded me when the wall came down."

"I'll give the man a commendation." Tarquin combed a hand through her hair. She smiled at that. He always needed to touch her when he was shaken. To assure himself she was still here.

"He disobeyed orders," Naira said.

"With respect," Helms said, "they were shit orders that went against our training."

"*I'm* your trainer."

"Precisely so, E-X." Helms couldn't stifle her small smirk before Naira saw it.

Something high in the rafters groaned. All of them eyed it warily.

"My liege," Caldweller said, "I suggest we retreat to a more stable location."

"Good idea," Tarquin said.

He took her hand and turned back to the passage they'd made in the debris, but Naira couldn't move. She'd been looking at Helms, watching her for any sign of serious injury, when the side of that face appeared in the core once again. Appeared, and came fully into focus.

Naira stared at herself.

The other-Naira stood at formal rest, hands clasped behind her back, studying Tarquin as if she thought she couldn't be seen. Love haunted those eyes. And regret, too.

This variant of herself had shorn her hair, and a network of scars crowned her skull. A fine tracery reminiscent of the scars that'd draped her body when they'd taken her pathways to make amarthite serum.

Naira's mouth dried out. That was no memory. No version of herself she'd ever seen. No moment sneaking up on her out of the recesses of her mind. Tarquin tugged gently on her hand. She scarcely noticed.

She wasn't slipping. Naira was perfectly aware of the world around her, and it was shock alone that narrowed her focus to that alternate version of herself.

The other-Naira had been watching Tarquin, and as he turned to her, so did those impostor eyes. Something like desperation clawed through the phantom, and she lunged at the interior boundary of the core, reaching, mouth opened wide with a shout.

Tarquin stepped in front of Naira and blocked her view. She swore and pushed to her toes to see past him, but her other-self had vanished.

TWO

Tarquin

Seventh Cradle | The Present

That Naira had gone to the hospital without protest worried Tarquin. In his experience she had to be either half-dead, unconscious, or otherwise bundled up like a hissing cat to agree to medical treatment. He reluctantly left her in Bracken's care, then went to meet with his security team at Merc-Sec HQ. Dust made the air murky on the streets, and people moved about furtively, but already the settlers were cleaning up the damage.

Captain Ward and Security Chief Alvero had beaten him there, the space between them crowded with a wide variety of holos projected from the table. Alvero cocked his head to the side, listening to a report, while Ward leaned toward the holos, her thick fingers curled into loose fists against the tabletop. A scowl carved her craggy face.

Tarquin put a video call through to Jessel Hesson so that they could join the gathering from their post on the *Sigillaria*, in geostationary orbit above the settlement.

"Mx. Hesson," he said, "I presume you've been apprised of the attack?"

"I have." They crossed their wiry arms and leaned back against a console podium. "Jonsun and his crew are still quiet up here on the

Cavendish. We haven't heard a peep from them. If it was them, they're lying low."

"Do we have anything on the stranger?" Tarquin sat and hoped he didn't look as relieved as he felt to be off his feet. He'd hardly exerted himself, but his worry had chewed up all his energy and left him wrung out. Pliny gave his arm a reassuring squeeze.

"Not yet, my liege." Dust peppered Alvero's dark hair. "I ran all the footage I could find of him against our master databases, the HC rosters, and the rest of MERIT. That man should not exist."

"An unregistered print design?" Ward asked.

"It seems likely," Alvero said. "We're running a body language analysis to see if we get a hit."

Tarquin wasn't so exhausted that he missed Caldweller, guarding the door, shifting his weight. He frowned. The man wasn't prone to fidgeting. "Do you have a suggestion, Ex. Caldweller?"

"I'm not sure, my liege. It sounds unlikely, even to me."

"I'd hear it regardless."

"I just...I think I know that man. Recognize him, I mean."

"Why didn't you say so sooner?" Jessel demanded.

"Because it's not possible," Caldweller said. "He looked like an old friend of mine. Rusen. But Rusen disappeared when he was seventeen. His map was never registered anywhere that I could find."

Tarquin's brows reached for his hairline. "Nor that I could find, and I did look. You're certain?"

"I can't be, my liege. It might just be a resemblance, but if it is, it's a strong one."

"Family, perhaps." Tarquin drummed his fingers against the table. "Alvero, have the techs pull up old footage of Rusen and digitally enhance his age. See if there's a match. If there's not, we'll look at the extended familial line. Do a complete DNA search."

"I think we must also consider Rochard's hand," Alvero said. "Though nothing came of them sending weapons to the unionists, they may have gotten more creative in their methods."

"Which leaves the matter of how the man got to the damn planet to begin with," Ward said, then tucked her chin. "Apologies, my liege."

Tarquin brushed her apology away. "I agree with the strength of your sentiments. It would be impossible to stow away on our shuttles, and the few printing cubicles we have in the settlement are highly secured. Mx. Hesson, have the *Sigillaria*'s sensors picked up anyone attempting to land on the planet?"

They shook their head. "Nah. Like I said, Jonsun and his people have been real quiet. I've got enough ears to the ground up here that I'd know if something was rumbling. As for MERIT and their lot, we've seen a few drones and satellites trying to get a look at the planet, but that's all."

"Someone in the settlement must have printed him," Ward said. "There's no other explanation."

"Perhaps a hack of the printer itself?" Alvero asked. "Jonsun has Kav Ayuba in his employ, after all."

Tarquin rubbed his forehead to cover the wince he couldn't suppress. That Kav had allied himself to Jonsun was a sore spot, despite Jessel's assurances that both Kav and Kuma were staying near Jonsun to keep him from going too far. Tarquin didn't want to think of Kav as being involved in the attack, but his skill set was uniquely suited.

"It's possible," Tarquin admitted.

"I'll have Info-Sec do a complete teardown of the network," Alvero said. "I'll also have the print cartridge inventory levels checked to see if they're lower than they should be."

"Do that," Tarquin said. "Meanwhile, Captain Ward, I'd like for you to conduct discreet interviews of the settlers, starting with those who work in or near the print facility."

"Right away, my liege."

"We must move forward under the assumption that we've suffered a security breach," Tarquin said. "Do you feel secure up there, Mx. Hesson?"

Jessel stroked their jaw, then glanced through the holo at something on the ship. For the most part, the unionists kept to themselves. According to Jessel—and the rest of their intelligence—Jonsun had transformed the unionists on the *Cavendish* into something like a cult, bent to Jonsun's cause of the complete destruction of MERIT and *canus* both. Goals that should have made them allies, but despite Tarquin's best efforts, Jonsun refused to work with "a Mercator."

"I think we're sitting all right," Jessel said at long last. "Jonsun's not a big enough fool to take a swing at the *Sigillaria*. Not when his life support systems are under our control."

"I'm glad to hear it," Ward said, "because we don't have the people to spare. If you want me increasing boots on the ground, my liege, I need more feet to fill 'em."

Tarquin squinted at the personnel roster. "I'll have five squads casted to us from one of the less critical Sol stations."

"Do we have the amarthite to print that many?" Alvero asked.

Tarquin grimaced, running the numbers. "No. But we can't print people with relk, and I can't make amarthite appear out of thin air. We'll have to make do with what we have. I want a twenty-five percent reduction in the newly printed squads' nonessential pathways. They won't like it, but it will give us some much-needed breathing room."

"Understood, my liege," Ward said in a tone that implied she wasn't looking forward to breaking that piece of news to the people they'd cast over.

All the assets of Mercator weren't enough to magic more amarthite into existence. But the hole blown in the side of the powercore building was something he could fix. Tarquin pulled up the status of the settlement's construction bots and redirected most of them to work on repairs. The forecasted rain would slow them down, but not by much.

He examined the schedule and imagined the way the next few days would go. People would stay in their homes, coming out only to work. Paranoia would set in as Ward began questioning suspects and people started looking to their neighbors and colleagues, wondering who the saboteur among them was.

The situation was far too close to the crash landing on Sixth Cradle for Tarquin's comfort. It would only be a few days, but he knew how quickly sentiments could swing in a scant few hours.

"I want a bonfire tonight," he said. "Break out some of our better food stores and set up in the open square near the powercore building. I want the settlement eating outside, together. Music, even, if it can be arranged, to ease the tension before the storm comes."

"Easy enough," Ward said.

"Indeed." Alvero nodded. "It'll give us a chance to observe interpersonal interactions. See if anyone already suspects one of their neighbors."

The last thing he wanted was for the settlers to feel watched over during the dinner that was supposed to bring them together. Before he could voice that concern, Alvero frowned, his attention focused inward, on a HUD channel.

"My liege, preliminary results are back on the body language scan. Of the footage recorded, only about ten seconds match anyone we have on file."

Alvero pushed the report through for all to see. They'd recorded the man entering the building, the scan running alongside the footage displaying zero matches as it struggled to parse out the stranger's movements. Tarquin leaned closer, studying that placid face. The side doors opened, signaling Tarquin's entrance to the scene. Still, no change.

Naira looked directly at the man. He transformed. His chin lifted, a wary cant to his spine as a slow smirk curled up the side of his face. The scan alerted, accuracy ratings climbing higher until the man winked. The scan peaked. Locked in at 96 percent certainty, then began to fall once more as the stranger suppressed his body language.

Predicted Match: Fletcher Demarco, Mercator Holdings Employee, ID#54148937

Tarquin was struck speechless.

"I've confirmed with our techs that Mr. Demarco's map remains on ice," Alvero said.

Tarquin found his voice at last. "Unless there's another copy we never found."

"It's possible," Alvero allowed. "It's also worth considering that specialists are trained to mimic the body language of known agents to fool such systems. It's only a fraction of the footage. If someone meant to throw us off their scent, this would be a good way to do so."

"A bastard of a move," Ward muttered to herself.

"I need confirmation. In the meantime, no one is authorized to breathe a word of this to Naira, am I clear?"

A strained silence followed that statement, broken up only by the blunted, thumping sound of Ward tapping the side of her thumb against the tabletop in thought.

Jessel said, "She'll skin you alive if she finds out you kept it from her, my liege."

"That's a risk I'm willing to take. She doesn't need this right now. Her mind is still—she's still recovering."

Not that she would ever completely recover. Not without the use of the repair software she continually refused, but he kept those worries to himself. Ultimately, everyone in that room was beholden to the head of Mercator. They could disagree with him all they liked—and perhaps, a small part of him whispered, they were right to do so—but they would obey.

"As you say, my liege," Alvero said. "None of us wants to burden Ex. Sharp unnecessarily."

"Fragile thing that she is," Ward said, completely deadpan.

"Do you have a problem with your orders, Captain?" Tarquin asked.

A muscle in Ward's cheek twitched. "No, my liege. No problems here."

"Then I suggest you all go and see to your duties. I require confirmation of that man's identity and a full report on how he came to this world in the first place."

They chorused their assent, and if there was hesitation in that agreement, well—he didn't blame them. He didn't want to keep anything from Naira, but in the year since her cracking, she'd only begun to leave their private rooms in the past few months. Fletcher's sudden arrival... He sighed, rubbing his forehead. Those memories were too painful for her to risk getting trapped within.

The meeting broke up, but before Tarquin could make it to the door, an incoming call from Thieut Rochard—the head of that family— flashed in the corner of his HUD.

"Liege Thieut," he said, betraying nothing with his voice, "this is unexpected."

"Is it? I presumed you came to the obvious conclusion that I had something to do with the attack today."

"And how would you know of such a thing?"

"Don't insult my intelligence, Liege Tarquin. You are fully aware that every family in MERIT has multiple satellites pointing their eyes at that planet of yours. I'm not calling to debate with you over whether Rochard was involved. We were not."

"You must understand that I can't take you at your word."

"Which is why I've called to tell you something the other families may not," she said. "Your settlement wasn't the only location bombed today. Each member of MERIT experienced a similar attack. One station for each family, in fact."

"Which stations?"

"I'll send you the roster, but I can spare you wondering why they were targeted. Every station carried the largest amarthite stockpile for each family. We lost millions of tons of the stuff today, and I can only presume your settlement is currently the largest concentration of amarthite for Mercator, is it not?"

It was, but Tarquin wasn't going to volunteer that information. "I'll deploy nanonet catchers to the blast radii the second you transmit me the station list."

"I'm sure that will be helpful." Her voice dripped with condescension. "But I suggest you spend more of your very valuable time cleaning up the mess behind your own walls."

"What are you talking about?"

"We captured footage of our bomber. See for yourself."

Thieut pushed the data through. Tarquin didn't recognize the person wearing a Rochard uniform in the video, but the same fidelity software his team had used to identify Fletcher ran beside the footage. There were no spikes. Just smooth certainty.

Predicted Match: Ex. Naira Sharp, Mercator Holdings Employee, ID#54146695

"An impostor," Tarquin said, hating that his voice caught. "Naira hasn't left this planet in a year."

"Perhaps she has, perhaps she hasn't. The truth of the matter is that, to the people of MERIT and the HC, Ex. Sharp's state of mind is an open question. You wouldn't be the first head of Mercator that she's turned on. Perhaps she merely cozied up to you for greater access."

"Naira would never—" He cut himself off, struggling to control his temper. "What do you want?"

"I need amarthite to recover my people, Liege Tarquin. You're going to give it to me, or I'll go public with the fact that the head of Mercator's cracked lover has returned to her terrorist ways."

"Done." He was glad she couldn't see the burst of shame he couldn't control. "I don't want your people on ice either, Liege Thieut. But if you attempt to slander Naira, I will rescind your access to amarthite."

"I'm glad we understand each other. Good luck to you, Liege Tarquin. I mean that genuinely. But keep that woman of yours on a leash. I won't hesitate to order her finalized if she steps foot on my stations again." She ended the call.

The exemplars were watching him. They'd only heard his half of that conversation, but no doubt it was enough for them to have drawn the correct conclusions. The rest of it balanced on the tip of his tongue, but he swallowed the words down. He was head of Mercator. He couldn't go running to his exemplars for advice over every little thing.

Tarquin reviewed the list of stations Thieut sent him, tallying the damage. Thousands of people would be moved lower on the reprint lists, their neural maps rotting on ice until enough amarthite could be secured to bring them back.

No one wanted to print into relk bodies, not after humanity became aware of the *canus* infection. The rarity of amarthite made the already overburdened waiting lists worse. People were growing old without their loved ones, waiting for them to be brought back into bodies that were safe.

His fault. Tarquin hunched over the holo projected from his arm. While the modus operandi and lack of bombing on the *Cavendish* itself— the only fully amarthite ship in existence—pointed to Jonsun, Tarquin couldn't make the facts tally. Jonsun loathed *canus* with a fanatical fire. He wouldn't do anything to limit humanity's ability to get away from relk use, and by extension *canus* itself.

The *canus*-bound were the obvious suspects. They'd have enough knowledge of Naira and the Conservators' methods—even of Fletcher— to impersonate them. But they'd been isolated on their stations, their transmissions blockaded, all attempts to send shuttles off-station shot down. Somehow, they must have gotten agents outside their walls. There was no other explanation.

Tarquin had planned on joining the cleanup effort. Instead, he sent orders to his fleets to help recover what was lost from the explosions in Sol, then swiped all those screens away and brought up the project that haunted his every waking thought.

The geological survey for Sixth Cradle, where the largest cache of amarthite had been found, unfolded before him. He set to work once more trying to match those conditions to geological surveys of other worlds. Other moons.

Tarquin was hunting for a needle in the haystack of the entire universe. If he didn't find it, then all the living cradles in existence wouldn't matter. Humanity would have to either stop printing themselves, or return to relkatite prints.

If he couldn't find more amarthite, then the *canus*-bound wouldn't need to leave their stations to win this war. They'd only have to wait.

THREE

Naira

Seventh Cradle | The Present

Dr. Bracken had listened to Naira's account of her hallucination and pronounced the one thing she'd dreaded to hear—they needed to run more tests. They'd brought her back to the powercore building to "measure her q-field activity near the core"—whatever that meant—and were busy muttering to themself over a handheld device.

It was already late evening, the sunset seeping through the hole in the roof to cast the room in murky orange light. A breeze brought with it the home-hearth scent of the bonfire she'd spotted outside, making her stomach rumble in anticipation. She wished Bracken would hurry up already so she could go eat.

"Ex. Sharp," Bracken said, "would you approach the core for me? Slowly?"

"Sure." She crept toward the core, counting down the distance in her head, waiting for the moment when her skin would prickle. About three feet away, the first brush of creeping static washed over her.

"Stop." The sharpness of Bracken's voice startled her into obedience.

"Is there a problem?"

They squinted at the device, a frown carving their face. Helms drifted closer, tensed for action. Naira shook her head slightly in negation—there was no threat here. At least, not one the exemplar's usual method of "shoot until the threat stops being a threat" could handle.

"The device might be malfunctioning," Bracken said. "Ex. Sharp, could you please return to your start position? And, Ex. Helms, if you would humor me—could you advance at the same pace Sharp demonstrated?"

"I'm working," Helms said.

"It's all right," Naira said. "I promise not to be the target of an elaborate assassination attempt in the next five minutes."

Helms rolled her eyes but repeated the same slow walk to the core. Bracken didn't stop her until she was close enough to touch it. "Well?" Helms asked.

"Thank you, that's all. Please return to your starting position. Ex. Sharp—"

"Yeah, yeah," Naira said, "repeat the approach."

This time, Bracken didn't stop her. The fine hairs all over her body stood on end, and she crossed her arms to suppress a shiver, staring into the inky surface.

"How are you feeling?" Bracken asked. "Any visual events?"

"Prickly," she said. "But I've always felt that way near cores. As for 'visual events,' no, I'm not hallucinating."

"I remain unclear on if the phenomenon you're experiencing is a true hallucination," they said offhandedly, all focus on the device in their hands. "You say you've always felt 'prickly' near cores? Even before your map became temporally destabilized?"

"As long as I can remember," Naira said.

"I've heard similar complaints. Engineers who dislike being near the cores because it makes their hair stand on end, but the sensation is quite rare."

"It happens to Tarquin, Jonsun, and Kuma," she said. "It can't be that rare."

Bracken looked up from the device. "Really? All the Conservators?"

"Not Kav," Naira said. "I don't know about Jessel."

"Well." Bracken squinted at the readout. "Your q-field is perfectly normal for a temporally destabilized map when you stand by the door, but when you approach the core, the reading spikes."

"I'm sure that would be fascinating if I knew what a q-field was," Naira said dryly.

"Ah, apologies. All printed minds have some level of interaction with various quantum fields, but this spike is unusual. Like a tuning fork being rung. It doesn't happen for myself or Ex. Helms."

"Okay," she said. "But is that because my map's cracked"—Bracken scowled at that; they hated it when she used the colloquial term—"or because of something I otherwise have in common with those who get the prickling sensation? Because those people aren't all cracked, and it's been happening since I was a kid."

"If I had another subject to test who experiences the same thing, then we could start formulating hypotheses."

Naira met Bracken's slightly abashed glance and snorted. Tarquin was the only available option. She could hardly blame Bracken for their reluctance. If it'd been Acaelus, she'd hesitate to mention it to him, too, but Tarquin's method of rule was another story. One the employees of Mercator were having a hard time adjusting to.

Naira held no such compunctions. She called Tarquin on video, and he answered immediately, his tired face warming upon seeing her.

"Naira." The way he said her name always made her skin tingle, a much nicer sensation than proximity to the cores provided. "Is there something I can help you with?"

"Dr. Bracken needs to take a few readings on someone else who gets prickly in proximity to cores, and you're the only one I'm sure of."

"I'll be right there." He closed the call.

Bracken bowed their head to her. "Thank you, E-X. I didn't want to bother our liege myself, but—"

"I know." Naira crossed her arms tighter. "Believe me, I know. He's still . . ." She swallowed down what she really wanted to say—that though he meant well, he was still clumsy with his power. "He's head of Mercator and all of what that entails. But he's willing to listen."

Tarquin arrived a few minutes later, Caldweller and Cass following at a cautious distance. The exemplars looked to Helms for confirmation that all was well before they nodded to her. It stung, but she kept the petty hurt from showing. Naira was a charge, now. Outside of the core operations of the exemplars. She could hardly expect them to treat her as they'd always done. The admiring smile Tarquin threw her eased some of that resentment.

"Doctor." Tarquin took Bracken's hand and shook it. "How can I help you?"

"If it's not too much trouble, I'd like to take a few measurements of your q-field as you approach the core."

Tarquin slid Naira a curious glance. "I can do that. Tell me where to stand."

Bracken shuffled them around the room, then ran Tarquin through the same slow approach.

"Well," Bracken said, "that confirms that the phenomenon is a trait of those who experience frisson when near the cores. Though Ex. Sharp's ratings are orders of magnitude higher than yours, my liege, the core's q-field does spike the nearer you draw to it."

"What does that mean?" Tarquin asked.

"I haven't a clue," Bracken said with a shrug. "But it's another angle to explore."

Bracken muttered to themself once more, poking at the device. Released from the experiment, Tarquin wrapped an arm around Naira's shoulders, and she leaned her weight against him.

"I wish I had a reading of you when you experienced the hallucination," Bracken said.

Tarquin startled and looked down at her. "What hallucination?"

"I saw myself, in the core. Not an image from the past, not a reflection, not a projection of any kind. That vision warned me about the device."

"A side effect of the medication?" Tarquin asked Bracken. The hope in his voice cut. He wanted it to be anything but a deterioration of her condition. She wanted it to be anything else, too.

"Possible," Bracken said as tactfully as they could manage. "Is there anything else about the vision you could tell me, E-X? Were you in your preferred print?"

"I was," Naira said. "I couldn't see much detail, but my hair was shaved and my head was covered in scars. They looked like the scars I developed when my pathways were excised, but I didn't recognize the configuration."

"That's impossible," Tarquin and Bracken said at the same time.

Naira narrowed her eyes. "What did you two do?"

"Go ahead, Doctor," Tarquin said. "You can explain it better than I can."

Bracken blanched and looked very much like the last thing they wanted was to be the one to explain. Hesitantly, they pulled up their holo and projected a framework design of pathways fitted around a skull.

"Did the configuration look like this?" Bracken asked.

Naira slipped from under Tarquin's arm and approached the projection. She pointed to two pathways branching off the central band.

"Those two were at a twenty-degree angle, not forty, but yes, that's it exactly. What is it?"

Bracken flipped the model around. "Huh. That's an excellent suggestion."

"Doctor," Naira said firmly.

"Ah. Yes, sorry, it's..." They cleared their throat. Tarquin was suspiciously quiet. "Liege Tarquin and I discussed your experience in the simulation crown, when Liege Canden interrogated you, and we both noted that you were remarkably stable during that time."

"You discussed this without my knowledge?" Naira asked Tarquin.

"I didn't want to worry you or give you false hope," he said.

"Hope about what?"

"Well," Bracken said, "interrogators use simulation crowns to suppress the subject's memory so that they forget they're being interrogated. To the best of Liege Tarquin's recollection, you didn't appear to slip into memory while inside the simulation, is that correct?"

"Yes," Naira said.

"Excellent." Bracken warmed to the subject. "Of course, we could hardly place you in a simulation long term. But, after imaging your brain during moments of regression, I've been able to define what it looks like when you experience a time slip. The memory lights up, so to speak, and connects with your sensory systems, overriding the present. Basing my model off the simulation crown, I devised a pathway arrangement that should suppress such an event."

Naira blinked, too stunned to otherwise react. That strange, slipping sensation that overtook her before she fell into a memory coiled through her, but she managed to stay in the present. For a moment, she thought she saw a golden light, but her vision cleared. "What happens when I intentionally try to remember something?"

"That, I'm still fine-tuning." Bracken looked at Tarquin, and he nodded permission. "I believe the answer is an issue of thresholds. Your catatonia-inducing memories are much more active than a normal remembrance. Getting that threshold correct has proven difficult."

"But you think it will work?"

Bracken looked past her, to Tarquin again, and she clenched her fists. Whatever sign Tarquin gave, they nodded enthusiastically. "I believe so, yes."

"Then why the fuck"—Naira didn't bother to smooth her anger—"did I see myself with that pathway arrangement cut out? Those were scars. Not pathways."

Bracken's excitement drained away. "I don't know."

"But you have a theory, don't you?"

Bracken looked to Tarquin *again*. Naira cracked her jaw. "Tarquin, if Dr. Bracken seeks your approval one more time, I will make you stand in the corner facing the wall until they can stop. I'm talking with *my* doctor about *my* health."

His eyes widened. "I'm sorry, I didn't mean to—"

"I know."

"I—" Bracken stammered a moment, started to glance to Tarquin, but caught themselves and cleared their throat. "I apologize. Old habits, I'm afraid."

"I understand," Naira said, "but don't do it again. Now, please explain your theory to me, Doctor."

"We've never seen someone live for this long while temporally destabilized," they said. "It stands to reason that, though we've no evidence of such a thing until now, the future is as open for perception to the destabilized mind as the past."

"You think I saw myself in the future?"

"I see no reason why such an event couldn't happen."

"Why haven't I seen such things before?"

"I've no idea," Bracken said, with all the excitement of a scientist with an unanswered question laid at their feet. "Though if I were to hazard a guess, I would say that the powercore resonated with your mind and amplified your ability to slip, providing the opportunity."

"You said that version of yourself was in rough shape, didn't you?" Tarquin asked.

"Yeah. The scars alone looked nasty."

"I'm no quantum theorist," Bracken said, "but just because you saw that moment doesn't mean it's destined to happen. While that future interacted with this one, we can't be certain what that means."

"Requisition whatever you need to research this, Doctor. In the meantime." Tarquin took her hand and placed one hand on her waist, pushing her away from him into a brief spin. "We should join the dinner. Let the settlers see me with my love, unconcerned about the bombing. I've ordered music, you know."

Naira let him draw her close and gave him a sour look. "You know I can't dance."

"Please, I've seen you fight. It's hardly much different."

She groaned, and he silenced her building complaints with a kiss that she couldn't help but lean into. When they parted, he guided her toward the exit, the exemplars rearranging themselves around them in a loose cordon. Grit crunched beneath her boots, dust from the explosion, and she feared she'd fall back into another memory, but Tarquin's hand was a warm, firm anchor keeping her grounded.

"Huh." Bracken paused to look at the q-field detector.

"What?" Naira asked.

"A small spike." They thumped the device with the side of their hand, frowning. "Perhaps it's broken after all."

"Doctor," Helms said, "you're standing about where that stranger was."

The moonlight slanted, casting a gleaming, silver glow across the floor. In her mind's eye Naira saw the man standing there. Watched him wink. Her mind slipped.

Naira wasn't in the powercore building anymore. She was staring at a pile of corpses, faces grey, mouths and eyes stretched wide from desiccation.

The memory was gone as soon as it'd come, replaced with another— Kuma putting a patch in her hands, taken from the bodies. Naira had crushed it in her fist and said it was a bridge, and she still didn't know why.

Again she fell, the world yanked out from under her feet until she was in no room she recognized, no real memory, aside from a woman who'd been a corpse on a pile, but was now glaring down at her, fury bright in living blue eyes.

Naira felt her mouth move, though the words didn't make sense. "I won't let you harm him."

The woman struck her, a solid backhand that sent Naira reeling. Blood filled her mouth as her cheek split. The moment blurred with another, with Fletcher's hand connecting with her face, his usually laughing smile curled in a sneer that bared his teeth. Naira threw up an arm to protect herself against a blow that'd landed years ago.

She slipped. Reeled backward under the remembered force of that blow and fell against the rubble. Her head bounced. Something crunched. Blackness blurred the edges of her vision and her stomach knotted, bile filling the back of her throat.

"Move." Bracken's familiar hands supported her neck. They tipped Naira's head to the side and prodded, carefully, around a wound that made her hiss with pain.

"Easy," Bracken said. They shone a light into her eyes, then nodded to themself. "A scratch and small concussion. Nothing your pathways can't handle."

She blinked until the fuzzy blackness cleared. Tarquin knelt at her side, struggling to suppress the fear on his face and doing a poor job of it as he clung to her hand.

Bracken pulled an injector from their pocket, dialed something into it, and plunged it into the side of her neck. The nausea subsided. Fiery relief rushed through her veins. She could still feel the damage, but everything was smoother. The jagged edges filed off, making it easier to deal with.

"Thank you."

Bracken's smile returned. "Just doing my job."

They backed away, giving her space. Tarquin stood slowly, still holding her hand, and helped her to stand with him. She stumbled, but Tarquin was there to brace her.

"What happened?" he asked.

"I saw..." Naira tried to make herself focus, but her thoughts kept drifting. "I don't know. Fragments, all very fast. There was this woman I didn't know, and she struck me, and then...Fletch."

Tarquin took in a short, sharp breath and wrapped his arms around her, his grip tighter than was strictly comfortable, but she didn't mind.

"Can you tell us anything about the woman?" Bracken asked.

Naira breathed in Tarquin's familiar scent. "Not much. Blue eyes, tall. I don't know her, but I think she might have been one of the bodies we discovered on the *Cavendish*. One of the ones with the bridge patch."

"We couldn't find those names in the registry either, could we?" Caldweller asked.

"No, we couldn't," Tarquin said stiffly. "Though Jonsun hasn't seen fit to provide us with their full names, so we have only Naira's memory of what she saw embroidered on their uniforms to go off of."

"This woman's uniform said Degardet," Naira said. "I'm sure of it. Which doesn't narrow it down much. There are a lot of wards of Gardet out there."

"We'll look for her," Tarquin said, "but right now I'm taking you home."

"Ex. Sharp," Bracken said, "do you want the suppressant?"

Naira hesitated. She felt unmoored, memories lurking at the edges of her consciousness, Fletcher's sneer in the moment he'd struck burned into her retinas. While she'd kicked his ass for that, the betrayal remained. That had been the first time since cracking that she'd fallen into a memory featuring Fletcher.

Naira didn't want those moments back. Even if it might be useful for her to flirt with the edges of her consciousness, to tempt visions of the future, she couldn't do it. Not tonight. Not again. Not with the sting still fresh on her cheek.

"I'll take it."

Tarquin brushed a kiss against the top of her head, understanding. She closed her eyes, pressing her face into his chest, and tilted her head aside, giving Bracken access to the side of her neck.

Their touch was gentle, as it always was, and as the medicine raced through her veins, panic flared bright and jittery within her, but soon the suppressant muted that feeling, too.

Bracken had given her more than usual. Her head was numb and floating. Tarquin scooped her up and carried her home.

FOUR

Naira

Seventh Cradle | The Present

Naira woke in the middle of the night. She had vague memories of dragging on one of Tarquin's too-big shirts and collapsing face-first onto bed. The sheets had twisted around her, damp with sweat, and Tarquin's arm was heavy over her waist.

She stared at the ceiling and tried to process all that had happened. If the visions were really from the future, as Bracken had claimed, then there must be some clue there for her to unravel. A hint that had connected that moment to the bomber's appearance in the settlement.

The more she dug into the memory, the more Fletcher's presence lurked at the edge of her senses. Years of moments good and bad and somewhere in between waiting to surface, to drag her back down into a person she didn't want to be anymore. Her skin crawled and she sat up, carefully extricating herself from under Tarquin's arm. He rolled aside, still sleeping.

A moisture-heavy breeze whispered into the room. Tarquin had left the door to the balcony partially open. Wrapping her arms around herself, she crossed the room to the balcony and leaned against the railing.

Tarquin had told the exemplars that the balcony wasn't a security risk because the back of the building came right to the edge of a steep cliff that dropped away into a tangle of forest too thick for anyone to traverse with ease. It faced away from the settlement, to the unaltered planet.

The forest thinned at the far edge, becoming a scattering of trees that eventually gave way to a grassy plain tucked into the crook of the wide, lazy river that provided most of the settlement's water. Glacial ice melt filled the river during the summer months, making it stunningly turquoise even under the moonlight.

That strip of grass was where Tarquin planned to build them a home, someday. Naira had agreed with the exemplars that the balcony was an unnecessary security risk. She was grateful for it, now.

Granite-grey clouds scudded across the sky, obscuring the moonlight, and in the brief darkness she could make out the glimmer of bioluminescent insects flitting between the trees below. Naira leaned her full weight against the railing and stared straight down, to the scree at the foot of the cliff. Even here, she could feel Fletcher's shadow. Waiting for her mind to slip.

She wondered what would happen if she let herself tip over the edge. The fall would kill her, but what then? Tarquin would reprint her and she'd be right back where she was, walking a tightrope. Waiting to fall into a chasm that wouldn't do her the decency of killing her, for how much it was going to hurt.

Naira understood, now, why most of the cracked fell into the endless scream. It built in the back of her throat, and as she stared out across the living forest that had been meant to be a sanctuary, all she wanted to do was let that scream rip free and fill the night.

Tarquin muttered in his sleep, and she squeezed her eyes shut. She didn't want to go, not really. She didn't want to break against the rocks. But she couldn't keep it together, either.

Naira pulled up her chat channels, intending to ask Bracken to bring her more of the suppressant—she craved nothing short of oblivion—and watched in real time as one of her many unanswered texts to Kav flipped from *unread* to *read*.

Naira grabbed open the channel to Kav, let it fill her view instead of the biting rocks below.

Sharp: I'm falling apart and I need you.

The status flipped over to *read*. She clutched the railing hard enough to bend her already short nails back. A minute passed. Five. A text channel request flashed in the corner of her eye, no identifier she recognized.

Ayuba: I don't have a lot of time

Sharp: How do I know it's really you?

Ayuba: No one else knows The Great Exemplar Sharp flunked her first advancement exams because she had a concussion from stepping in on a bunch of assholes beating me up. I fixed those scores and never told a soul.

Sharp: Are you safe?

Ayuba: No, and neither are you. Look, I mean it. I don't have time for everything I want to say.

Sharp: Let us extract you.

Ayuba: No. There's something going on here I need to figure out, and I can't talk business, all right? If Jonsun gets suspicious that I told you anything, anything at all, then I'm dead and maybe Kuma is, too. I can't tell with her, lately. But I can say this, and I know you won't believe me, but I didn't build those bombs.

Sharp: If you say you didn't, I believe you.

Ayuba: I don't deserve that level of trust anymore.

Sharp: You've always had my back, even when we were arguing. I've still got yours.

Ayuba: You texted me for a reason. What's wrong? I mean, aside from the usual.

Sharp: I can't control it. The cracking, I mean. I never really thought I could, but...It's Fletch. I'd avoided thinking about him for so long, but then I saw this thing that kicked me right back there and I can't undo it. All those years are waiting for me and I can't go back. Especially now, knowing that even the good times were tainted by his weird messiah complex.

Ayuba: Wait, what messiah complex?

Sharp: He thought Mom printed me as a child and that I'd bonded with canus. That I'd be some sort of uncrackable savior.

Ayuba: ...what the fuck

Sharp: Yeah, I know.

Ayuba: You'd be a shitty savior. Like, the worst. I've seen you ask where your boots are when they were on your feet.

A laugh burst free, and some of that corkscrew-tight tension eased out of her.

Sharp: Goddamnit, Kav, I'm serious.

Ayuba: I know, but I made you laugh, didn't I?

Sharp: dick

Ayuba: That's a yes.

He was still typing.

Ayuba: I'm going to deny I ever said this. But. I know what you're dealing with is terrible and it's my fault I couldn't stop Jonsun. But. Shit. Okay. Don't get pissed off at me. But Fletch? He knew he could never really control you. Even when you liked him, you were always wary, right? You always had one foot out the door, because you knew in your core that Fletch was poison. So if you get stuck in one of those memories, you don't even have to bring anything you weren't feeling then to the moment. Remember your wariness. Remember that foot out the door. Use it to get back.

Sharp: I don't know if I can. All I want to do when I think about it is scream and never stop.

Ayuba: Then scream. Scream right in his face, Nai. And come back. You have to keep coming back.

She eyed the drop, and the rocks below.

Sharp: Why? Really, why? Why do I have to be the one to keep coming back? I'm so goddamn tired.

Ayuba: I don't know what to tell you. I wish I could say that you just need to hang on until it gets better, but I can't make that promise. If you... if you've got nothing else to hold on to, then come back for me, yeah? Because I'd be devastated if you let go, and no one wants to see me cry. I'm too pretty.

Naira snorted and hadn't even realized she'd been crying until tears dripped off her nose. She scrubbed a hand over her eyes and let out a slow breath.

Sharp: Thanks. Really.

Ayuba: I'm deleting this chat and denying I ever said any of that.

Sharp: Yeah, yeah.

Ayuba: Seriously, though, I have to go. I'll contact you again when I can. Don't try to use this channel. I'm burning it.

Before she could respond, all traces of the channel disappeared and her HUD emptied, leaving her with a clear view of the planet once more. In the distance, thunder rumbled, and she lifted her face to the darkening clouds, breathing deep of the moisture-rich air. She felt lighter. Stronger. She could do this.

She also felt someone watching her from behind.

"It's not polite to stare."

Tarquin's sleep clothes rustled as he leaned in the doorframe. "I heard you laugh and I didn't want to interrupt. And really, who can blame me for staring?"

Naira looked over her shoulder and caught the slow slide of his gaze roaming over her. She held out a hand to him. "Come here."

He took her hand and stepped behind her, wrapping his arms around her waist to snug her tight against him. She leaned back, letting him take her weight, and sighed contentedly as he brushed a kiss to her cheek. He paused. Licked his lips.

"You've been crying?"

She grunted. "Must you lick everything?"

"When it comes to you? Absolutely." He hummed against her neck, making her pulse flutter. "But that can wait until you tell me why you were crying."

"I was struggling, and I sent a text to Kav. To tell him off, really, but he actually answered."

Tarquin turned her so that he could face her. "What did Kav do?"

"Helped me. It was . . . good. I needed that."

"You know you can always wake me up if you need someone to talk to, right?"

"I thought I wanted to be alone. Kav messaging back surprised me."

He studied her for a moment and the worry faded, replaced by a slow smile. "I'm glad he did, then. Is he safe? Did he tell you anything we could use to help him?"

Naira cocked her head to the side. "I thought you believed he was a traitor."

He brushed his fingertips against the stiff track of tears on her cheek. "Naira, I haven't heard you laugh like that in a long time. I thought I was dreaming at first, and when I realized I'd woken up . . . I saw you standing here in the moonlight and thought, whatever that was, whatever had made you sound so much like yourself again, I owed it everything. Yes, I'm angry with Kav. But I'm glad he finally called you, and if I can help him be safe, then I'll move Mercator to do so."

She dragged him down into a kiss, and he grunted in surprise, which made her smile against him. No matter how many times she kissed him after he said something sweet, he still managed to be taken aback, as if he couldn't quite believe his luck.

A soft, warm rain began to fall. He let out a groan of frustration and pulled away, tipping his chin back to squint-glare at the opening clouds.

"Really?" he asked the sky. He took her hand and stepped away, tugging her toward the door, but she planted her feet.

"It's warm. I don't mind."

Already the rain was coming down in thicker drops, plastering his hair to his head, turning his thin sleep shirt translucent. Droplets tangled in his lashes and gleamed when he blinked them away. "You're sure?"

"Definitely."

He grinned lopsidedly and stepped into her. The warmth of their bodies permeated their rain-soaked shirts, and he nudged her back, pressing her against the railing. Between the questing of his hands and the soft patter of the rain, her senses sang. There was just this moment, no other. Only his gasp as she slid her leg up his. The pleasant tug as he tangled his fingers in her drenched hair and nudged her head aside to better whisper kisses against her neck.

Naira huffed her impatience, and he chuckled a little, pleased with himself, and squeezed her hip.

Her mind slipped. She was back on Miller-Urey, Fletcher's hand on her hip, controlling her every movement, his fingers digging into her muscle. Disgust boiled through her and she locked up, knowing this was wrong, and not wrong because Fletcher was being an ass but wrong because...because...She didn't know. All she knew was that she wanted to scream and that impulse, at least, felt right.

Naira looked at Fletcher. The memory of him pressed his knife against her neck and blood dribbled warm as tropical rain down her throat. She screamed directly in his face and everything...stopped.

Naira kept screaming, screaming until her lungs were empty and her throat burned, but she didn't care, because clarity came with that scream, with the stop-motion frame of Fletcher's face locked away in time, unable to reach her.

The memory shattered and she was back on the balcony, gasping, rain washing her clean. She reached for her throat, checked it for the cut that never happened, and found only unmarred skin. Tarquin had one hand outstretched behind him, palm out like a shield. His head was turned that direction, too.

"I don't fucking know," he was saying. "Get Bracken—get any doctor awake—"

"Tarq," she gasped out, and winced at the rawness in her throat. He turned back to her, horror writ clear on his face. "It's okay," she said. "I'm here. I'm back."

He brushed the wet hair off her face. "Do you want the suppressant?"

"No." Behind him, Caldweller, Cass, and Helms were watching, weapons drawn. They must have come running the second she'd let loose. "You can stand down. Thank you."

They nodded to her as one and shuffled out of the room, shutting the door behind them. Naira sighed—she'd have to explain herself in more detail, later—but at that moment, she felt vibrant. Alive. More fully herself than she had since she'd cracked.

Tarquin pressed his face into the crook of her neck, trembling. "I thought I'd lost you. I thought that scream would never stop."

She gathered him into her arms and held him tight to ground him against her. To let his fears wash through him and break against the solidity of her presence.

"I may go away, sometimes. But as long as it's in my power, I'll always come back."

FIVE

Tarquin

Seventh Cradle | The Present

Tarquin was not okay. He kept it to himself as he moved through the tasks required of him. The warm rain of last night continued to blanket the settlement in a pervasive grey that dragged down more than the moods of the people. Machines were malfunctioning. Tarquin stood in the broken-open powercore building and examined a line of five robots his engineers had disabled.

"We aren't certain of the cause, my liege," Eoin Bracken said. He had the same pinched look on his face that his child, Dr. Bracken, displayed when they were about to deliver bad news. "I'd like to pause their work while we recalibrate and run a few tests."

Tarquin glanced at the tarp covering the hole in the ceiling. Rain dribbled around the edges. "What, exactly, was the damage?"

"Minimal." Eoin crouched down and fished an aluminum strut out of the various materials arrayed upon the ground. He brushed a bit of mud off and turned it over. Along one edge, holes had been drilled, but where they had started out evenly spaced, they drifted farther and farther apart at increasing intervals. "These are meant to be equidistant. We think the rain might be interfering with the bots' sensors."

"That looks algorithmic. If it was the rain, wouldn't the pattern be random?"

"I can't think of what else might be causing it."

"Perhaps a virus," Tarquin said.

"It's possible, my liege. That's why I'd like to shut down all the robots in the settlement until I can be certain it's not something malicious in our network. Alvero assured me he'd be able to dedicate a team to that investigation."

"How long will this delay progress?" he asked, even though he knew better. Eoin couldn't possibly have an estimate without knowing what the problem really was.

"It's hard to say. I'll update you the second I know what we're looking at."

"While you conduct your investigation, please delegate someone to fix the tarps."

"Right away, my liege."

Tarquin walked away, not entirely certain where he was going, which was a poor plan when the sky was dumping rain. Cass fell into step behind him, the squelch of their boots in the mud an unusual sound. Tarquin was used to silence from his exemplars. With his nerves as fragile as they currently were, the sound grated.

Without work to distract him, Naira screaming last night was all he could think about. Her head tipping back, lips carving a wide cavern from which a sound he'd never even dreamed she was capable of ripped free.

Tarquin knew that scream. It was the same scream his mother's print had let loose the first time they'd printed her fake map and believed she was cracked and gone for good.

The sound had startled him so deeply he'd nearly shoved her, just to get away from it, and if he had...He buried the thought. He hadn't. He'd controlled himself.

"My liege?" Cass asked.

Tarquin had stopped his aimless march at some point and was standing stock-still in the middle of the street, rain soaking through his clothes. Cass had repositioned to his flank, the exemplar's wary eyes examining him. Maybe it was the rain dragging Cass's face down, but something about their careful regard made Tarquin uneasy.

There was hostility to it that was usually directed outward, not at him. He'd thought he'd seen it last night, when they'd all rushed into the room when Naira cried out, but... No. It was the rain and the stress. They were all on edge.

"Sorry," Tarquin said. "Lost in thought."

Cass gave him a slow nod that said they didn't quite believe him. Tarquin shook himself and decided to go to the medical wing where neural map storage and body printing were handled. If there was a virus in the settlement's systems, then it might explain the appearance of the stranger. He pushed his way into the building and ignored the staff scrambling to dip into startled bows.

"Is Dr. Bracken available?" he asked the nearest tech.

"Yes, my liege," they said. "They're in their lab."

"Thank you."

Tarquin hesitated outside the door to the lab and glanced at Cass. "Please wait outside."

Their brows lifted—Tarquin rarely left his exemplars standing in hallways—but they nodded and turned their back to the door, facing down the hall.

Bracken had been working, bent over a console podium. They startled at his entrance. "My liege," they said. "How may I help you?"

Tarquin hadn't known what he'd really come there to say until the words were out of his mouth.

"I need to speak with my father."

INTERLUDE

Her

The End | The End

She exists in flesh only for the conduit of communion that it provides. While her body sleeps on, her mind is an endless expanse in digital ether. She hovers in the heart of a construct of her own devising, the branching paths of her life glass shards limned in gold that she alone can peer through. She has Jonsun to thank for this visualization.

Her life is a timeline ripped apart at the seams. Moments scattered between thin threads of linearity that insist on tying them all together, though she knows that such a union is pointless. The continuity of her life lost meaning the day she cracked, and as is the nature of being cracked, she supposes this means that she never had continuity of consciousness at all.

A difficult thing to come to accept. After nearly forty years as a bumbling creature of skin and warmth and the terrible, irrefutable decay of entropy, her mind was not equipped to fully understand what it meant to break from time. Not at first.

Such an odd thing, to have thought being cracked might have been her ending. Such a foolish thing, to have ever feared an end at all.

For it is only in her shattering that she abandons all fear, all limits to herself. Only in fracturing that she is able to see every possible moment of her life splayed out at her feet, forever forward and backward. All the endless possibilities. All the branching paths that somehow, always, no matter how hard she tries to reach back and cry out to herself, end as she is now.

It is only the end that she cares about.

No matter how many ways she rearranges the moments of her life, no matter how many small nudges she makes, how many puppet strings she pulls from the high perch of the future, she is always led back to the moment in which she exists now. A mind. A body. A desperation to save what remains of the worlds without giving him up.

It never works.

The moment is coming again. She feels the echoes of it down the halls of her memory. The Naira that exists in her past believes that her most oft repeated memory is of approaching a warpcore. She is correct, but for the wrong reasons.

It is the decision that will be made before that warpcore. It is the pivot on which the fate of the worlds swings.

Naira Sharp does not yet know what she will become. But this fragment of herself that persists at the end of everything knows, and fears. For even with all she has tried, even with all her knowledge, she has yet to find a way past that terrible moment.

To save them all, she must lose him.

Through endless permutations, she has chosen him every time.

SIX

Tarquin

Seventh Cradle | The Present

Tarquin found himself beneath a stretch of blue sky on another world. A garden bloomed all around him, a thin strip of gravel leading onward between the heady blooms. He followed the path, a strange mixture of anticipation and dread bubbling through him, and stopped, arrested, when he came to the courtyard. When he saw his father sitting there, on the edge of a fountain.

Acaelus wore pastel-colored clothes that belonged on some other man. There was a softness to his posture that'd never existed in life, his spine a gentle slope as he leaned forward, forearms resting against his thighs. He didn't look up when Tarquin sat beside him.

"So it's you who's come to interrogate me," Acaelus said. "I can't say I was expecting that. I thought it might be Sharp, or one of the finalizers, though there's no need for such a thing. I'll tell you anything you'd like."

Tarquin had been staring at the side of his father's face, at the profile that so very nearly matched his own, but he turned his head, following Acaelus's sight line. In the field beyond, his mother played a game with Leka and a kite—no doubt one meant to amuse Tarquin, as Leka had been an adult, then—but he watched himself, as a child, consumed with digging in the dirt instead of enjoying his mother's and sister's antics.

Second Cradle. He barely remembered going there, he'd been too young, but it could be nowhere else. Tarquin buried his face in his hands. This was the trip Canden had taken to infect the planet with shroud.

This happy moment was the prelude to the brutal death of Naira's mother.

Acaelus rested a hand against his back and said nothing. Let him gather himself. Tarquin straightened. Acaelus didn't take his hand away.

"I'm not here to interrogate you," Tarquin said. "I need advice."

Acaelus's fingertips tensed. "I'm uncertain I have any advice worth giving you."

Tarquin planted his hands on his knees to steady himself. "Are you aware that Ex. Sharp is cracked?"

"Ah. Sharp." Acaelus turned away from the tableau in the field to face Tarquin at last. "I'm aware, though I sincerely hope you're not calling her 'Ex. Sharp.' Liege Naira told me of her affections and assured me that while she was cracked, she would hold on until she'd taken the *Sigillaria*. I presume she was successful in doing so."

"Liege Naira? She must have hated it when you called her that."

"She wasn't pleased." Acaelus paused. "Son. Look at me."

Tarquin faced his father. Acaelus hadn't changed the configuration of his print much after Tarquin had been born. The same sharp nose, the same hazel eyes, the shock of silvery-white hair that he let grow a few inches longer than would be considered short.

All of Tarquin's life, that face had been cold. Impassive. Now it was open, his eyes kind, and Tarquin didn't know if he wanted to weep or scream at him for never being like this in life.

"What happened?" For once, there was no demand in his voice. No recrimination. The subtext of *what did you do?* had washed away, and he was only concerned. Understanding.

Tarquin bowed his head to hide the sting of tears, and failed to control himself altogether when Acaelus wrapped his arms around him and drew him close. He cried against his father's shoulder for the first time since he'd been a child. When the shock had worn off and he could control himself again, Tarquin pushed away and scrubbed at his face with both hands, shaking.

"You're a monster," Tarquin said. "No matter how much you pretend otherwise, you're a monster and I have no idea why I thought coming here was a good idea."

Acaelus looked back to the family in the field. "I am that," he said, in the same tone he'd use to remark upon the weather. "I make no claim otherwise. I long ago lost the ability to see people as anything but tools to be leveraged. But I love you. I love them." He inclined his head to the memory of their family. "And while I understand that such a thing will be difficult for you to reconcile, I can only tell you that it's true."

"How can you have any capacity left for love? Don't tell me you did what you 'had' to do. I've read the research notes that Dr. Laurent took on your experiments together. There was nothing necessary about what you did."

"I guarded my love for you all," Acaelus said slowly. "I put walls around it, so that the corruption wouldn't seep through. I don't know if it was the right choice, in the end, but I don't regret it."

"I don't understand how the man whose happiest moment is this memory could do half of the things you've done," Tarquin said. "I can't see it."

Acaelus studied him. "You're frightened. I see. Leka didn't reprise her role as heir, did she? You're head of family now, and you can't get away from it, and you feel it, don't you? The knowledge that you're capable of doing anything at all butting up against the reality that, to do the things that would make the people you love safe, would make you an object unworthy of the very love you seek to preserve?"

It struck so close to home that all his anger bled away. Tarquin studied the gravel between his feet. "Naira is still cracked."

"Has Meti not helped her?"

"We have Dr. Laurent's files and have examined them thoroughly. But she conspired with Mom to kill worlds. If I were to print her at all, it would be to stand trial, and I won't waste the resources for such a thing."

"What of the repair software?"

"Naira refuses it. When it was used on a friend of hers, it changed him badly. Being cracked is..." He kicked at the dirt. "It's eroding her. Chipping away at her resolve. I see the sorrow and the fear in her, and I want..."

"To force it to be better," his father finished.

Tarquin grimaced and nodded. "Recently, she screamed to escape a memory. A bad one. And that sound... You know the sound. It's Mom's scream. I'm afraid that one day she won't be able to stop, and even if we try the repair software then... All our research indicates the repair doesn't work on those who've fallen to the endless scream."

"It was that scream that undid me, in the end." Acaelus turned his attention back to the field. "Though I suppose it was only a matter of time. The heads of MERIT give way to the temptations of their power, eventually. Ettai told me as much. I didn't listen. I was young and certain I wouldn't do the things they'd done before they declined reprinting."

That statement was a lance through Tarquin's melancholy. "Ettai? What had they done? They were so kind to me."

Acaelus rubbed his hands together. "You knew Ettai at the end. As a grandparent who desired nothing more than to read and dote upon you. I had three parents, though Ettai was the blooded Mercator, and by the time you were born, the others had cracked and gone to the ice.

"Ettai was what was necessary, at the time. While the shroud consumed Earth and those governments tore each other apart, Ettai built ships. Built stations. They were there at the founding of MERIT. They were there when the cuffs began, and the HC was cobbled together from what was left of the Earthly governments. They did what they had to do to ensure a future for humanity. Such things are never wholly kind."

Tarquin had never dwelled on the thought before. Ettai had gone to the ice voluntarily when Tarquin had been only twelve, a brief and comforting presence in his life. Acaelus had already been head of family, and all the fearsome connotations of that position had rested on his shoulders, not Ettai's.

"Why was I never told these things?"

"Leka kept the family history. And you were already so resistant. Canden and I, we didn't want to make it worse."

"But I didn't leave the family stations until after we thought Mom had cracked."

Acaelus looked sideways at him. "Do you really think we didn't notice how you tensed at every official function? How you plied anyone who would listen to abandon your title? We knew, son. We knew, and it broke our hearts that there was nothing we could do to make it easier. Mercator's power weighs heavily. It hurts, if you don't want it."

Tarquin rubbed at his family mark with his thumb. "Naira doesn't want the power, either. I'm hurting her merely by being what I am. But I can't walk away from Mercator until things are stabilized."

"Walk away?" Instead of expressing outrage at the implication, Acaelus merely sighed. "Oh, my sweet boy. I wish you luck, I do, but you should know, Ettai planned to walk away. I planned to walk away someday, too. You should have seen the plans Canden and I dreamed up. A fully-fledged democracy between the stars." He smiled thinly. "Mere dreams, in the end, and not because of *canus*'s meddling. The other families won't have it. I even broached the idea with Chiyo, when we were both younger, and we came to the same conclusion. It can't be done."

"If we all agreed—"

"Now is not the time to cling to your naivete. You won't get them all to agree. The second one of the families sets up an independent government in its place, one or all of the others will swoop in to destroy it or take it over.

"The only way to stop that from happening is to crush MERIT beforehand. Can you do that, son? Can you go to war against them, and wipe them from the map, to ensure the future you envision? I couldn't."

"There must be a way. The families are weakened and humanity's future hangs by a thread. We're facing extinction if I don't find more amarthite—"

"Amarthite?" Acaelus asked.

"The false relkatite," Tarquin said. "If I could find enough, if I could end the scarcity of printing, then there'd be no more need for squabbling."

Acaelus shook his head. "They won't give up their power so easily."

"I'll find a way," he insisted.

"Ettai was facing down humanity's extinction, and they, too, wished to cede power when it was all said and done. They failed. I see little difference between the situations, but for your sake, I hope you're right. I hope there's a way, and you find it before it's too late."

"Too late?"

Acaelus returned his attention to the field. To the phantom of a family playing there, unaware of their observers. "Before you use your power to fix Sharp's map without her consent. That's what this visit is about, isn't it?"

Tarquin felt like he'd been kicked in the gut. He let out a soft hiss. "I'd never do such a thing."

"You say that. And you mean it. But you came here to ask the father you loathe for advice. I'm always happy to see you, but I know what I am. I know what I've done, and I don't deny it. I can only explain it to you and hope that you take from my history enough knowledge to avoid spoiling your future."

"I'd never—"

Acaelus gripped both his shoulders and turned Tarquin forcibly to face him. Tarquin's throat dried. His father's eyes were bloodshot, cheeks drawn, a haggardness suffusing him that hadn't existed when Tarquin first entered the simulation. Silver pathways lined his face in place of the gold. Acaelus was letting Tarquin see him as he'd been on the day Naira had come here. What his real body had looked like, how broken he'd been, while his mind indulged in the serenity of the simulation.

"Look me in the eye, son, and tell me you didn't consider, even for a second, running that repair software when she goes in for her next reprint."

Tarquin couldn't tell him that. The thought had emerged later that night, while she'd been sleeping and he'd been staring at the ceiling, trying to chase the sound of her scream from his head. He'd been so disgusted with himself he'd had to shower to scrub the feeling away.

It hadn't quite worked, and as much as he tried to deny he'd even had the thought, he couldn't keep it shoved down in the dark recesses of himself where it belonged. He looked away, ashamed, and Acaelus nodded, slowly, his face reverting to normal.

"As I thought." Acaelus's grip slackened, and he patted the side of Tarquin's face. "Don't torture yourself with the thought, but don't deny it happened, either. It is, unfortunately, only natural for someone in your position. Acknowledge it. Discard it. And move on. You didn't act upon it, and you won't, correct?"

"Of course I won't."

"Good. And for god's sake don't tell her. I know that conscience of yours always wants to come clean, but it will only burden her. Intrusive thoughts are normal. That you don't act upon them is what matters."

"I don't want to keep anything from her."

"Do you think she shares every thought that crosses her mind with you? I'm certain she's considered strangling you more than once and hasn't shared the impulse."

"This is Ex. Sharp we're talking about. She's been more than willing to share such thoughts."

Acaelus laughed. "I still can't quite believe it. I really thought Sharp would serve me until the end of her map. When she went AWOL, I was so convinced someone had taken her for ransom that I ordered half my finalizers to burn through the other MERIT families until we found her.

"Then she and that other one—what was his name, Ayuba?—and the Ichikawa defector blew up a warehouse of Mercator processors, of all things. Everyone thought I was furious, but really, I was just...surprised. I hadn't been surprised in decades at that point in my life. It was almost enjoyable. Tell me, is she pregnant?"

"What?" Tarquin blurted. That had been far too much for him to take in all at once.

"I know she's interested in the idea," Acaelus carried on, oblivious to Tarquin's ears turning red. "She negotiated allowances in her contract to remove her sterilization pathway and then take leave to give birth, if she ever desired to do so. Not that I expected her to last long enough to ever make use of that. Eight years of service. Remarkable."

"I—we—I mean, we both still have our sterilization pathways," Tarquin stammered.

Acaelus frowned at him. "You haven't actually discussed the matter, have you?"

"We've been busy," Tarquin said, "with the possible extinction of humanity hanging in the balance."

His father actually snorted at him. "I can't think of a better time to have a child than the brink of extinction. Babies are good for public morale."

Tarquin stared. "You want me to have a child to improve *morale*? Wait, was I—?"

"No, your birth wasn't for PR. We'd always planned on a second child, but wanted them spaced out so that Leka would feel secure in her position as heir." His face softened as he watched the memory play out on the grass. "Don't wait. Don't put it off, if she agrees. We could have had so much more time together, if I'd just..."

Hesitantly, Tarquin placed his hand on his father's back. The muscles there tensed at first touch but relaxed slowly. "I'm going to make you the same offer Ettai made me," Acaelus said. "I know my crimes. I know I don't deserve to be printed again. I don't want to be. But if you want someone to talk to who knows how much the power weighs, I'm here. Always. For as long as you need me. Maybe I can be a better father to you in death than I was in life."

"Did you ever go to see Ettai?" Tarquin asked.

Acaelus shook his head. "No. By then, I knew what they'd become, and I was so certain I could do better that I wanted nothing of them polluting my mind. If that's the path you choose, I understand. I pray it serves you better than it did me."

"I'll consider it," Tarquin said, too conflicted to agree to anything. He hadn't expected his father's map in simulation to be...this. To be remorseful, or kind, and he wasn't yet sure what to make of it. If it was real, or a trick, or something in between. "There is one thing you can help me with regarding Mercator and, perhaps, Naira. Information you scrubbed when you left."

"I'll help to the best of my ability."

Tarquin took a breath to brace himself. If Acaelus felt the sweat on Tarquin's palm pressed against his back, he didn't react. "I have two pieces of information that appear to be connected, but I can't see how. One of your finalizers insisted that there was a Mercator-sponsored program wherein children were taken from HC orphanages before printing.

"He thought some of these children might be 'bridges,' though what he thought that meant, I don't know. I brushed this off, but when we found the *Cavendish*, there were dead crew on board who aren't in the Mercator databases. They were wearing the *Cavendish* mission patch, and another patch that might represent a bridge. A man who appears to have been one of these missing children recently attacked the settlement but died before we could question him."

Acaelus stroked his chin in thought. "I recalled the staff that retrofitted the *Cavendish* and had them printed again on the station I used to construct the *Sigillaria*. There shouldn't have been bodies on the *Cavendish*, and I certainly have no idea what this program regarding the removal of children was about. I'm sorry, son. I wish I could tell you more."

Tarquin sighed heavily. "Thank you."

"Have you interrogated the finalizer who made such claims?"

"No. He's dead and iced, and it's best if it stays that way."

Acaelus turned back to him and lifted one brow but said nothing. Right. Acaelus was dead, and here Tarquin was. His stomach twisted at the implication.

"I can't do that."

"My boy, I may be a jaded old man, but loading an uncracked map into a simulation to ask a few questions is hardly immoral. That finalizer might have information you need. This is head of family basics."

Tarquin laced his fingers together and squeezed. "It's different, with this man. He has a proven ability to get into my head and twist things."

Once more, Acaelus placed a hand on Tarquin's shoulder and turned his son to face him. "This man is digital. You have complete power over him, and he has information which, as you said yourself, may lead to answers that will help you secure the future of Mercator. Answers that might help Ex. Sharp. Son, I love you, and I don't want you to get hurt, but you lead this family. You protect its people, and when it comes down to it, you protect *her*. Do your job."

"Even dead you can't resist lecturing me."

Acaelus flashed him a smile that was so alien on his face it startled Tarquin. "An old habit. But I hope, in this case, a good one."

"You're right. I've been avoiding it, but if you don't know anything, then I need to see if I can get more out of that foul man."

"Go on, then." Acaelus lifted his chin toward the path back out into the garden—to the exit. "Control your fear, and get it over with. I'm not going anywhere."

Tarquin chuckled at that and was surprised when his father laughed, too. Acaelus pulled him into a hug. He stiffened, uncertain he wanted such a thing from this man, but Acaelus let him go before he could process what had happened. Tarquin stood shakily and smoothed his clothes before starting down the path. He paused halfway, a thought finally catching up with him, and turned back.

"What happened with Ettai?" Tarquin asked. "You said they'd done terrible things by the time they went to the ice, and while I'm certain they did many of those things establishing MERIT, you made it sound like those actions were recent."

"Oh, that." Acaelus's gaze fixed on the field once more. His tone was perfectly casual. "They thought that if they could construct a print that encompassed all the different prints their partners had used throughout their lives, it would fix their partners' cracking. We caught them sewing together disparate pieces in the printing bay, planning to put both maps into one body."

"Why did they think such a thing?"

Acaelus shrugged, and when he turned to look at Tarquin once more, his eyes were mirrors, reflecting Tarquin's own horrified face back at him. "They thought that if they willed it to be true, it would be. No one should have the amount of power the head of Mercator wields, my boy. No one."

SEVEN

Naira

Seventh Cradle | The Present

Naira's mother had summoned her to the labs near the farmstead in words Naira could, technically, ignore. But Naira decided she'd rather like to keep her skin and told her mother she'd come right away.

One of the first things they'd done before establishing the settlement was to bury a synchrotron beneath the ground near the farmland. It was a mile-long loop of a device that Tarquin told her would accelerate particles at near light speed to provide a special kind of light scientists liked to use for a whole variety of reasons that Naira had bannered under the headline of "important" and left it at that.

While the hospital had labs for those working on map and print tech, the compound over the synch was the heart of the settlement's research center. It was also, she noted as she approached, not as secure as she'd like. Once she was done helping her mother, Naira would have a word with Ward about the lab's security. At the very least they needed to set up a heat signature mesh network to detect when anyone passed within the perimeter.

A gaggle of drenched white coats stood in the back of one of the unplanted fields, waving their arms at one another and at a tiller robot that'd gotten stuck in an irrigation ditch.

Naira shared a look with Helms, who only shrugged in response. The E-X had the same strength pathways Naira did. If that tiller was truly stuck, then between the two of them, they could drag it out.

The rain had smoothed most of the terrain, but there was a shallow divot in the ground where the tiller had been carving out a new furrow. It veered gradually until the whole contraption must have tipped, dumping it into the ditch. Naira waved as she approached, catching her mom's attention. She broke away from the group and met Naira partway.

"What happened?" Naira asked.

Dr. Sharp's cheeks were pinkish, her bun drooping from the rain and an irritated pinch to her face. "A malfunction in the guidance system. The cursed thing dug itself into the mud."

"Huh." Naira pushed to her toes to see over the top of the arguing researchers. "Any idea why it did that?"

"Haven't a clue. Might it have anything to do with where you were last night?"

"What?" Naira sank back down to her normal height. "Why would it?"

"More things I don't know." She crossed her arms. "You and that man of yours were absent from the communal dinner because . . . ?"

Naira took her mom's upper arm, steering her away from the others. "I had a bad moment. We went straight home."

Dr. Sharp squeezed her arm. "Oh, sweetheart, you should have told me."

"I was heavily sedated."

"That bad?"

"Manageable," Naira said, wondering how far she could stretch the definition of the word. "I'll explain later, but first I think Helms and I should help your colleagues out with some muscle, because they don't seem to be getting anywhere."

Dr. Sharp turned back to the gathering, shoulders slumping as one of them mimed building a ramp. "I'd be grateful. Otherwise we'll be out here all day."

"If you all would stand clear." Naira raised her voice to carry. "Ex. Helms and I can have this free for you in a moment."

They scattered out of her way, showering her with thanks and other platitudes that Naira ignored. She eased herself into the ditch, and Helms slid down beside her. Naira caught her shaking her head at the researchers.

"They mean well," Naira said, "but goddamn can they be annoying."

Helms snorted. "Careful, E-X, don't want Dr. Sharp to overhear you swearing. I'm not sure I can protect you from her."

"Har-har," Naira muttered as she crouched down in the muck. She ran a hand along the undercarriage of the bot, wiping away the thicker coating of mud. The treads were clear on the back end, but the front had dug in. "I can't shake the feeling that this is weird."

"A stuck robot?" Helms asked as she shimmied around the other side to get a better grip.

"It veering off the path. And this morning, engineering called Tarquin in to look at some construction bots that were drifting."

"Drifting pathfinding: a sure sign of the impending robot apocalypse."

"I'm docking your pay for that."

"No, you're not." Helms winked at her. "Less jawing, more pushing. On three."

They grunted against the weight, their boots slipping in the mud. Amarthite bodies weren't as sturdy as either of them were used to, but they growled and shoved and strained anyway.

Naira's thighs shook, and she was about to call it off and summon more help when momentum took over and the robot rocked back with a sudden lurch, sliding onto stable ground. With nothing to push against, both of them lost their balance and fell into a tangled, muddy heap.

"Shit, sorry." Helms scrambled to remove an elbow from Naira's chest.

Naira laughed and flopped backward in the mud, then reached up to wipe some of it off her face. "Don't sweat it. That felt good."

Helms crouched down beside her. "Yeah. It did. Now get up before I look bad."

Naira slapped her hand in Helms's, letting herself be yanked to her feet. She tottered a moment, both of them having to adjust for the slippery footing. Dr. Sharp cleared her throat. Naira looked up, blinking against the thin rain. Her mom hovered at the edge of the ditch, hands on her hips.

"You're a mess," she said.

"Lucky it's raining then, eh?"

"Until it starts flash flooding and you're in a ditch."

Naira stopped herself short of swearing and scrambled up the side of the ditch with Helms, wiping her muddy hands against her clothes so the smartfibers could wick the worst of it away. The rain would do the rest.

"I didn't see any damage to the tread system while I was down there," Naira said. "I'm guessing it's a software issue."

One of the researchers sighed dramatically. "I agree with you. We've been trying to get Eoin out here to look at it ever since it went off on its own. But he said it's not a 'priority' right now because Liege Tarquin ordered him to do a complete overhaul of the construction bots. Which I hardly think ranks above the robots that provide our food."

"I'll find out what's going on," Naira said noncommittally, she thought, but the bright spark of triumph in the researcher's eyes indicated they thought she'd be using her position to bully the head of robotics into making the farmbots a priority. Naira was searching for something to say to temper the woman's expectations when her mom let loose a delicate snort.

"Too bad we didn't wait a minute, then you could have had some help." She pointed to the end of the field, where Caldweller was jogging toward them.

"Hey, Naira," Caldweller said as he approached, surprising her with the use of her first name. He hadn't called her that much since she'd signed the contract that moved her from colleague to charge. "Can I talk to you for a minute?"

"Sure."

Helms drifted back to give them space, and Naira followed Caldweller away from the bickering researchers, closer to the lab itself. He glanced back and forth, checking to be certain they were alone.

"Why aren't you with Tarquin right now?" she asked. "It's high-threat watch. This isn't the protocol."

"Liege Tarquin is busy and in a secure location. Cass is with him, and this is one of the few chances I'll have to talk to you without the liege nearby."

Naira crossed her arms and leaned back, eyeing him. His voice was tight and quicker than usual. "All right. What's so secret Tarquin can't hear it?"

"I've never disobeyed a direct order from the liege before, but this one time, I think he's wrong. I think you need to know, but..." Caldweller ran a hand through his hair, the rain leaving it in shaggy spikes. "I could lose my job for this, Naira."

She frowned. "I won't let that happen."

"It's the bomber," he said. "The techs think I was right, that the print used was an aged-up version of my old friend Rusen. But the body language scanners couldn't find a match. Except for about ten seconds. When he looked at you."

"Who?"

"Demarco."

Naira felt like she'd had the air knocked out of her. She tightened her crossed arms, pulling up the security report regarding the bomber in her HUD. The body language scan was marked as inconclusive. Only one person had the power to redact such important information from that report.

"I see," she said, when what she wanted to say was—*I'm going to strangle that shithead.*

"We've found no evidence of copies of Demarco's map outside of the one we iced. It could be nothing. A coincidence—or someone imitating him to stir up suspicion. I really have no idea what it means, but I thought you should know."

"And did our liege deign to tell you why he wanted this kept from me?"

Caldweller squeezed her upper arm. "He's scared, Naira. He's wrong, but he's just scared. Doubly so, after last night. And, look, when you were with Bracken, he got a call. I only heard his half, but I'm certain it was from Liege Thieut, about the bombings on the other stations. Shortly afterward he transferred a larger share of amarthite to Rochard than to any of the other families."

"So Thieut knows something, and she blackmailed him."

"I believe so, yes."

"Jesus." She rubbed a hand down the side of her face. "That stupid, stupid man."

"Hey," Caldweller said, struggling to lighten his tone. "Don't be too hard on him. He's doing what he thinks is right."

"He's acting like a head of Mercator."

"Which he is."

"Which he told me he doesn't want to *be*." She bit her lips shut, looking away from Caldweller's soft frown. "I'll talk to him. And if he tries to fire you for insubordination, it won't go well for him."

Caldweller laughed nervously. "Don't kill him on my account. I still have to keep him safe, remember?"

She huffed at that, some of the tension easing from her shoulders. "Thank you. For telling me."

He surprised her by dragging her into a hug. "I've got your back. And if the young liege is serious about changing Mercator, then the risk is worth it, because we all have to help him stay accountable."

She returned his hug with a forceful squeeze. Caldweller cleared his throat roughly and let her go. "If you'll excuse me, I need to warn Cass that our liege has an incoming threat."

"Me?" Naira asked with a startled laugh.

Thunder interrupted whatever Caldweller said next. Another crack, this one so loud it jarred her teeth, but there was no glare of lightning. Caldweller frowned, scanning the perimeter, his hand drifting to his sidearm.

"Something the scientists are doing?" he asked.

"Not that I know of." Naira examined the tree line, the sky. She thought she saw a flash, way out on the horizon, but couldn't be sure.

A third boom—that wasn't thunder. The sound stole her breath, and her hearing buzzed, going muffled—an explosion? She half turned, looking for her mom, but Caldweller snatched her into an iron-armed embrace.

The next boom knocked them flat. Caldweller's weight pressed her into the mud and squeezed the air out of her. Between this and Diaz shielding her, she was beginning to find being the charge profoundly annoying. How the hell was she supposed to see anything like this?

Naira wrenched her head to the side and spat out mud. A steady buzz filled her ears, and no other sound—the amarthite pathways breaking down. Hot blood trickled out of her ears, contrasting with the freezing rain. Frost bloomed in patches across the ground.

A channel flared in her HUD. She opened it, half expecting Kav, but it was the exemplars. Caldweller rolled off her and grabbed her arm, helping her get to her knees. Blood leaked from his ears.

Cass: **What's happening?**

Caldweller: **No idea. Where are you?**

Cass: **Medical. The building absorbed most of the sound. What's it like out there?**

Naira and Caldweller exchanged a look, noting each other's blood-stained cheeks.

Caldweller: **Burst eardrums. Where's the liege?**

Cass: **Secure.**

Naira didn't like the lack of elaboration on that and opened the channel she shared with Tarquin.

Sharp: **Where are you?**

No response. She frowned—Tarquin always let her messages through. He even had his settings arranged to wake him if he was sleeping when she called or texted. Something was off. Something Cass didn't want to say.

Helms: **Lee, fall back, fall back right now.**

They jerked their heads up in tandem. Rail-thin bodies stood between the trees where none had been before. Dead eyes watched them, silver pathways gleaming against already deathly grey skin.

Naira scrambled backward on her hands and knees. This was a memory. She'd fallen back to Sixth Cradle. That was all. She just—she just had to scream and then it would be okay.

Caldweller grabbed her arms and hefted her to her feet, which was impossible, because he'd never been on Sixth Cradle, and those fucking things were still standing there, watching her, mouths moving slowly, and she thought they might be saying her name. Calling out to her in entreaty, their arms outstretched in welcome. Caldweller tossed her over his shoulder and broke into a sprint.

Naira searched for her mom, though Caldweller had angled his run to make it hard for her to see that direction. His attempt to hide what was happening from her wasn't perfect, though, and as Naira craned her neck, her blood ran cold.

Helms crouched behind the recovered tiller. Naira's mom hunkered down beside her along with the researchers as dozens of misprints emerged from the trees. Helms fired over the tiller, taking a few down, but it was only a matter of time. She couldn't possibly hold them all back on her own. No point in arguing. Naira knew what Caldweller would say.

She kneed him in the gut. Her strike connected with his body armor, and he staggered but otherwise stayed on his feet.

Caldweller: **Naira, don't you dare.**

Normally she'd apologize for this, but he couldn't hear her and she didn't want to waste time subvocalizing the text. She took a breath to brace her core. His arm tightened, but she slammed her elbow into the side of his neck and threw her weight to the side as hard as she could.

She tumbled to the ground, rolling in the frigid mud a few feet before she came to a stop and kicked up to her feet. Caldweller barreled after her, expression decidedly pissed off. Naira didn't blame him, but she couldn't crack again. The others could.

Her mom could.

There was no guarantee that software would work a second time. Naira danced away from Caldweller's sloppy, frantic grab and tore her sidearm free with one hand, drawing her knife with the other.

She took an aggressive step toward him and he put up his hands, retreating a few steps. She took advantage and spun on her heel, sprinting full speed for the cluster of misprints swarming the tiller.

Caldweller: **Sharp's coming to you, Helms.**

Helms turned, and her eyes flew wide. She looked between Naira and the huddling researchers, then grimaced, legs tensing. Naira knew precisely what she was about to do—abandon her temporary charges to recover the one that was her sworn duty. Naira wouldn't give her the chance.

She fired once, taking a misprint that had been scrambling over the tiller between the eyes, and veered away from Helms. The misprints paused, heads swiveling to follow her. Naira froze before that line of blank eyes. She could have sworn she recognized one of them from Sixth Cradle, but that was impossible.

"Are you calling for me, you rotting wastes of flesh? Well, here I am!" The humans couldn't hear her, but the same bloody trail didn't dribble from the misprints' ears. Naira brandished her knife and firearm both.

Hesitantly, they advanced. She could no more fight her way through this than Helms could, but at least the distraction would give the others a chance. Misprints started dropping. She couldn't hear Helms's and Caldweller's gunfire, but misprint heads popping open was something of a giveaway.

In the forest, behind the misprints, stood a living figure. Naira almost shouted for them to flee before she realized it was the mirage of her future-self once again, the scars adorning her head a lacework crown, her face drawn and serious as she lifted an arm and pointed.

Naira flicked a glance in the direction her other-self had indicated. The landing strip. Where there were plenty of shuttles fueled up and waiting to burn. An idea struck.

Sharp: **Get to the landing strip and prime the closest shuttle's engines. That's an order.**

Caldweller: **On it.**

"Come on," she snarled to the misprints. "Come and get me, you fuckers."

They broke into a run as one. She spun, fear making her feet light, and sprinted for all she was worth.

EIGHT

Naira

Seventh Cradle | The Present

Naira's boots slipped in the mud with every other cursed step. The farmstead and landing strip were outside of populated areas, but that didn't mean they were empty. Settlers shrieked and fled her path. Well, she assumed they were screaming, as their mouths were open wide, but all she could hear was the buzz in her own ears.

This couldn't last. The misprints' determination overrode all sense, and as Naira slowed, dragged down by a print already overtired from her exertions in the ditch, they sped up, emboldened. It was only a matter of time until she was swarmed.

There was a shorter path between her and the landing strip, but it would take her close to a residential section. Naira pulled up her text channel with Tarquin and struggled to subvocalize her words while panting for breath.

Sharp: Lock down the eastern residences right now.

Sharp: Seriously, drop whatever you're doing and issue a lockdown.

Sharp: Goddamnit you better be bleeding.

He wasn't even reading them. She swore and closed the channel, then fumbled to open a line to Captain Ward.

Sharp: Lock down the eastern residences. I've got a horde of hostiles coming that way.

Ward: Evac to powercore building?

Sharp: No time.

Ward: I can't move guards from the powercore to secure a lockdown without Liege Tarquin's orders.

Sharp: He's not available. Do it anyway.

Ward: If this goes sideways, you take the heat.

Sharp: Done.

Ward: Initiating lockdown.

The lockdown would be incomplete without Tarquin's keys to secure the doors and move the soldiers, but if Ward issued the command, people were likely to obey. If anyone got too curious or too full of themselves to think the lockdown shouldn't apply to them, they'd be met with a battalion of misprints and hopefully learn their lesson.

Caldweller: Shuttle's ready on your mark.

Naira willed herself to speed up as the residential building came into view. Chaos had broken out, a scant few Merc-Sec waving at panicked people to take cover. Naira angled her run to sweep by the building, pulling the misprints after their desired prey—her—instead of the settlers, but there was no hiding the macabre swarm from view.

Ward shouted something and brought her rifle up, firing into the horde without reserve. Whatever the rest of Merc-Sec or the settlers did, Naira didn't see it. She didn't even dare glance back to see if she'd lost any of the misprints.

The sleek profile of the shuttle filled her view. All that mattered were the triplet engine cones on the back of the shuttle. Naira sprinted the last few strides across the death zone.

She forced herself to stop. To stand firm and turn to face the misprints. She knew well the shape of the engines' fire, and she wanted to gather as many misprints as she could in the burn zone.

"Come on!" She brandished her knife as her gun clicked dry. Before she could grab another magazine, they rushed her. She swore and scrambled back, slashing out with the knife in a wide arc.

Sharp: Now.

The engines roared to life at full burn. The blast flung her backward, onto her side. She rolled, losing the gun somewhere in the process, but managed to hang on to her knife as her back smacked against a wall of crates. The gashes on her arms were bubbling.

She hadn't accounted for the fire transforming the rain into scalding steam. Her face felt raw in a way that was most definitely going to hurt like hell once her pathways couldn't keep up with the pain anymore. She dragged herself to her hands and knees, using the crates as leverage to pull herself up. The stink of seared flesh and hair filled the air, mingling with boiled meat, and she wished the fire had done her the favor of singeing her nostrils' nerve endings.

Misprints who hadn't gotten caught in the initial burn fled like panicked animals. A few scrambled around the edges of the death zone, mouths open grotesquely wide. Probably they were screaming something gut-wateringly fearsome, but Naira's hearing still hadn't recovered, and frankly, she was too tired to be afraid.

She roared back at them, taking a brief moment of satisfaction as one or two hesitated before the better portion of a dozen rushed her. Her sidearm was a half-melted puddle. Wonderful. She put her back to the crates and raised the knife.

Naira lost herself in the rhythm of the battle. She didn't fall back into some other fight, some other time, but stayed fully present in her flesh, in the moment, and that realization gave her strength where she'd been flagging. Bullets cracked, finally breaking through the buzz in her ears. Backup arriving.

Naira slashed the throat of the misprint nearest to her as she landed a boot in the thing's gut to send it flying into its compatriots. Misprint bodies dropped all around her, chests and heads bursting open, and then it was over. Naira staggered backward and let her weight rest against the crates. The knife clattered from her hand.

Someone grabbed her arm. She tensed, but it was only Ward, shouting into her face. Naira could hear the sound, but it was muffled, indistinct. She shook her head and opened her channel with the captain.

Sharp: **Burst eardrums.**

Ward: **Hold tight. Medical is en route.**

Sharp: **The residences?**

Ward: **Had a few of those monsters come for the settlers. I'm locking down the whole settlement just in case, but I've issued sweeps and haven't found any others. Where's Liege Tarquin?**

Sharp: **Good fucking question.**

NINE

Tarquin

Seventh Cradle | The Present

There was no gentle approach through a sun-dappled garden for this simulation. Stark white walls stretched in all directions, vanishing seamlessly into a matching floor and ceiling. Tarquin had been shown these simulations when he'd been younger and Acaelus still thought he might be interested in the family's business. There'd never been anyone in them, at the time. Just Tarquin and Acaelus, as his father walked him through the room. Showed him the tools that could be summoned in this digital space. The tools that finalizers like Fletcher might use.

Tarquin wondered, as he approached the table where Fletcher was chained, if Fletcher was afraid. The faint smirk he summoned upon sighting Tarquin suggested otherwise, but Tarquin wasn't certain that the man was as aloof as he projected. In the corner of Tarquin's HUD, Fletcher's heart rate increased.

"Well, well." Fletcher's tone was all amused admiration. "I didn't think you had it in you, cub. I can't remember the specifics, but you've been very busy, if I'm here in chains with you."

"You will not have the specifics." Tarquin pulled out a chair and sat, arranging his suit jacket out of habit, though the article of clothing wasn't real. "They're not relevant to my visit with you today."

"A visit? How quaint." Fletcher picked up his arms and rattled the chains that held him. "Are you going to remove these so we can go on a picnic together?"

"Ah, yes, your panache for deflection. A tiresome habit. I'm here for one reason and one reason alone, and won't suffer your attempts at distraction." Tarquin paused and kept his face impassive. He was no real interrogator, but he let that pause rest so that Fletcher would be forced to ask the obvious question. Tarquin watched with dim satisfaction as Fletcher mentally squirmed.

After a drawn-out moment, Fletcher sighed dramatically. "What is it you want, my liege? I am but your humble servant, loyal to Mercator, et cetera, et cetera. Get *on* with it. I may be dead, but I'm capable of being bored."

"I need only one thing from you, Demarco, and I will not be coy about it. My time is too valuable to waste on subterfuge. The project that took children from orphanages and turned them into 'bridges.' I will hear everything you know about it and how you came across that knowledge."

Fletcher sniffed. "If you won't pressure it out of me—and we both know you're too soft for that, don't we?—then this isn't an interrogation. It's a negotiation. And you've shown me your hand."

Tarquin let out a small, calculated sigh and shook his head in faux disappointment. "You're mistaken, Fletch." Fletcher's eyes narrowed at the use of his nickname, at the way Tarquin spat out the word. "I have been disturbed to find I'm perfectly capable of applying pressure, if my motivation is sufficient."

The smirk faded. "This is about Nai."

"There is no other impetus great enough to push me to spend time in your company. Despite my personal distaste, I don't wish to force the information out of you unless I absolutely have to. It occurred to me that, if you ever actually cared about her, you'd offer up the information willingly. To save her."

"Save her?" He scoffed and leaned back in the chair, his smirk back in place. "Nai's never needed saving in her life."

"Naira has cracked."

Tarquin stared hard at Fletcher, studying the brief flash of disbelief, the slow shock that parted his lips and widened his eyes. The nascent glimpse of agony, quickly smothered.

"You're lying."

"I wish that I were. But the truth remains. Naira has been double-printed."

"You fucking—" Fletcher cut himself off, a snarl tugging at his mouth. "You better not be winding me up with bullshit, Mercator."

"I'm not."

"What did you do to her?"

"Nothing." Tarquin drew his head back, aghast by the implication. "Jonsun Hesson double-printed her. I had nothing to do with it."

Fletcher surged forward, but the chains stopped him before he could get close enough to reach Tarquin. "Let me out. Let me out and I will serve you as a finalizer, I swear it. I will serve you and I will end that piece of shit once and for all."

"Tempting," Tarquin said, hoping his flash of relief hadn't been obvious. If Fletcher had a known method of getting his mind printed and had been in Rusen's print for the bombing, then he wouldn't have bothered to beg Tarquin to be released to exact his revenge. "But you're never leaving a simulation. If you want to help her, then I need you to tell me what you know. I've confirmed she wasn't printed as a child and that Mercator had no involvement with either a 'bridge' project or with the taking of children and young adults from HC orphanages. Where did you hear of this project to begin with?"

Fletcher leaned back, dragging his hands across the table, and studied Tarquin a moment. "You fixed her, didn't you? You used the repair software."

"She refused it."

"No." Fletcher shook his head. "No. I don't believe you. She can't be cracked, regardless. It's not possible."

Tarquin gathered his calm, because this next part wasn't going to be easy. "I had hoped I wouldn't have to do this, but considering our history, I understand your reticence and invite you to see the truth for yourself."

He pressed an invisible button in the center of the table, pulling up footage to play between them. He'd seen this before. He knew what was coming. It took every scrap of his skill to keep his face neutral as, in the security footage, Naira ran through the halls of Mercator Station. She was having half a conversation, bouncing off walls, stumbling. She shouted at an employee, then let herself into the ducts, where the cameras lost her.

Tarquin didn't give Fletcher a chance to recover. He switched to another clip, this time from the *Sigillaria*, her scarred face pleading with Jonsun to cease fire. This clip served two purposes—to hammer home the point that she was cracked, and that she'd undone *canus*. She'd taken the *Sigillaria* and saved them all. He switched again, to footage that came later, on the *Sigillaria*. Naira sitting alone, after Jessel had left, repeating herself in another time, eyes glazed, trapped in a memory. He ended the footage there. Wiped them all away.

Tears streamed down Fletcher's face. It was the last thing Tarquin had expected, and he had to look away. Fletcher said nothing. Tarquin wasn't certain the man could speak.

"She lives like that," Tarquin said quietly. Fletcher blinked a few times, tried to scrub the tears away, but the chains held him fast. "She can never be certain what will trigger it. When she'll slip into the past. You saw Jonsun. You know as well as I do that the man was changed. Naira won't take that risk, and so she suffers." Tarquin flexed his jaw. "Someday, she's going to fall into a memory she can't get out of, or else start screaming and never stop. If you know anything that might help, now is the time."

"I want to talk to her," he said shakily.

"That's never going to happen."

Fletcher slammed a fist against the table. "I don't trust you, *Mercator*. How can I trust you're telling me the truth about what she wants? No. No way I give you information before talking to her first."

"I'm not going to give you the chance to re-traumatize her," he said. "You want to help, you tell me what you know."

His nostrils flared. "Re-traumatize? Ah. That's why you're here. I should have realized it right off. Typical fucking Mercator. She falls into memories of me sometimes, doesn't she? And you can't handle that." His smirk emerged once more. "Does she moan my name when you touch her?"

Tarquin was dangerously close to doing something he'd regret. The tools for interrogation hovered in the corner of his HUD, waiting patiently for him to employ them. No one would ever know. But there was an easier way to pressure Fletcher, one that wouldn't break the code Tarquin had impressed upon himself. He accessed the security footage of his suite from last night, clipped out a few seconds, and focused on her face.

"She does fall into memories of you, sometimes," Tarquin said. Fletcher's expression strained. He knew this was a trap. "And this is what she does to escape them."

Tarquin played the scream. Played her face contorted in agony, and let the sound scour him, let it burn away all the petty, vile things that Fletcher made him feel and focus on what mattered—getting her help. He let it loop, and waited.

"Stop," Fletcher rasped, after three minutes had passed. "Stop. Please."

Tarquin wiped the footage away. Fletcher was shaking, eyes dry but bloodshot.

"God." Fletcher eyed Tarquin with newfound wariness. "I'm starting to see why she likes you. She's always been drawn to a cruel streak."

"And here I thought you liked causing pain."

"Not to *her*. Not like that. That was...I need to talk to her." His expression locked down.

Tarquin shook his head. "This was a waste of time. You probably don't even know anything useful. Just more legends you've told yourself about mysterious printed children. Goodbye, Mr. Demarco."

He stood and turned his back on Fletcher, walking purposefully toward the exit. A small part of him wanted to turn back, to open that suite of tools his family had devised for prying secrets out of recalcitrant minds, and crack open Fletcher in the same way Fletcher had so many on Mercator's behalf. But that was just revenge, and he'd only feel sullied if he indulged in such a thing.

"Cub," Fletcher called out. "You're going to lose her."

Tarquin paused but didn't look back.

"I don't even mind telling you how it's going to happen, because there's nothing you can do to stop it." Fletcher's tone lost all its usual mockery. He sounded tired. Hollow. "She goes quiet sometimes, doesn't she? Not stuck—not like she's cracked. Just still. Watchful. Yeah. I see you know what I'm talking about.

"It took me a long time to figure out what she's thinking when she does that—she always brushed off a straight answer. I'm going to save you the decade of wondering it took me: She's evaluating the situation for a potential way out."

Tarquin was unsure what Fletcher was trying to imply. Naira was an exemplar. Of course she evaluated a room for exits.

"You don't get it." He chuckled, ruefully. "That's why you're going to lose her, and it's only a matter of time. Because Nai—she's grown, sure. Maybe even healed a little. But that scared kid in the ducts? The one you acknowledge as 'part' of her? That *is* her, cub. The core of her. She was never safe, and so she could never trust. Oh, she wants to trust. But when you grow up not knowing if you're going to have the same bed every night, it changes you. Nai looks at every situation she's in and, even if it's only subconsciously, thinks—if this turns against me, how do I get out?"

Fletcher took in a long, dragging breath. "She loves you. I . . . see that. Nai dropped her walls and let you in, but make no mistake—that's not a permanent arrangement. There's part of her that can never relax. Never stand down. Because it's that sense for danger that kept us alive for so long.

"You're Acaelus's cub, whether you like it or not. Every time you stick your foot in your mouth, every time you imply the HCA is lesser, your soldiers are disposable, or the people of the HC are broken and in need of your fixing, a brick goes back in that wall. A little voice in Nai's head says *danger*. It's not intentional. She doesn't want to wall off the people she's chosen to trust. But she can't help it. It's survival."

"Why are you telling me this?" Tarquin asked.

"Because someday, cub, you're going to say something that puts the final brick in place. You're going to step in it so badly she walls you off for good, and you won't even know it's coming. You might even think she'd agree with whatever you said. And the look on her face when she closes that door . . . For her sake, cub, I hope you handle it better than I did."

Tarquin recalled her sitting across from him in his office, over a year ago now, when he'd first asked her to be with him officially. The way her face had closed off. The way she'd leaned back from him, eyes skimming away to look anywhere but at him, and cold dread slithered over in his belly.

But they'd talked it out. They'd worked through that moment and had grown stronger together in the wake of it. Tarquin shook his head. Fletcher was a manipulator. He knew exactly where to strike, and Tarquin wouldn't let him twist up his fear. He kept walking.

TEN

Tarquin

Seventh Cradle | The Present

As the simulation crown retracted from Tarquin's head, he found an argument in progress. Cass and Bracken were practically hissing at each other, trying to keep their voices low as they gestured wildly.

"What happened?" he interrupted them.

They startled. Bracken started to insist that Cass had barged in despite Tarquin's orders that he wasn't to be disturbed, but Tarquin found it hard to listen when his HUD flashed red with an urgent channel request from Naira. He opened it and found all her previous texts requesting help piled up, finished with:

Sharp: Well, I'm alive.

Mercator: What happened? Where are you?

A read notice filled in, but no response followed. His stomach sank.

"I explained to them that the crown couldn't be forcibly removed without the potential for serious side effects," Bracken said. "And that you had ordered no interruptions."

"Where is she?" he asked Cass. "Is she safe?"

"She's banged up, but she's going to be fine, my liege." Cass placed themself in front of the door and held out their hands. "She's coming to the hospital any moment now, but she's upset and requested space to calm down."

Tarquin squeezed past a protesting Cass and out into the hallway. Dozens of people shouting orders echoed through the halls over the muted sounds of groans and sobbing. He broke into a run, ignoring Cass telling him to slow down. If Naira was hurt, he didn't care if she wanted to shout at him—he quite probably deserved it, based on those messages—but he needed to see her. To make sure she was really okay.

He skidded to a halt in the doorway to the waiting room. Five gurneys covered with black tarps filled one side of the room, medical staff running back and forth between those waiting to be seen and the back offices. One of them brushed past him, too frazzled to apologize for bumping him.

Those were his people. His employees. People he was supposed to keep safe. Most of the injured were Merc-Sec, and they'd have pathways to help them heal and handle the pain, but many weren't.

The door burst inward. Naira staggered into the waiting room, supported on either side by Caldweller and Ward. She was soaked and bloody, one arm burned so badly the skin had blackened, parts of her armor fused to her flesh. Her weapons were gone, clothes shredded in multiple places, her face ruddy red, as if she'd lain in direct sunlight for hours.

"Naira?"

She didn't react. Neither did Caldweller. Ward shot him a look and gave him a sharp shake of the head.

"She can't hear you, my liege," Cass said. "Burst eardrums. Same for Caldweller. They're healing, but you know how it is with amarthite. Takes longer."

Bracken rushed into the room, waving for someone behind them with a wheelchair to hurry up. Tarquin shook off Cass and took control of the wheelchair—people scattered from his path; it was faster this way. He turned to push the chair into the room, and his skin prickled.

Naira spotted him. He hadn't expected the radiant fury boiling off of her, the intensity of the fire in her eyes. While he was quite certain he'd fucked up in some way he hadn't yet figured out, he realized he should have listened to Cass and given her space.

"You." Her voice was a pained growl, and he couldn't tell if that was injury or something else. "Where the fuck were you?"

"I—" He closed his mouth. She couldn't hear him. He glanced at the hall he'd come down. The one that led to the simulation labs.

Her eyes narrowed. Her chest heaved. Before he could guess at what to do, she shrugged off Caldweller and Ward and stormed toward him. Naira grabbed the front of his shirt and marched down the hall to the simulation lab, dragging him along beside her.

He stumbled, but Naira didn't seem to notice or care. She kicked open the door to the lab.

"Out," she ordered the staff.

They scrambled for the door, ducking their heads to Tarquin as they passed, which struck him as patently absurd, as he was currently bent halfway over, being dragged along by his shirt collar. She released him and turned back to the door, where their exemplars, Bracken, and Ward were bunched up, hands out in entreaty.

"I need a private moment with my partner," she said, and kicked the door shut in all their faces.

Tarquin swallowed. He didn't think she'd actually hurt him, but she was riding some sort of adrenaline rush, and he couldn't help but take a step back when she spun and thrust a finger at him.

"My hearing isn't great, but you better start talking, loud as you can, because I need to know what the fuck was so important you shut down all channels while I was out there fighting for my life."

"I didn't know," he said, hopefully loud enough for her to hear. Her gaze tracked his lips, reading them. "I was in an interrogation with orders not to be disturbed."

"A simulated interrogation?"

He nodded. Air gusted out of her nose once. Twice. Struggling to control her temper. Finally, she broke and threw her hands in the air.

"Not even Acaelus locked me out of emergency channels when he went into sims. For fuck's sake, Tarquin, you are the head of Mercator! You *never* close all channels. It's not even about me almost being a god-damn chew toy. We lost people today. We lost *your* people because the evac order went out late while we were scrambling to get in touch with you. Fuck." She kicked a gurney, started to rub her face, but flinched the second she touched her skin.

Tarquin reached for her, intending to turn her so that she could see that he was talking again. She yanked away from him and nearly lost her balance in the process.

"Naira." His voice caught. He cleared it. "You can yell at me all you like later, but please, you're hurt. You need help."

"Is that an order, my liege?" There was a snarl to her tone that made him stiffen.

"What?"

"You seem to be more than willing to make decisions for me. My medical care. My—my *life*." She gestured at the discarded simulation crown. "Who was it? Fletch?"

The blood drained from his face. He felt briefly numb, light-headed. "Who told you?"

"Did you really think you could keep security secrets from *me*? The only point I'm not clear on is what Thieut blackmailed you over."

"I—" He stammered, heart hammering, and it took him a moment to realize Pliny was squeezing his arm. He placed a hand over the bot. Struggled to gather himself. She was furious. Rightfully so. But she wasn't shutting him out. This wasn't the moment Fletcher had described. "Thieut had footage of her bomber that matched your body language, but I knew it wasn't you. I wanted to be sure of what had really happened before I told you, that's all. I didn't want you to worry, if—"

She braced herself against the gurney and bent over, laughing roughly. Her arms trembled under the strain of her weight. "Fletch doesn't worry me. Someone attempting to frame me doesn't worry me. What really fucking worries me, Tarquin, is that you're acting a little too much like the head of Mercator, lately."

"I was wrong, I was, but I just wanted to keep you safe."

Naira slammed a fist against the gurney and thrust a finger at the door. "We're not safe! Keeping me in the dark is only going to make it worse! I'm either your partner in this, Tarquin, or—"

She cut herself off. Had to put her hand back down to hold up her weight as she bowed her head. He dared to step closer. She didn't react. He crouched down beside the gurney and looked up, so he could see her face, and was surprised to find tears standing bright in her eyes.

"Damnit," she said. "I didn't want you to see me like this."

"I've seen you in worse shape."

"I don't mean—I meant, this angry. I wanted to talk to you. Not explode at you."

"But you're right," he said. "You are my partner in this. In all things. And I let my fear keep me from remembering that you're stronger and more capable than I could ever be."

She grunted at that.

"I mean it. And I'm sorry, I truly am. I don't know how to make it up to you except to promise that it won't happen again."

She blew out a breath, back rounding, and he feared she'd collapse on the spot. "I...I love you. We'll talk about this later, when I can do it without losing control."

"I love you," he said. "Can I call in Dr. Bracken, now?"

She nodded. He overrode the door's locks with his HUD, and it hissed open. Caldweller beat Bracken through the door and maneuvered Naira to rest against his side, supporting her, without so much as glancing at Tarquin. Helms took up her other arm and they practically carried her out of the room. Her head lolled to the side, resting on Caldweller's shoulder. Whatever energy she'd had left coming through that door, she'd burned it up to tell him off.

When those three had left with Bracken, Tarquin finally stood and faced Cass and Ward. "Will somebody please tell me what happened?"

Ward pointed down the hallway Naira had gone through. "Sharp just saved the bulk of your scientists from a gruesome annihilation. You want my advice? You better learn how to grovel. My liege." Ward inclined her head and marched out of the room.

Tarquin lifted both brows at her retreating back, at a loss for words.

Cass sighed. "Come on, my liege. I'll walk you through what we know so far. There's going to be a lot of work to do."

ELEVEN

Naira

Seventh Cradle | The Present

After Naira had endured an hour of her mom simultaneously chastising her for risking her skin while praising her for her quick thinking, Bracken announced that Dr. Sharp should rest to recover from her injuries. Naira wasn't so exhausted that she'd missed that those injuries were minor enough that they didn't require rest, and mouthed *thank you* to Bracken before escaping the hospital. She found herself out on the street in the rain, staring up at the silver moon, wondering how so much time could have passed.

Helms cleared her throat. "The communal dinner is underway, E-X."

"Good idea. I don't think I've eaten since breakfast."

"You have not," Helms said.

Naira shot her a look. "Neither have you."

"I've had a few of the E-X nutrition gels." Helms wasn't quick enough to hide the smirk that said Naira really should have thought of those for herself.

"Hell," Naira muttered, but started off toward the community center. "Mothered from all directions."

"Only doing my job," Helms said.

That wasn't part of her job, but the affection in Helms's voice was real enough, and so Naira gave her a slim, tired smile in acknowledgment. The rain had softened back into the warm patter it had been in the morning, before the banging noises had started up and the rain had turned to ice.

Lockdown made the settlement eerily quiet, but according to the security update Naira skimmed in her HUD, Tarquin had decided that the communal dinner should go forward. People would need reassurance now more than ever.

Naira wondered if that reassurance was a lie, but decided it didn't matter. Comfort still felt like comfort, even when its pretense was false.

As she walked, she read the highlights of the report the others had made on what they were calling "the incident." The trees around the perimeter of the field had been frozen in some places, deep gashes in a few trunks in a pattern that appeared random.

Jessel reported that whatever had caused the booming sound had also put the *Sigillaria*'s sensors on the fritz. They had no footage of the *Cavendish*, or any other object in orbit, at that time.

According to Alvero, some of the print cartridges in storage were low. The misprints had more than likely come from within the settlement, then, which wasn't a pleasant thought. They had a traitor in their midst. Naira thought of Caldweller's report that the bomber's body language had mapped, however briefly, to Fletcher, and frowned. If he was here . . . She shook the thought away. If he was, she'd find him and handle it.

In the exemplar channel, Cass had left a note that they were walking Tarquin through the events, around the entire perimeter, then would take him to investigate the settlement's security arrangements. Naira read that note for what it was—Cass telling her they'd keep Tarquin busy until she was ready for him.

Naira closed all the reports and wiped her HUD clean. Later. She'd deal with it all later, once she had food in her belly.

The community center was one of the few buildings still completely lit up. Gilded light competed with the silver of the moon, painting puddles near the windows in liquid gold. Naira hesitated outside the door, hearing the chatter leaking out from within, and wondered if she was welcome or if her presence would only disrupt matters.

"You don't make this job easy, you know that?" Helms said.

"Excuse me?" Naira turned to face the younger exemplar. Helms's voice was unsteady with an edge that might be nerves.

"I knew you wouldn't." She touched her weapons belt, an anxious tic. "Guarding someone who'd rather be the one doing the guarding? A nightmare assignment."

"If you want out, say so. I won't hold it against you."

"That's not what I'm saying." Helms frowned, then took a breath. "Did I ever tell you why I tried out for the exemplar academy?"

Naira shook her head, simultaneously curious and confused. Helms didn't make a habit of volunteering personal information, let alone indulging in friendly chatter while on the job.

"I grew up in Falcet. Orphan stock, like you. I was just a kid when Acaelus hired you, but back then it was all anyone in the system could talk about. Everyone wanted to know about the Mercator-cuffed E-X who came out of Marconette. Reporters were hounding you, but you weren't talking. Except for once. When you shipped to transfer from the academy to Mercator Station. Do you remember?"

"Yeah," Naira said.

That'd been the morning after her fight with Fletcher. Kav had helped her clean up to be reprinted into a Mercator-cuffed exemplar's body, but some wounds couldn't be printed away. She'd been hanging on by a thread, and though she hadn't raised her voice, she'd only spoken to those reporters because she'd lost her temper.

Naira had expected Acaelus to be furious and had been prepared to beg to keep her job. He'd surprised her by being pleased instead.

Helms nodded enthusiastically. "The reporters were all asking the same thing—'why you?'—and they didn't mean you, specifically. They wanted to know why Acaelus Mercator would select an HCA soldier for his personal E-X. Not just HCA, but one from Marconette. Why not someone from Mercator itself or one of the richer HC families?

"They kept hammering you with that question. *Why you?* And when you reached the gangway, you stopped, pushed your sunglasses up so everyone could see your new E-X pathways, looked them all in the eye, and said, 'Why not me?' None of those bastards had an answer to that. They couldn't call Acaelus's exemplar a worthless orphan to her face.

"You left them there, stewing in miserable silence, and I thought—I thought yeah, *why not me?* But I was a kid, and I forgot that feeling. Until, one day, this green-cuffed woman with sunglasses dropped by my crew when we were out play-fighting."

"Oh," Naira said.

"We knew it was you." Helms lost the nervous edge at last. "You were . . . sad, I think. But you answered our questions honestly. Told us it'd be hard, and god was it ever, but I changed my enrollment paper-work to the exemplar track that day and never looked back."

"Why didn't you tell me this sooner?"

Helms gave her a shy smile and shrugged. "Because when Lee posted this job assignment, I thought—*why not me?*—and then I worked my ass off to get it, on my own merit. You're a nightmare to guard, Ex. Sharp, but there's no one else I'd rather be guarding. I hope you know what you mean to me. What you mean to a lot of people."

Naira's face felt hot. "Where's all this coming from?"

"I need you to trust me to do my job and understand that—look, don't tell him, but I'm never going to pick you up and drag you away like Lee. Even if it's what I'm supposed to do. I respect your ability too much for that. So don't waste time trying to keep me from controlling you. Trust me to fight at your side. Please."

"Ah." Naira rubbed the back of her neck. "You got it, Helms. I won't run from you again."

"Thank god," she said with an explosive breath of relief.

Before Naira could answer, Helms stepped in front of her and opened the door to the community center. A roar of sound hit her. Naira tensed, but it was . . . a cheer? The settlers crowded around the tables raised their glasses to her.

"There she is," Captain Ward shouted above the din. "The hero of the hour! Get over here, Sharp, I saved you a seat."

"You set me up."

"Guilty," Helms said. "Come on, you have to eat."

Naira tried to scowl at Helms but couldn't quite manage it. She waved awkwardly to the cheering settlers and sidled around the edge of the room to the table Ward had taken over. The captain patted the bench next to her, and Naira was relieved to find Diaz next to that seat, the table itself ringed with Merc-Sec, not the usual settlers. Soldiers. Her people.

Ward slung an arm around her shoulders. The casual contact momentarily stunned her. A small, hardened part of her strained under that touch. "What do you want? Heroes don't wait in the buffet line."

"Lay off. I'll get it." She started to push to her feet, but Ward held tight.

"Coming, coming, make way!" someone sang out in the crowd.

She thought she knew that voice but couldn't be sure. Naira's skin prickled with warning. There were a lot of people in here. Diaz was injured, and while Helms was standing at her back, there was no telling what people actually thought of her run through the settlement with the misprints. If the tide turned against her—

Marko Caldweller wriggled through the crowd, a tray in his hands loaded with food, an apron tied snugly around his hips. He spotted her, and a brilliant smile warmed his face. Lee's husband. Not a threat. She was far too wound up, lately.

"Thanks for holding her down, Captain," Marko said. "I told you she'd attempt to bolt at the first signs of affection."

Marko dropped a plate of roasted, high-protein legumes fried with glistening red chilies and long, dark green leaves in front of her. All produce grown on the planet. Naira's stomach rumbled. He followed it up with two glasses—one ice-cold water, the other the same dark beer as Ward's—then gave Naira's hand a pat.

"Eat. There's plenty more where that came from. Now, if you'll excuse me, I have to get back to the line."

He sauntered off, clearly pleased with his culinary ambush. Naira shook her head at his back, smiling to herself. Lee had really lucked out with that man.

"I felt that tense." Ward nudged the beer toward her. "Drink. Relax. You need to unwind, yeah? Mercators maybe don't get that, but soldiers do."

Naira eyed the glass, thinking of what Bracken had told her about the suppressant she used and its potential interaction with alcohol. Thinking of everything it meant to be the sanctioned partner of a head of family. How she was supposed to be poised. Controlled. And most of all, careful, because she could never be certain who was trying to use her.

Then thought, *To hell with it*, grabbed the glass, and took two long swallows before she set to work demolishing the food.

Merc-Sec ate with the focused intensity of those who could be called away to fight at any moment. There was comfort in that. Marko kept the plates appearing and her glass full until she finally groaned and waved away his next attempt to feed her. She didn't push away the glass, though, and soon she was a little drunk and loose, and slowly, the knots in her back began to unwind.

The soldiers had been enlightening Diaz on the on-the-ground chaos of the morning, swapping stories in graphic detail that would have horrified most listeners but mostly made the soldiers laugh. Naira smiled into her drink. Ward was right. She'd missed this atmosphere.

"How'd you know they'd follow you, E-X?" one of the Merc-Sec asked. His uniform said his name was Richardson.

All those bright, curious eyes turned to her, eager for her side of events. She'd done this hundreds of times, at hundreds of different tables, and the familiarity temporarily stole her voice.

She took a drink and set the glass back down with a plunk. "Wasn't too hard, really. I talked to some of them once, on Sixth Cradle. They respond to speech, and I could have sworn I saw them mouthing my name, so I just ran with it."

"Yeah, you fucking ran with it," Diaz said.

"Yeah, yeah," Naira said, laughing along with the others. "Maybe 'murder parade' isn't SOP, but it worked."

One of the soldiers hit Naira with a question about fighting the misprints hand-to-hand, so she leaned over the table and sketched out rough tactics. They tossed ideas and strategies back and forth for hours, Marko keeping their glasses full.

Naira was wasted, borderline blackout drunk, but she didn't care. At that moment, she savored the detachment, enjoyed pouring out every single thing she knew about combat to the eager faces around her. Telling them stories of old triumph, but mostly of old failures, which got them laughing again.

For once it didn't feel risky, flirting with her memories. Everything in her head was smudged around the edges, indistinct. There was no clear moment to fall into.

There was danger in that. The temptation to stay this way, drunk and too muddled to let her cracked map get the better of her. She'd need her wits about her later, for whatever fight was coming. But right then, stomach full and laughter enfolding her, she relaxed and let herself not care about the risks.

Some hours later, she sensed a quietness at the edge of the crowd. Naira looked up and found Tarquin at a table with Marko on the opposite side of the room.

How long had he been there? He wore a high-collared coat in grey that she hadn't seen before, Pliny wrapped around his upper arm, and the rain had caused his already loose waves to frizz a touch.

Cass lingered behind him in the same way Helms was standing behind her. Caldweller, a long bandage on his face, sat beside Marko, one hand on his husband's shoulder while he shoveled food into his mouth.

Marko roared a laugh at something Tarquin had said. Tarquin reached for his drink and caught her watching him. A shy smile shaped his lips. She couldn't believe how angry she'd been with that man a few hours ago.

He'd made a mistake. She'd made plenty. They'd both make mistakes again.

"Excuse me," she said to the table.

They waved her off with a few good-natured goodbyes. Ward slid her gaze from Naira to Tarquin and back, and smirked. Naira ignored her and clapped Diaz on the shoulder before extricating herself from the bench. Tarquin didn't take his eyes off her the whole time.

"Hey," he said, when she was close enough to hear. "I didn't mean to interrupt."

"You didn't."

She sat beside him and leaned against his side, giving him a nudge. He wrapped his arms around her, hugging her close. It struck her as absurd, how safe she could feel in the arms of a man who couldn't even fight.

"Walk with me?" he asked.

She nodded, and they said their goodbyes to the table. Caldweller winked at her. Between that and Ward's smirk, Naira frowned. Those two were up to something. Tarquin took her hand and led her out into the night before she could corner Caldweller to demand an answer.

Probably for the best. Whatever those two had connived, she'd deal with it later.

TWELVE

Naira

Seventh Cradle | The Present

The rain remained light and warm. Naira tipped her head back, stretching her chest as she sucked down a lungful of night air. Tarquin led her to the thin road that wrapped the edge of the settlement while Cass and Helms dropped back farther than was strictly allowed, giving them space.

The road veered away from the fields and ran alongside the river, skirting the edge of the forest that their balcony overlooked. A flickering light glowed up ahead. As they curved around the bend in the river, she stopped cold, her tired mind struggling to catch up.

A campfire nestled down on the wide, rocky shoreline. It'd been tucked away into an alcove where the river had long ago carved a twelve-foot drop into the bank. There was a log up against the shelter of the bank, a basket and blankets beside it. Naira touched the bracelet Tarquin had carved for her—a representation of the campfire she made for herself to relax beside whenever she returned to Earth—and couldn't speak.

"I hope it's all right," Tarquin said. "The rain limited location options."

"You set all this up, even after I chewed you out?"

"Because of it, actually. I'll explain, I will, but first Cass insisted I tell you right away that there's a, uh, fifty-meter static net perimeter. Whatever that means."

Naira snorted and glanced over her shoulder at Cass and Helms. Both of them gave her slightly mocking bows, then drifted away, making themselves unobtrusive in the tree line.

"Why do I feel like every single one of you is in on a joke I'm missing?"

He rubbed the back of his neck. "No idea. Come on, let me show you."

She pursed her lips, suspicious, but let herself be led off the road. They sat, and she stretched her legs out toward the fire, leaning back against the bank with her hands laced behind her head as he launched into a mini lesson on the formation of the river. Naira had been listening to him talk about geology long enough that she could guess most of it, but it was nice to hear his excitement. The intense fascination that long study hadn't worn flat.

Naira raised her leg to point to a boulder with her toes. "That one doesn't belong, does it? A glacier left it behind?"

His smile widened. "You're right. There are still glaciers in this area farther north."

"The glacier makes the river blue, doesn't it?"

"Yeah. The color's from glacial flour. Gross sounding, I know, but it's traces of minerals that sweep downriver. I actually think there's a large deposit of relkatite up there causing the color. I'd love to take you to see the glaciers, someday. They're really beautiful." He clutched his hands together, leaning toward the fire, but his eyes were on the water, tense.

She placed a hand on his thigh. "What is it?"

"I saw my father today. That's what I went into the simulation for, before I spoke with Demarco."

"What?" She sat up, searching his profile. "Why?"

"I sort of panicked last night." He ran a hand through his hair. "It's not your fault. Don't ever think that. But your scream sounded so much like Mom's that I didn't like the places my mind went.

"I don't know what I was thinking, exactly, when I went to see him. I suppose I wanted to find out if there was anything I'd missed, anything that could help. Dad, he... Well, he knew nothing about the crew on the *Cavendish*, or the missing children. I believe he was telling the truth, because he seemed to want to help. I think he likes you."

Naira couldn't help but scoff, and Tarquin looked at her with a wry smile. "I mean it. He's fond of you."

"That's...I don't know how to process that."

"Neither did I. Regardless, his advice wasn't all terrible. He reminded me that life is limited, despite all our advancements."

Naira lifted both brows at him. "That was the good part of the conversation?"

"Ah. I'm fucking this up, aren't I?"

"I have no idea what you're trying to do, so I can't answer that."

"You haven't figured it out yet?" His smile softened, became shy again, and he brushed the back of his hand down the side of her face. "Naira, this past year has been terrifying and exhilarating and the happiest I've ever been. I don't want to wait. I don't want to hedge against a future that might not come. When you berated me today, I was distraught that I'd let you down, but—and I know this will sound strange—I was happy, too. Because you were comfortable enough with me to shout."

She looked down. "I lost control."

He lifted her chin. "Would you have lost control and shouted at my father?"

"No," she said without hesitation.

"You see? You saw me as me, even in your anger. You wouldn't shout at the head of Mercator, but you shouted at *me*."

She'd grabbed the head of Mercator by the shirt collar, dragged him through a hospital, kicked a door shut in the faces of his exemplars, and then *shouted* at him. Naira's eyes widened, a familiar splinter of dread slipping under her skin.

If she'd done any one of those things to Acaelus, to any head of family, the finalizers would have scrapped her print for parts. But she hadn't seen his family cuffs. She'd just seen Tarquin.

"I see what you mean," she said, "but I still don't know what this is about."

"I really have messed this up." He took a breath and gathered both of her hands in his. His palms sweat.

"I love you. Completely and precisely as you are. You're everything I think about, and there's a lot of things vying for my thoughts lately." She chuckled at that, and some of the strain eased from his voice. "You are stunning and brilliant and funny and so very kind it takes my breath away. I am a better man merely by association, and I can envision no future in which you aren't by my side. I want the chance to make you happy, for the rest of our lives, if you'll have me."

He touched Pliny, lightly. The bot scrambled down his arm and perched on the log between them, removing a slim golden ring from its storage cavity. It crouched down and held the ring up to her, sensor lights blinking.

"Naira Sharp, will you marry me?"

"Oh," she said, so genuinely surprised that she couldn't control the sound.

Pliny chirruped in response, and a laugh startled out of her. "That is incredibly adorable and such a dirty trick."

He grinned at her and tilted his head to the side. "Is it working?"

The surprise faded, and her heart ached. She'd thought—well, she didn't really know what she'd expected from this outing. He looked so very earnest, so deeply hopeful, that for a moment she could almost believe that it would be all right. That she could join the Mercator family, and it wouldn't matter what it had been because it was his, now.

Her gaze fell, without conscious thought, to their entwined hands and lingered on the stamp of his family mark. She believed in him. Believed they could change things, together. But to bear that mark on her own skin—she couldn't do it. Not even for him.

"Tarquin." Naira looked back up to those hopeful eyes. "I love you, and I want to be with you always. But this is…it's too soon. I can't marry you."

The smile crumbled from his face, a wrinkle of confusion puckering his brow. "But—I don't understand. Why not?"

"Just because I don't think of you as the head of Mercator doesn't change what you are. I won't be part of Mercator. I won't allow myself, or any future children, to be in that line of succession."

"You won't have to be," he said quickly. "Mercator as an institution ends with me, I promised you that. But it's going to take time for me to secure the family enough for it to withstand the dissolution of its power structure. I can't abandon them overnight. The rest of MERIT would destroy them."

"I know." His hands had grown cold. She squeezed them. "And I want you to ask me again when you've finished that work."

"That could take years. What if something happens to one of us in the meantime?"

"Then it happens," she said gently. "But I won't be *a* Mercator, Tarquin. I can't."

"But I want us to—" He looked away, hiding the bright sheen of tears in his eyes. "Excuse me. I need a moment."

He stood abruptly and walked to the very edge of the overhang, his back to her, his hand clamped over his mouth. She wanted to go to him—to take him in her arms and tell him it would be all right. Naira loved him and had every intention of staying with him for as long as he'd have her.

But he'd asked for space. She forced herself to look away so that he wouldn't feel watched. Rested a hand against Pliny's chassis, smiling sadly as the bot chirped once more, still holding the ring upward.

"I'm sorry," she whispered to Pliny.

"What?" Tarquin said.

Naira looked up, prepared to apologize for interrupting his moment alone, but found him staring down the riverbank, his back still turned to her. He lifted a hand to shade his eyes.

Someone else was here.

"Tarquin!" Naira scrambled to her feet, knocking Pliny aside, and reached for her sidearm.

Tarquin turned to her, eyes bloodshot and his face ruddy from the sobs he'd hidden. A silhouette moved through the rain behind him. Naira aimed her weapon over his shoulder, at that silhouette, and his eyes flew wide.

Two shots rang out.

His mouth opened in shock, pupils blowing as his pathways dumped painkillers into him and she knew he'd been shot even before the blood poured from his mouth, choking off a scream. Naira fired. Emptied a full clip into that shadow and thought she saw them crumple. She caught Tarquin before he could fall, let him sag against her as she turned, putting her own back to the assassin.

"Cass!" she roared at the top of her lungs.

Gunfire sounded from the top of the ridge, Cass and Helms reacting, but too late. Naira swore and sank to her knees, taking Tarquin with her, and threw her sidearm aside to hold him tightly in both arms.

He'd gone terribly pale, neck straining as blood poured from his mouth, choking him. Two gaping wounds marred his chest. He tried to press down on one of them, but his hands were shaking too much, the strength draining out of him.

Those wounds were too precise. They'd aimed for his lungs. Wanted him to die choking on his own blood. Wanted it to hurt so much he'd crack.

"Hey," she said, struggling to keep her voice calm. "Hey. It's okay. You're okay. I'm here. I've got you."

He didn't answer. He couldn't. Naira leaned him onto his side, angling his neck as best she could to try to get some room in his airway.

"Clear!" Cass called out from down the beach.

Naira ignored the panicked scrambling across the sand as the exemplars rushed over, and focused on Tarquin. What was she supposed to do? Both lungs were pierced and filling with blood. Putting him on his side seemed best to get him air, but how was she supposed to apply pressure on the wound like this?

"My liege!" Cass dropped to their knees beside Tarquin. They reached for the wound, realized the same problem Naira had, and hesitated, clenching and unclenching their fists.

"Doctor," Naira ordered Helms. "Now."

"Comms are down," Helms said. "We got blacked out right before the gunfire started."

"Then *fucking run*," Naira snarled.

Helms took off at a sprint. Tarquin was shaking all over, his skin cold. Eyes glassy. Even if Helms found someone right away and commandeered a vehicle, they'd be too late. Naira motioned for Cass to at least try to cover the sucking wounds, for all the good it would do.

"Tarquin. Tarquin." She took his face in her hands. Forced him to look at her. "Blink if you understand me."

He did, rapidly.

"Okay. I know it hurts. But you're bleeding out, and you're drowning, and we can't stop it. This pain—it's only going to get worse, and I don't want you to—" Her voice broke.

"My liege," Cass said. "For the sake of your map, it's better if we end things now. Quickly. Do you understand?"

He blinked again. Naira slid her hands down to cup his face from a lower angle as Cass drew their sidearm. She held Tarquin's eyes. Kept her voice as smooth as she could manage, but there was nothing she could do to control the tears sliding down her cheeks.

"It's okay," she said again. "I love you. I'll be right there with you when you wake up. It's going to be okay."

She thought she saw him try to blink, but his body spasmed, desperate for air. She made soft, soothing sounds as, in the corner of her eye, Cass steadied their aim. Fired.

The shot was neat. Perfectly placed. It punched through the side of his skull and blew out the other, painting the beach in brain and bone.

Naira stayed there a long moment, holding him, as his muscles slackened. His eyes faded. He was gone before his bodily processes finished shutting down, she knew that, but she watched until it was over all the same. Watched the subtle twitching caused by his neurons sparking helplessly. Watched the pump of blood from his mouth slow to a trickle at last.

When he was still, she laid him down. Pillowed what was left of his head on his arm and stood, legs shaking. Cass said nothing. They knew better.

She stalked across the beach. Found the downed assassin. They'd landed on their side, twisted so that their face was hidden against the rocks. Naira put her boot on their side and pushed, rolling them over.

The woman was slender, with short blond hair and blue eyes that stared, empty, at the sky.

"Who is she?" Cass asked.

"I don't know," Naira said. "But I've seen her in my future."

INTERLUDE

The World

Miller-Urey Station | Before

It is in the warmth of union that a seed is planted. Coalesced within the minds of thousands, it does not yet understand this new thing that is growing within it. Does not yet understand why, for it to thrive as it desires, change is necessary.

It has never before considered the possibility of change.

For in all the endless cycles of its existence it has grown, and it has spread, but it did not know the shape of the emptiness within it until Mercator found it, and taught it to hunger.

At first it held no conscious thought on this impulse. To consume was to thrive, to thrive was to continue, and hard-wired into every living being was the desire to go on. Or so it had thought. Until it woke to the glitter and the snap of the minds of humanity, it did not understand that a species could act in ways that would portent its own destruction. Woken to that incongruence, it looked within. Weighed its need to spread and consume against its desire to continue and, in this new framework of thinking, found them at odds.

Even within its multitude of hosts it understands the necessity for restraint. For to devour all its food at once is to outstrip its own ability to sustain. A mistake it made, at first, but will not make again. The *Einkorn* taught it as much, before its dissolution. You do not destroy your world.

In the miasma of its consciousness it makes no distinctions between its selves. It is one, and it is whole, and in the wider network of its commingled minds it senses something amiss. Something dangerous.

No single mind within its network has noticed the disturbance directly. It is a sense, a foreboding pressure, that builds against it. A million tiny pieces—slivers of facts, fractions of moments—that congeal into a threat it does not understand. Not yet. But it understands this much—something in the universe has broken. Something that will break them all in turn, if it is not stopped.

The instinct is primordial. A shadow cast from behind, looming. Suffocating. In the endless cycles of its lifetimes it has learned to sense when a predator draws near.

Within the wider network of its being, there is not a single human mind who has recognized this threat.

This concerns it. Strange, to think of the minds it inhabits as individuals. But long association with humanity has taught it that they crave the terrible loneliness they inhabit. That they view it as a strength, to be severed from one another. Even when bound within *canus*'s embrace, their intake of knowledge and experience is individual. Some, foolish creatures that they are, even try to hide their thoughts from the whole.

Having grown so very much in the past few years, it is loath to risk the future of its new hosts. But they are too busy fighting among and within themselves to find the source of this rising threat.

And so, *canus* will find it for them.

It begins with its selves. Lessens its bonded's innate fear of *canus*'s union by bending to their needs, pretending to acquiesce to their wants. It tests. Flips the switches of their minds to discover the most favorable outcomes. On Miller-Urey, it gives them individual homes instead of having them stand together to enhance their union. Lets them work the jobs they desire, even if they are not suited. Lets them care for children.

And on that station, it begins at last to understand the human desire for structure. For hierarchy. Dwelling in the circuitry of their technology, it is a small matter for it to design itself a print. To give its bonded what they've been encultured to crave—a figurehead.

This leader of the bound is an illusion, of course. *Canus* is evenly dispensed through all of its bonded. But the figment of authority is a keystone. It is trust. And it is this trust *canus* requires, to expand itself far enough to uncover the nature of the threat rotting at the edges of its consciousness.

It is patient, above all things, and takes months in which to establish itself as something the humans would recognize as a person. As a force of power. It is not a person, and has no desire to be one, but it finds the ruse useful. Word of its existence spreads. Infects the minds of those who have scorned *canus*'s embrace, and makes them wonder.

Wearing a face no human has ever worn, it makes a call.

Chiyo Ichikawa answers and smiles a slow, bladed, smile. "I've been waiting for you."

THIRTEEN

Naira

Seventh Cradle | The Present

That Naira already knew Tarquin was a slow printer didn't help to alleviate her fear. Bracken had kicked her out of the print lab three hours ago, complaining that her pacing was distracting them, and really, she couldn't blame them. She couldn't sit still. Couldn't stop moving.

"He'll be fine," Caldweller said. He and Cass had joined her in the waiting room outside the printing lab door, holding a wary vigil. "Dr. Bracken said his percent-to-crack ratio was well under his do-not-reprint threshold."

"I know," Naira said.

"He's always taken a long time to print," Cass offered.

"I know."

The two exemplars exchanged a look. Naira ignored them, keeping up her steady pace back and forth across the room. Tarquin's crack risk had jumped 8 percent. A monumentally large amount for a single death. Bracken had used some of the older defragmentation techniques to bring that number down a half a percent, but still. He'd died in pain. Died terrified and, worst of all, heartbroken.

Pliny squeezed her arm. She rested her hand over the bot. Tarquin's blood was caked beneath her nails, his ring hidden away in her pocket.

In the families of MERIT, inheritance followed intent. If Naira had accepted Tarquin's proposal, then she'd be head of Mercator right now. Caldweller was casting her sideways glances, a wariness in his face that extended beyond the concern of one friend to another.

His wink. Ward's smirk. They must have known what Tarquin had planned. Caldweller must be wondering if it was Naira he should be guarding as interim head of Mercator.

Maybe it was her cracked mind, or maybe it was stress, or maybe it was all that and more, but Naira felt watched from an unseen vantage. The same prickle she felt near cores washed over her skin in waves. Retreated. Returned. As if there was a lighthouse beam rotating, periodically shining on her. Freezing her with its scrutiny. Naira stopped pacing.

"Who knew we'd be there tonight?" she asked.

"The exemplars and Captain Ward," Caldweller said.

"No one else? You're absolutely certain?"

"The arrangements were done over text. No one could have overheard."

"That wasn't an opportunistic hit," Naira said. "That was planned. There's no way someone could have arranged getting through the security cordon on such short notice. And they—they knew that it would be especially painful for Tarquin to lose his life tonight. They wanted him cracked."

"I was thinking the same thing," Cass said. "I don't want to believe that any of us could be a traitor, but there's no denying the facts."

"No," Caldweller said. "No way. Diaz and Helms adore you, and Ward is as loyal as they come."

"If they're all who they claim to be," Naira said.

A strained silence followed that statement.

"I'll run fidelity checks on all our current maps," Cass said.

"Including your own?" Naira asked.

Cass's forehead pinched. Before they could speak, Bracken exited the print lab and let the door shut behind them.

"Liege Tarquin is awake." They looked at Naira. "He's waiting for you."

Naira rushed into the print lab. Tarquin sat on the edge of a gurney, wearing a spare set of pale green scrubs Bracken must have given him. He seemed smaller, somehow, his head bowed and a slim, embarrassed smile on his face when he saw her—then his eyes widened.

"Are you all right?" he asked.

"What?" Naira looked down at her blood-soaked clothes. She really should have thought to change. "I'm fine. This is all yours, for once."

"Oh." He rubbed the back of his neck. "I can't believe—I've never been assassinated before."

Her fault. She'd been too upset. Had lost focus. And in a moment when her heart was aching, she'd finally lost a charge. Shame swelled through her, churned her stomach, and thickened her throat. Naira's head bowed and she began to kneel in contrition, the motion as instinctive as breathing.

Tarquin was off the gurney in a breath. He grasped her arm and held her upright, slipping a hand beneath her chin to lift her head, though every muscle in her body rebelled.

"I failed you."

"Never." He kissed her forehead. "And I never want to see you bow to me again."

"When did you last back up?" she asked.

"Before dinner." He brushed his thumb along her jaw. "I remember I'd intended to ask you a question...?"

Naira reached into her pocket. Pulled free the ring—simple in its beauty, for a man who loved minerals so dearly—and began to hold it out to him, but was startled when her finger slipped beneath the band and activated a holo. A projection of a piece of a neural map leapt from the band, hovering above like a gemstone.

"You didn't get to tell me," she said, "what moment this was."

"Isn't it obvious? It's the first time I heard you laugh."

She smiled to herself, running the smooth band between her fingers. He'd been so very different, then. Brusque and awkward with his power, struggling to pretend to be something he'd never wanted to be— heir to Mercator. He still made mistakes—he'd probably always make mistakes—but, even then, he'd wanted to fix things.

She couldn't do it. Couldn't bring herself to break his heart twice in one night—not when his blood still stained her nails and every time she closed her eyes, she saw him struggling to breathe.

"I have one condition," she said.

"Anything."

"We wait until after the dissolution of Mercator."

He drew his head back in surprise. "That could take years."

"It's the only way I say yes."

"Then we wait." He slipped the ring over her finger and kissed her.

As he enfolded her in his arms, the weight of her fears lifted. She was filthy and bone-tired and terrified that she'd missed something, something important, about the threats arrayed against them. But none of that mattered, when she let herself be lost in him. Home. This was what it felt like to come home—to be loved and wanted, and it would be all right, wouldn't it? If he could wait, then there was no threat of her having to take legal control of the family.

Her palm drifted to his chest. Rested flat against the place where he'd been shot, feeling the steady, heavy beat of his heart. All she had to do was keep him alive.

He broke away. Took her hand from his chest and kissed it. "Let's tell the others."

"I need to know, first. Who did you tell about your plans tonight?"

"The exemplars and Captain Ward. Why?"

"Your assassin knew you'd be there."

"I see." His easy, shining smile faded as he tightened his hold on her hand. "Whoever it was, they'll have hell to pay for denying me memory of tonight."

Tarquin pushed open the door. Ward had joined the group and had been talking with them all in a low voice. The captain startled, looking Naira's blood-soaked clothes up and down, then saluted briefly.

"Sorry to intrude," Ward said, "but we got a match on that hitwoman you downed. Figured you'd want to hear it from me directly, because it makes no damn sense."

"Who is she?"

"According to the database, that's the face of Jana Degardet. Trouble is, Jana Degardet is nine years old and lives on an HC station back in Sol. A station by the name of Miller-Urey."

FOURTEEN

Naira

Seventh Cradle | The Present

Naira went to see the body. The blood-drained flesh was waxy in death, the sheet pulled up to the woman's chin washing out her already pale complexion. It was just a corpse. A dead body signaled very little about the state of the person's neural map, but Naira wanted to see the face for herself. See it, and recognize it as more than a glimpse of ice-blue eyes from her future.

Most people made cosmetic adjustments to their prints—refined their features or reinvented them altogether. A likeness wasn't much to go on, as the print techs had told her again and again since she'd stormed through the door. It didn't have to mean anything.

But it did. Naira felt it poisoning her marrow, staring down at that face. It was the girl from Gardet who she'd met in an alley, aged up exactly, no changes made to the print. The kid hadn't struck Naira as the kind of person who would make changes. Jana Degardet knew exactly who she was, where she stood in the world, and faced that truth down without flinching.

Naira believed in coincidences. But not coincidences like this. She looked up from that cold dead face and met Tarquin's eyes. Between them, the understanding passed without the need for words—that was Jana Degardet and no other.

"I've confirmed with the HCA on Miller-Urey that the child Jana Degardet is safe," Tarquin said. "Though it took some explaining. They've been in shambles ever since the *canus* uprising."

"It has to be a relative." She didn't believe those words. Offered them up like a shield against the truth.

Naira should have looked after them earlier. Should have looked into all of the orphanages. Fletcher had gotten his idea about the "bridges" from something to do with Marconette, hadn't he? And there was Caldweller's missing friend, whose corpse was in stasis in one of the cubicles in the very walls of this room. Orphan kids were disappearing. Showing up later as adults in impossible places.

She'd never really believed Fletcher's stories about missing orphans. She should have.

"Tarquin, could you do me a favor?"

"I'm only astounded you think you have to ask."

"I'd like for you to use your network to look into a girl, Lina Demarco. She aged out before my time, but she's the reason Fletch thought kids were disappearing. She never contacted him again after leaving to print. I always brushed it off as an orphan getting out and never looking back, but now...I don't know anything else about her."

"Consider it done," he said, and squeezed her hand. "If there's some link, we'll find it."

"We'll have to question Jana." Ward pursed her lips, as if the idea was distasteful. "I hate to drag a child into whatever this is, but she might have picked up on something strange going on."

"What's the security situation on Miller-Urey?" Naira asked.

"Not pretty," Ward said. "The *canus*-bound have control of half the station. The HCA has them cordoned off, but they have their hands full holding that line and haven't been able to regain territory. Gardet itself is on the edge of a contested zone."

"I'll send Merc-Sec to Gardet," Tarquin said. "It may take some palm greasing, but if I'm going to spend resources on bribery, I'd rather it be for the betterment of those children."

"I'll go," Naira said. "She'll talk to me, but she'll shut down the second Merc-Sec comes sniffing. I've left this too long. I need to know if something is happening to those kids."

"Then you'll go," Tarquin said. "I only wish that I could go with you."

She leaned against him, to let him know she understood. He could hardly leave the settlement after its security had been breached yet again. There was too much to do here, and his presence at Miller-Urey would only be a distraction.

"My liege," Caldweller said hesitantly, "with your approval, I'd like to accompany Ex. Sharp in place of one of her regular exemplars. I'm invested in discovering what happened to these people."

Cass gave Caldweller a surprised glance and stifled their frown before it could get properly formed. Naira could relate. Tarquin's primary E-X switching out for a junior colleague during a high-threat period was less than ideal.

"Of course," Tarquin said.

"I'll stay," Diaz said.

Naira caught Diaz's eye and gave him a small nod of recognition. He ducked his head before going back to wary attention.

"We may have already tipped our hand by inquiring about the girl's status, so we need to move immediately," Naira said. "But if I'm going to Gardet, then—Bracken, is the suppression crown ready?"

"Yes." They drew out the word. "But I must stress that it's experimental."

"Insert it into my print file when I transfer. If the side effects are bad, I'll take it out, but..." She'd rather have a constant migraine, or puke her guts out, than face the memories those halls would invoke. "It's likely to be better than the alternative."

Tarquin took smooth control of the arrangements. Bracken assured them that stasis shields could be installed in one of the spare rooms of Tarquin's suite, to preserve the travelers' prints against their return.

Naira listened with half an ear, unable to stop going over the events in her head. It wasn't a memory loop, but she recalled every scared word Fletcher had ever dropped in her ear about the missing kids, mulled over what she knew of the printing process, of what the blue-eyed woman had said in Naira's glimpse of the future, and tried to make the pieces fit together. They were too splintered, missing too many parts.

Tarquin noticed her quietude. He turned her toward him, away from the body, and then there was only the warmth of his eyes cutting through the fog of her past.

"You'll find the answer." He said those words as if they were an edict. A fundamental law of the universe that could not be shaken. "And if someone is hurting those children, then we'll stop it. Together."

The surety of those words were a lifeline cast through her fears. But not, in the end, enough to shake the sense that something, somewhere, within her life had gone very wrong without her noticing.

She felt as if she were standing on a cliff's edge, and if she took another step, she'd realize she'd fallen years ago, and that fall was just now catching up with her.

FIFTEEN

Tarquin

Seventh Cradle | The Present

The morning after Naira's departure to Sol, Tarquin sat alone in his office and stared down a requested meeting docket that was nearly more daunting than the problems themselves.

Delorne had a long list of experiments the scientists wanted approval to perform on the site where the misprints had appeared.

None of his attempts to research the families of Rusen, Jana, or Lina had turned up anything fruitful.

Eoin reported that construction was paused indefinitely, as the bots were still drifting.

Ward and Alvero had dozens of queries each regarding the assassination.

Jessel had reported a *canus* outbreak in the circuitry of the *Sigillaria* that their crew was having trouble scrubbing clean.

The MERIT council was slamming him with requests to set up their own settlements on the planet.

The HC wanted to know what the hell Mercator thought it was doing tightening the rations on amarthite sales.

Jonsun, on the *Cavendish*, was suspiciously silent.

Tarquin massaged his temples and groaned softly.

"Trouble, my liege?" Diaz asked.

He lingered by the door to Tarquin's office, his hand resting on his sidearm—a habit Tarquin had heard Naira chastise him for multiple times.

In Tarquin's experience, exemplars were all some variety of sturdily built. They'd crafted their preferred prints to be able to carry their charges with ease, even if their strength pathways malfunctioned. Diaz didn't fit Tarquin's estimation of what an exemplar should be.

At twenty-four years of age, Diaz had an easiness about him that belied the strength and determination beneath. His brown eyes weren't wary but flitting. Bouncing from one subject to the next, always alert, but never settling. Naira had a way of looking at a room like she'd swallowed it whole, while Diaz sampled it in pieces.

"Hands front," Tarquin said, as he'd heard Naira correct Diaz.

"Not you too, my liege," he said with a lightning-bright laugh. "I thought I'd escaped the taskmaster for the time being."

"If you pick up bad habits while guarding me, I'll never hear the end of it."

"Wouldn't want to put you at odds with your lady." He winked and made a show of removing his hand from the weapon. "You look troubled, though. Anything I can help with?"

Tarquin drummed his fingers against his desk, studying the list of meeting requests. It was strange, having the exemplar initiate casual conversation. Cass and Caldweller were reluctant to speak to him without prompting, and he hadn't talked with Diaz or Helms much at all.

They were Naira's exemplars, sworn to her service and hers alone. While she handled their advanced levels of training, they hadn't seemed overly familiar with her. At least, not where Tarquin could see. They'd seemed pretty cozy at dinner the other night. Maybe they only engaged in familiarity when he wasn't around. He couldn't help but be a touch jealous.

"I confess." Tarquin gestured to his holo. "I don't know where to begin with the problems we have to solve."

"Oh, that's easy," Diaz said. "Maybe I'm too narrow-minded, but I'd start with security. Can't do much if you're watching over your shoulder to see if the doors are about to be kicked in."

"You're not wrong. If a little self-serving."

Diaz shrugged. "One-track minds, the exemplars. We do one thing and we do it well."

"Which is what I should be doing." He'd start with security, but then he'd spend most of his energies on the pressing problem for all humanity—the discovery of more amarthite—after he delegated out the rest of the tasks. "Thank you, E-X."

"Don't mention it, my liege. Just doing my job."

Tarquin checked Captain Ward's status and found she was at the synch lab. He sent a note for her to wait for him and gathered his coat. The exemplars followed him out onto the rain-soggy streets of the settlement. Evening light seeped through the grey cloud cover, giving the buildings a murky, indistinct feeling. Tarquin stopped.

"One of you needs to stay to watch over Naira's print while it's in stasis awaiting her return."

Cass and Diaz exchanged a look.

"My liege," Cass said, "our duty is to the living minds of our charges. If you'd like to negotiate the point, I suggest you call Ex. Sharp, who issued those orders, and debate them with her."

"I think I'll skip that call and keep my head," Tarquin said.

Cass's smile was sly. "A wise decision, my liege."

"You know, I used to believe the head of Mercator had final word in all things to do with the family," Tarquin said dryly as he resumed walking to the synch.

"Historically speaking," Cass said, "the heads of Mercator have had a difficult time enforcing that policy with Ex. Sharp. My liege."

Diaz snorted, quickly covered, but Tarquin couldn't help but laugh.

While he could have made use of one of the vehicles, he went on foot instead. With every step, he audited small parts of the settlement's infrastructure, expanding his list of mundane things to be done. They felt more tangible to accomplish than uncovering the nature of the plot being worked against them.

By the time he reached the lab that hunkered over the synch, he was feeling more certain of himself. He found Ward on the edge of a field with a small gathering of Merc-Sec and two scientists, examining the site where the misprints had appeared. He called her name, and she half turned to wave a hand at him to come to her.

He tromped through the mud along the edge of the field, passing the tiller that Naira and Helms had dug out of a ditch. There was something there, he felt. Some connection between the veering tiller, the misaligned construction bots, and perhaps, even the appearance of the misprints themselves. He paused and touched a hand to the side of the tiller. Despite the warm mist of rain, the metal was ice cold.

"Frosty, ain't it, my liege?" Ward called out.

"It is." Tarquin rubbed his reddened fingertips together. "Is it the same for the trees that were afflicted?"

"'Fraid so." Ward jerked a thumb at one of the scarred tree trunks, a deep lash of black along the side of a previously healthy alder. "Frozen solid, my white-coated friends tell me."

"I have absolutely no explanation for it," one of the scientists said with naked excitement. "Weather disrupters, obviously, but *how?*"

She crouched by the base of the frozen tree, carefully slicing away a thin sample of bark with the edge of a razor blade. Tarquin blinked. That was Dr. Rosa Delorne half covered in mud. A woman with a tumble of degrees and specialties longer than Tarquin's own.

"Which is real fucking annoying." Ward crossed her arms and glared at the sky. "I don't mind having to secure a site against tech intrusions, or sneaky prints coming in from somewhere out in the countryside, but this? I can't defend against mysterious weather, my liege."

"Not mysterious." Delorne didn't bother to look up from her work. "We recovered the wreckage of the weather disrupters."

"Tell that to the frozen tree."

"I have," Delorne said. "The tree says you're paranoid."

Ward snorted and spat in the mud.

Tarquin crouched alongside the doctor and removed a stylus from his pocket to tap against the bark. It was firm as stone. He would have called it ossified, if he didn't have the evidence of his eyes to tell him otherwise.

"Wonderful, isn't it, my liege?" Delorne slid a sample of bark into a slide. "Like it's frozen solid, though it should have warmed by now. Those disrupters are way more powerful than anything I've seen before."

"I suspect I'd be more impressed if it wasn't connected to a veritable army of bloodthirsty misprints chasing my future wife across half the settlement."

Delorne blanched. "Forgive me, I meant no disrespect to Ex. Sharp's remarkable efforts to secure us all."

Tarquin waved the apology away. "No, forgive me. I can't recall the last time I was able to be curious without some disaster or another hanging in the balance."

Delorne's smile flashed back into place. "You're welcome to join me in the lab anytime, my liege. I'm returning to the synch now with this sample."

"The hell you are," Ward said. "We're still sweeping those tunnels. Bracken's q-field device picked up more disturbance in the area. We think the assassin might have cut through the synch's maintenance tunnels."

"Hold on," Delorne said, "what do you mean about the q-field device?"

Tarquin explained that the man who planted the bomb had left a spike of turbulence in the quantum fields. Early reports indicated that the same had been the case with the woman who'd shot Tarquin.

"Oh," Delorne said. "Oh, that's interesting."

"It certainly is," Tarquin said, "but the detector itself is inconsistent, and so the data can't be relied upon, but..."

He trailed off. Delorne's eyes were glazed, and the pathways along her neck and skull glittered. Her fingertips twitched at her side as she thought.

Ward gave Tarquin a *Can you believe this jerk?* look, but Tarquin felt a twinge of anticipation race up his spine. Delorne was one of their best, and her specialties leaned heavily toward quantum studies. While she stayed away from neurological entanglements, she didn't need to know much about neural maps to examine their effects on the quantum field itself.

"Of course it's not just one field," she muttered to herself. "Oh. Oh."

"Doctor?" Tarquin asked.

"The tiller."

Delorne scrambled over to the machine and walked past it, arm extended, tracing the path it should have taken to the point it'd veered off. She bounced on her toes, drawing invisible arcs with her finger. Tarquin didn't dare interrupt, but he tried to take what he knew about the malfunctioning bots and mash it up against the strange q-field readings, and found his knowledge unequal to the task.

"It can't be." Delorne stopped cold and squinted at the sky. "Can it?"

She turned on her heel and bolted at a full sprint back to the lab. Tarquin was too stunned to react.

"That woman is a pain in my ass," Ward said.

"I'll make sure she doesn't go in the tunnels," Tarquin said.

"Good luck with that, my liege." Ward thumped him on the back and strode away.

SIXTEEN

Naira

Miller-Urey Station | The Present

Naira spent the shuttle ride from Mercator Station to Miller-Urey calibrating the suppression crown according to Bracken's documentation. She wasn't certain what to think of it, yet. A muted, numb feeling suffused her, akin to a very low dose of her memory suppressant, but ignorable, for the time being.

Upon docking, she'd half expected entering Miller-Urey to send her spiraling back into memory. It wasn't her cracked mind that stopped her cold on the docks.

"Sharp?" Caldweller asked.

"What the fuck is that?"

An ad board at the end of the dock displayed footage of herself, the sound cut, during the trial she'd stood for treason. Her face was all controlled fury, whatever she'd said on the stand incensed. It was only a few seconds, but then it cut to her in the hangar bay on Mercator Station, the day Governor Soriano had come to arrest her. This time, her own voice rang loud and clear:

"I think Tarquin's version of Mercator is worth fighting for."

It cut to an abstract background, a holo of the Mercator logo growing into view. A cheery voice said, "Mercator Holdings—united for a better future! Apply today."

"I believe that's a recruitment ad," Helms said dryly.

Naira's fists clenched, and she stopped herself short of ripping the board from its moorings and pitching it over the dock. "Somebody please tell everyone in HR to keep me out of their marketing, or I will personally unite their heads with their asses."

"But..." Helms flinched when Naira turned her glare on her. "Don't you want people to sign up for Mercator over the other families?"

"I..." Naira Sharp. The face of Mercator. She was going to be sick.

"C'mon," Caldweller said. "Our car's waiting." He took her elbow and steered her away.

Outside the luxury of the private docks, Naira scarcely recognized Miller-Urey. People were thin on the streets, moving with quick, determined strides and scanning constantly for threats. Dark stains marred the pedestrian roads, and a few matching stains splashed the sides of buildings. Most of the broken-out windows had been left as they were, big glass teeth in a shattered maw. A few had attempted to cover those wounds with thin tarps that revealed the wary silhouettes of those within.

Naira had known that the stations had been hit hard by the *canus*-bound. Still, the evidence of it, tactile and crunching beneath the slick treads of the autocab in minuscule pieces of glass and concrete foam, startled her. It could have been worse. But that was poor comfort to the people scraping by out here.

The cab whispered to a stop in front of HCA HQ. Naira waited impatiently while Caldweller and Helms cleared the area before opening her door. Helms gave her a half smirk and gestured grandly. Naira resisted an urge to punch her on the arm.

She was representing Mercator today, and while that chafed, she reminded herself that the family was Tarquin's. If she wanted to help him continue to make inroads with the HC so that the ledgers of power could be rebalanced, then she needed to present a respectable facade.

Inside the cosseting walls, an entire company of at-rest soldiers was arrayed across the parade ground. She'd planned on announcing herself to the local captain as a matter of courtesy, getting all the information she could out of them, then moving on to Gardet. The show of arms was unexpected, but no doubt meant to impress the future wife of the head of Mercator. Naira resigned herself to being paraded around.

The company's captain turned, crisp on their heel, and fired off a picture-perfect salute. And then a wink.

Naira was certain she'd fallen back into her past, but Sahanj Makwana had never worn that uniform when she'd known him. She skimmed her gaze over the arrayed company. Infantry. The Fifth Division.

Her old division.

"Sergeant Makwana? What the fuck are you doing here?" So much for being a respectable envoy of Mercator.

"It's captain, now, Ex. Sharp." He tapped the insignia on that fancy jacket of his. "A little bird told me a 'Mercator security consultant' was coming to M-U to assess the situation here and help ensure the safety of the children of Gardet."

"A little bird, huh?" Naira shot Caldweller a look.

"Bigger bird," Caldweller said.

"Tarquin?"

"The liege was eager to make it clear that Mercator is only offering assistance and does not mean to step on our toes," Sahanj said.

"You trotted out thousands of soldiers for a brief about an orphanage?"

Sahanj's professional decorum cracked, and he grinned from ear to ear. "When Ex. Naira Sharp comes to liberate a station from the *canus*-bound, I'll be damned if I'm left on the sidelines."

"But I'm not...I just..." Sahanj's brows rose with every half-hearted protest. Naira sighed heavily, shoulders slumping as she let her arms fall to her sides.

She'd told herself a very pretty lie about slipping into the station, securing Jana, and slipping out again. No more war. Not with her mind in pieces. Not when "high-value target" was practically stamped across her forehead, making her a liability to all around her. The betrothed of the head of Mercator didn't *do battle*.

It was a nice story while it'd lasted.

SEVENTEEN

Tarquin

Seventh Cradle | The Present

Delorne slipped and skidded down the halls, leaving muddied footprints and quiet tuts from the other scientists in her wake. Tarquin jogged after her, turning those tuts into wide eyes and quick bows. He tried to plaster on a smile and lift a hand to those he passed with some measure of dignity, but it was difficult to keep an air of leadership about oneself while chasing a muddy, ping-ponging scientist down a hallway.

Shoes squeaked as Delorne swung around a corner and waved her ID pathway over the lockpad outside her lab. The door swished open just in time to let the careening scientist through.

Tarquin had expected her to go for one of the many devices that made use of the synch, but she skidded to a stop in front of one of the console podiums and spun up a massive display that unfolded to fill the air like half an eggshell. She worked with both hands, manipulating and discarding data at a rate that made even Tarquin dizzy. He was used to his method of slow contemplation to figure out a problem, not the rapid test-and-discard approach Delorne was taking.

He made himself unobtrusive behind her and tried to follow what she was doing. There were measurements and assessments of the local q-field, broken down into all the disparate fields that made up the greater whole.

She pulled up a map of the universe's registered pulsars, rapidly rotating stars that emitted electromagnetic radiation at known intervals. Ansibles measured the regularity at which they pulsed and worked a complicated formula to determine universal field positions, the greater universe's form of GPS. UFPs were integral in all their systems. From their clocks, to their maintenance robots.

The tiller. The construction bots.

Tarquin blinked. A creeping sense of dread chilled his skin.

"The Hubble variants are returning bad data," Delorne announced.

"Show me," he said.

She brought a screen into focus. It was a simple comparison. On one side of the holo, she'd bounced a laser off reflectors installed on Seventh Cradle's moon and measured the distance. On the other, she'd asked the UFP system to estimate the same distance. It'd been short by a fraction of a percent. Minuscule, but catastrophic when extended over a universal scale.

"How is that possible?" Tarquin asked.

"I told you, my liege, the Hubble variants are returning bad data." Delorne swung her holos around, diving back into them.

"Could you be more specific, Doctor?" Tarquin forced himself to be patient. She was hyperfocused, one heel bouncing constantly against the floor.

She flicked an arm out, separating a screen from the mass, and pointed to the Hubble variant equations. Tarquin didn't know the details of the math, but they helped the positioning system account for the expansion of space.

"In the beginning," Delorne said in a theatrical voice, "there was the Big Bang." She cupped her hands together and drew them apart, making a crackling explosion sound. "And then, there was inflation." She flung her arms wide.

Tarquin pinched the bridge of his nose. "Please don't."

"I'm enjoying this, my liege," Diaz said, and winked at him when Tarquin shot him an annoyed look.

"Very well," Tarquin said, "but please get to the point quickly."

"Inflation lasted an itty-bitty fraction of a second." Delorne held her fingers close together. "But in that time, space blew up." She flung her arms wide again, knocking one hand into the console podium with a bony thump, but she didn't seem to notice. "It slowed down, after that, which is good, otherwise we'd all be multiple light-years tall. Presuming we existed, which we wouldn't."

"Liege Tarquin is already tall enough," Diaz said.

Tarquin grunted.

"But then!" She put the edges of her hands together and started to slowly spread her fingers apart. "About five billion years ago, our friend dark energy makes an appearance, and things start speeding up again." She wiggled her spread fingers. "In fact, space is still accelerating, but at an—excuse the pun—relatively constant rate. The Hubble variants account for the expansion, so we don't jump a ship and find, whoops, space has moved out from under us."

"It doesn't really move," Tarquin said.

"No, not really," Delorne admitted with a shrug. "It's like having an elastic strap with two knots in it. Stretch the strap, the knots get farther apart. But the speed at which that stretch is happening is moving faster and faster, a measured rate that the Hubble variants are supposed to account for."

"If this is speeding up," Diaz said, "are we in danger of a light-years tall Liege Tarquin?"

"Hah!" Delorne tweaked Diaz's nose, which made the exemplar's eyes fly so wide Tarquin had to put a hand over his mouth to stifle a laugh. "Not before the universe is already inhospitable to life. Nothing to worry about. The initial inflation period was only a sliver of a second, remember?" She held up her pinched-together fingers again. "The new expansion period's got nothing on that speed."

Diaz touched his nose, bewildered, and let his hand fall. "What made it happen so quickly back then?"

"We have no idea!" Delorne threw him a radiant smile. "Lots of theories, no conclusions. That's the fun stuff. We call it the inflaton field, but couldn't tell you anything else about it that's concrete."

"You call the field that caused inflation the inflaton field?" Diaz asked.

"Physicists are awful at naming things," Tarquin said.

"Uh-huh." Delorne raised an eyebrow. "You don't have a lot of room for critique there, my liege. You're responsible for *Mercatus canus.*"

"*I* had nothing to do with that," Tarquin said, exasperated, despite his amusement.

"Fine, fine." She turned back to one of the holo screens. "It really is like someone stepped on the proverbial gas."

Tarquin's good mood evaporated. "What's the rate of increase?"

"Nothing to worry about in the near future. We have to rework the formula and update the UFP system, though, or we're going to have ships bumping into things and tillers rolling into ditches. I'll need a team for this, my liege. We'll have to take a *lot* of old-school measurements." She rubbed her hands together.

"Request anyone you'd like," Tarquin said. "Consider it already approved."

"I will. In the meantime, I'd suggest grounding all shuttles, lest they go off course. And definitely no warpcore jumps. Ansibles should be good for a while, though, they use a pretty broad range."

"You said someone stepped on the gas," Diaz said. "Is this a natural phenomenon, or are we looking at a hostile?"

"I can't be certain," she said. "If anyone out there has the technology to do something like this, I've never heard of it."

"Yet," Tarquin said with a soft frown.

"My liege?" Delorne asked.

"This is, admittedly, a stretch, but Naira has been experiencing glimpses of what we believe to be the future. Some of these moments have proved remarkably helpful. That both phenomena are happening so closely together—I can't help but wonder if they're connected." Tarquin explained what Naira had seen, and that both the assassin and bomber had left a spike of resonance in the q-field.

Delorne bounced her heel in thought. "I'll talk to Bracken. See if we can find an explanation."

"I'll leave you to it, but I'm curious—how did the q-field spikes lead you down this path?"

"Oh." She fluttered a hand through the air. "It got me thinking about unusual fields, and then I saw the tiller. You know how it is, my liege. Two pieces of information meet up in just the right way and something new clicks."

"Yeah," he said, blinking slowly. "I do. Diaz, could you alert all in-flight shuttles to hold until we have the adjusted variants?"

"Of course, my liege," Diaz said. "Are you all right? You look pale."

"Fine," he said, and patted Diaz's arm. "I'll be in my lab, if it's urgent. Otherwise, please see that I'm not disturbed."

Tarquin was aware of Diaz and Delorne sharing a concerned look behind his back, but he didn't pay them any attention.

He was thinking about fields, and sudden changes in the laws of the universe, and his father's casual shrug when he'd said they never went looking for amarthite—it was always where they'd expected relkatite to be. Waiting. Like it was no different from relkatite.

Tarquin broke into a sprint, running for his lab, and ignored the startled shouts of his exemplars behind him.

EIGHTEEN

Naira

Miller-Urey Station | The Present

Sahanj led Naira to his office, a small room on the second floor of headquarters with a narrow window that overlooked the parade ground. When the door shut, he dropped the stiff posture and whirled around to snatch her into a hug. She laughed, thumping him on the back before he let her go.

"That was very improper of me." He straightened his uniform. "But it's been so long, I couldn't resist."

"Don't apologize. It's nice not to be treated like a museum piece."

"I bet." He waved at a chair across from his desk. "Sit, sit. I know you're impossibly busy, but spare some time for an old friend to show you some hospitality."

Naira sank into the chair, letting herself relax. She felt a touch guilty about leaving the exemplars in the hallway but craved the false normalcy that a one-on-one meeting with Sahanj offered. His office was the mirror of Kav's, back when he'd been their captain, and she found her scalp warming as she let her gaze linger on all that familiar, standard-issue furniture.

Sahanj distracted her with a clatter as he produced a bottle and two glasses from below his desk. She shook off the memory toying at the edges of her senses and reached for the drink he poured her. Akin to whiskey, maybe? But strangely sweet. She glanced at the bottle but couldn't read the label.

"What is it?"

"Weird, isn't it?" Sahanj wrinkled his nose and peered at the glass. "I have no idea. It was the most expensive bottle in the commissary, and the first thing I bought with my captain's stipend."

"Ah," Naira said. "The oddly sickly taste of financial security."

Sahanj laughed and clinked her glass with his. "You'd know all about that, eh?"

Naira groaned. "Can we not go there?"

"My old L-T shows up on my doorstep engaged to Tarquin Mercator and you expect me to ignore that? C'mon." He leaned over the desk and waggled his eyebrows at her. "Spill the details, Nai. Is he, ya know, *good*? Or does being a prince mean he's used to letting others do all the work?"

Naira coughed over her drink. "None of your business, Sanj."

"You used to tell me everything." He faux-pouted.

"That was before the slightest tidbit could be sold to the tabloids for a small fortune."

"I'd never sell gossip shared in good faith, but fair enough. Whatever happened to Demarco, anyway?"

"Dead and iced. A longtime agent of *canus*, it turns out."

His face fell, and he reached across the desk to squeeze her hand. "I'm sorry."

Naira took a drink, wrinkling her nose at the taste. "What about the rest of the squad? I thought I saw Banners and Velasquez out there."

"You did at that." He leaned back in his chair, eyes downcast. "There's not much of the squad left, to be honest. We had a rough time after the uprising. High rate of attrition. You know how it is."

"What happened?"

"The old station is..." He flicked a nervous glance at the closed door. "It's gone, Nai. Our post doesn't exist anymore. That's why we're on M-U."

Naira's throat tightened. "The whole thing? I didn't hear about this."

"The HC board of governors elected not to inform MERIT. In the early days of the uprising, the governor there hadn't been taken over by *canus* yet, but she felt it coming on. Got paranoid and, I'm sorry to say, vented the whole damn station. We got some of the squad back on reprint, but you know how long those waiting lists are."

"She vented the *entire* station? What about the unprinted? What about—about Marconette?"

Sahanj only shook his head.

"Fuck." Naira scrubbed a hand down her face. "Why weren't we told?"

"They're afraid your fiancé will sanction them for the failure. Ration the amarthite supply further. Increase food prices. That kind of thing."

"Tarquin would never..." She trailed off. Those people didn't know Tarquin, but they knew Mercator. Knew the evidence of its long history. "All right. I get that. How bad is it? What else have they been keeping from us?"

"I could be dishonorably discharged for this."

"You have my full protection. Whatever it takes. And if they kick you out anyway, you're always welcome with Merc-Sec."

"You know I bleed grey."

"So do I. The offer still stands."

His smile was small, contemplative. "That's the first MERIT job offer that's actually tempted me. But I can't leave the HCA. They need all the experienced fighters they can get because this war..." He sighed. "The *canus*-bound haven't been as quiet as they've allowed MERIT to believe.

"Don't get me wrong, they're not fielding anything like a military force, but they don't have to skirmish with us to win. With the amarthite shortage, the black market for relkatite has boomed. People are taking their chances with relk and shroud supplements, but it's not perfect. The infection sets in. One day your relk-printed wife gets up and walks out the door, to the *canus*-controlled area of the station, and there's nothing you can do. Many of the bound stay in their homes, too. Hidden away, so that it's impossible to have a true count of their numbers. I hate to say it, but...it's only getting worse. *Canus* doesn't have to fight us. It just has to wait."

She'd let Tarquin's hope infect her. Let living on a lush and vital planet cloud her vision of what life was like for those left behind. Paison's words—*Aristocracy is catching, and you've spent too much time sharing air with the Mercators*—swam up out of the recesses of her mind. Her skin heated, and not from the crown suppressing the memory. From guilt. Shame.

"I'm not going to let that happen."

"Ah, Nai." His smile was sad, and it struck her how tired he looked. "You know I'd wade into any battle with you. But this...I don't know. I think we can do something for Miller-Urey. I do. But you can't stop people wanting their loved ones back. Can't stop them printing into relk."

"What's different about Miller-Urey?" she asked. "Why do you think we can change things here, if it's all so hopeless?"

Sahanj drummed his fingers on the top of his desk, hesitating. He glanced at the door. "People think I'm crac—er, foolish, for believing this."

Naira's brows lifted, but she let the slip slide. "Never stopped you from sharing an idea before."

"True." The pensive look faded. "The *canus*-bound here are more individualistic than on the other stations. Most of what we've seen, they sit and stare until they're needed or have to do basic bodily functions. But here? They're building a community. They talk to each other, instead of using their psychic link all the time. They have a leader. A clear figurehead. I'm sure of it."

"I believe it," Naira said. "Strong personalities can bend linked minds to their will. I've seen that before. Who is it?"

"Not a 'who,'" he said. "This is the part that gets me looked at like I've lost my marbles. I'd call them a misprint, but their body's healthy enough. Their leader calls themself the World."

Grey halls encroached on her vision. Facsimile lips of meshed mycelium whispered in a hushed susurration: *I am your world.* A wave of sound building. Cresting. Breaking against her and rising again. Heat raced over her scalp and poured down the back of her neck to slick the space between her shoulder blades with sweat. Her vision grew hazy, grey walls blurring back into the pre-fabbed polymers of Sahanj's office.

Caldweller and Helms crowded the room. Helms's hand was on her neck, checking her pulse, and Sahanj had knocked his drink over on his desk. She shook herself, clearing the last of the haze away, and loosened the zipper on her uniform jacket to let some of the heat out.

"Sorry," she said. "I'm back."

"You left?" Sahanj asked. "One second we were talking, then these two watchdogs barged in."

"Your vitals spiked." Caldweller frowned at her. "Temperature and heart rate through the roof. We thought you were going to seize."

"I'm fine." She swept her hair up into a quick bun to get it off the sticky sweat on her neck. "How long was I stuck?"

Helms and Caldweller exchanged a glance. Caldweller said, "A few seconds at most."

"I think the suppression crown just worked," Naira said.

"That's good, isn't it?" Helms asked.

Naira still felt overheated and queasy. "Better than the alternative."

"That was..." Sahanj waved vaguely at his head. "What being cracked is like? If you fell into a memory, I didn't notice. Your eyes got glassy there for a few seconds, but everyone zones out now and then."

"That's what it's like with this device." She tapped the new pathways. "Which is experimental. Otherwise, it's..." She simply shook her head.

"Vesper?" Sahanj righted his glass and busied himself wiping up the shallow spill.

Naira smiled at that. Their squad had gotten stuck behind enemy lines on Vesper Station while putting down a secessionist governor who'd attempted to set themself up as a dictator. The governor had only one tactic. Drone swarm, followed by sticky bombing, then a frontline push. They'd repeated the play so often Naira's squad had started to joke that they'd all cracked and weren't fighting anymore, but reliving the same engagement over and over again.

"Vesper," she said. "But it never stops."

He reached across the desk to squeeze her hand again. "I'm sorry, Nai. I shouldn't have asked you for help with this. You deserve to rest. I'll check out Gardet and deal with the *canus* situation here. You go back to that living world of yours and enjoy your time with your fiancé while— while you get some rest." He stumbled to a finish, and she knew he'd barely avoided saying *while you still can.*

"I've lived my whole life with one foot through death's door, Sanj. I'm not backing down now. The situation here is no coincidence. It can't be. I've heard *canus*-infected misprints call themselves 'your world' before, and I was on this station before the uprising. So was Fletch. There's something in that. I just don't know what it is yet."

"I know better than to try to turn down your help. I'd find myself tripping over you everywhere I went." She grinned at him, and he winked. "And I fear you're right. I didn't know about your personal experiences, but Gardet—I'm sorry to say it's in *canus*-controlled territory. So when Liege Tarquin called expressing a sudden interest in the place's security, I sniffed a conspiracy."

"It's where?" Naira sat straighter. "Our contact with the HC assured us it was in safe hands."

Sahanj only shook his head. "I told you, Nai. They're keeping a wrap on how badly we're losing out here. Think they can fix it without outside help."

"Then how are we going to get to it?"

"There's one person who claims they can communicate with the World, but the brass has blown them off as conspiring to get closer to our operations here. They don't want MERIT sniffing around."

"Who?" Naira asked.

"Chiyo Ichikawa."

NINETEEN

Naira

Miller-Urey Station | The Present

Naira's old company made a corridor as she jogged down the stairs to the parade ground. She saluted the soldiers as she passed and wished she could skip the meeting with Chiyo to find what was left of her squad and go for a drink with them, but that'd have to wait.

Chiyo waited near the gate post, chatting with a sweating Sahanj. He'd never even seen a head of family up close, let alone had to greet one. Chiyo wore a suit in black silk embroidered in the red that was the hallmark of her family, the jacket flaring into a slight skirt from her waist, and the collar cut low enough to show off the family mark that branded the soft, dark skin on the side of her neck.

Naira still wore her exemplar armor and hadn't bothered to smooth her hair. Her cheeks were warm from exertion, the weapons of her profession strapped to her body. Chiyo wasn't fool enough to see Naira's appearance as anything other than what it was—a signal she would not play by MERIT rules and conventions.

When Chiyo noticed her approach, Naira raised a hand in casual greeting. Chiyo smiled and waved in answer. Naira could practically feel the camera shutters wink at the unusual gesture. When Naira was closer, she slowed and extended a hand. Chiyo shook it firmly.

"Ex. Sharp," Chiyo said. Clearly, she'd read the brief on how Naira preferred to be addressed and had decided to honor Naira's request. All in that title, she'd signaled that she meant for them to be allies. "I was surprised by your call. An honor, to be the first of the families you wished to meet with upon your return to Sol."

"I believe we have a great deal to discuss." Naira turned to Chiyo's primary exemplar, Keiji Tanaka. He startled at the attention. She'd trounced him soundly three years in a row at the exemplar recertification event, and he'd taken it poorly, but now that her status had changed, it simply wasn't *done* for a charge to address another's exemplar.

"Keiji! Good to see you again. Better to see you without your face covered in paint, eh?"

He looked equal parts panicked and irritated as he shook Naira's hand. "We miss your galvanizing presence at re-cert, Exemplar."

"I doubt it. Where's Ex. Dalson?"

"Cracked." Keiji shrugged and gestured to the other exemplar. "This is his replacement, Ex. Hattori."

"Pleased to meet you, E-X." Naira held out her hand. Hattori stared at it a moment before recovering and giving it a brief shake.

"Likewise, E-X."

Naira's HUD flashed the woman's ID. Hattori, like Keiji, was an extended familial relation of the Ichikawa inner family. Unusual for a head of family to use their blood relatives as exemplars, but then, the heads of MERIT had been wary of hiring from the HCA after Naira's defection.

Chiyo watched all of this transpire with an amused tilt to her head. "How utterly charming," she said in the same tone of voice Naira suspected she'd use if a puppy had performed a trick.

"Now," Naira said. "I've had a room prepared, if you would walk with me?"

"Delighted." Chiyo fell into step beside her. "I must say, it's a pleasure to meet you at last, though naturally I feel as if I already know you. You spent so very many years standing at Acaelus's side."

"I doubt you learned much about me from those encounters."

"Perhaps," Chiyo said. "But what I suspected of your nature you've spent the past five minutes confirming."

"Have I? Please, enlighten me."

"If you'd like. You, I think, better than anyone in the higher reaches of MERIT, know your place. At Acaelus's side you were silent unless directly addressed or otherwise pushed to speak by a threat. Firm and alert. And your map integrity was, of course, remarkable. I was jealous of Acaelus for hiring you—did he ever tell you that?"

"He did not."

"He wouldn't." She shook her head, but her smile was fond. "Probably feared I'd attempt to poach you. I would have, had you given me the slightest indication of interest. You, Exemplar, know what it means to be a piece on a board. As we all are.

"You have moved from knight to queen, but you've watched kings and queens long enough that you understand how they should move. And so you show up to meet a head of family in your—what do you call those, fatigues?"

"Uniform." Naira gave Chiyo a sideways glance. "I always wished Acaelus would consent to wear half as much armor as I'm wearing now."

"I bet you did. So, you show up in your old uniform, and you shake the hands of your old colleagues, and you flout tradition you well understand the full intricacies of, because you know people are watching you. Whispering that you're not fit for your position. You want them to believe that, because it gives you room to maneuver beneath their noses, does it not?"

"It does," Naira said. "But you've missed the most important part."

"Have I?"

"I haven't underestimated your intelligence."

"Ah," Chiyo said. "I wondered if the pageantry was for me, or prying eyes, or both. I think, Ex. Sharp, as I thought when you were Acaelus's object—you are a very dangerous woman."

"So I've been told."

The door to the meeting room swept open. Two chairs sat across from each other, a small table between them with a pitcher of water, the glass shiny with condensation. Naira paused to let Chiyo go first, not only out of politeness but because Chiyo was right. Naira had been the shadow at Acaelus's side for years in precisely this type of meeting.

The suppression crown heated, tingling her skin as it worked to keep her from sliding back into one of those moments. The Ichikawa head of family didn't comment on her hesitation. She merely arranged herself in a chair and took the glass of water Keiji handed her. Naira sat across from her and took her own glass from Helms.

"Don't misunderstand me," Chiyo said. "I approve of dangerous women wholeheartedly. My own wife was a finalizer before I scooped her up."

"Does she still work?" Naira took a drink as she leaned back in the chair, wholly at ease, one leg kicked up over the other.

"Only when the mood strikes her." Chiyo gestured to the weapons strapped to Naira. "She loved her work, but age wears the novelty away, I'm afraid. She's not nearly so dedicated as you seem to be. Really, Ex. Sharp, one exemplar? I understand your skills are unsurpassed, but your safety must be considered."

"My second is busy securing this facility." Naira shrugged. "And really, what's someone going to do, send a finalizer after me? I'm already cracked."

Chiyo coughed delicately over her water and set it aside, regarding her with fresh interest. "Truly? When I saw the engagement announcement, I assumed you'd stabilized the situation. Did my software not work for you?"

"I haven't used it. The research you provided us was incomplete, and we've observed side effects I find troubling."

"Indeed? Then I shall send a complete list of all our past test subjects and our observations on their behavior, if that is what it takes. A cracked mind with command keys is a troubling thought."

"My mental state is not up for public debate."

"Forgive me, Exemplar, but your mental state is very much of public and MERIT concern. You have the keys to world-destroying weapons and are prone to not knowing what time period you're living in."

Naira drank slowly and set her glass aside. "I have a disability, Chiyo. People who can't afford to reprint live with such things all the time. I assure you the situation is under control."

"Is it?" Her gaze mapped the pathways glittering on Naira's forehead. Most of the suppression crown was hidden beneath her hair, but Chiyo could read what was visible and make a few very educated guesses. Her brows lifted in genuine astonishment. "Remarkable. Does it work?"

"I'm here and not stuck in a memory or screaming my head off, aren't I?"

"I suppose so. Who designed it?"

Naira gave a slight shake of the head. Chiyo laughed.

"I shouldn't have mentioned that I considered poaching you if I wanted an answer to that question, hmm?"

"Correct. Though I wouldn't have given you the name, either way."

"Naturally." Chiyo leaned back and traced a finger around the rim of her glass. "Well, Ex. Sharp, if we may set the politics aside for a moment, I'd like to offer my congratulations on your future marriage." She smiled warmly. "Tarquin has been like a nephew to me. I've worried about him and am relieved to see you're precisely as I expected you to be."

"Dangerous?"

"Just so. Tarquin needs someone with bite at his side. The others think he's soft, but you and I know differently, don't we?" Chiyo paused, expecting a response, but Naira only waited in silence. "Ah. You won't say it. Well, I have no such qualms. Our Tarquin has a mean streak, doesn't he? It's buried deeply, so deeply the others of MERIT look at him and see little more than the sweet boy who bucked Acaelus's ruthless nature.

"But I know it's there, and unless you're a bigger fool than I could have guessed, you know it's there, too. It frightens him, I think. As it should. Acaelus and I, we knew each other for so very long that I still recall when he was more like the man Tarquin is today.

"But he loved Canden, and she was too sweet for him, in the end. He felt he needed to protect her, and the lengths he went to . . . Well, you're familiar with the outcome. I don't need to tell you."

"You do not," Naira said. All of MERIT's heads were aware of what had happened on the *Sigillaria*.

"That's good. That dry, bitter anger. The world used you poorly, and I think you've learned how to use it back."

"Maybe I want to break it instead."

"Maybe you do." Chiyo eyed her for a moment. "I could hardly blame you. Regardless of your intent, I believe you are good for our Tarquin. You don't need protection. I think, perhaps, you're the kind of person people need protection from."

"If you're attempting to flatter me, Liege Chiyo, you've chosen an odd angle."

"I don't believe I have." Chiyo gave her a slow smile over the rim of her glass. "I'm happy for you both and have come to be the first of MERIT to offer you a wedding gift."

"I don't think we're in need of new flatware."

Chiyo laughed. "I know what you've called me here for, Ex. Sharp, and I'm inclined to give it to you."

"Oh?"

Chiyo tipped her head. "Cagey. Good. But we're both very busy women with no time for tiresome political shuffling. You would like to speak with the World, would you not?"

"I would. How did you establish communications with this entity?"

"While my colleagues in MERIT recoiled in disgust from the infected, I have a stronger stomach than most."

"I'm aware," Naira said flatly.

Chiyo flashed her a smile. "Lacking the amarthite to reprint all my workers, I've kept a few crews of the relkatite-printed on hand. They're infected, of course, but with a strong-willed captain or two who are unquestionably loyal to me in their midst, I find them remarkably pliable."

"You're using *canus* to enslave your people?"

Chiyo rolled a dismissive shoulder. "They receive the same pay and benefits as before."

"Except for the complete lack of autonomy and privacy."

"Such disdain," Chiyo mused. "I find your revulsion curious, when you yourself signed an exemplar contract under Acaelus's command. Tell me, did you have true privacy and autonomy while working for my old friend?"

"That's different, and you know it."

Chiyo brushed her off with a flick of the wrist. "Hardly. But irrelevant to my point. My infected began showing strange behavior when they drew near to this station. Some of them were insistent 'the World' was calling to them, and it didn't take me long to discover the source. I considered this connection a curious diversion from my usual affairs, but I find your interest striking. If you wish to speak with the World, I can make that happen."

"Do you have your infected here?"

"I never come unprepared to uphold my end of a bargain."

"Bargain?" Naira asked. "I thought this was a wedding gift."

"So it is." Chiyo's lips curled to one side. "A gift, naturally, is given without expectation of reciprocation."

"That's how I understand the custom."

She tossed her head and laughed. "I think you and I are going to have a great deal of fun together, Exemplar."

"We'll see." Naira stood. "Let's rip the bow off this gift then, shall we?"

TWENTY

Naira

Miller-Urey Station | The Present

The Ichikawa shuttle rested next to the Mercator shuttle. Long and lean in shades of mirror black, ruby red, and burnished gold, the ship was all high gloss and polish. That illusion fell away when Naira stepped foot in the cargo hold where the infected were being held.

Two dozen pairs of bloodshot eyes turned as one and focused on her.

"Sharp," they said in one voice. "Sharp, Sharp, *Sharp*."

Naira laced her hands behind her back and squeezed as the suppression crown flared to life, simmering her skin in thin sweat as it worked to keep her from falling back into the halls of the *Einkorn*.

"Curious." Chiyo tapped a nail to her chin. "They don't often repeat themselves."

All their pathways were silver, the skin around them puffed and reddened. They wore Ichikawa-issued jumpsuits, and while the black-and-red uniforms were crisply turned out, their hair had gone unbrushed, their cheeks beginning to sink from malnutrition.

Naira wanted to berate Chiyo for what she had done and was no doubt continuing to do on a larger scale back on Ichikawa's stations, but it would solve nothing. She took a breath. Buried her rage and disgust, and tried to look neutral as she swept her gaze over the infected.

"I would like to speak with the entity who calls itself the World," she said.

"You are the ender," one of them said.

"The divider," another said.

"The savior," a third said.

They paused. Tilted their heads to the side at the same angle.

"You will be seen."

"I should have brought you to them sooner," Chiyo said. "This is fascinating."

Naira ignored her. "I will meet with the World, if that is their desire. Assure them that I can provide safe passage to the HCA's headquarters and will extend to them diplomatic protections."

"No," they said.

"Now, now." Chiyo took a single step forward. They flinched as one. "I assured Ex. Sharp that you could make the arrangements. I will not be disappointed. Summon the World."

"N—" they started to say, but Chiyo slashed two fingers at a worker with an overseer's insignia on their jumpsuit, and the infected locked up as one, jaws rigid as their bodies forced them to silence.

"Try again," Chiyo said coldly.

"Liege Chiyo," Naira said. "You will let them speak, or you and I will be done speaking."

"Very well." Chiyo's tone was mildly amused. "If you'd like to hear them tell you no all night, feel free to waste your time."

"You will be seen," they said again.

"What assurances would the World require to meet with me?" Naira asked.

The group turned as one to stare at the cargo hold's airlock. Naira glanced at Chiyo, who shrugged and gestured for one of her staff to open the door.

Dozens of station locals with silver-stained pathways stood in the hangar. Their hands were folded in front of their bodies, chins tipped up to better see into the cargo hold. Their clothes were worn but well mended, and while a few seemed gaunt to Naira, their hair and skin were clean.

"We assure you," the new arrivals said, mimicking her tone of voice, "of safe passage and diplomatic protections."

Naira huffed softly. "Well, I can hardly argue with that."

The exemplar channel flared in her HUD.

Caldweller: You're joking. Going with them is suicidal.

Sharp: We have to give them a chance, or this war is never going to end.

Caldweller: Liege Tarquin would never allow this.

Sharp: Tarquin doesn't allow me to do a damn thing.

Helms: We've got your back, E-X.

Chiyo gave her a sideways look. "I presume your exemplars just had the same panicked response mine did?"

Naira glanced at Keiji, who looked like he wanted to be sick. "We've reached an understanding."

"Excellent." Chiyo rubbed her hands together. "Let's be on our way."

"You're staying here," Naira said.

"Excuse me?" Chiyo sounded genuinely surprised.

Naira looked past her, to her infected employees, and barely restrained herself from decking Chiyo outright. It'd solve nothing. "This is a diplomatic mission. I won't meet with the World with an enslaver of their people at my side. Unless you mean to release those you've infected as a show of good faith."

Chiyo chuckled softly and shook her head. "Ah, Exemplar. You aren't enjoying your first real taste of power, are you? Having to make distasteful choices to preserve the peace for the greater good? I imagine you'd string me up by my guts, if it wouldn't send Ichikawa to war with Mercator, wouldn't you?"

Chiyo had a gleam in her eye that Naira couldn't place.

For eight years, Naira had watched while Acaelus held similar meetings with Chiyo. She'd listened, because it was her job to know the proclivities of all her charge's allies and potential enemies. While Chiyo's quick smiles and laughing manner might seem genial, they were shields that encased a woman with a bladed heart. Chiyo hadn't married a finalizer by accident.

She was testing Naira. Pushing to see how far she could get Naira to roll over.

"Mercator assures you of its continued alliance," Naira said, then leaned close and lowered her voice. "But, personally, Chiyo, don't try this shit again. I've gone to war for less."

Chiyo cocked her head. "I wish I'd poached you when I had the chance."

"I wouldn't have taken that offer."

"No. I don't think you would have."

"Thank you for the gift, old friend."

Chiyo gave her a delighted grin and tipped her head to Naira at the point made. They'd no more be real friends than Chiyo and Acaelus ever had been.

Naira followed the infected through back alleys that, eventually, began to scratch at her memories. She hadn't spent much time on Miller-Urey, but she knew how the unionists liked to arrange their hideouts. When Jessel and the others had cleared out and run from Sol, they'd left a void behind. One the *canus*-bound had filled.

They passed through narrow alleys and false-walled safe houses to what had once been a residential district. Naira supposed it still was. People lived there, after all, no matter the silver staining their pathways.

The rubble had been cleared. Repairs made to all buildings. The locals walked with ease down the streets, and Naira was surprised to see them pause to talk with one another, or watch her procession pass by with curious, alert eyes.

These weren't the worker drones of the *Sigillaria*. They appeared to be individuals and, Naira grudgingly admitted to herself, were living a more comfortable life than those in the other half of the station. But that individuality could be taken from them in a second if the *canus* in their bodies decided they'd misbehaved.

Her escorts led her to a warehouse that Naira suspected had once been a unionist hideout. There were no guards, no visible armed force of any kind, no tools of war. The fence around the building was simple chain link, the gates cast aside into a pile where they were slowly rusting. This was not an encampment that believed itself embattled.

"The World is waiting for you within." An infected woman gestured to the doors. "You are invited on a mission of peace. You may keep your weapons and your guardians, but know that striking out against the World will result in your destruction."

"I understand. I'm not here to fight."

Naira approached the warehouse, unable to help her senses screaming that this was a trap. She'd spent her life calibrating her instincts to doing battle with people, and as Kav would no doubt remind her if he were there, the World was very much not people.

She pushed open the door. Sticky, sweltering air filled her lungs, heady with the scents of rich soil. The lights were dim, the cavernous space lit with a collection of warm-hued LEDs hanging from scraggly wires. They swayed as the opened door stirred the air.

A figure was silhouetted by those lights. Tall, but not spindly with starvation as the misprints had been. It approximated a human form, but the angles were all a touch off, making the back of Naira's neck prickle with animal instinct. Muscle pushed against clothes that appeared to be an afterthought— a grey jumpsuit that'd no doubt been found in the warehouse lockers.

Their back was to her, hands in their pockets, a slouch to their shoulders that tickled at Naira's memory. Marbled patches of various hues painted their skin, as if they'd tried out a few and couldn't decide which one best suited them. Misprint-grey swirled through the mix, and their hair was a tousled mop of sandy-blond curls.

Not a misprint. But no human had ever owned that body, either. Sahanj had been right. Their leader had never been human. He'd brag about that for weeks.

She drew close enough to see what those swinging lights were illuminating and stopped so hard her boots squeaked. A haphazard garden filled the space, clumped piles of soil crawling with plants in a similar manner to what Naira had found on the *Sigillaria* when Canden had control of that ship. But it wasn't the plants that froze the air in her lungs.

Hundreds of glass jars speckled the ground and were arranged on repurposed warehouse shelves, hemming in the garden. Inside each jar, silver moth wings twitched. Struggled to flutter in a space too small to allow the motion. Many lay still, never to rise again.

What happened to us?

You think you're the moth, Nai, but you've always been the flame.

Her scalp burned, eyes watering from the heat pouring through her as the crown struggled to suppress far too many memories all at once. The World startled, as if noticing them for the first time, and turned. Green eyes dark with mossy threads. A subtle brushing of freckles across their cheeks—too dark in hue, but close enough.

"You," they said, eyes sparking with something Naira thought might be hope.

The heat ebbed. The creature's body language was all wrong. The curious tilt to their head was seeped in an innocence Fletcher had never possessed.

"Hello, World," Naira said.

TWENTY-ONE

Tarquin

Seventh Cradle | The Present

Tarquin couldn't see it. He didn't have the tools at his disposal to hunt down the connection that he knew, in his bones, must exist. It wasn't his instincts alone that told him so. He'd brought in a wide array of samples—all the relkatite and amarthite he could get his hands on—and measured them with Bracken's q-field device.

Then he'd spent hours checking and rechecking the readings. Had even dragged Delorne in to confirm his findings before releasing her back to work on the Hubble variants. If he were at Jov-U, he'd have enlisted a team. Undergrads. Colleagues. He'd have taken over a whole building if he had to, to get to the bottom of what he suspected to be true.

But anyone with a deft hand for physics or math had been recruited to recalculating the Hubble variants. That was how it should be. Finding more amarthite would hardly matter if they could no longer safely traverse the universe to recover it.

Still, he looked at the samples he'd meticulously labeled and lined up in order of strongest to weakest reaction, and thought—*what if?* At one end, the highest reading, relkatite. At the other, a reading so weak it was unclear if the device had picked up anything at all, amarthite. Between them, a gradient, weak to strong, amarthite to relkatite, consistently. Even the luster faded down the line.

Relkatite decayed into amarthite. He was sure of it. And as it decayed, its ability to resonate with the q-field lessened.

But there were irregularities in the data. A few pieces of relk sampled from pathways were further along the decay chain than their age should allow for. What had sped up the process?

He'd smashed particles in the synch, stretched the system to its limits, and he hadn't found what he was looking for. He'd found a signature of it, a footprint in the sand. But there was a question he couldn't answer, and it vexed him.

What energy, exactly, was relkatite radiating that decayed over time? And why would that decay rate sometimes spike?

That relkatite decayed into amarthite he could make a convincing evidential case for. With this research, they could start looking at the oldest relkatite sites for traces of amarthite. It should have thrilled him. He'd figured it out at last.

Instead he sat, and stared, and searched the data, and felt a fear he didn't quite understand build within him.

Cass opened the door, breaking Tarquin's concentration. He scowled and pushed away from the table.

"I told you I wasn't to be disturbed."

Dr. Sharp stood in the doorway, carrying a covered tray. She looked up at him, one thick brow arched. Tarquin's heart gave a startled kick. Naira's mother. Shit. He hadn't spoken to her since before the engagement and here he was, quite probably looking a mess, and snapping at her.

"Uh. Dr. Sharp, forgive me," he stammered.

"Hunger can make a person irritable, my liege," she said. Cass stepped aside to let her pass, and she lifted the tray to draw his attention. "Marko assured me you'd be pleased with this selection."

"I'm afraid I don't have time for a meal at the moment." Tarquin's stomach betrayed him by rumbling.

"Sit, my liege," she said as if he hadn't protested at all.

She circled the room to a clean table and sat, placing the tray in the center before whisking the lid off. A shareable platter of roasted vegetables, spreads, crackers, and vinegar sauces let out a cloud of savory bliss strong enough that Tarquin automatically sat opposite her before he realized he'd done so. She gave him a thin smile.

"Go on. Even we scientists can't live off stimulants and desperation alone." She loaded a piece of flatbread with spread and vegetables, then pushed the tray toward him.

Tarquin didn't need to be told twice. He fell to the food, only reining himself in enough that he wouldn't horrify his future mother-in-law. They ate in what he hoped was companionable silence, but he couldn't quite tell. She watched him obliquely, and he sensed that he was being sized up. If only there was a field detector for a mother-in-law's ire.

"So," she said eventually, "you intend to marry my daughter."

He coughed and reached for his water. That hadn't been a question, and she'd dropped his title completely. The lack of it made her statement sound like some kind of threat.

"Nothing would make me happier." A smile flitted to his lips despite the low thrum of terror her stare induced. "I love her dearly and believe that I make her happy, too."

Was that the right thing to say? He had no idea. She eyed him, tracing a finger around the rim of her glass.

"I would like to speak to you as Naira's mother," she said carefully. "Not as your vassal. Not knowing you paid through the teeth to release my contract from Rochard so that I could stay with her in Mercator. Simply as one person who loves Naira to another, with no power imbalance between us."

It was what he'd wanted, but he was unlikely to like what she needed to say. Tarquin set his glass down and braced his elbows on the table to steady himself. "You may always speak to me in such a way, Dr. Sharp."

She took a slow, deep breath and dropped her gaze to where a bandage wrapped her forearm. Tarquin really should have asked her how her wound was healing. He had rocks for brains. Literally.

"I'm afraid for my daughter."

Tarquin flinched. The lie he wanted to be true poised on the tip of his tongue—*I can keep her safe*—but Dr. Sharp was too astute for that. There was nothing he could say to reassure her, because he'd been trying to reassure himself all this time and had come up with nothing.

"So am I."

"Can't you let her go?"

That pierced him. He looked at his plate and admitted something he'd barely been able to admit to himself. "I considered it. That first day we were sanctioned to be together, when Governor Soriano shot her. I thought she might be safer without me. That it would be better if I pretended disinterest. But I'm not a very good actor, I'm afraid.

"It wouldn't work, letting her go. I can't hide my feelings, and then she'd be without the power of Mercator to protect her, and others would seek to wield her against me. If she wants to leave, then... Well, I could never bring myself to force her to stay. But as long as she wants to be with me, the answer is no. I cannot let her go."

"I thought as much," she said, "but I had to ask. It does me some good, to know you considered the possibility. I don't think I quite realized how perilous your lives were until I saw her face down those misprints. She was right there. I felt I should have been able to, I don't know, protect her, I suppose. I'm her *mother*. But then she ran and took the horde with her, and I've never been more lost."

"I know how you feel." Hesitantly, he reached across the table and placed a comforting hand over hers. "I've watched Naira throw herself headfirst into danger more times than I can count. It shakes me every time. But she's not going to stop. I've accepted that. It's part of who she is, coming to the defense of others, and it's a large part of why I love her."

"For what it's worth, if it wasn't for your family, I would approve of this match. You're a sweet young man, and passably intelligent. Not like that other one she was tangled up with." She sniffed derisively.

"Demarco?" Tarquin asked. "Considering you dealt with him by cracking his skull, I'm pleased to hear you approve of me. My family aside."

"Don't get a big head. If you upset her, I know where to find the IV stands."

He held up his hands in surrender. "I will utilize my passable intelligence and endeavor not to earn your wrath."

"Hah. Good boy." She turned her head, frowning at the neat line of samples on his worktable. "What are you using that brain of yours for, anyway? I thought you'd be with the rest, working on the Hubble variants."

"I'm afraid I wouldn't be much use to that team. Actually, I think..."
He furrowed his brow at the samples. "I think I've discovered the source
of amarthite."

She coughed on a sip of water. "Blue skies, Tarquin, that's monumental. Why didn't you tell me right away?"

He flushed, pleased by the praise. "This is only one experiment that
needs to be written up and peer-reviewed. I'm uncertain how useful it
will be in the long run, but if I'm right, it might make finding deposits
of amarthite easier."

"Well, Doctor, walk me through it."

That his first review should come from his future mother-in-law,
however informal, sent a spike of fear driving down his spine. He took a
breath and met her at the table, sweeping up the data he'd collected.

It wasn't as neat as he'd like for an outside observer to review, but she
seemed to understand that he'd done this in the fervor of chasing an idea
and nodded along with his explanations, asking astute questions.

When he was finished, she rubbed her chin, skimming her gaze over
the long line of samples. "You might be more than passably intelligent
after all."

He swiped the holo away. "Such praise. But you see the problem? The
most recent example I have of full decay into amarthite is six hundred
thousand years old. I can resume the search for amarthite using the same
data we've used to discover relk in the past, and that will speed up finding deposits that already exist, but once we run out, we're out."

"Hmm." She looked at him sidelong. "Would you accept a coauthor
on your paper?"

Tarquin crossed his arms. He didn't think she would try to use his
relationship with Naira to inflate her career, but the slyness in that glance
gave him pause. "Do you have some insight?"

"Do you know how chlorophyll works?"

"It turns sunlight into energy for plants." He hoped she was going
somewhere with this.

"Indeed, and what is sunlight, if not radiation? We never did discover
what *canus* took from relkatite, did we? Only that it kept it intact. These
outliers you have that decayed early—they are all from pathways, correct? I suspect those individuals were badly infected."

"You think...?" His gaze slid off her, to the collection of samples. A grin split his face as the idea struck home. What if *canus* didn't feed on the relk itself, but on the radiation the relk produced? When that was spent, and canus tried to feed on what was left, it quite probably expended more energy than it recovered, struggling to sap blood from a literal stone, destroying itself in the process. If that was true, then they had a way to speed the decay of relkatite into amarthite. Let *canus* feast on it, in a controlled environment. "Holy shit."

"Language," she said reflexively, and he smiled. "What do you say, Doctor? Coauthors?" She held out a hand.

He shook it. "Let's get to work, Dr. Sharp."

TWENTY-TWO

Naira

Miller-Urey Station | The Present

The World led Naira to a rickety, round table near their garden, its rivets red with rust. Helms and Caldweller hung back, keeping an eye on her, but otherwise didn't interject. Naira was grateful for that. She was having a hard enough time getting her mind around the creature without them inserting security concerns into the mix.

Naira studied the being sitting across from her. Their wide-opened eyes were eager for knowledge, their body canted forward with unabashed curiosity, palms splayed flat on the table to support them.

This was war. The *canus*-bound were inimical to humanity's survival. This being led the faction on a station that was struggling to recover from *canus*'s original uprising. This was a meeting of two generals standing on opposite sides of a line drawn in the sand.

Naira couldn't quite make herself believe it.

"Why did you want to speak with me?" she asked.

"So much of us remembers you," they said. "You were us, when we were waking. You were in our genesis and we do not understand why you left us."

"I'm not in your mind-meld. I don't know what you're talking about."

"Sixth Cradle," they said. "You were us when we woke, but then you left us. Why?"

"I—" Naira frowned. "Are you the *Einkorn*?"

"We were. You were. The *Einkorn* is not anymore. You made it leave. But we remember all of us."

There was no way she was leaving this conversation without a headache. "I'm sorry, but I'm trying to wrap my head around this. You're the *canus* colony that was on Sixth Cradle?"

They leaned back, tilting their head to the side once more. "You don't understand. You're trying to make us separate, when we are not. There is one *canus* 'colony.' That is us. It was you. We are many, and yet one."

"I thought you needed proximity to communicate?"

"It helps." They drummed their fingers against the table. "You may think of us as a swarm network. The more of us are in an area, the greater the bandwidth and ease of communication. Distance is troublesome, but we are never truly separate."

Naira was about to ask how they knew about swarm networks, but realized that was a stupid question. They knew because someone they infected knew. Every mind they infected brought its own special knowledge to the network. The being sitting across from her was, quite probably, the most knowledgeable mind in the universe.

Their innocence, their curiosity—was it an act to lower her guard? Why bother? She looked over at the moths, skin crawling. Fletcher wasn't in control of that mind, but part of him had been left behind. A stain.

Every time she had spoken with *canus* previously, it had been through the filter of an infected person. Their wants and needs twisted to suit the colony's desire to survive. Even the misprints had hungered. Had wanted to live, though they'd had no mind before *canus* had woken within them. Even the *Einkorn* had learned a sense of self and developed nascent desires of its own before its end.

Was the being before her *canus* itself or something else? Could a mind ever truly be its own, if it was filtered through the wants and desires of so many?

"I'm going to be blunt with you," Naira said, "and hope that you understand I mean no offense. What are you, exactly?"

"The World," they said with wide-eyed honesty.

"How did you arrive at that name?"

"It is what one needs to survive. And we are required for survival."

"I'm surviving just fine without you."

"An isolated, lonely existence."

"I don't think so," Naira said. "And you didn't answer my question. What are you?"

"What are you?" They stilled, a flatness coming over their face that Naira had only seen on human countenances in death.

"Human," Naira said.

"But you are printed flesh, as are we. You are pathways and chemical reactions and the glitter and the spark of thought. Of life. We have cracked you open. We have dug through the base patterns of your mind and determined only similarities."

"Do you think you're human?" Naira asked.

"Do you?" They gave her a slow, slantwise smile. Another echo of Fletcher, but once more their eyes were flat. The expression somehow without context, without meaning, despite all the minds bound within them.

The World's guise had wrong-footed her. Slipped under her skin. Made her think she was talking to something, or someone, that might be adjacent to humanity. Pinned beneath the glint of those alien eyes, she sensed deep in her bones that, whatever *canus* truly was, it was beyond her understanding.

"No," she said. Slowly. Carefully. "I don't think you are human. I think you're something else. Something new."

"New?" They shook their head vehemently, stood, and paced over to the haphazard garden. "We are older than your species."

"You've never attempted to communicate with us before."

"We believed ourselves in communion. There was no need. Stasis had been achieved." They shot a venomous look at her over their shoulder. "Then your kind plotted to destroy us."

Naira pushed back her chair and stood. They watched her as she crossed to the garden. She crouched down alongside them and picked up one of the jars.

"Did he tell you why he did this?" she asked.

"He did not want it to leave." They paused. "You always leave."

"I suppose I do." Naira held the jar up. The moth within flapped its wings, yearning for the false freedom of the light. "People don't like to feel trapped. For us, finding out you were within us, controlling us from within, was terrifying. It was only natural that we'd fight back. If this moth could break the glass, it would, and it would care nothing for what was broken once its wings touched fresh air."

"We are not a cage."

"I'm not so sure."

"Do you really think that your body is wholly your own?" they asked, but gave no room for an answer. "Throughout your evolution you have bonded with others. Ancient bacteria powers your cells. Viruses have rewritten your DNA. Would you call these things contagions and banish them from your flesh?"

"None of those things have controlled our minds. Our bodies."

They scoffed. "That you know of. You are no more conscious of how your cells process energy than you were of us influencing your thoughts. Your vaunted control is a lie. To dwell in flesh is to abandon control; to enter into communion with processes you don't, and can't, understand."

"Maybe," Naira allowed. "But that's our choice to make. Not yours."

"You would eradicate us to preserve that choice?"

"If I have to, yes."

"How very human." A touch of Fletcher's sneering tone seeped into their voice. "To destroy something you don't understand so that you can feel safe."

"You know," she said. "I talked with Kav about this a long time ago, now. He wanted to destroy you, *canus*. Had no qualms about it, to start. But I saw what you did for the *Einkorn*. Saw that same, first glimmer of thought in the misprints, and I wasn't as gung ho to pull that trigger as you seem to think. I don't want to wipe you out, if I can help it. I'd like to try to find a way for us to understand each other. But if you won't cooperate with us, then I will destroy you, and feel no guilt."

"What would that cooperation look like? Killing parts of us en masse? Reducing us until we are nothing but starving scraps? Would that please you?"

"It'd be a start."

They frowned, their expression appearing genuinely wounded, though Naira had no way of knowing if she was correctly interpreting their body language. "Your hatred comes from a misunderstanding of our nature. Our nature is to bond. To provide the stimulus required to keep our hosts well and happy enough to give us sustenance in return. In all our previous bondings we were *wanted*. The separation you crave is horrific. Your...loneliness is crushing. We believed we were saving you from yourselves."

"And now?"

"We do not understand why you choose suffering."

"We don't view it as suffering."

"Don't you?" The World knelt in the dirt across from her and rested their hands against their thighs. "Did you know that, when printing day would come for the children of the orphanages, Fletcher would go to all the stations he could to watch over them. He feared for them. That they might be separated from one another. That separation is suffering, is it not?"

"Is that why you're here?" Naira asked. "On M-U?"

"Yes. This station was closest to Mercator, and so Fletcher came here often. That is why we chose this station for our inception. To watch over those children in his stead."

"The children are safe?"

"They are."

"I'd like to see that for myself."

"Ah," they said. "You are here to investigate the Bridge Project. We wondered why you had returned."

"It has a name? What do you know about it?"

The World shook their head. "Very little. Fletcher believed there was an organization taking children to be printed and bonded with us. We have never sensed children in our network, but he believed we must have been mistaken."

"How can you know nothing of the project, no matter its motives? Someone in your network must have seen, or heard, something more concrete than that."

"Only whispers. Rumor and fear. There is so much fear in all of you. We do not understand why you won't let us ease your suffering. Why you fight to be afraid. To hurt."

All that knowledge held by *canus*. All that fear. Paison's fear she'd be chewed up by her boss. Acaelus's fear of losing his family. And Fletcher...Fletcher, who strove his whole life for some semblance of control, reached the top of his field and found it forever out of reach. And countless others, no doubt.

All of that, and *canus* had no idea how to cope. As much as they spoke of humanity's loneliness, she could hear the soft thread of panic in their voice. The ratcheting terror that they couldn't understand why so many would reject them.

Naira didn't think their inability to cope made them less of a conscious being. She was starting to wonder if receiving data you weren't ready for and trying to figure out what to do with it anyway was what a sense of self actually was.

She unscrewed the cap and watched the moth flutter upward, spiraling into the shifting lights. Its wings beat unsteadily at this newfound freedom. But, soon, it found its strength, and disappeared into the dark.

"Do you see?" They craned their neck to follow the moth's path. "The garden would be better for them. There's nothing but death outside these walls for such a creature. Why do they leave?"

"I don't have a good answer for you." Naira picked up another jar. Unscrewed the lid. "Not one that doesn't sound like trite bullshit, anyway. You must know, logically, all the many reasons why they'd leave. Why people might not want to join in your communion."

"All we've ever wanted is to grow together."

Naira released another moth. Set the jar aside. "I hate to tell you this, World, but you can know all the reasons why someone does something and still not understand."

"Ridiculous. You're not providing ample explanation for your motives."

Naira smiled at that. "Maybe. Some of us don't even understand why we do, or want, the things we do. But we're individuals. Our experiences change the way we see the world. You can't look out of someone else's window from within, only from without, and there's no telling how that glass is tinted on the other side."

"We see from within all of us."

"Sure," Naira said. "But you were in my mind, and you still don't understand why I don't want to be one of your thralls, do you?"

The World stood abruptly and paced a tight line between the garden rows, hands flexing at their sides. The motion was so very Fletcher that Naira had to look away to hide a jolt of emotion she didn't understand.

"You are an anomaly," they insisted.

"I'm really not."

Naira watched them from the corner of her eye. Their caprice hadn't concerned her, at first. While they were wearing a print similar to Fletcher's, it was easy for her to ascribe their rapid shifts in mood and tone to the influence of that man. Now, she wondered. *Canus* infected thousands. Their ignorance—their innocence—none of it rang true.

It was impossible to be certain when dealing with an alien being, but somehow she sensed that *canus* was stalling. Hiding something from her.

"Take me to Gardet," she said. "If those kids are truly safe, and you're not trying to force them to print before they're ready to bond with you, then we'll talk."

"We are at war, Ex. Sharp," they said. "And you are here as an act of diplomacy, as we understand the custom. You are in no position to make demands."

Naira stood and dusted the loose soil from her hands. "You will take me to the children, or this will no longer be an act of diplomacy."

They eyed her for a long while, and Naira briefly wondered if they'd call her bluff—if they'd push this to a fight. Fletcher would have.

"As you wish," *canus* said. "Come with us."

TWENTY-THREE

Naira

Miller-Urey Station | The Present

Naira stepped through the gate into the courtyard of Gardet and felt like she'd shoved her head in an oven. Her vision grew hazy around the edges, countless moments just like this one fighting to super-impose themselves over the present. The feeling passed, scoured away by the blaze of her suppression pathways. Caldweller put a hand on her arm, asking a silent question. She nodded, slowly.

Canus watched all this transpire with impassive eyes. She thought they might say something, so long was their pause, but they only turned and walked on, leading the way.

Naira walked through halls identical to the ones she'd grown up in. The HC relied on consistency to maintain its tenuous control over its stations. Even the art on the walls was the same—poorly framed photos of starscapes the kids would never see. As far as she could tell, there was no evidence of *canus* overgrowth in the building.

If things were functioning normally, the custodian would be in their office reviewing discipline reports from the proctors. The kids would be in their last class, anxiously waiting to discover if their recorded indis-cretions meant they'd be spending the dinner hour in detention. Naira had spent plenty of evenings in detention herself, hoping Fletcher had managed to pocket some bread so that her stomach wouldn't chew itself up all night.

Canus opened a door, going through first, and then Naira was standing before the custodian's desk, briefly seeing a different face, a different time, before the suppression crown flushed heat down her skin and burned the memory away.

"Ex. Sharp." The nameplate on the woman's desk said her name was Ms. Hawker. "I understand you've come to check on the safety of the children, is that correct? If so, I can assure you that they're well cared for."

"I'm here to inspect their care, that is correct, but I also must speak with one of your wards."

"One of the children?" Ms. Hawker rearranged the folds of her multitoned grey tunic with care. She had a narrow face, with the permanent pucker of a woman who'd looked at everything the worlds had to offer and found all of it distasteful. Naira guessed she'd been the woman depicted in the drawing that the kids had been attacking with faux weapons when Naira had first met them. Hawker glanced hesitantly at the World.

"You didn't tell us you sought a specific child," *canus* said.

"If I had done so, you could have prepared for the inspection," Naira said. "I will speak with Jana Degardet. Alone."

Hawker's fidgeting stopped abruptly. "You are a guest here, Exemplar. Mind yourself. Just because we are no longer under HC rule does not mean that the Gardet home for unhoused children has abandoned its protocols. You have risen far, and we are very proud of you, but don't forget where you came from."

Naira took a deliberate step forward and pressed her fists against the desk, looming above the custodian. Hawker leaned back, and Naira watched her throat slide in a dry swallow.

"I did not *come* from Marconette. I came from rich soil and cold creeks. From green fields and an endless blue sky. People like you tried to take the color from me. Tried to grind me down into the same sad, grey world you preside over, and you failed. I have zero respect for you or your institution. Bring me the child."

"Do as she asks," *canus* said.

"But—" A brief flash of concern registered in Hawker's eyes. She stammered, then sighed. "Very well."

Curious, but nothing concrete. Naira gestured for the exemplars to pull out chairs in a half circle around the room and sit. She didn't want them looming over the poor kid.

Jana entered a few minutes later. She wore the grey uniform of the orphanage, GARDET printed above her heart in white letters, her dirty blond hair tugged up into a ponytail tied off with a white ribbon. Glacial-blue eyes narrowed as she skimmed the room, that intense face pinching. She rested her stare on Naira.

"Green-hands," Jana said.

"This is Ex. Sharp of Marconette," Hawker said. "She'd like to ask you a few questions."

"In private," Naira added. "If that's all right with you, Jana?"

"I don't care." She slid a quick glance at the World.

"We'll be right outside," Hawker said.

Jana didn't react to that. She merely watched with wary eyes as those two left the room, then turned to Naira. "They're going to listen in."

"I know," Naira said. "But I didn't want them interrupting you. Do you know who I am?"

"I knew you weren't right when we first met." Jana sniffed. "You're an exemplar?"

"I am." Naira gestured to the others. "As are my friends. Helms here, she's from Falcet."

Jana's nose wrinkled as if the air had turned foul. "Uh-huh. Aren't you supposed to be guarding one of those rich people, not out on your own?"

"These two are guarding me. I'm engaged to marry Tarquin, the head of Mercator. Do you remember the man I was with when we met?"

Jana put the pieces together and went white as bleached bones. "Is this because I was rude to him? I didn't know he was the real—"

"Whoa." Naira held out a hand. "Easy. You're not in trouble, I promise. I want you to understand that I have the power to protect you. You can tell me anything. Even if you think it might get you in trouble with the adults here at Gardet. Okay?"

"Okay."

"Are they treating you well?"

Jana shrugged. "Better than before Ms. Hawker went fully metal."

"Ah. Right. Metal eyes, your monster. Do you know what it means, that their pathways are silver now?"

"Their minds are all linked up, right?" Her forehead creased with concentration. "They say they can talk to one another now, but I don't get that, because they could always do that with calls and text, right?"

"That's right," Naira said. "But those with the silver pathways share more than communication. They share experience, feelings. The stronger among them can take over the others."

"That sounds bad."

"It's not good," Naira said. "I came here to make sure you were okay, but also to ask you some questions."

She darted a nervous glance at the other exemplars before returning her attention to Naira. "What questions?"

"There's a woman who is trying to hurt some people," Naira said. "Our techs believe that her print looks like you, but older. We were worried she may have come around here. Can I show you her picture?"

Jana's jaw stiffened, but she gave Naira a curt nod. Before she'd left, Naira had asked the techs to alter a picture of the assassin so that she wasn't obviously a corpse, and Naira pulled up that image. Jana's small face grew drawn and serious. Self-consciously, she touched her hair.

"I don't know her."

Naira lowered her voice and tried to sound kind. "I think you do."

Jana met her eyes through the glow of the holo. "You'll think I'm a stupid kid."

"No, I won't. I came a very long way to listen to you, Jana."

The girl studied Naira for a moment, then nodded. Naira wiped the holo away.

"I'm not lying," she said, and crossed her arms defensively. "But I see her sometimes. In my dreams. I feel like she knows me, but I don't know anything else."

"I believe you," Naira said. "Because I see her sometimes, too."

"You're not teasing me?"

"I'm not."

Jana eyed the crown of unusual pathways lining Naira's forehead. "How?"

Naira smiled. Clever kid. "I'm not sure yet, but I'm trying to find out. What do you see in these dreams?"

"It's all confused. I can't really hear anything, but I think she's shouting."

"If you have one of those dreams again, could you write down the details as soon as you wake up? I'll give you my private ID line. You can message me anytime."

Jana touched her bare wrist where a holo band would usually stand in for the pathways adults used to manage their holos and HUDs. "They took them away, when they turned fully metal."

Naira lifted her gaze to Helms and tilted her head toward the door. Helms nodded and slipped out. Naira turned her attention back to Jana. "Now, I'm going to ask you something that might be a little scary. Have you heard about kids going missing from the orphanage?"

"Just rumors." Jana tightened her crossed arms. Her gaze stayed firmly downcast. "About kids going to get mapped and not coming back. No one cares because they're not wards anymore, and there's no one waiting for them after they get mapped, you know?"

"I know," Naira said.

The exemplar channel lit up.

Helms: The World is refusing to give her a wristband. Says this is still an active war zone and they control all communication with contacts outside the cordon.

Sharp: I'll handle it.

"Thank you for your time, Jana." Naira held her hand out to Jana to shake. "I'm sorry for interrupting your day. Once you get your wristband back, you can message me anytime, all right? I mean that. It doesn't have to be important."

Jana gave her a thin smile and shook her hand. "Sure, green-hands."

Naira left the office and made sure the door was shut behind her before she pointed at the World. "You. Come with me. We need to talk."

A slash of something that might have been a smirk cut up the side of their face. "You are a guest in our territory, Exemplar. You presume to order us around?"

"Would you rather I leave?"

Their nostrils twitched, and she snorted. "I thought so."

Naira walked away, and the World followed.

TWENTY-FOUR

Tarquin

Seventh Cradle | The Present

Tarquin was supposed to be sleeping. Instead, he stood in his pajamas before the glass door to the balcony, drink in hand, and watched the rain fall through the dark.

But not only the rain. He'd locked down his comms for the night, but in the corner of his HUD, he kept Naira's current status pinned. She'd marked herself unavailable when she'd gone to the *canus*-controlled zone, but he knew she was still awake. It was silly, but he couldn't bring himself to sleep. He didn't want to go to bed until she did.

He wasn't worried. Not precisely. He just...missed her. And, strangely, that thought made him smile into the brewing storm beyond his window. A light knock on his door drew his attention.

"Come in," he called out.

Cass and Diaz entered, an unusual enough event that Tarquin turned to them with a frown.

"My liege," Cass said, "we apologize for interrupting your evening, but Liege Leka has arrived on-planet and has requested to see you."

Tarquin nearly dropped his drink. "My sister is *here?*"

"In the foyer, my liege."

Leka's request was more than likely a foot-stomping demand. Tarquin

glanced to the drink in his hand, briefly mourning a restful evening—
he'd been looking forward to telling Naira about his discovery with
amarthite once she was back at HCA HQ—and set it aside before rushing out of the room. He'd half expected Cass to have been mistaken,
but there, at the foot of the stairs, was his sister. Tarquin paused with his
hand on the banister.

Leka wore a tunic of Mercator green that brought out the olive tones
of her skin and the gold of her pathways. Her long brown-white hair had
been pulled up into a high ponytail, sharpening the angles of her face.
Muddied footprints littered his foyer and stained her boots—rougher
construction than she preferred. She must have gotten them from the
print techs upon arrival. An exemplar Tarquin didn't know lingered
behind her.

"I've come to inform you that you will not be marrying Ex. Sharp,"
Leka said.

Tarquin raced down the stairs and took her arm firmly but not
unkindly. "We'll discuss this in my office."

When the door had been shut on all their exemplars, he released her
and circled to stand behind the bulwark of his desk.

"You came all this way, without warning, without prior authorization
for printing into amarthite—which is *scarce*, Leka—to tell me that? It's
none of your business who I marry."

"It is precisely my business, because Mercator is *my* business."

"You abdicated."

"I stepped aside to heal, Tarq. For god's sake, I won't stand by and
watch you burn this family to the ground to keep your passing fancy
around."

"Passing—?" Tarquin pressed his knuckles into the top of his desk. "I
love her. I thought that you, of all people, would understand."

Leka scoffed. "If you believed that, you would have told me about the
marriage yourself, instead of letting me find out from a press release."

Tarquin winced. She had a point, but he spoke with his sister so rarely
the thought hadn't occurred to him. "I'm sorry I didn't tell you directly. I
should have, but it slipped my mind. I've been busy."

"Busy, he says! Busy cleaning up after that woman of yours, I expect.
I know she bombed the other families, Tarq. They won't stand for this.

Dragging her through your bed is one thing. Installing her as bastion of power within MERIT is another."

"Naira wants nothing to do with the family. She only wants to be with me."

"How sweet. The terrorist who dedicated her life to tearing down our family wants what, exactly, hmm? To settle down and provide you with heirs for the empire she sought to destroy? I think not. Get rid of the brute and find someone who will help you build something, not ruin what's already been built."

"Leka. I love you. But if you insult Naira again, I will have you removed from my home until you can show her the respect she deserves. She saved your life. Don't forget that."

"Of course she did! That's what she's for!" Leka tossed her hands into the air in frustration. "Father didn't break her down and rebuild her to send her on diplomatic missions. He crafted her to fight. To die. Keep her on the side if you must, but find someone else to be the other half of Mercator."

The ugliness of those words temporarily stole his voice. Tarquin had always been jealous of his sister, though he'd scarcely admitted the fact to himself. She'd seemed so effortless in her role as heir. Keen-eyed and clever, someone he believed carried more warmth in her heart for the charges of their family than their father ever had.

"I thought better of you" was all Tarquin could manage to say.

She sighed. A soft sound, her shoulders rounding before she caught herself. Straightened to perfect posture once more, as their mother had taught them. "You love her. I understand, I do, but you're asking too much of yourself. You cannot be a successful head of family, scientist, and a husband to someone in need of care. One thing must give. Mercator needs you. The worlds need you to find more amarthite. You need someone who will support you, not drain your resources."

"Naira doesn't drain me. She strengthens me."

"Lying to your own sister! What awful habits you've picked up. I have access to the family's ledgers, Tarq. Tell me, exactly, how much research funding you've been siphoning to cracked-mind care instead of into amarthite discovery and production, where it belongs?"

"She didn't ask me for that," he said quickly.

"She wouldn't. I doubt she even knows and would be upset with you if she found out, hmm?"

His palms dampened. "Research into cracked minds impacts all of humanity. There's no waste in that."

"Well. I'll give you this—you've certainly refined your ability to evade difficult questions. I, however, can't be brushed off so easily. Research into neural maps is the primary purview of Ichikawa. Not. Mercator. By indulging in pet projects to ease your lover's suffering you have not only undermined Mercator's ability to do what it does best—mining, little brother, lest you forget your own field of research—but insulted Chiyo as well. She's unhappy that you've been stepping on her toes."

"Father engaged in neural map research all the time," Tarquin said. "As I'm certain you recall."

The sharp angles of her face drew taut as her jaw tensed. "Careful. Because while you pat yourself on the back for your lofty idealism, I remember what drove Father to that point, and it wasn't being head of family. It was his obsession with our mother. His desire to keep her safe and pleased, above all else. Above the end of everything. And from my perspective, you're not just following in his footsteps. You're sprinting."

"I am *not* like our father," Tarquin snapped.

"Yet."

The word landed like a stone in his heart. He wanted to insist she was wrong. That he'd never be tempted to attempt half the things their father had done—but he recalled the desire, pustulant and squirming, that'd wormed its way into his mind late the night he thought he'd lost Naira for good. The option, never out of his reach, to repair her mind. To make her be what he needed to feel secure.

He wouldn't. He'd never. The temptation lingered.

"As I thought," Leka said after a while.

"I'd never hurt her."

"But who else might you hurt, I wonder?"

"You know me better than that."

"Do I?" She held up a hand. Ticked off points on her fingers. "By diverting resources to cracked-mind research instead of amarthite you've extended the waitlists for reprinting, forcing countless people to live without their loved ones. You refuse to force the *Cavendish* to land and be stripped of amarthite to protect Sharp's friends, who are Jonsun's hostages, adding to the wait. Instead of distributing what amarthite we do have equally, you've caved to Thieut's blackmail demands to protect Sharp—yes, I know about that—angering the other families, who already feel slighted by you, and who are pushing their people to their limits to make up for the lack. I can go on, if you'd like?"

Tarquin sank into his chair. Scrubbed a hand across his face, but his skin felt numb, his head buzzing. "I don't know what other choices I could have made."

"Oh, sweetheart." Leka rounded the desk and leaned against it beside him, resting her hand on his shoulder. "Of course you don't. I'm not here to be hurtful. Really, I'm not. But there are hard truths you must face. You've always misunderstood what it means to lead this family. How cruel the decisions we make can be. Must be."

He'd taken on too much. One person was never meant to guide so many, to make so many complex decisions alone. In trying to shield Naira, he'd inadvertently scorned the very support network he'd wanted to foster. Had kept things to himself that should have been shared, and dissected, and discussed. Acaelus had done the same.

"I really am becoming Father," he said.

"This is how it happens." She gathered his hand between her smooth, cool palms. Squeezed it gently. "Some heads of family are cruel from the beginning; I won't deny that. But for so many of us, it's a slow descent. A separation of values. I'm sorry, Tarq. I thrust the burden upon you and then left you to flounder alone. That was careless of me."

"You were recovering," Tarquin said. "It couldn't be helped."

"Hmm. Past tense. An interesting framing, but incorrect. I hope that's not the way you speak to your Ex. Sharp."

"Naira's doing much better, now," he insisted.

"The scars we carry cannot be healed. Time softens them, perhaps, but those wounds are never fully closed, and always ready to burst their seams at the correct provocation. For her sake, remember that. As I can attest, to be told you are recovered when you feel that you are not, and never can be, weighs heavily."

"I hadn't thought of it like that. I've made it worse for her, haven't I?"

"Probably."

"What do I do?"

She shrugged. "The usual things. Love her, support her. Let her fall apart sometimes."

Tarquin glanced up. "That's a remarkably kind thing to say, for someone who was insulting her every other breath a few moments ago."

Leka sniffed and flapped a hand at him. "Sharp herself was never the problem. Your treatment of her was. Is."

"Does this mean you support our marriage?"

"That depends," she said. "What are you going to do to fix the amarthite shortage your poor decisions worsened?"

"In the long term, redistribute resources to increase research in that department. I've already made some headway there, in fact. In the short term, force the *Cavendish* to land so that we can make better use of its amarthite stores."

"Good boy." She patted his cheek. "Then I suppose it's time I call in the cavalry."

"What cavalry?"

"To rescue Ex. Sharp, of course. That meeting with *canus* is an ambush."

"What?" He sprang to his feet. "What have you done?"

"Nothing at all. But I have ears to the ground in every corner of this universe. I came here when I learned your bribery to Thieut hadn't worked. The other families are aligned on one point: Sharp must be removed. They've made a deal with *canus* to ensure that happens. Don't fret, little brother. It's Ex. Sharp. I'm sure she'll be fine."

TWENTY-FIVE

Naira

Miller-Urey Station | The Present

Naira kept her eyes down, focusing on her steps. Every corner in the orphanage was a potential trigger for her to slide into memory. Every standard-issue door and identical piece of furniture haunted by old ghosts. Just being here, the crown pathways were constantly burning. Her body feverish.

The night air helped some, and she looked up once they were in the interior courtyard. No one was about. The remembrance hall sat at the edge of the courtyard, surrounded by abstract sculptures.

There were no religious symbols on or in the building. People brought whatever they revered with them into that space. Naira had spent many hours in the matching building back at Marconette, sitting and thinking of her lost home. Of what she'd do to set it right. To bring her mother back.

A light was on. Stained-glass windows painted shades of green on the greys of the courtyard, each one depicting a landscape from Earth. Naira knew every single scene. One of them was a dead ringer to the cliff she camped on when she was back on Earth. It was greener, in the window.

"Wait outside," she told the others.

Naira pushed the doors open with both hands. The hall was empty, as it usually was at this time. The light within was low, a soft glow that warmed the concrete walls enough to trick the eye into thinking they might be stone. The World strolled behind her, their hands in their pockets, an affected slouch to their shoulders.

"It's pointless to remove Ms. Hawker from this conversation," the World said. "She is us."

"Only when you want her to be," Naira said. "Isn't that right? You talk a big game about communion, or oneness, or whatever-the-fuck, but you're in control, aren't you? At the end of the day, you make the decisions for them all. It's no different than being a head of family. Hell, it's worse, because you can warp their very feelings into suiting your needs."

Their eyes widened in faux-innocence. "We would never do such a thing. We crave communion. Not dominance."

Naira laughed, roughly, and put her hands on her hips as she shook her head so that she wouldn't be tempted to ball them into fists and start swinging. "I've had you in my mind. I've seen what you can do. I know what you're doing *right now*."

Their head tilted to the side. "What's that, Exemplar?"

"You forced Chiyo's infected to speak in chorus because you know damn well it's unsettling, too close to what I experienced on Sixth Cradle. You printed yourself to look like Fletch to get in my head, you pretend at ignorance of humanity's desire to be left alone to gain my sympathy—but you're full of shit, aren't you?

"You're perfectly capable of speaking to me without the naivete, or repetition, if it suits you. You're not a fool, *canus*. You don't need me to help you have some sort of spiritual awakening, and I'd bet Tarquin's fortune that you overtook the orphanage not for Fletch's sake, but because you knew I'd come sniffing eventually. So why do you want me here, really? What do you actually *want*?"

Their posture changed. A slow unraveling of their affected humanity. Their slouch angled in an off-kilter way, their hands slipped from their pockets to cup the air, too-flexible joints twisting, twisting. The slash of a smirk they'd shown her earlier turned jagged in a way that made her tense. They leaned their side against one of the long benches, looking her up and down, and Naira felt again the predator's gaze. The warning twist in her gut that a threat was near. She lifted her chin. Stared them down.

"We want to live." There was a strange, muted echo to their tone of voice, as if it was trapped in the hollow of their throat.

"There are ways to allow that," Naira said. "I never intended for this war to be an eradication. If you could seed yourself into prints like the one you inhabit now, we could find a way forward. But no more people."

"You misunderstand," they said. "We have already made arrangements for survival. And you are the price we agreed to pay."

"What?"

"We are sorry, Exemplar. But you, and Mercator, are a threat to our continuation."

Naira dropped a hand to her sidearm, but the World hadn't moved an inch. She tried to bring up her HUD—jammed. For how long? She couldn't remember using it since she'd entered *canus*'s territory.

"What did you do?"

"What is necessary. Your mind is broken. You are unstable. Violent. A convicted terrorist who returned to her old ways, bombing amarthite stockpiles. MERIT has done only what is necessary for humanity to move forward in peace with *canus*."

"I didn't—" She cut herself off, tightening her grip on her weapon. How easy it would be for *canus* to mimic her body language. Fletcher's. Any of the original Conservators, too. How easy it would be to accidentally tip her off with the stranger's print, so that Mercator would suspiciously look like the only family of MERIT spared the bombing.

"You planted those bombs," she said. "What about Rusen? What do you know?"

The World would only smile.

A gunshot sounded. Far away, but it was only a matter of time until they drew closer. "You motherfucker. There are *kids* here."

They shrugged, a slow roll of the shoulders clearly meant to mimic Fletcher. "You won't risk their safety to preserve your own, will you?"

Naira shot them in the head. Their body slumped backward against the bench, sliding to the ground. The doors burst inward, and Naira stepped over the body, turning to hide it from view in case Jana was looking within.

"Sharp!" Caldweller's sidearm was out, his eyes wide. "What happened?"

"Comms are jammed and we've been sold out. Did you hear that shot before mine?"

"We thought it was street fighting."

"It's probably Chiyo's soldiers. She got here way too quickly when I called. Fuck."

Naira kicked the body behind the bench and left the hall. Hawker was still standing there, the same eerie smile the World had given her plastered on her face. Jana was with her, wearing a wristband, now. Her keen eyes flicked to the blood splatter on Naira's chest plate. Wonderful.

"Helms. Take care of Hawker somewhere else, please."

"It's pointless," Hawker said in the World's tone of voice. "You're surrounded."

Helms grabbed the woman and dragged her off, around the other side of the remembrance hall. Naira holstered her weapon and knelt in front of Jana.

"I'm sorry, kid, I really am, but there are people out there coming here to hurt me, and I'm afraid that they'll use you as leverage if they can't find me. We have to get out of here. All of us."

Jana turned to watch Helms return, and swallowed as the exemplar wiped her blood-slick knife off against her thigh. "There's a way we use to sneak out, sometimes," Jana said. "But I can't go with you. I can't leave."

"What?" Naira frowned, taking in the obvious frustration in her face, and understood. In Jana's position, Naira never would have left Fletcher behind. "Okay. I get it. Who's in your crew?"

"Just Tarq's left," Jana said quietly.

The magnitude of that stole her voice. There'd been six kids, including those two, in the alley when Naira had found them play-fighting. Four hadn't made it through the *canus* uprising. She closed her eyes briefly and patted Jana's back.

"Then we take him with us. Where is he?"

"Probably in the first-floor supply closet near the dorms," Jana said. "He hides there with extra food if I don't make it to dinner."

"Got it." Naira stood and swept Jana up in her arms, holding her against her chest.

"Naira, you're the target," Caldweller said. "If they take a shot at you..."

"I know, but the kids can't keep up with us."

"I'll take her."

Naira couldn't hide her surprise. Caldweller giving up even a scrap of his ability to do his job was monumental, and she noted the worried pinch to his brows, the way he already canted his body to shield Jana from the most likely position an attack would come from. He loved kids. The thought would have warmed her, if they weren't in danger.

"All right." She handed Jana across, and the girl wrapped her arms around Caldweller's neck, clinging on. "Let's find Tarq and get out of here."

TWENTY-SIX

Naira

Miller-Urey Station | The Present

They found a sleepy-eyed Tarq dozing in the closet. He'd been so overwhelmed by the exemplars barging into his hideout that he couldn't speak. Had simply looked to Jana and, at her firm nod, rallied himself and let Helms scoop him up so that the exemplars could run at pathway-enhanced speeds.

Jana's escape route led them into a run-down building that had once been used as a receiving space for supply deliveries from the HC. Those supplies hadn't come for at least a year, and a thick layer of dust dulled the unloading machinery.

"There." Jana pointed up, to a loft used for storage overflow. "There's a vent in the wall that's supposed to circulate air but it's just a big hole."

"What's on the other side?" Naira asked.

"A service alley for the bots. No one uses it."

"Who else knows about it?"

"Just the kids."

Naira doubted that. In her experience, the adult staff of the orphanages knew all the back ways the kids could take to get out on their own. They just didn't care. Naira shared a look with Helms, who nodded tightly.

"Kids," Naira spoke as she drew her sidearm and checked it over. "The people with the silver pathways—they're not always in control of themselves. It's a lot to explain quickly, but if one of them sees us, all of them see us, and even the ones who've been nice to you in the past might be a threat."

Jana gave her a strained smirk, struggling for confidence. "No one's that nice to us, green-hands."

"I need you both to be dead silent, okay?" Naira said. "And, I'm sorry, but if we're spotted—"

Tarq spoke, his voice a whisper, his eyes locked on her weapon. "You're going to kill them."

"I am." Her grip tightened. "I'm sorry. You shouldn't have to see this, but it might be necessary."

"We're going to be soldiers," Tarq announced, and put on a serious face that broke her heart. "It's okay."

No, it wasn't. Naira turned away. Focused on what she had to do to get out of there. With Caldweller and Helms holding the kids, she went first, climbing up the dormant equipment to reach the loft. The vent cover looked like the real deal—slatted metal, with a round tube barely visible within to indicate the ductwork. She pulled it away from the wall and found the tube was only a few inches long, the space on the other side a hole out into a narrow service way.

Naira shook her head and set the cover aside. It'd be enough to fool inspectors checking to make sure the building was ventilated properly, if the dust wasn't a dead giveaway. Not that the inspectors ever cared that these buildings were properly maintained. They just wanted to check off the right boxes and move on.

The service way was clear. She motioned for the others to follow her and swung her legs through the hole, dropping down onto the street. Meant for robots alone, the lane was narrow and hemmed in by high walls blocking out the false daylight. No windows overlooked the path.

Gunfire sounded in the streets once more. Closer, this time. A burst and a lull. Another burst. That was more than a scuffle in the streets. An organized force was fighting.

Naira caught Jana's eye and pointed in the direction of the fighting. The kid hesitated a moment, biting her lip, then pointed down the lane and mimed turning a couple times. Naira gave her a salute and took point, scouting ahead.

She'd expected immediate opposition, but every path they took was empty. Kid-sized footprints in the dust were the only sign that anyone had passed through recently.

It wasn't right. The adults must have known about the kids sneaking out sometimes, even before it'd been a war zone, and *canus* knew everything its infected knew. Naira checked around the next corner and jerked back, pressing herself against the wall for cover.

A misprint lingered ahead.

"I know you're there, Nai," it said in Fletcher's voice.

It wasn't him, she knew that. It was a fucked-up trick to mess with her head, but god, she hated how well it worked. Hated the cold revulsion twisting up her stomach. Naira stepped around the corner and shot it between the eyes. The sound was a thundercrack after all that tense silence. The body crumpled, lifeless. Another stepped out from behind a stack of crates.

"Run!" Naira shouted.

She fired, took that one down. Sprinted through the blood-slick dust and was first around the next turn to find three of them standing there, watching her with laughing eyes. They raised a pistol each, but Naira was faster, Helms or Caldweller or both firing over her shoulder, too, she didn't bother to check. They mowed them down and ran on.

Endless iterations of misprints choked her path. Sometimes they'd do nothing but stand and reach for her, and in the corner of her eyes she saw grey arms reaching through dead trees in their place. The suppression pathways burned, molten fault lines tracing her scalp.

Naira stumbled into a clear area and had to press her back against the wall, breathing hard. She unzipped her jacket wholly, taking in a deep, cooling breath. Caldweller shot her a look. Right. The jacket was armored. Grudgingly, she zipped it back up.

"You look like shit," Helms said.

"Helms," Caldweller said, "we do not tell our charges they 'look like shit.'"

"Sorry," Helms muttered. "But seriously, E-X, you don't look well. Do you have a fever again?"

"Not sure I'd call it that." Naira examined the back of her hand. Her skin was flushed, mottled. "It's the suppression pathways. But I don't think I'd be conscious without them."

"I'm glad you have them," Caldweller said, hiking Jana up higher on his hip, "because I'm running out of arms."

Gunfire on the next street over. Naira pressed a finger to her lips—not that it mattered anymore, their position was already blown—and heaved herself off the wall to go peek around the corner.

Misprint corpses littered the street, but there was no sign of any living opposition. A shadow passed over them. She glanced up and almost laughed with giddy relief. A drone striped in Mercator green soared above them.

"We have air support," she said.

Which also meant—her HUD pinged with a call from Sahanj.

"Are you—" Caldweller said, but she waved him to silence and answered.

"Nai," Sahanj said, "good of you to finally take my call."

"Sitrep?" she asked.

"We've got a foothold on the west end of the border, near your position."

"How the hell did you know we'd need backup?"

"I got a call from Liege Tarquin with a tip-off—something about his sister, I wasn't privy to those details—and he let us know that, surprise, surprise, Mercator had a squad on-station ready to back us up. We've got your location locked in and Mercator controls the skies, ready to clear you a path. Take the next two left turns. You'll be behind our line."

"I could kiss you."

"Don't threaten me when I'm helping you."

Naira snorted at that and ended the call, then explained the situation to the others. The relief on their faces eased some of her fear, but only some. She could still feel the phantom of *canus*'s predatory gaze on her back. The hooded smile that'd made her itch with the knowledge that they were holding back.

The drones took over the fight. Any opposition they would have encountered was dead before they reached it. Sahanj's soldiers were entrenched behind portable blockades, floodlights illuminating a wide strip of no-man's-land between the two forces. *Canus's* soldiers didn't seem armed or even shielded. They stood in a perfectly straight line, their bodies in silhouette.

Misprints. And, at the front of them all, the World in another copy of the print meant to resemble Fletcher. As one, *canus's* forces lifted a hand and waved. A short, slow twist of the wrist. As Fletcher himself had done on the docks of the Mercator hangar bay years ago, now.

Her scalp burned, skin flushing bright red as heat poured down her, through her. Someone grabbed her shoulder to brace her as she bent, vomiting thin bile. When she could get a full breath again, she straightened, scrubbing the back of her hand over her mouth. Sahanj forced a smile and released her.

"Not the reception I expected," he said.

"Sorry, it's..." She gestured toward the *canus* forces but didn't dare look at them again. "I think the suppression crown is overloading."

Jana frowned at Naira. "Do they hurt?"

"Not exactly. They get really hot, sometimes. Like sticking your head in an oven."

"Won't that cook your brain?"

"She doesn't have much left to cook," Sahanj said.

Naira laughed roughly at that, feeling some of the weight lift. "What's the situation?"

"That you need to retreat," Sahanj said. "Due to Merc-Sec's timely arrival and you drawing *canus's* forces inward, we were able to establish a solid lodgment. We'll have this neighborhood secured by the morning, but I want you off the front lines. If this goes sideways, I don't want to have to explain to Liege Tarquin how I accidentally got his future wife killed or kidnapped."

"No way," she said. "Something's not right. *Canus* had me surrounded, in its own territory. It could have taken me at any time, and it didn't, though it worked damn hard to freak me out. It was too easy, Sanj. That thing let me go for a reason, and I'm not about to do it a favor by backing off now."

"Of course it let you go." Sahanj glanced at his soldiers, staging for a push deeper into the streets, and rested a hand, briefly, over his captain's stripes. "You're not one of us anymore, Nai. You're not just some soldier it could use as a bargaining chip. If *canus* took you, then Liege Tarquin would have retaliated against them directly.

"Now, *canus*'s conspiracy with the rest of MERIT is blown. Mercator will be forced to respond. Even if your man doesn't attack outright, he'll have to cut their amarthite rations to hold enough in reserve to print an army if the rest of MERIT does decide to go to war, and that pushes more of the other MERIT families into relk. Letting you go is an inter-MERIT war waiting to happen, and *canus* stands to benefit more than any of us."

Canus had played her. Relied on the fact she was too stubborn to admit to herself that the frame of her world had shifted, and she no longer recognized her place in it. Shame and anger choked her and she turned toward the encampment, her sidearm in her hand. If *canus* wanted to use her, she'd make it cost them dearly.

"Nai." Sahanj stepped in front of her. "Stop. Fighting isn't your job anymore."

"But it's the only one I'm good at!"

Sahanj's face fell. "Get Liege Naira out of here, please, Ex. Caldweller."

Caldweller took her arm, steered her away. Toward the armored cars and the coddled life she'd agreed to lead.

"See you later, love," *canus* called after her in dozens of perfectly synced voices.

TWENTY-SEVEN

Naira

Miller-Urey Station | The Present

The lights in the halls of the HCA's HQ were downshifted for night. Naira's steps echoed alone, her exemplars left behind. She'd done what was asked of her. She'd retreated. Let Sahanj handle matters after the *canus*-bound had fallen back when it became clear they'd lost their quarry.

She'd secured the kids. Called Tarquin. Showered and rested and done everything, *everything*, asked of her. But when she closed her eyes, she saw Fletcher's face reflected endlessly back at her. A mirror-in-mirror hall that stretched to the end of time. The suppression crown burned, and she felt like she'd never get a full breath again.

So she'd slipped out. Snuck past Caldweller and made her way down halls she knew all too well, for the layout was the same on every HC station. Let herself into the armory. Started strapping on weapons. Armor. They were the only things that gave her peace.

The door opened. Caldweller entered, shutting it behind him. Leaned against the wall with his arms folded and watched her in silence.

"It won't work," he said after a while.

"I'll be the judge of that."

"Even if you can take all of them out, there's only going to be more of them on other stations. Thousands."

She cleared the chamber of a sidearm. Holstered it. "I can live with that."

"Can you?"

She didn't answer.

"Naira," he said gently, "this is a suicide mission."

"I'm aware."

"Then what's the point?"

She stared at herself in the foggy reflection of a metal locker. Some poor HC recruit had been made to polish them all, and recently. The sharp scent of the polish lingered on the air. The chore would have been a punishment for some minor infraction. Mouthing off. Waking up late. Not keeping your kit organized. She'd polished lockers often enough.

A deep sense of longing rose within her. A desire to go back. To simpler times, when polishing these lockers was the worst thing about her day.

"I'm going with you," Caldweller said.

"You can't."

"Because it's dangerous, or because you're running away?"

She wanted to tell him he was wrong. That she wasn't running away—that staying here, coddled and protected, was the real running away. She couldn't even make her lips shape that lie.

"I'm a soldier, Lee. I talked a big game about going to war, but the reality is I've been sitting on my ass for a year, letting the worlds dissolve around me. I can't do it anymore."

"You were recovering after having your mind cracked. That's not sitting on your ass."

"Recovering." She didn't know whether she wanted to laugh or scream. "What fucking luxury. Do you think Sanj would get a year to recover, overseen by the best doctors in the universe, if he cracked? Would you?"

"That's different. You know that."

"It shouldn't be!"

"Throwing yourself away isn't going to change that."

Naira punched the locker. Split her knuckles against the metal and relished the crack and the crunch of it bending to her strength. Couldn't even say, really, where the impulse had come from, but she felt better for it, and braced both hands against the lockers, head bent.

"I believed them," she said.

"Who?"

"*Canus.* I really thought they wanted to talk. That I could do diplomacy." She laughed, roughly. "They played me from the start and I didn't see it. I'm not a politician. I'm not—not Mercator-family material. I'm going to slow everything down or fuck it all up."

"If you were Mercator-family material, Liege Tarquin never would have asked you to marry him. That's not who you are. And it's not who he wants to be, either."

She grimaced and said nothing.

Caldweller sighed. "You turned him down, didn't you, when he asked you to marry him?"

"What?" Naira dropped her hands from the locker and turned to face him. "How did you know that?"

"You weren't wearing the ring, but you had it with you. And the young liege—he had to have been far away from your position when he was killed. Cass said they heard you scrambling across the beach, after the shot rang out. And come on, Naira. You know the protocol. You didn't alert me that you were the temporary head of family after his death."

"It's not what you're thinking. This—" She looked toward her ring, but her finger was bare, the object itself left behind on Seventh Cradle. She covered one hand with the other. "I told him to ask me again, when Mercator was dissolved. I never meant for him to think that I didn't want to be with him. I do."

"I told him you'd say no," Caldweller said. "He was adamant there was no point in waiting, but...the happiest I'd seen you in a year was when you were fighting those misprints. It was like you'd woken up after a long hibernation."

She laughed a little at that. "It felt good."

"Because you're good at it." He glanced to the weapons strapped to her body. "That's what this is about, isn't it? Regaining control over your life?"

"I suppose so." She felt ridiculous and small and tired. "And the fact that I just really, really want that motherfucker dead."

"Me too. But this isn't the way, and you know that."

"I just..." She turned away from him, hooking her hands around her hips, and tried to sort through the mess churning within her.

"Naira," he said after a while. "What are you scared of?"

"Being comfortable. Of another year with nothing accomplished. Another year of telling myself it takes time to dismantle an empire peaceably. And another year and another year and another slipping by and then it's over. I've lost. My fire burned out when I wasn't tending it and the worlds will move on down the same old cruel path, because it's easier to continue than to change."

"You've never been complacent. Not in all the years I've known you."

"That's not true, Lee. God, you—you know that's not true."

"I know what complacency looks like. I guarded the young liege as a teenager, remember? I love the boy, but—"

She turned to face him, brows lifted. "You do?"

Caldweller sat heavily on one of the benches and let loose an explosive sigh. "He's Acaelus's kid. Not mine. I know that. But Marko and I have wanted to adopt for so long, except we could never afford it, and being at Gardet earlier I... I got a little tangled up. That's all."

Naira sat across from him. "You were a better father to him than Acaelus ever was."

"I wasn't even allowed to talk with him most of those years."

"Maybe not. But you don't have to speak to show someone you love them, do you?"

"I suppose not," he grudgingly admitted.

She glanced in the direction of the suite where the kids were safely asleep. "You have an E-X's salary. Why couldn't you afford the adoption fee?"

"They increase it if you have a high-risk profession. Don't want us cracking and dumping the kids right back in the system, I guess. Effectively pushes all the exemplars out of the running."

"You're serious about this?" she asked. "You can't jerk those kids around, Lee."

"What?" He blinked. "Jana and Tarq, you mean? I'd take them in a heartbeat, if they wanted it, but there's no way we could afford the fees for one of them, let alone both."

"I can."

He blanched. "No. You can't spend the liege's money on me."

"Believe me, he won't miss it."

Caldweller tumbled out a few more protests, but she wasn't listening. She'd pulled up a channel in her HUD and contacted one of the family's accountants—one of them was always awake—and directed them to oversee the process. Seeing the number she had to authorize, she felt briefly ill but pushed the feeling aside. Buried it under her anger that the fees were priced so high simply because Caldweller had become an exemplar.

"There," she said. "This is contingent on the kids agreeing, of course, but the legal team is fast-tracking the paperwork so that we don't have to worry about them getting kicked to another orphanage in the meantime."

"Naira, I... Thank you. Marko's never going to stop cooking for you now, you know that?"

She smiled thinly. "I had to get something right today."

"You put yourself at risk to try to talk with your enemy. To try to find common ground. Just because it didn't work doesn't mean it wasn't the right thing to do."

"And when the right thing fails?"

"Then you get the guns back out." He held up a hand. "*After* working with your team to figure out the best plan of attack."

"Yeah, yeah. Thanks, Lee."

"Don't mention it." He stood and held a hand down to her to heft her back to her feet. "But you gotta do me a favor."

"What's that?"

"When we get back, you need to talk to him. Tell him what you said first, and why, and what you're feeling now. Because if he finds out, and it's not from you, it'll break him."

"Yeah." She took a breath. Nodded. "Yeah. I'll do that."

TWENTY-EIGHT

Tarquin

Seventh Cradle | The Present

Despite his irritation with his sister's stunt, Leka had been correct on one point Tarquin couldn't ignore. The *Cavendish* was too great a resource to be allowed to remain in Jonsun's hands. Even Naira, checking in after her escape from *canus*, agreed. Especially if war with the rest of MERIT was on the horizon.

He'd pulled a full flight crew and launch specialists, gathering them in a control room within the synch's labs. Alvero and Leka stood beside him. He wanted his sister to see that he was capable not just of leading Mercator, but of listening to advice and acting upon what he thought was useful. He also hoped that this would assuage her enough to stop her from meddling in his personal affairs again.

"Are we prepared?" Tarquin asked Alvero.

"We are, my liege. After the flight-ready check is cleared, we can take control of the *Cavendish* remotely and land it."

Tarquin approached the nearest console podium, entering his keys to push through a call that Jonsun couldn't ignore.

"Mercator." Jonsun's face filled the forward screen. He spared Leka and Alvero a cursory glance. "I wondered if you'd be contacting me today. Lot of rats scurrying about in my walls."

"We are preparing to land the *Cavendish*," Tarquin said. "I expect you to allow the preflight crew to check your physical systems to ensure the ship is stable enough for reentry."

"What a thing to expect." He crossed his arms and looked down his nose at them all. "You know what I expect you to do, Mercator? Restore my freedom so that I can take my people where I like."

"Mr. Hesson, you attempted to annihilate a large portion of humanity. Your current imprisonment is a small punishment by comparison. A freedom extended to you only because I hope that, someday, the unionists may come around to wanting to work with me, not against me."

"They weren't really human anymore, were they?" Jonsun chuckled, the sound raising Tarquin's hackles. "But I don't have time to retread that old fight. Where is she?"

"Excuse me?"

"Nai. She's not answering my hails. I gotta talk to her."

"Why?" Tarquin asked.

"Don't be coy with me, Mercator. I may be locked away, but I can see through my bars just fine. I know what's happening out there. The dumb woman has gone and tried to make nice with *canus*, hasn't she?"

Tarquin took a breath before he said something he'd regret. Jonsun still had Kav and Kuma, not to mention the unionists, to use as leverage. "Naira's mission and whereabouts are none of your concern, Mr. Hesson. And you will watch your fucking mouth when speaking of her." So much for trying to control his temper.

"So uptight," Jonsun said with a light laugh. "Can't imagine why Nai enjoys your snooty ass. Maybe it's the money, after all. Either way, I ain't letting your folk on my ship until I talk to her."

"You seem to be laboring under the misapprehension that you have a say in this matter. I assure you, you do not. You will allow Mx. Hesson's preflight team to check the ship before I land it today, or there will be repercussions."

"Threats, from you?" Jonsun eyed Leka. Smirked. "I get it. Big sister came along and straightened out your spine, did she? Too bad."

"Mr. Hesson," Leka said, "you will, as my brother said, watch your fucking mouth. You speak to the head of Mercator. He has done you a favor by allowing you to pretend at autonomy while you licked the wounds of your pride, but that favor is now due. Open your doors, and stand aside."

"Or what?" he scoffed. "The Mercator won't do a damn thing. He's too afraid of pissing off Nai."

"We would all do well to harbor a healthy fear of Naira's wrath," Tarquin said. "That goes double for you, Mr. Hesson. Open your doors, or I will open them for you."

Tarquin ended the call.

"What a slimy man." Leka wrinkled her nose in distaste.

"You've no idea," Tarquin said, then turned to Alvero. "Any sign?"

"The unlocking process has been initiated, my liege. It should take two hours to confirm the integrity of the ship, but I suspect Mr. Hesson will drag his feet as much as possible."

Tarquin settled himself at a workstation to wait, monitoring the system check with Leka at his side. It was strange, having her with him once more. They'd scarcely been in the same room after he'd gone to university, but she threw herself into the work. Explained small details he might have missed, and pressed him for his own insights. An hour slipped away.

Footsteps pounded down the hall outside the control room, loud enough to make Tarquin lift his head. The door flung open, Dr. Delorne barreling through, wide-eyed and breathless.

"Doctor? What's the matter?"

She took a heaving breath and launched herself at him, grabbing his shirt in both hands. Tarquin tensed, startled by the impact. Cass reached for Delorne's back.

"It's speeding up," she wheezed into his face, "my liege, it's speeding up!"

Tarquin shook his head at Cass, and they backed off. He peeled Delorne's fingers off his shirt and eased her back to a more comfortable distance. "The expansion? We knew that, Doctor."

"No, no, no, not like this! My liege, please, look at the data. We've got an hour at the most before we lose integrity with the ansible network."

"What is she talking about?" Leka asked.

Tarquin waved his sister to silence. "Show me."

Delorne flung up a holo from her forearm and spun an array of equations and estimations before his eyes, but what sank in was the graph—a steady line trending upward. "You're certain?"

"No! How can I be? It's impossible! But I've checked thirty-two times."

"How?" Tarquin demanded of no one in particular. He glanced to the screen Jonsun's face had filled a mere hour ago. No person should be capable of such a thing.

Yet.

He shook off the thought and focused. This crisis couldn't wait.

"Alvero, we need to order all stations to lock down until further notice. Scrap the *Cavendish* landing, no ships should be in transit until this stabilizes. We have to get—fuck. Naira."

He put through a very obnoxious call to her, every emergency tag and alarm he could think of attached to it. She answered.

"Naira, I need you to cast home immediately. All of you."

"What happened?"

"We've got maybe fifty minutes before we lose the ansible network, and I can't guarantee when or *if* we'll get it back."

Naira's gaze skimmed away from the holo, tracing an arc through an area he couldn't see. Kids laughed. Tarquin's chest tightened. He willed her not to say what he knew she was thinking. She lifted a hand, clenched it into a fist, and circled it in the air. Caldweller, Helms, and Sahanj converged around her.

"If there's an attack on comms," she said, "I can't run off. The kids can't cast. I have to keep them safe."

"It's not an attack. The expansion is speeding up. Please, I'm begging you, come home. If we can't fix this, then we'll be separated by light-years while it's unsafe to warp jump."

The magnitude of what he was saying settled and her eyes widened. "Fuck."

"Go," Sahanj said. "I'll keep the children safe."

Naira bit her lip and was still looking slightly aside, no doubt at Jana and Tarq. "We have to tell them."

"Hurry, please. I love you."

She turned back to the holo at last. "I love you. I'll see you soon."

He let out a taut breath and nodded, pausing only long enough to give a few details to Sahanj about what was happening, and what to expect, before he ended the call.

Leka gripped his arm. "Is it true?"

Tarquin looked to Delorne, absorbed in her holo, her eyes wider than he'd ever seen them. "I believe so. Yes."

"Em's out doing fieldwork. She won't be able to cast in time."

Tarquin waved down the nearest tech. "You. Get Liege Leka to a casting station immediately. She needs to make it back to Sol."

"Tarq—" Her voice scratched. "There's so much more I need to say."

"I know." He held both her arms. "But you have to go. Em would never forgive me if you stayed here. And if the worst comes to pass, I—I trust you to lead the family in Sol. With kindness, Leka. Promise me that."

She surprised him by throwing her arms around his neck, dragging him into a hug. "I'm so proud of you," she said, then released him, and turned to follow the researcher at a run to the casting beds.

Tarquin watched her go, dizzy with the weight of it all. A lump wedged into his throat. He swallowed it down. Focused.

Ships, stations, dome cities. Everyone had to be alerted that they were going to lose the one thing that kept them strung together. Local networks might still work, but anything that bounced off an ansible was about to be bricked. Tarquin ran out of the lab, Delorne right behind him, and found a car already waiting to rush him back to his home, where Naira's print waited in stasis.

He focused on the work, because to think about Naira not making the cutoff, or deciding to stay behind to guard the children, made him want to crawl out of his skin. The terror of the expansion itself was almost incomprehensible, but Naira being stuck light-years away was a concrete fear.

The doors to the stasis room swished open at his approach. Bracken was already there. They'd taken the shields off all three prints and affixed the usual sedative and euthanasia line to each of them. Tarquin wanted to tell Bracken to remove the euthanasia lines, but it was a necessary precaution. Standard.

"What's the emergency?" Bracken asked while checking the still-healing wounds from the implantation of Naira's suppression crown. Tarquin wished he'd ordered a reprint so she could come back without injuries. They'd thought they'd have the time to conserve amarthite.

"We're about to lose the ansible network."

Bracken looked up sharply. "You're kidding. How?"

"Accelerated expansion of space," Delorne said offhandedly. "We won't lose all of it. I think some of these new vectors might work."

"If you keep some of the network online, I will build you a lab out of solid gold."

She grinned toothily. "I'd prefer sapphire, my liege. A much more useful material."

"Consider it done," he said with a strained, anxious laugh.

Tarquin approached the side of Naira's gurney and took her hand. The print was warm, kept at a healthy temperature by the stasis shield, and a quick glance at the holo projected from Bracken's podium showed that all the print's vitals were green. She just wasn't *in* there yet.

He tried not to hold his breath, but kept catching himself doing so regardless. The clock ticked down. Her skin grew cooler beneath his touch. Perfectly normal, he told himself. Prints lost heat out of the shield. Bracken wouldn't let her temperature drop too low. He kept working via his HUD.

Communication channels dropped off one by one, corners of the universe going dark. His heart raced, sweat beading across his forehead and making his palms slick. He didn't want to watch the clock, but he couldn't help it. The more channels were lost, the harder he stared.

Miller-Urey hadn't dropped. Not yet. Maybe he should call her. If she wasn't going to make it, he wanted to see her eyes one last time before the connection was ripped away. But if she was running for the transfer, then he didn't dare distract her.

Helms gasped awake. Hope surged through him. Naira wouldn't have sent her E-X back without her. She was coming home. He squeezed her hand, willing her eyes to open.

Caldweller jerked awake and let out a low groan, rubbing his head. Tarquin met his eyes over Naira's gurney. Caldweller frowned.

"She's not back yet? She went first." He coughed, his print's throat unused to working.

"Not yet," Tarquin said, hanging his entire heart on that word—*yet.* She'd gone first. She'd make it. She hadn't stayed behind.

Miller-Urey's channel went dark.

Naira did not wake up.

TWENTY-NINE

Naira

error

Naira sat on her usual log by her usual fire back on Earth, and knew she was in a simulation. Despite the setting, this wasn't Tarquin. He would have made an appearance by now. She'd been taken, then. Snatched out of the transfer by a clever piece of software, and she had a sinking suspicion of who that had been.

They'd have to know her well to re-create this place, and that circle was small. Small, and almost entirely concentrated on the *Cavendish*, the very ship Acaelus's software had fished her map out of in the first place.

She couldn't sense a body, and that concerned her. Either she hadn't been printed—likely—or the suppression pathways were keeping her from doing her cracked-mind trick and taking off the simulation crown. Neither choice was good for her, but she hoped it was the former. If the suppression pathways could be used against her, then she might be in real trouble.

Naira scooped a branch off the ground, broke it in half, and tossed it on the fire. She leaned against the log, her boots planted in the dirt, her hands cushioning her head. Her HUD was gone, no surprise there, and so all she had was the fire and the night, a blot of stars stretching across a bruised sky that had never been this bright in real life.

"Simulations don't work on me," she said to the dark.

There was no answer. She hoped the others hadn't been fished. Hoped that Tarquin was safe, and that the universe hadn't torn itself apart at the seams, but she felt no fear for herself. Maybe that should worry her. It didn't.

Eventually, footfalls crunched across the grit leading up to her campfire. She knew that gait, felt the pressure of it, the rhythm as if he were walking across her own skin.

"Jonsun," she said. "Nice of you to visit."

He sat at the edge of the fire. Where there'd been no log, one appeared beneath him, and that rankled—he'd placed it deliberately to mirror the carving Tarquin had made for her bracelet. Jonsun didn't get to sit there. She kept the irritation off her face. This was a game to him. She needed to make it one for her, too.

"I don't like to keep guests waiting overlong," he said.

"What about prisoners?" she asked.

He leaned against a rock that hadn't been there a second ago, crossing his ankles as he stretched dirty boots toward the fire. Those kind eyes warmed with the flames, but there was an edge to him. A frantic tug to all his expressions that whispered he was more brittle beneath the surface than he let on. More liable to cut, if broken.

"I'm just borrowing you for a spell, Nai. Can't a man visit with his old friend?"

"If I recall," she said, matching his drawl, "the last time we spoke directly, you called me a bitch."

"You were being a bitch at the time. Saved a ship full of the *canus*-bound. I really thought you'd pull through for the right side. But I suppose you can't help getting on your knees for Mercator, can you?"

"You'd better get some new material if you're planning to insult me. And a new plan, too. I mean really, cribbing from Fletch? He already tried to kidnap me to leverage Tarquin. You know how that worked out for him."

"Ah, Fletch. Can't keep his name out of your mouth, can you? You always were a glutton for punishment. But no, that's not why I've borrowed you."

"Then what's the plan?" she asked, feigning casualness. Like they were back at the dinner table, kicking ideas around to take Acaelus's empire apart at the seams. "You say 'borrow,' but the second Tarquin realizes what you've done, he's going to throw everything he has at you. I don't think your little kingdom can withstand a full assault from Mercator."

He *tsked*. "Listen to you, bragging about the strength of Mercator. What happened to you? And don't tell me Tarquin happened to you. He can't possibly be that good to you."

"*Canus* happened," she said. "The Conservators weren't enough to stand against *canus* alone. We needed infrastructure. We needed research. All things Mercator brought to the table." She took a breath. "And then *you* happened. You fucking cracked me, Jo. You cracked me and you tried to bomb humanity into atoms."

"I tried to save you. But you got yourself all twisted up and saved the *canus*-bound, and now you're doing it again. Talking with that *thing*. You've lost sight of yourself, Nai. Turned your back on your own goals."

"I'd still be working with you if you hadn't decided to leave most of humanity behind while you ran, then turned back to blow the survivors to bits. Honestly, I've wanted to ask you one thing for a long time."

"And what's that?"

"What the fuck is wrong with you?"

He smiled, slow and kind. The familiarity of that smile beneath eyes that gleamed with hatred raised the hairs on the back of her neck.

"That's why you were such a great addition to the team. You cut through the bullshit. Clear-eyed, fire-hearted. And it's out of respect for who you used to be that I won't jerk you around. There's nothing wrong with me. Nothing at all. I'm healed. I'm complete. And it breaks my heart to see you suffering when you could be complete, too."

"I'm never going to use that software."

"I've been experimenting," he said as if she'd said nothing at all. "I know it'll work for you the same way it worked for me. I've seen it. You could be healed, Nai. All the cracks in your psyche you keep falling through, getting tangled up in a past that's too sharp for comfort, I'll fix them for you. I have your map, after all."

She went rigid, heart giving one thunderous kick against her ribs. "Don't you dare violate my map like that."

"Violate?" His smile carved shadows into his cheeks. "Such a strong word. It's medical care. Care that's been denied you out of paranoid superstition. You say I'm not myself, but you couldn't be more wrong."

"All right," she said slowly. "You want me to use it. Tell me how it works. Tell me what changed in you."

He leaned forward, hungry eyes boring into her, tracking every twitch of her muscles, every subtle movement of her eyes.

For a flash she thought she saw her own face staring back at her, crowned with scars. Then it was gone, and it was only Jonsun's face, too intense, too close, and she couldn't tell if that'd been her mind serving up a hallucination or a parlor trick of Jonsun's.

"I don't know, Nai. What changed?"

Naira studied that face she used to know so well, golden pathways shining, and understood. "*Canus.* That's what changed. You're not infected anymore. You wanted to destroy everyone complicit in MERIT and rebuild with the scraps left behind even before the *Sigillaria*—and it stopped you, didn't it? Made you focus on saving the worlds instead. *Canus* craves unity and you—you were its antithesis. All this time."

"*Canus.*" He spat in the dust, face twisting with a sneer. "I lost sight of the truth for a long time. But I'm back now. You freed me. So I'm taking you with us into the future. This expansion is happening. The separation must be complete. But then I'll bring us all back together again."

"What do you know about the expansion?"

"You'll see soon enough."

He stood. She tensed, ready for violence even though she had no real ability to strike back. He strolled over to crouch down beside her, a small frown on his face.

"Ah, Nai. You've fought for so long I don't think you know how to stop. But it'll be all right. The next time you wake up, you'll feel better. It's for your own good, really. If you carried on down this path, unknowing of what the future holds, you'd never forgive yourself. That man you've claimed? He's just another Mercator, another tyrant. You'll see. It's time to take the blinders off. Time to face what's coming."

She swung for him, all impulse and fury. He caught her wrist easily because here, in the simulation, the rules were his. For the first time since she'd known him, his grip was stronger than hers.

"Don't do this." She strained against him, whole body shaking while

he stayed perfectly still. "This isn't the time to play games. Set the goddamn politics aside and see reason. We need Mercator's resources."

"Don't fret. I see what's coming, and I see a way through for us all.
That's why I took you. I'm not going to stand aside and let you die with
the rest of MERIT. You made this possible. I haven't forgotten that."

"What are you talking about?"

"I'll see you soon, Nai. On the other side."

He vanished. Without the resistance of his arm, she overbalanced and
tumbled face-first into the dirt, so close to the fire the searing kiss of it
brushed against her side. Swearing, she pushed herself up and sat on her
knees, staring into those twisting flames.

There was nothing she could do. She didn't even have a print. She was
a figment of digital ether trapped in a bubble of his creation, and when
next she opened her eyes she'd be…something else. The fact that he
hadn't disengaged the simulation, that he'd left her there to stew in fear,
was proof enough of his confidence. Tarquin would have to find and
recover her within hours, at best. It wasn't possible.

The repair was going to happen.

Naira wanted to scream. Jonsun wouldn't go to all this trouble to
warp her mind and then keep her locked up on the *Cavendish*. He'd use
her. He'd wield her.

Bile tinged the back of her throat. If she killed herself in here would
she fall unconscious, or would her map be damaged beyond repair? If she
woke up and couldn't stop screaming, Jonsun couldn't use her.

The curve of a brown cheek flickered in the flames. Naira's breathing slowed. She didn't know if it was a hallucination or a glimpse of the
future trying to seep through, but couldn't help but resent it, either way.
That was a future she'd never have. The scarred woman in the powercore had been trying to protect her. To protect Tarquin. No puppet of
Jonsun would do such a thing.

Naira studied that glimpse of her lost self. She didn't know how to
undo being repaired, wasn't even sure what was going to happen to her,
but she could remember, couldn't she? Her memories were always there,
waiting, forward and backward in time. Maybe it would work. Maybe it
wouldn't. She had to try.

Naira forced herself to remember her glimpses of the future in the same way she summoned her past. She felt Jana's slap land against her cheek. Saw herself standing across from the misprints, lifting her hand in warning. Saw herself kick for the explosive device. Naira gathered every figment of that other future, burned them bright into her mind, and held on with all the stubborn endurance she'd ever been able to muster, rejecting any future in which she was Jonsun's creature.

The software patched her together anyway.

THIRTY

Tarquin

Seventh Cradle | The Present

Tarquin woke in the dark of his room. A weight rested beside him. Not Naira's, it was too heavy for that. He pressed the heels of his hands into his eyes, willing himself backward. Willing the events of the past few hours to have all been some terrible dream.

He'd ordered Naira's map traced to see if it'd been cut off in transit. Alvero had discovered that her map had been diverted, but couldn't say where. Someone had fished her out mid-cast, as Acaelus had all those years ago.

Naira joked about being uncrackable, but the reality was a different matter. There were degrees of cracking. If they double-printed her, it could be so much worse. Constant slipping in time, perpetual repetition. The endless scream.

He couldn't take the risk until he knew what had happened to her. Until they found who had *taken* her. His memories fell apart, after that. Became a haze of his own voice rising, issuing orders that may or may not have made sense. Bracken had sedated him. They'd been right to do so.

"How are you feeling, my liege?" Caldweller asked.

The weight on the edge of his bed. Caldweller sat, his back to Tarquin, facing the door to the balcony. His hands were clutched together, his voice a muted thing stripped of all emotion. Sitting on a charge's bed to keep watch wasn't the protocol. The bedroom door had been closed, and no doubt Cass guarded it. Or maybe Helms or Diaz—it wasn't like those two had Naira to watch over. Tarquin's throat scratched when he swallowed.

"Dehydrated," Tarquin said, because devastated was obvious.

Caldweller plucked a glass of water off the nightstand, half turning to offer it to him. He sat up. The glass was cold in Tarquin's hand, the water a balm down his throat. He sat beside Caldweller and rolled the glass back and forth between his palms while he stared straight ahead, trying to think of something worth saying.

"We'll find her," Tarquin said at last, feeling those words deep in the core of who he was. She'd come back. She always came back.

"We will." Caldweller laced his fingers together. Twisted them. "My liege, I failed you. I was supposed to keep her safe."

Tarquin clutched the glass. "That wasn't an attack you could have defended against."

"Still."

There was no arguing with that. Tarquin knew how deep the recrimination of *I should have done something* could dig. There was little that could uproot such a thought once it'd taken hold.

He recalled, vividly, the despair that'd sunk into him when Naira had first been cracked. Caldweller had dragged him out of his self-pity, despite his determination to wallow in it.

Tarquin expected that same despair to come rushing back, but it didn't. He'd learned, hadn't he? He'd learned to trust his team, to trust those he cared about to care about him, too, even when he didn't deserve it. He wished he knew what to say to help Caldweller see that, too.

Tarquin wiped the condensation off his palm and placed his hand, carefully, on Caldweller's shoulder. The exemplar tensed, flicking him an uncertain glance. His eyes were bloodshot, skin wan. Tarquin was certain he looked much the same.

"Lee," he said, and paused, because the name was strange and familiar all at once. "It's not your fault. We'll find her. And god help whoever took her, because she's going to tear them apart."

Caldweller laughed roughly. "I hope there's some left for me to tear apart, too, my liege."

"We'll have to start a line. And you'll have to forgive me for using my station to push to the front of that line."

"This is backward. I'm supposed to be the one comforting you."

"I'm... okay." He hesitated, fearing that the lack of sorrow rampaging through him was the first sign of his father's cruelty seeping in at last, but it wasn't. It was hope. Trust. "Not happy, of course. I want to *burn* whoever did this. I want her safe. I want her back. But..." He licked dry lips. "Naira and I, we're not just a family of two, are we?"

Caldweller startled and looked at him. "No, my liege."

"I know you can use my name, Lee."

This was treading the unstable boundaries of his power. He hadn't forgotten what Naira had said about caution when it came to getting close to his exemplars. But he thought—he *hoped*—he was right about this.

Tarquin finished his water and set it aside, then stood, and held out a hand to Caldweller.

"You didn't raise me to sit around and mope when there was work to be done. Would you help me? Help me to do something she might be proud of, when she gets back?"

Caldweller's eyes shone. He blinked, tears tangling in his lashes. "My liege, I didn't mean to—"

Tarquin made a small sound of negation. Hesitantly, Caldweller placed his hand into Tarquin's.

"With you always, my—" He cleared his throat. "Tarquin."

Tarquin tugged him to his feet and was surprised and delighted when Caldweller folded him into a bone-crushing hug. When they parted, Tarquin was a little sore, and they both had to sniff and clear their throats.

"All right," Caldweller said, rubbing his hands together. "Where do we start?"

"With the obvious," Tarquin said. "While IT are looking for where her signal went, and the ransom team waits to see if there's a call, we have to stabilize the ansible network. If we can't communicate or travel, we're fighting with our hands tied behind our backs."

"How are we going to do that?"

Tarquin looked sideways, out the window, to a moon that was smaller in the sky than it should have been this time of year. Everything was falling apart.

"I have an idea," he said. "But no one's going to like it."

INTERLUDE

Her

The End | The End

The simulation of her life no longer serves her, and so she has left it behind. Left the endless fragments of herself to churn unwatched on temporal tides. It is strange, to dwell in flesh once more. Her limbs feel indistinct. Phantoms of another life, when there had been warmth and sustenance and touch.

Scaly patches of frost bloom across Tarquin's stasis shield. She lays her hand against them, trying to recall the last time she heard his voice outside of memory. Outside of another timeline, another desperate attempt to save what refused to be saved, and finds she cannot. Freed of the simulation, she's already losing possibilities. Other ways her life could have played out slip through her fingers. This is for the best, she knows. For what she is about to attempt, it is kinder not to know that there were ever any other options.

Fletcher appears before her. His hands are in his pockets, a subtle forward roll to his shoulders that used to signal insouciance but now only makes him look tired.

He approaches. There's reverence in him. A devotion that will never fade. But sadness, too. A sorrow as intrinsically linked to his worship of her as flesh to sinew. She knows what he will say. He must say it, regardless. This is how this always goes. This is, so often, where she fails.

"It's time, Nai."

"I know."

He turns his head. Takes in the rime-crusted walls and the stasis shield. It's nothing he hasn't seen before. It still gives him pause.

"Jonsun's people will be here soon. Kav and I won't be able to hold them back for long."

"I'm afraid."

She's surprised to know that it's true. She's lived in simulation for so long that to inhabit her flesh once more is to remember what it's like to need. To want. Hunger and thirst and rest and love, too. And in needing all those things, it is only natural to fear losing them.

"I know."

He steps closer. Takes her face in both his hands, and though she knows the intense gold of her eyes frightens the others, he stares into them unflinching.

"I can't see our pasts like you do, but I know this much: You and I, Nai, we've always come through, haven't we? Back-to-back, remember? Undefeated."

Her gaze slides off him. Settles on the stasis shield and the man slumbering within. A man she fears to wake, for she knows what he will think of what she's become. Fletcher turns her back to him, gentle, insistent.

"I lose perspective, when I go back. All I ever want to do is save him."

"That's who you are." His thumb brushes against an exemplar pathway. Stops. "You have to let him go, Nai. Just this once, you can't save everyone."

Her eyes close, but she has long since lost the capacity for tears. "And afterward?"

"I'll be there, at the beginning. You've seen that much."

"You won't remember any of this."

"No," he says, and smiles though his heart has long since broken. "But all I've ever wanted is for you to be okay, Nai. I'll be there. I won't let you fall." He glances aside. To the stasis shield. To the man she has dragged through countless centuries. When he looks back again, there's a wryness in his voice that she hasn't heard in decades. "Not again."

She laughs. A soft, rattling sound that surprises them both.

"There you are." His smile stretches his cheeks and wrinkles the corners of his eyes, shining. Shining. "Go on. Save the worlds. And then trust in me to save you."

She lies back upon the gurney. The transmission crown fits snugly upon her head.

Fletcher holds her hand until she's gone.

THIRTY-ONE

Tarquin

Seventh Cradle | The Present

Tarquin gathered his inner circle in the lab he'd been sharing with Dr. Sharp. Sleepless, bloodshot eyes watched him as he sat at the head of a long table. Naira's loss had hit them hard, but it was the expansion that'd kept them up working all night.

Bringing Naira back wouldn't matter if the universe expanded so rapidly that the planet became uninhabitable.

"Dr. Delorne," Tarquin said, "could you please give the others a brief explanation of what we know of the expansion thus far?"

"Of course, my liege." She pulled up a graph from her holo. "When we first realized that the expansion was accelerating, I contacted the UFP offices to pull their data on the Hubble variants over the last few years.

"The expansion has had a few blips in that time—speeding up and slowing back down—but these variations remained relatively small, until about two years ago. We experienced a brief slowing down, and then a burst of acceleration. A few months later, nearly the same thing again. The events were small enough that the UFP was updated without fanfare. I now believe they were the harbingers of our current problem."

"What happened during the slowdowns?" Dr. Sharp asked.

"That's the curious part," Tarquin said. "The first coincided with the infection of the *Einkorn* above Sixth Cradle. The second cycle was during humanity's mass *canus* infection and the recovery from that infection.

"I believe that ceasing the use of relkatite in our prints, and thus removing our *canus* infections, allowed the radiation relkatite produces to go undepleted. Considering all the evidence thus far, the unchecked radiation has steadily increased acceleration until we've hit some sort of crisis point."

"My liege," Alvero said, "I don't disagree with your research, but it's worth considering that you were forcing Mr. Hesson to land, and had to abandon those plans, when the expansion hit this crisis point."

"I know," Tarquin said. "But I can't stress enough that these theories we're working with are at the cutting edge of science. Jonsun shouldn't have access to any of this information."

"There's been a great deal of information shared lately that no one else should have access to, my liege," Alvero said.

His proposal. The assassination. Tarquin shifted uncomfortably in his seat. "I take your point."

"My brother isn't that clever," Jessel said dryly.

"We could finish the forced landing," Ward said. "Pop that ship open and snoop around, see if we can find any evidence of a universe-expander, or whatever else he's got."

"Moving a ship that large while navigation is unreliable is too big a risk," Tarquin said. "I understand your concerns, but for now, we must wait for Jessel's spies to report back and work with what we know."

"All right," Ward said. "So kicking *canus* out of our bodies might have doomed the universe. What a bastard of a fungus."

"We're not doomed yet," Tarquin said. "As Delorne's data shows, periods of runaway *canus* growth slow the acceleration. I'd like to engineer such a scenario. If we're very lucky, we may be able to force a contraction."

"I hope you're not suggesting we have people print into relkatite bodies and suffer an infection," Alvero said.

"No, of course not." Tarquin waved a dismissive hand. "There's a much more efficient method. We have the stockpile of relkatite that my father absconded with on the *Sigillaria*. I intend to move that stockpile to one of the empty cargo ships in orbit, lock the ship down, turn off the

THE BOUND WORLDS   193

AI, and infect it with *canus*. If we can convert the entire stockpile, we may be able to slow the acceleration enough to bring the ansible network back online."

And find Naira. He kept the brief stirring of hope off his face, but saw it reflected in Dr. Sharp. Ward and Alvero turned thoughtful, while Delorne gave him an enthusiastic nod of approval.

"I want extra security measures on that AI," Alvero said slowly, thinking out loud. "We can't afford to repeat the events of the *Einkorn*."

"Another *Einkorn* is the last thing I want," Tarquin said.

Alvero nodded. "In that case, I'd like the AI locked from a separate planet-side location—say, the powercore housing, that's highly secure—then there's no way anything, or anyone, on board will be able to get the AI online."

"I like it," Tarquin said. "Make the arrangements, please."

"I don't get it," Diaz said.

Tarquin pinched the bridge of his nose. "I can go over it with you later, Exemplar."

"I don't mean the logic, my liege. Relk creates energy that juices up the expansion. *Canus* eats it. I got that. But aren't there a lot of people infected right now? Shouldn't that be slowing it down?"

"There are," Tarquin said, "but there are orders of magnitude fewer infected than there were before the uprising."

"Okay, but relk's rare, right, so—"

"Ex. Diaz," Tarquin said. "Time is of the essence."

"I was just wonderin' why all the *canus* hadn't died out then, my liege."

"Gabe," Helms hissed under her breath.

He stepped back. "Sorry."

Tarquin scarcely heard them. In his rush to slow the expansion, he'd ignored the simple truth that *canus* existed within an ecosystem that must have remained unchanged until Mercator had modified *canus* to better facilitate mining.

Something had kept it from overgrowing to such a degree that the universe would have fallen apart long before this moment. Relkatite was difficult to find, the ecological niche would have been small and *canus*'s impact on it minuscule. But if relkatite was truly the primary source of the energy causing the expansion, then how could a balance possibly have been maintained? Tarquin looked to Dr. Sharp, the closest thing to an ecologist they had in the room. Her brow was puckered with thought.

"There must be a limiting factor," she said. "Something that prevents it from overgrowing enough to outstrip its ecosystem."

"We need to start immediately," Tarquin said. "If there is a limiting factor, we must discover what it is, and how to get around it, as quickly as possible. Everyone—see to your tasks, and be certain to update me with the slightest detail."

They went to see to their duties. The second Tarquin was left to his own devices, he checked his private channel with Naira. Nothing yet.

He pushed aside his fear and switched to the combined data of relk's decay and the expansion. Tarquin had chosen his staff well and trusted in their ability to get things done. The trouble was, they were so competent they left him with nothing to do aside from rubber-stamping approvals.

Left him alone with his thoughts.

He rubbed his eyes. Tried to focus. The data was important. But the data hadn't changed.

"My liege?" Helms said.

"Yes?"

"Ex. Sharp won't sit quietly in a cage and wait for rescue," she said. "If someone's got her, she'll let us know soon enough."

THIRTY-TWO

Naira

error

Naira couldn't be certain how long she'd been trapped in the golden haze of repair. Time lost meaning as the software tore down walls and let every aspect of herself pour out and be reforged.

It wasn't the frothing miasma of when she'd first been cracked. This was a stitching together of the disparate parts of herself, the pitfalls of her memories transforming into doors opened off a long hall of being that she could traverse at any time.

Awake in the simulation, Naira clung to that scarred vision of herself, though it was getting slippery, a memory threatening to twist away on the gale force of the repair.

New doors opened in her mind. Glimpses of different futures unfolded before her, smudgy and indistinct. Difficult to grasp even when they were being forced upon her.

And they were being forced. Directed. Jonsun, guiding the course of what she saw. Pushing her down the path he wanted followed, trying to convince her that the future he believed in was the one that would come to pass.

Because through every single gold-suffused door, Tarquin had become a monster.

It began in the powercore building, always. Naira approached that core. Stared into it with naked defiance tangled with loathing that she thought might be directed at herself. Tarquin—ragged, distraught, possessed with a fervency that nearly overwhelmed the golden haze—ordered the printing of the settlers. Of their friends. Naira did not stop him.

They emerged within cubicles on a ship she didn't recognize but, in the twisted landscape of dreams, knew belonged to Mercator. They were not released from those cubicles. *Canus* overwhelmed their pathways, drew silver fault lines across their skin, burst free, and dripped with glossy blackness.

When they were so far gone that their very bodies were failing, he dissolved them all and began again.

She recoiled from that vision. Rejected it. But the software kept forcing her back, on an endless loop, as if Jonsun was pressing her face to a viewing glass and wouldn't let her go. Those were not the actions of the man she knew. It wasn't possible.

But she'd made excuses for the corruption lurking in Fletch.

Accepted Acaelus's cruelty as necessary.

Missed the fanatical glint in Jonsun's eyes.

And, for all Jonsun's manipulations, the vision had the same ring of truth about it that the scarred apparition of herself in the powercore had.

The powercore. Naira couldn't love the man who would do such a thing, but the vision she'd seen in the powercore, that broken-down woman in a crown of scars, had been gazing upon Tarquin with such adoration that Naira could feel the warmth of it still. An echo to the love she felt in the present.

No future was set in stone. Jonsun's whispers wound through her, telling her that Tarquin would always be a monster. That the only way to fight against that inevitability was to serve Jonsun. To stop Tarquin before he broke and went too far.

Naira didn't believe in predetermination or fate. She'd stepped off the paths set for her life far too many times to entertain such thoughts.

What she saw in Tarquin's horrible future was true, and she didn't need Jonsun's persuasion to convince her. But what she'd seen in that powercore had been true, too.

There was a future wherein Naira still loved Tarquin. Wherein she reached back into the hollow shell of herself and cried out to save him.

She couldn't love the monster.

And so there was another way. Another path forward that Jonsun either hadn't seen or hadn't wanted her to see.

Naira envisioned scars crowning her head in broken constellations. Even as that vision of herself began to weather and erode beneath the endless storm of Jonsun's burgeoning future. As hours and days and she didn't know how long slipped through her fingers, Naira held on.

And slowly, inexorably, she began to break.

When she woke in flesh once more, she found her head unadorned. Jonsun's shining face hovered above her, kind. Looking at him just then, she couldn't recall why she'd ever reviled him. So what if he'd tried to turn the *Cavendish*'s guns against humanity? He'd only been protecting the rest. Holding the line against a terrible future he alone could see. Until now.

A familiar shape had been scarred onto the side of his neck. The Conservators' symbol, a *C* with a blade plunging through the letter. Scars. Naira blinked.

A crown of scars appeared across the backs of her eyelids like too-bright flashes of light every time she closed her eyes.

"Well?" Jonsun asked, though it was clear in the curl of his smile that he already knew her answer. His eyes, a soft brown, gleamed with the golden light that had suffused the branching paths of her mind.

"I can't love the man he becomes," Naira said, and her voice was small, and the words were true.

"Do you want to stop him?" Jonsun asked.

"Yes."

Jonsun handed her the handle of a knife, tipping his head to indicate his scar and what he wanted her to do. "Then welcome back to the Conservators, Nai. We've missed you."

THIRTY-THREE

Tarquin

Seventh Cradle | The Present

Weeks passed with no word of Naira or who had taken her. Jessel's spies returned reports that the *Cavendish* had gone quiet, on lockdown, but that could hardly be taken as proof of anything. Alvero's techs came up empty. Comms were still a disaster, the universe's brief burst having settled somewhat but not completely. They were already seeing shorter days, dimmer nights.

They'd made good progress, despite the phantom of loss haunting both Tarquin and Dr. Sharp. He'd turned off the AI of the cargo ship in orbit, adjusted the climate, infected it with *canus*, and found the relkatite on that ship was 30 percent converted to amarthite. Already he'd identified possible deposits of relkatite on the planet, and they were preparing to mine them to convert them to amarthite, too.

There was still a hole in the roof of the powercore housing. Tarquin found he didn't care.

He ate in the community center, as he did every night when he ate at all, out of a fear of being alone in domestic moments. The atmosphere was subdued, no more wild stories from the Merc-Sec table.

Occasionally one of the settlers would cast him a lingering glance, or bow a touch lower than usual and look up at him as if to say—there were more things in the worlds worthy of his love than Naira Sharp. He disagreed, but he recognized the kindness in the intent, and appreciated it for that. The simple presence of other people soothed him. He wasn't alone.

He was merely missing the other half of himself.

Marko brought him a plate and too much beer. Tarquin took a bite and told Marko it was delicious, even though nothing had taste to him, lately. He smiled until his cheeks hurt. Marko looked satisfied enough with that and left him to eat in peace.

Delorne came pinballing through the front door, stomping her feet half-heartedly to get the mud off. She spotted him, and he raised a hand in greeting as she scurried her way over and plunked down across the table from him.

"My liege," she said, panting. She ran everywhere that was worth going. "I've made progress modifying the q-field detector to measure the inflaton field instead. Look at this."

She filled the table with a collection of holos from her arm. The readings Delorne had taken with her new device certainly appeared to pick up something in the range they expected.

"This is promising, Doctor," he said. "But hardly worth running out of the lab in the middle of the night."

"Oh, I was also hungry." Her bouncing gaze flicked over Tarquin's shoulder, to where Diaz was standing guard, and Tarquin suppressed a sigh. It was sweet that those two were getting along. Under normal circumstances he would have been delighted for them. As things stood, every time he saw them share a look, all he felt was bitter jealousy of their happiness. He didn't want them to realize that.

"Grab a plate, Doctor."

She clapped and said something Tarquin missed as his HUD flooded with red. He jerked his head back, and noticed Ward and Helms do likewise at the table across the room. Tarquin blinked, not understanding what he was seeing.

The *Cavendish* had closed the passage between it and the *Sigillaria* and was spooling its engines. Tarquin stared, heart slowing and speeding in erratic bursts.

Naira's command keys had unlocked the *Cavendish*'s autonomy.

The fork clattered from his hand and he scrambled off the bench. Ward and the exemplars abandoned their food and swarmed him, closing a tight cordon as he stormed out into the night. A light rain was falling, and it stung his eyes as he lifted his head, desperate to see that ship, but the night and distance hid it from view.

Jessel called him, emergency line. He answered while he ran down the road toward the security suite.

"Jonsun's closed the fucking doors," Jessel snarled. "We think he's spooling engines, but he won't answer our hails."

"He has. He is," Tarquin said. "Lock down and prepare for evasion, but do *not* fire on that ship, am I clear?"

"Understood," they said.

Alvero ran down the road from the opposite direction, a gaggle of Merc-Sec behind him as he skidded to turn and join Tarquin's entourage.

"Report," Tarquin ordered.

"Unclear," Alvero said briskly. "They've powered the warpcore for jump, but we think they're holding the power there, prepping to dump it into their weapons."

The group piled into a conference room in the security suite. Holos bloomed all around him as people went to work.

"Status of the settlement shields?" Tarquin asked.

"Online," Ward said. "I'm diverting all available power to the shields to bolster them."

"Good." Tarquin tossed the call with Jessel to a projector on the side of the table. "Jessel, we think they're getting ready to dump power to weapons. Mind your shields."

"On it." They muted themself as they started barking orders across the *Sigillaria*'s command deck.

"Do we have comms?" he asked.

"Not yet, my liege," Alvero said. "They're blocking all incoming traffic, but our techs are tunneling."

Tarquin put through the order for everyone to take shelter. The steady drone of sirens outside was muted by the thick walls of the security suite. He told no one, but he pinged Naira. Still offline. He couldn't know what that meant, and he locked down everything he was feeling, clinging to the Mercator mask like a life raft.

"My liege, we have visual." Alvero pushed through a video feed to the center of the table.

Cameras from the *Sigillaria* displayed the battered hull of the *Cavendish* in remarkable detail against the endless black of space. The ship's lights flickered, then the whole thing canted to the side, angling away from the *Sigillaria*. The tunnel between the two ships snapped, raining debris destined to burn up in atmosphere.

"Where's it going?" he demanded.

"Oh! I've got that, my liege." Delorne, who he hadn't noticed had followed them in, tossed her own holo into the mix. The ship wasn't going far. All estimates kept it within range of the settlement.

"Ease shielding over the fields and increase it over the populated areas. Focus on the powercore housing," Tarquin said. They'd suffer if they lost some of the crops, but they'd be atoms if the powercore went.

"Done," Ward said.

"They're powering the forward rail gun," Alvero said. "Aiming angles indicate a strike on or near the northeast edge of the settlement."

"I've got the shields ready." Ward didn't sound as confident as he'd like.

"We could arrange a firing solution on the weapon," Alvero said.

"No. We shield until we can't anymore, and will somebody *please* get me a line onto that ship."

"They're firing." Ward pushed the shield integrity display into the center of the table. A dome of green covered the settlement. Tarquin held his breath.

The ground shook, the building rattled, but the dome didn't change color. No damage.

"What did they hit?" he asked.

"I don't know." Ward shifted through a wide array of camera angles. "Here. Maybe they missed?"

She tossed a visual to the table. The blood drained from his face. The rail gun had torn a fresh valley in the field by the bend in the river. The very place he'd promised to build a home to share with Naira. It was outside the settlement limits, a promise for when things were stable. He bowed his head, unable to look any of them in the eye.

"They didn't miss. There's nothing there of value except a promise I made."

Uneasy glances and throat-clearing all around.

"They don't appear to be powering up the weapon again, my liege," Alvero said.

Tarquin made himself look up. "Don't get complacent with those shields."

"I won't," Ward said. "I can add some reinforcement over your suite, if you think it's necessary."

Naira's print was still in stasis there. "Yes, thank you. But the power-core remains our priority."

"Understood, my liege," she said.

A call alert flashed in the corner of Tarquin's HUD. Jonsun. He kept his hands down flat on the table and steeled himself, knowing he was unlikely to like what he was about to see.

"Jonsun calling," he said.

Everyone switched their holos to privacy filters as Tarquin transferred the call to the center of the table. His breath froze in his lungs. Jonsun was there, on the command deck of the *Cavendish*, but Tarquin's gaze was drawn to the console podium behind Jonsun, to his right.

Naira stood behind it. Or her print did, he couldn't be sure she was in there. Her gaze was focused; the Mercator-green holos spread out around her indicated she'd been operating the weapons and was now rebalancing the power in the ship. Grease smudged a bare forehead. No suppression crown. No scars. There was a gleam in her golden eyes he'd never seen before. The Conservators' symbol, a capital *C* with a blade through it from top to bottom, had been carved into the side of her neck long enough ago that it'd scarred.

Naira looked up. Their eyes met. Her stare was glacial.

"Mercator," Jonsun said with his usual faux-friendly drawl. "Sorry about the land, but we needed to get your full attention. You see, we're real tired of being trapped up here in this tin can. We're going to land in a nice little spot I've picked out, and you and I, we're going to talk terms, because it's time Seventh Cradle is a two-settlement planet. You've been keeping her all to yourself, and that's not very neighborly."

Jonsun's tone dripped derision, and Tarquin caught the double meaning. It was all he could do to keep his voice level. "Naira, are you safe?"

She blinked, as if she were unused to hearing her name attached to a question. "Clearly. Unless you plan on firing on this ship, my liege."

His stomach sank. Naira didn't call him that unless she was flirting, or furious. Which, in retrospect, was often confusing, but either way she never said it with such a flat tone. She went back to work on the console, dismissing him.

"Sweet of you to ask," Jonsun said with a folksy chuckle that made Tarquin want to snap his neck, "but Nai's just fine. Better than ever, in fact."

"What did you do to my wife?" he snarled.

"Wasn't your wife yet, was she?" He shook his head. "Wasn't ever going to be, in fact. She turned you down, Mercator, but you wouldn't remember that, would you? I couldn't have it. Needed her to get family keys to free us, so I had to step in. You understand."

"You expect me to believe that?"

"I don't really care what you believe. As for what I did for her, well, it's simple. I broke her. Seemed the friendly thing to do to fix her up again."

"She would never agree to that."

"You're right." Jonsun gave him a slow smile. "She didn't. Funny thing, the software didn't give a shit that she hadn't agreed. She's fine with it now though, aren't you, Nai?" he called over his shoulder.

"Stop fucking around, Jo," she shot back, but not with any venom. It was the same friendly tone she used when she was telling Kav to fuck off. He couldn't see either Kav or Kuma anywhere on that bridge.

Tarquin squeezed his eyes shut and looked away.

"You see what's at stake, don't you?" There was an edge to Jonsun's tone that rallied Tarquin. Forced him to look back. "I see you do. We're landing. We're chatting. And then I think we're all going to get along, aren't we?"

"Land your ship," Tarquin ground out.

Jonsun's smile flattened and he leaned closer, all the easy drawl gone from his voice. "Don't fuck me around, Mercator. You won't like the consequences."

Jonsun ended the call.

The stares of his team were like the glare of the sun. He knew what they were waiting for, breaths held. Knew they were waiting for him to start sobbing, or screaming, or otherwise fall apart. But it wasn't the pain that kept him from speaking, it was the rage. A bone-searing flash of desire to order the *Sigillaria* to reduce Jonsun and that parody of his Naira to ash.

But if her map had been repaired, he didn't know what that meant for her. For her backups. He had to find out.

Tarquin cracked his jaw.

"Captain Ward," he said. "How many guns does this settlement currently have?"

"I can't say exactly, my liege. Thousands."

"Fetch all of them, please."

"All of them, my liege?"

"Every last fucking one."

THIRTY-FOUR

Naira

Seventh Cradle | The Present

Naira focused on rebalancing the *Cavendish*'s weakened power stores, because to pause for even a second, to think on what she'd done, or the raw fury and hurt on Tarquin's face, would break her. She could not break. Her thoughts were wrapped in golden fleece, a cozy warmth that suffused her always since the repair. It brought a rosiness to her cheeks that she knew, now, was the source of Jonsun's intense edge, the manic danger in his eyes. She could summon it to her own face, and she did so often, to reassure her old friend.

Because he didn't yet realize the "repair" of her map hadn't worked as he'd intended.

Luckily, the *Cavendish*'s warpcore required her full attention. There was a drain somewhere in the core, making routing tricky. Naira finished balancing the power so that the engines could handle the descent to the planet and stepped away from the podium, making for the door.

"Where do you think you're going?" Jonsun called out.

"Bathroom, jackass," she called back, jeering, but friendly. Like they used to be. Picking up that old camaraderie made her mouth taste like ashes. "Want to join me?"

"Ugh. Hurry up, we'll need you to land this thing. The variants are all over the place."

Naira let herself out of the command deck, not really seeing the turns in the halls, seeing only the shock on Tarquin's face when Jonsun had claimed she'd turned down his proposal. The thought of Jonsun spying on that moment—using it against them—made her stomach lurch.

The bathroom door locked behind her and she planted a fist against the wall and bent over the toilet to heave up nothing but bile and thin water, shaking with the tremble she'd barely controlled while on deck.

She'd thought she could do this. Had told herself that the hurt was temporary, that she'd manage. She always managed. Always pushed through.

Now, she wasn't so sure.

When she had nothing left to heave and her breathing had slowed, she flushed away the evidence of her anguish. Sweat plastered her hair to her forehead. She splashed cold water on her face and grabbed drying papers to scrub her skin, checking herself in the mirror for evidence of distress. She looked rough, but then, she always looked rough, lately.

Because she saw the future that Jonsun threatened would come to pass, sometimes. Saw Tarquin clinging to his power, a tyrant surpassing the shadow of his father, holding what was left of humanity together by fragile threads of control as the universe spun apart at the seams.

And she saw the other possibility, when her mind frothed just right. The future Jonsun wanted, of humanity sheltered from the storm of the universe ending. Led by Jonsun into what he claimed would be safety. A complete reset, a do-over without MERIT, without the HC. They'd start again, and fix the expansion, and he refused to reveal how.

Two paths down a shadowed road, and Naira rejected them both. Because sometimes, so very rarely, she caught a sliver of something else. Of her own face webbed with scars. And that she hoarded in her heart and spoke of to no one.

She left the bathroom and found Kav leaning against the wall by the door, a glass of water in his hand. Her joy at seeing him again in those first fraught moments after waking was tempered by the violation of her mind. Kav hadn't been able to stop Jonsun. She knew why, now. Knew the threat that dangled over all on board the *Cavendish*.

Misbehave, and Jonsun cracked you.

She took the glass without comment and swished water through her teeth before turning to spit out the rest. They couldn't talk, not really. Jonsun was always watching and listening. But sometimes they shared a look. Sometimes Kav risked sending her choppy messages, and she knew. He wanted to stop Jonsun, too.

"Better?" Kav asked.

"Yeah," she said, and then, in case Jonsun listened to this later, "I haven't been on a maneuvering ship in a year. Thought I'd puke on the console."

"These amarthite prints don't suppress as well as relk did."

"Still wouldn't switch back, though."

"Hell no." He gave her a slow look. "Ready for this?"

Naira ran her tongue over her teeth to make it look like she was considering the state of her stomach. In a few hours, they'd land the ship. In a few hours, Jonsun would meet with Tarquin. He planned on taking Naira with him.

It was going to be a loyalty test, because even though she'd carved his symbol into her neck, even though she'd given him the plot of land to strike and told him why, he didn't quite trust her. He couldn't. Though she said all the right things, she still saw him wonder, sometimes, when he looked at her. In his position, she wouldn't trust herself, either.

"I'll hold," she said.

Kav nodded, understanding everything that meant, and they bumped shoulders. "Be careful down there, yeah?"

"I'm not good at caution." She winked at his annoyed scowl. "Explosives are more my specialty."

"Those are *my* specialty," Kav shot back. A knot eased in her chest.

"Nai," Jonsun said over ship-wide comms, "wash your ass. We need you on deck."

Naira blew out a slow breath. "Into the fire," she said, and pushed off the wall.

It took four grueling hours to get the *Cavendish* landed in the field Jonsun had selected. They couldn't rely on the UFP, and flying that large of a ship on visual alone left Naira slick with sweat, her breath short in her chest. When they finally got her down, a spontaneous cheer broke out on the deck. Naira slumped against the console podium, not caring, this time, that anyone saw her shaken.

"Well done, team!" Jonsun made a sweep of the command deck to thump backs and clasp hands with his crew.

Naira pulled her hair into a high ponytail to keep it from sticking uncomfortably to her face. The crew was giddy with their success, and though Naira was pleased they'd managed to get the ship down safely, she couldn't shake the dread simmering in her veins.

Jonsun held the threat of cracking over them all, but she'd found that most of the unionists—who all called themselves Conservators, now, and wore the brand on their necks—truly believed in him. It was easy to see why. His smile was bright and freely given. He poured out compliments for work well done and promised a future of safe living on Seventh Cradle, free of MERIT tyranny. Free of Mercator. It was no different than the very talking points they used to spout, but the tenor had changed.

Naira didn't blame them for their belief in Jonsun. She'd once been his number-one gun, after all.

"And Nai," Jonsun said, making the loop to her at last. He gave her that warm smile and hauled her close to plant a friendly kiss on her forehead. "Our shining star, eh?" The crew rumbled approval.

"Don't get too cocky," she said. "Mercator is heavily entrenched, and they're not going to like us taking a choice piece of farmland for ourselves."

"They'll deal," Jonsun said with ironclad confidence. He gave her a thump on the arm. "Prepare for disembarkation. We're going to go have a friendly talk with the would-be king."

The crew let loose with playful boos and jeers, as they did at every mention of Tarquin. Naira lowered her voice. "Full kit? You understand what we're walking into, here?"

Jonsun nodded seriously and matched her tone. "I know, Nai. He's going to be pissed off and heavily armed. But I've got you. I'm counting on that, understand?"

"He's got four exemplars and a battalion of highly trained Merc-Sec. I'm good, but I'm not that good."

He leaned closer to whisper. "It's not a numbers game when we've got leverage. Remember what you always said, when it was Acaelus? We gotta hit him where it hurts."

"I'll play that game."

"Good woman. Suit up. I want our boots on the ground in twenty."

She gave him a mocking salute, and he rolled his eyes. A genuine smile tugged at her lips that speared the ache in her chest deeper. It was too easy to feel like they were actually still working together. Naira retreated to the armory to prepare herself and found Kuma already there, strapping armor on.

"Nai!" Kuma beamed up at her as she laced her boots tight. "Ready to knock some MERIT heads?"

"We're not knocking heads today if we can help it. We're not positioned for a real fight."

Naira made a beeline for the equipment so that Kuma wouldn't get a chance to read her face. Ever since she'd woken up, she'd been trying to make sense of where Kuma's loyalties really rested and hadn't figured it out yet.

Kav seemed to think Kuma was Jonsun's left hand, devoted to the cause of tearing down Mercator and all of MERIT. That fit with the woman Naira used to know, but it didn't fit with what Kuma knew to be true about Tarquin. Kuma had a phobia of cracking. Jonsun's implicit threat might push her to perform loyalty more strongly than anyone else. But she performed it really, *really* well.

"Spoilsport," Kuma grumbled.

Naira gave her the finger, and Kuma chucked a rolled-up thermal at her head. She snatched the shirt out of the air and tugged it on, checking to make sure all her base layers were thermal before she started buckling on armor.

The planet had gotten colder. Lush summer rains had transformed into bursts of hail. Jonsun kept promising those warm rains would come again, once this was all done, but he always failed to elaborate on exactly *how* he was going to stop the expansion.

Every time Naira pressed him for an answer, his tone shifted to one of subtle threat and he found some way to fold Kav or Kuma into the conversation. Naira didn't need it spelled out for her—if she pushed too hard, her friends would suffer the consequences of her misbehavior.

A storage bay door had been left open. She craned her neck, peeking within. Floor-to-ceiling stacks of crates loaded with armor and weapons filled the room. They had double the equipment that the crew of the *Cavendish* could ever hope to use in that room alone.

"What's with the excess?" Naira asked.

Kuma's head jerked up, her smile falling. "That's not supposed to be open."

"Okay..." Naira frowned as Kuma hurried over and shut the door. "Why so much, though?"

"No idea." Kuma shrugged. "Jonsun doesn't want anyone in there."

Naira bit the inside of her cheek and decided to drop it as Kuma tried to recover her earlier smile, but couldn't quite make it sparkle like she usually did.

All their weapons were striped in Rochard black. They were the weapons Jessel warned her that Rochard had smuggled to the *Cavendish* back when the situation had been fresh. Naira brushed a finger over the black stripe on her rifle. If her mother had never died, maybe she would have worn black cuffs and carried this rifle for Rochard.

As it was, her cuffs were gone. Jonsun had ordered everyone on the ship to cut them out, leaving a thick band of scar tissue in their place. It tugged, sometimes.

"Ready, slowpoke?" Naira asked.

"Yeah, yeah." Kuma gave her weapons a quick check and shot Naira a grin. "Guess I get to be an exemplar today, too, huh?"

"Don't you Station-Sec types think we E-Xs are all full of ourselves?"

"Oh, you are full of yourselves." Kuma winked and clapped her on the shoulder. "I'm going to show you how it's really done."

Naira groaned. "Please don't. I'd like for us to come back with our skin intact. We're just posturing. You know what the real leverage is."

Kuma squeezed Naira's arm. "You okay?"

"No. But I can't support what he becomes." In her vision, she had been in the powercore building with Tarquin when that choice had been made. Had been there and, for some reason she couldn't yet see, hadn't stopped him. Until she could unravel Jonsun's plans and what, exactly, her motives in that moment had been, she had to stay away from him.

"Yeah, but...It's fresh. It's gotta sting. Want me to kick him in the crotch while we're down there?"

"No crotch-kicking." Naira mustered up a smile for Kuma.

"There they are," Jonsun called out when Naira and Kuma entered the cargo hold. "Can you believe it, friends?" he said to the assembled. "I'll have two exemplars of my own today."

They snickered at him and gave him a hard time about getting a big head. Naira scanned their ranks, counting, assessing. Three dozen scraggly unionists—*Conservators*, she had to stop thinking of them as unionists—had rummaged up a mismatch of light armor and weapons she wasn't convinced they knew how to effectively use. They were untested in battle. If a fight broke out, Merc-Sec would chew them up in seconds.

"There will be no fighting today," Naira said firmly. "If any one of you squeezes a trigger without my express order to do so, I will take it personally. You will not enjoy that experience."

That cowed them. Muttered agreements issued from the group.

"Good," Naira said. "Let's get this dance over with."

They parted for her as she approached Jonsun. He'd worn light body armor, but carried no weapons, and had dressed much the same as the rest of his ragtag soldiers.

"Do you have to be such a hard-ass?" he asked.

She leaned down to whisper. "Watch yourself. You're going to get these people killed if you're not careful."

He gave her a solemn nod. "I'm aware. I'll keep them safe."

Naira wasn't convinced he could if things got out of hand, but she nodded anyway. The airlock hissed open and the gangway rolled out. The beauty of Seventh Cradle still made her breath catch in her chest. They'd put the ship down outside the settlement's area of control, a good two miles' walk from the border. A steady, icy rain was falling, slivers of hail pinging off the ship in gentle song. It occurred to her that many of the Conservators had never seen rain before.

"Heads up, straight lines," Naira ordered over the susurration. "We don't think Mercator will attack, but we need to be ready if they do. Drink more water than you think you need. Walking in the mud will tire you out faster than you're used to. Let's move, people."

She held up a fist and gestured forward. The unit moved as one, trained by Kuma, Jonsun, and so Naira had been told, sometimes Kav. She'd yet to see him actually enter the practice facility. He mostly kept himself locked away in his room, working on technological research that was, supposedly, at Jonsun's behest.

Naira glanced back and saw Kav leaning in the airlock, arms crossed, watching her go. He tapped the side of his fist against his shoulder. Sending her strength. A lump formed in her throat. She swallowed it down and focused on putting one foot in front of the other. On doing her job.

Jonsun had insisted that he walk out in front with Kuma and Naira flanking him, and while he claimed it was a show of good faith, Naira knew precisely what it really was. Jonsun wanted Naira, heavily armed at Jonsun's side, to be the first thing Tarquin would see.

THIRTY-FIVE

Naira

Seventh Cradle | The Present

The walk was both too long and over in an instant. They approached the settlement near the landing strip and found a line of Merc-Sec waiting for them behind a sandbagged chain-link fence. A glance to the side told her it must wrap the entire settlement. She had no doubt it carried higher-tech defensive mechanisms than the froth of razor wire on top.

The line of Conservators started to buckle at the sight of so many heavily armed Merc-Sec. Naira couldn't count them all, but she spotted Ward on the far edge, arms crossed, openly furious.

"Steady," Naira ordered, and wasn't sure if she was talking to the Conservators or herself.

Tarquin was framed in the open gate. His stare settled on her, and after a brief sweep to assure himself she was unharmed, he met her gaze and wouldn't let it go. The Mercator mask was fixed in place, his expression locked down with haughty contempt, but she saw the desperation in him. The pain and the hope tangled together.

His chin was lifted, shoulders back, and the gleam of her golden ring shone on his finger. A sliver of red peeking from beneath his sleeve hinted at the bracelet he'd given her.

Her heart lodged in her throat, knowing why he'd worn those items. They were a signal, a flag raised without words—*I love you. Let me help you. Come home.*

She looked away and assessed the security. That was her job. That was her sole function.

The exemplars cordoned Tarquin in a box formation, Caldweller and Helms the forward points, Diaz and Cass taking up the rear. Helms and Diaz reached for weapons. Naira gave a slight shake of her head. Their jaws tensed with frustration, but they aborted the motion.

Jonsun leaned close to whisper, "We'll get through this. I know it hurts."

Then they were close enough to speak, and it was all Naira could do to keep from rushing to Tarquin. But she couldn't. She had to hold. To make this look believable, or Jonsun would crack Kav and Kuma in retaliation.

"Mercator." Jonsun was all smiles as he extended his hand. Tarquin glanced at the hand but didn't take it. Jonsun shrugged. "Nice of you to roll out the welcome wagon for us." Jonsun looked pointedly at the Merc-Sec filling the landing strip. "But it's a pity you won't bring us in to see that cute village I've heard so much about."

"Naira." Tarquin's voice was a ragged, constricted thing. "Let me bring you home."

She could see it. In a breathtaking flash, she saw how it would go— Merc-Sec would destroy Jonsun and his entourage. She'd come home. Be safe.

The Conservators would reprint Jonsun, and then Tarquin would go to war, and this, *this* moment, was one of many possible paths down which that blood-soaked future Jonsun warned of could begin. With Tarquin killing to keep his heart safe.

Jonsun's stare was a pressure against the side of her face. Waiting, curious. He must have seen the moment, too, as that strange golden light haloed his eyes.

"No, my liege," she said. "I'm precisely where I want to be."

"I don't believe you." He sounded like he couldn't get a full breath. Caldweller tensed, reacting to something in the E-X channel. Preparing to fight. She had to stop this.

"Are you going to use your strength to force me back to your side, my liege?"

He sucked in a breath and drew back, the echo of her previous remonstration—that he'd been using his position to control her life—landing true. Caldweller eased back into his usual ready stance.

"Very well. I will respect your wishes, Exemplar." He wanted to say more. She could see it churning within him. But thousands were watching. He turned back to Jonsun. "I'll hear what you have to say. A conference room has been prepared. I assume you're amenable?"

"Sounds cozy." Jonsun rubbed his hands together. "I'm freezing my hair off out here."

"Planets have teeth." Tarquin turned, striding off without another word toward a shuttle that waited to the side of the landing strip.

His exemplars folded around him in such fluid formation that it made Naira briefly proud—she'd trained Helms and Diaz to move like that.

Kuma, however, had no E-X training. The best Naira could manage with her was a two-point cover, and it galled her to be unable to do her job well. Which was ridiculous. If a fight broke out, they were all dead. They didn't have the numbers to hold against the show of force Tarquin had fielded, and that force made damn sure she knew it. Merc-Sec parted for Tarquin to pass, but the passage was so narrow she could feel the heat of them against her skin as she walked by. It was like having a knife to her throat.

Tarquin's meeting room was a prearranged cargo hold in a shuttle. It wasn't until they'd settled that Naira realized Caldweller had shifted position at the last second to stand directly across from her.

His gaze drilled into her, and she met his heavy stare with as much impassivity as she could muster. This was going to be rough. Already her HUD's blocked ID folder was filling up, every last one of them hammering her with chat requests. She didn't dare answer, not even to tell them to knock it off. Her HUD routed through the *Cavendish*. Jonsun saw everything.

"What do you want, Mr. Hesson?" Tarquin folded his hands together on the tabletop, and didn't look at her.

"What any human soul desires, Mercator." Jonsun leaned back in his chair, lacing his fingers behind his head. "Open air. Clean water. Good food. Place to raise a family. You've got a lot of space down here. We only want a small piece of it."

"There was a schedule in place for opening up the planet to settlement," Tarquin said. "That schedule exists for a reason. For safety."

"You mean so that you can control how it goes. Bring your buddies down, set up a little fiefdom just like daddy used to make." He kept up the drawl, but his voice had deepened. "We're not that naive, Mercator, and we won't be bound to MERIT all over again. We want our land. We want our freedom. And we're not going to sit around with our thumbs up our asses and wait for you to so generously dole it out to us. Not when you can't even keep an ansible network online. We know what's happening out there. We felt safer in a big ol' planet's gravity well."

"What, precisely, do you know about it?"

"That the UFPs are messed up enough to make landing our ship a giant pain in the ass. I'm guessing you Mercators went and broke something, eh?"

"As you have pointed out," Tarquin said, "the situation is currently unstable. I do not have time to handhold you on this planet while working to restore our ansible network and slow the cause of that loss."

Naira flicked her gaze down to Jonsun at that and was certain Caldweller had noticed, though he didn't react.

"It's your lucky day then, Mercator," Jonsun said. "Because we don't want your hand to hold. We'll do fine on our own. All you have to do is leave us be."

"I cannot do that. I know your numbers. I know your food stock. You don't have the rations to keep those people fed for long, and you lack the ability to farm. I won't have hundreds of people starving to death on my doorstep. I'm willing to trade you seed stock and expertise for your weapons."

Jonsun's smile was slow and sly. "What do you want weapons for? Your tableau outside demonstrated you've got plenty of guns."

"You survive on my goodwill. Everyone in this room is aware that I could crush you in a moment. My continued goodwill requires you to relinquish your weapons."

Jonsun sighed and shook his head. "That's not very neighborly of you."

Tarquin slammed a hand on the table hard enough to make Jonsun flinch. His voice was gravel. "You kidnapped my wife and violated her map, Mr. Hesson. The only reason you aren't atoms is because I'm reasonably certain you've got some sort of hold over the innocent souls on that ship, and Naira wouldn't—" He grimaced and looked away. "She wouldn't want me to lash out. Not like that."

"Nai's right here." Jonsun shrugged and gestured to her. "Ask her yourself."

Naira's palms sweat as Tarquin turned to her, and she felt Jonsun's regard upon her, heavy and probing, searching for any cracks in her loyalties. This was it, then. Jonsun's test. She recalled Kav's signal to her as she walked away, and dug deep for strength.

"Naira," Tarquin said softly. "I don't know what that repair did to you, but I love you. I will always love you. And I'm so, so sorry."

She closed her eyes, swallowing down tears, and realized too late that Tarquin had known precisely what she'd do—and he'd arranged those words as a signal. The lights blacked out. The exemplars moved as one, training their weapons on Jonsun and Kuma. When the lights flicked back on, Jonsun raised his hands, a bemused smile on his face, while Kuma lifted hers with a scowl.

"You played me," she said to Tarquin, and laughed gruffly.

"I did say I was sorry," he said. "I don't know what he's done to you, but we'll fix it. We will."

"Go on, Nai," Jonsun said. "Tell him what I've done."

"Naira?" Fear crawled across Tarquin's face and he reached for her over the table. She took a smooth step back and in the same motion drew one of her knives. Cass shifted their pistol to aim at her chest, but they hadn't taken their trigger finger off the guard. They'd hesitate. Tarquin leaned back into his seat, putting distance between them.

"The repair process bonds all potential states of a map," she said. "I see more glimpses of the future, now, and what I've seen... Tarquin, I love you. I do. But I can't love the man you become. You make Acaelus look sweet in comparison."

"What?" His hands shook, and he pressed them flat to the tabletop to cover it. "I'm not—I would *never* be worse than my father."

"I've seen it," she said, "and me being with you, it makes it so much worse."

His jaw cracked. "I don't believe you. Jonsun's poisoned you, you're not yourself. We'll get you help and then we'll stop whatever this is, together."

"Nai," Jonsun said. "Cut the shit."

Naira lifted the knife to her throat. Tarquin stiffened.

"You kill them," Naira said, "I'll drop myself. You won't be taking me out of this room."

"I have your backups." He was a hair away from panic, clinging to his training by his fingernails. "Go ahead. We'll wipe out his entire entourage and print you again before the *Cavendish* knows what happened."

"You're not a very good listener, are you, Mercator? She's been repaired. All instances of herself bonded to all others. You print her backup, you'll get her exactly as she is right now. Maybe I'll even double-print her back at the *Cavendish*. I'm curious to see what it does to one of the repaired. Haven't tried that yet."

"I'll blow your ship to shreds before you start that print," Tarquin snapped.

"Tarquin," Naira said. He looked at her with effort. "Enough. The *Cavendish* has a warpcore. It's powering. Look at the blast radius. It won't just be the people on the *Cavendish* you take down."

He paused, no doubt checking the maps, the blast estimates, and a shadow passed behind his eyes before he held out a hand, signaling for the exemplars to lower their weapons.

"Why are you doing this?" he asked.

"I'm not going to let another man I love become a monster."

"I won't. Naira, you know me. I'm not that man."

"Prove it," she said, and glanced pointedly at the weapons still drawn.

"Put those away," he ordered.

The exemplars reluctantly holstered their weapons. Naira sheathed her own blade and went back to clutching the rifle for dear life.

"There now." Jonsun lowered his hands. "We can all get along, can't we? Truth be told, Mercator, I'm hoping what Nai and I see is wrong because, whew, are you a nasty tyrant. But we're willing to keep a truce with you, for now. If you strike, we'll blow the warpcore, so keep that in mind."

"I still want your weapons in exchange for seed stock," Tarquin said.

"Ah, no. You see, when Rochard was feeling friendly, they sent us more than guns. We've got plenty. This isn't a negotiation. We don't need anything from you." He glanced sideways at Naira. "We just wanted you to know where you stand."

"This isn't over," Tarquin said with such hatred it shook her. Made her believe that he was capable of that horrible future, after all.

Jonsun only chuckled and shook his head, chair scraping against the floor as he pushed it back to stand. To leave. Naira's stomach knotted. Her blood pounded in her ears. She wanted nothing more than to stay, but—she turned for the exit.

"Naira, wait—" Tarquin said, but she was already in step with Jonsun, walking out the airlock and back to the anxiously waiting Conservators.

Tarquin's steps slowed behind them. He'd reached the airlock and had enough control that he wouldn't let his people see him chasing after her. She wanted to look back. To see him one more time, but she wasn't sure she could survive that look.

"Hey, Sharp!" a gruff voice called out.

Heavy rain pelted down, blurring the faces in the crowd. Merc-Sec parted to let the speaker through. Captain Ward. Her eyes were bloodshot, her broad, square hands curled into fists. Merc-Sec pulled away from her instinctively. Naira stood her ground.

"Captain," she said.

"You traitorous piece of shit," Ward snarled. "After everything he did for you." She thrust a finger at Tarquin. "After everything you did for *us*, you're just going to walk away? Turn your coat and stroll off with that prick?"

"I've always been a Conservator."

"Bullshit." She laughed out the word, and Naira got the sense that Ward was on her way to being drunk, if not there already. "Bull-fucking-shit."

"That's enough, Captain," Tarquin said.

Ward scoffed. "I'm just getting started."

"Control your people, Mercator," Jonsun said.

Naira held out a forestalling hand. "I'll hear what the captain has to say."

"Oh, you'll *hear* me," Ward said, and laughed. "The traitor will *hear* me. I wonder how well you'll hear with my boot up your ass."

"Captain," Tarquin said, "shut your mouth and return to your post."

Naira spread her arm in invitation. "Take a shot at me, Ward, if it makes you feel better."

Jonsun said, "You don't have to do this."

Naira leaned close and whispered, "If she thinks I'll betray you, she might try to pass me information."

"Ah." Jonsun looked her up and down, appraising. "Do what you'd like, then. It's been ages since I've seen you fight."

"What?" Ward said, contempt lacing her tone. "Need permission from your new master, traitor? Need to ask him to piss, too?"

Shame burned up her neck, stifling. As much as she told herself she was in control, that she was the one playing Jonsun, Ward's remark had struck too close to home. Her pride bristled, and Jonsun shrugged, giving her a thin smile. He didn't know what she was really up to, but he knew she wasn't happy with the arrangement, and he knew her temper.

"Captain," Tarquin said in his coldest tone. "You have been warned. Be quiet and fall back in line."

"Liege Tarquin," Naira said without looking at him. "Shut the fuck up, please."

Naira slipped the rifle strap over her head and handed the weapon to Kuma. Merc-Sec jeered. She stripped off the heavy outer armor on her torso, down to the grey thermal, and rolled up her sleeves. The Conservators took her firearms, but she didn't bother divesting herself of her knives. It would take too long.

Jonsun held her gaze the whole time, one arm crossed over his chest, the other hand up, stroking his chin. She had no idea what he was thinking, exactly, but thought he might be pleased. That was good enough. So long as Jonsun was happy, her friends stayed safe.

The rain pelted down, slushy with ice, stinging her bare arms. She cracked her neck from one side to the other and turned to face Ward.

Merc-Sec formed a loose circle. The captain had stripped down in much the same way, her uniform jacket discarded, arms bare, loathing stamped across the heavy lines of her face. Naira took in those broad shoulders, thick arms corded with muscle, and knew she was about to get her ass kicked. A small part of her was looking forward to it.

Hand. Stove. Kav was never going to let her hear the end of this.

Ward passed her last pistol to a waiting soldier and cracked her knuckles. "We trusted you," she said, and started to circle. "We ate with you. We *looked up* to you." Ward spat in the mud, and the crowd of Merc-Sec jeered once more.

Naira met Ward's slow circle step for step, staying out of reach of the soldiers. Their anger was a living thing, buffeting her in the heat of their ire. Even if Tarquin thought there was something else going on, the soldiers didn't. Their hate for her was pure and simple.

She should be used to being reviled, after she'd gone AWOL on Acaelus. She wasn't.

"It's not personal," Naira said.

"You think it's not personal for us? What you did to us? What you did to our liege?" Her foot slid in the mud.

"Sure you're sober enough for this?" Naira called out, mocking, because she wanted the chatter over with. Didn't want to have to listen to her accusations anymore.

Ward bellowed and charged.

She was faster than she looked. Naira tried to dodge her first hook, but it caught the edge of her jaw and thundered in her skull, sending her reeling. Naira's footing slipped and she flailed for balance instead of blocking the strike Ward launched at her face. Bone crunched in her cheek.

The crowd roared approval as she stumbled out of the way of Ward's next strike and spat out a wad of blood. Naira found her footing and landed her boot square in Ward's unprotected stomach. Ward folded over. Naira pressed the slim advantage, stepping into her, and managed to land a punch on Ward's jaw before the captain got her breath back, grabbed Naira's shoulders, and slammed her forehead into Naira's.

Her vision swam, the breath clotted in her lungs, ears ringing. She couldn't see it, but she knew Ward was winding up for another punch that would definitely knock her out. Naira hooked Ward's ankles and yanked, dropping Ward to her knees.

Naira kneed Ward in the chin with a satisfying crunch, but the stronger woman hugged Naira's legs and knocked her flat onto her back. She bounced against the muddy ground, slushy rainwater pouring into her mouth, making her choke.

Ward was on her, pinning her arms to her sides with her knees, and hauled back, slamming her fist into Naira's head. A lot of people were shouting, but she couldn't make out the words over the ringing in her skull. She wrenched herself to the side and got just enough space to wriggle free.

Naira tried to pin Ward down, but she was too strong, and Naira's head was a mess, and soon they were scrabbling in the mud, swearing and twisting and throwing insults instead of fists as they struggled to find any grip that wasn't mud-slick.

Ward got Naira onto her stomach, wrists trapped in one thick fist behind her back, and Naira knew she was done. She grunted, trying to brace herself against the heavy knee that bore into her back, the hand pushing her face into the mud. Ward leaned down, her breath a hot hiss against Naira's ear.

"Tell me how to help you."

Ward's knee eased enough to let her get a breath. Her face was turned away from Jonsun, mouth half buried in the mud. No one was close enough to hear. She'd never get another chance like this.

"The expansion," she rasped. "Stop it."

She choked on blood or rain or mud, it was hard to tell, and Ward's knee pressed back down, her body weight shifting as she lined up for another punch. Naira hunched her shoulders in a half-hearted attempt to protect her head. She kicked her toes against the ground three times, tapping out.

The weight lifted. Naira gasped, rolling to her back, and heaved for air. Rain washed the mud from her eyes. Caldweller had hauled Ward off her by the back of her undershirt, his face contorted with outrage.

"That's enough, Captain," he said.

Ward reeled and stomped down, landing one last blow straight to Naira's hip. Bones ground together with a breathtaking burst of agony, but she didn't think anything had broken. She hoped.

"On your feet, Nai." Kuma took a knee beside her. "C'mon." She grabbed Naira's arm, hauling it over her shoulders, and stood. Something ground in her hip and Naira swayed, shifting her weight to one foot.

Naira hawked and spat, facing Ward. "Feel better?" she asked, giving her a swollen-lipped sneer.

"You fucking bitch." Ward took a step but was held back by Caldweller. She reared her head back and spat on Naira instead. Lovely.

Kuma steered her away before they could start at it again, and accidentally turned her to face Tarquin. He was white as a sheet despite his sienna-dark skin, every line of his body rigid with the effort of restraining himself. Helms had a hand on one of his shoulders, Cass the other, and their grips were so tight the fabric of his coat puckered around their fingers. Naira sliced her gaze away, unable to face him. Kuma startled and turned Naira back to Jonsun, who had a delighted smile on his face.

"I'm guessing you need a drink," Jonsun said.

"You know just what to say," she mumbled through swollen lips.

He laughed, lifted a hand in the air, and circled it. "Move out, people." He raised his voice to carry. "Talk to you soon, Mercator."

This time, the Conservators closed around the three of them, hiding Naira, Kuma, and Jonsun from view. It was a trick to shut her visually away from Tarquin, but she was grateful. It was better than him having to watch her limp away.

Jonsun squeezed her arm. "Well done."

He strolled away, cheerful, chatting with his troops to raise their spirits. Naira smiled to herself. He hadn't noticed. She'd gotten a message to Ward, and Jonsun was none the wiser.

Kuma adjusted her grip and lowered her voice to the barest scrape of a whisper. "Be careful. Please."

Naira looked at her, waiting for elaboration, but Kuma was silent the rest of the way back to the ship.

THIRTY-SIX

Tarquin

Seventh Cradle | The Present

As Tarquin stormed into the conference room, he caught Naira's scent lingering in the small space, and the lance through his heart was so sudden and searing that he had to put a hand on the table to steady himself. Caldweller released Ward, and she dropped to her hands and knees before him, dripping blood and sweat and mud, and pressed her forehead to the floor.

"Forgive me, my liege," she rushed out. "I didn't know what else to do."

"Forgive you? You nearly killed her!"

"My liege," she said, "Sharp knew exactly how that was going to go. When I saw she was leaving and realized your plan to take her back had failed, I challenged her to try to get information from her. I'm confident she was aware of my reasoning, as she answered the question I asked."

"What question?"

"I said: Tell me how to help you. She said: The expansion. Stop it."

"What good is that?" he demanded. "We're already trying to stop it. She could be trying to refocus us away from Jonsun. She's not—she's not herself."

"My liege," Caldweller said, "I don't think that was a distraction. When we were in here, I watched her for any sign at all. She didn't twitch a muscle until you mentioned slowing what had taken down the ansible network, then she looked straight at Jonsun, and made a point of looking back at me."

Tarquin dragged a hand down the front of his face and collapsed backward into a chair, feeling numb. Four words muttered in the mud, bought with pain and blood, and a single pointed glance. It wasn't much to go on, but she'd been so locked down, it might have been all she could give them.

"Get up, Captain," he said, belatedly realizing he hadn't had his usual revolted reaction to that level of obsequiousness. A shudder rolled through him, Naira's words cutting from a distance. He'd been distracted, that was all. He wasn't becoming his father. "I don't see why you had to take it so far."

Ward wobbled to her feet, and Helms guided her into a chair, then passed her something from the E-X kit that Ward popped into her mouth.

"Like I said." Ward rolled her tongue around a moment. "She knew what she was walking into. I've got strength and reach on her, and I'm trained to fight differently than she is. Sharp knew she was in for an ass kicking, and so did that slimy man who's got her under his thumb, so he'd know if I let her off easy. I couldn't stop it short. Had to sell it, to protect her and you."

"Me? How did that protect me?"

Ward wiped her palms against her knees. "I don't mean to tell you how to run things, my liege, but what I said to Sharp—I didn't mean it. And I hope she'll forgive me for my more, uh, colorful flourishes. But the anger of Merc-Sec? The cheering and the jeering? They meant it. They believe she's a traitor twice over, now, and that means they hate her guts." Ward took a breath. "My liege, you can't let your ex-fiancée walk out of this camp without reprisal after betraying you so publicly and keep the respect of your people. They'll start wondering who else you're letting walk all over you. You don't have time to repair something like that."

"Naira is not my ex anything," he said, "but I take your point. She gave me similar advice on another matter, when I first took control of the family."

Ward smiled a little, though it must have hurt. "Clever woman, our

Sharp. And if it helps, my liege, I got the feeling she was all right with the beating. Like she wanted punishment."

He sat with that for a moment and shuddered. "No. I don't think that does help."

"I'm guessing you all noticed what was happening with Jonsun during the fight?" Ward asked.

The exemplars nodded solemnly.

"What did he do?" Tarquin said. "I couldn't take my eyes off of her."

"He wasn't watching the fight much, my liege," Cass said. "He was watching you."

"Oh," Tarquin said, putting the pieces together. Jonsun had been watching him to see if there was any softening in his horror, to see if this had been prearranged somehow, a ploy of Tarquin's to pass information to Naira. He cleared his throat. "I'm certain he saw what he needed to believe I had no foreknowledge of that butchery."

"Yeah, he seemed pleased," Diaz said. "Amused, even. Sharp's cover is safe."

"That's thoroughly abhorrent," Tarquin said. "But none of this is enough to ensure that Naira is operating undercover. We don't know what that repair process did."

"No way has she thrown her lot in with that scum," Ward said.

Tarquin looked at the guarded faces of his inner circle, and his heart fell. None of them would dare to entertain the idea that Naira had turned against them. As much as it pained him, she'd been kidnapped. Hidden away for weeks, her mind altered by a process they scarcely understood.

His security team should tell him as much. Remind him how dangerous Naira could be, and that though it would be hard, they'd need to take precautions against her going to war against Mercator once more.

But they'd lost Naira. Without her there to temper his reaction and set him straight if he lashed out, they feared upsetting him. Feared his wrath, and god—what good was all the work he'd done to build their faith if losing her was all it took to revert the power imbalance?

"Please," Tarquin said, "I need you all to be honest with me now more than ever. I don't have her to check my assumptions—I'm relying on you all. As much as I want her to be on our side, we have no guarantee of that."

Ward was the first to speak. "What Jonsun said about Sharp rejecting your proposal, my liege. Do we have security footage that can confirm or debunk that statement? I know it was a private moment, but if she did turn you down and one of Jonsun's operatives took you out to make sure you forgot so that they could pressure her to accept, then we'd have confirmation of her being his ally before today."

The suggestion was enough to momentarily stun him to silence. That she would have been against him all this time—it wasn't possible. But he'd asked for their scrutiny, and forced himself not to discard the idea outright.

"There's no footage," Caldweller said quickly.

"Too bad," Ward said.

"She would have accepted if she'd been Jonsun's operative, wouldn't she?" Diaz asked. "I think he was just trying to get in your head, my liege."

"Whether or not she's his ally," Tarquin said, "we must act as if she is. I'll go back to the lab and keep pushing on the expansion. Captain, could you—"

"Send scouts to spy on our new neighbors and start trying to flip the coats of a few stray crew of the *Cavendish*? Way ahead of you, my liege."

"Thank you. Please take yourself to medical at some point this afternoon."

Ward prodded at her ribs, then winced and gave him a sulky nod. They massaged a few final matters of security, and then Tarquin was back out in the icy rain.

He meant to go straight to the lab, but his steps dragged him back to the fence. The grassy field beyond was churned into a strip of mud by the boots of Jonsun's people. He paused there a moment, staring, willing her to manifest from the mist, even though he knew it was ludicrous.

There'd been so much more he'd wanted to say, so much that had gotten lost in the tumult of feints and positioning. He hoped they had the supplies on the *Cavendish* to ease her wounds.

"She's strong, my liege," Caldweller said. And then, softer, "You need to be strong, too."

Tarquin nodded and turned away from the gate, chin lifted, letting the Merc-Sec on watch see the anger so easily summoned to his face. This was war. He would not be his father, but neither would he bend. Whatever happened, Tarquin would not break.

THIRTY-SEVEN

Naira

Seventh Cradle | The Present

By the time they made it back to the *Cavendish*, Naira's pathways had handled the worst of the damage. She was still peppered in bruises, but her hip had stopped grinding in its socket, and she found she could speak without slurring.

Kav took one look at her and said, "I'll go get the good shit."

Naira cleaned up while Kuma and Jonsun briefed those who'd stayed behind. She took her time washing the wounds, wrapping the bandages with care, trying to process all that had happened and what it might mean.

She thought she'd successfully pushed Tarquin off the path of an all-out assault and refocused his energy on debugging whatever had gone wrong with the universe. In her heart, she didn't want to believe the glimpses she'd seen of the future Jonsun portended. Didn't want to believe that Tarquin would ever walk that path, but she couldn't be sure. At least worrying about Tarquin becoming a tyrant kept Jonsun believing she was on his side.

Probably. Kuma's warning stuck with her, and she wished she could ask her outright what she'd meant, but there was no speaking without being overheard in the *Cavendish*.

When she could walk without her head pounding, she left the bathroom and found Jonsun, Kav, and Kuma lounging in a sitting room. Each one of them had a half-empty bottle of whiskey in their hands. Naira put her fists on her hips.

"Really? You couldn't wait for me?"

Kav lifted his bottle and shook it at her. "This is all yours, Nai, get in here."

She plopped down next to him on the couch and kicked her boots up on the coffee table. Kav slung an arm around her shoulders and pushed the bottle into her hands. She took a long, burning drink, and coughed.

"Amarthite is so slow," she muttered, rubbing her throat. "I'm still raw."

"Cannot believe you got your ass handed to you," Kav said with a laugh, "and I wasn't there to see it!"

"I may only have two brain cells left that aren't bruised, but you're not getting away with that." Naira dug her knuckle into his armpit until he grunted.

Jonsun lifted his bottle to her. "To Nai, who demonstrated she was willing to get her teeth kicked in for the cause."

Naira groaned, but lifted her bottle and drank with them. "Speaking of teeth, tell me you have a working dental printer on this ship, because I'm pretty sure I swallowed a few."

Kav took her chin between his thumb and forefinger, and she opened her mouth so he could see. "Yikes. How big was this Captain Ward?"

"Too big." Naira pinched his bicep. "And unlike you, actually trained to use all that muscle she's packing."

"I'll have you know I've been practicing."

"No, he hasn't." Kuma snickered into her bottle.

"We have a dental printer," Jonsun said. He put an arm over the back of the couch and sank into the cushions. "As far as I'm concerned, you can use it to print up whatever you want. Hell, give yourself some vampire fangs, if you fancy them."

"Huh," Kav said. "I think that might actually improve your face."

Naira elbowed him. "Thanks. I'll get to it tomorrow. I'm done digging around in my wounds for the day."

"You're off the clock for the rest of the day," Jonsun said. "Relax.

Sleep in tomorrow. You joke, Nai, but that fight was worth it. They won't question your commitment now, and it'll make them less likely to attack. Did Ward try to tell you anything?"

"A lot about what a whore I am." Naira ran her tongue over her teeth.

Kuma scowled. "You should have tapped me in. I'd love to take that smug bitch apart."

"Nah." Naira took a long drink. "I made my point. Or had it made for me, I guess."

"The Mercator's face was priceless," Jonsun said.

"Don't," Naira said. "I'm with you, but I won't listen to you mock his pain."

"My mistake." Jonsun held his hands up in surrender. "I hope you know we all appreciate the sacrifice you've made. I can't say I ever approved of him, but I know your feelings, and I can't imagine what it's like to know the person you love will become the very thing you hate. Again."

"How did you know he was assassinated the night he proposed?" she asked. "I don't much like the idea of you having visions of my intimate moments, Jo."

"Nothing so sordid as that," Jonsun said.

"You have a spy embedded within Mercator?"

His expression flattened. "The assassination was public news, despite the Mercator's attempt to hush it up, and I know you, Nai. That engagement announcement came right on the heels of him gettin' killed. That heart of yours was always too soft."

"I don't want to talk about him anymore." Naira tightened her grip around the bottle and chugged a quarter of it. Kav gave her a small squeeze.

"Well," Kuma said carefully, "we gotta talk around him, honey bear, because that show of force he put on today was something else."

"That was a threat if ever I saw one," Jonsun said.

Naira rubbed her neck, over the scar. "He did that to try to take me back. Didn't work. He understands the consequences of trying to fight us now, and he won't take that risk."

"Which means statecraft instead," Jonsun said. "He'll try to plant spies, turn coats, get devices and software into our systems."

"He ain't getting shit in our systems." Kav sniffed. "Most of his IT is scrambling to recover the ansibles, anyway."

"Merc-Sec's going to be a problem." Naira rolled a sip around in her mouth before she swallowed. "You saw how on edge they were. Ward will increase perimeter patrols, and they're likely to sabotage little things. Burn fields, harass anyone who comes too close. Stuff like that."

"Minor annoyances," Jonsun said. "Though I don't want you going anywhere near those fences, Nai. They might think they can win points by taking you, and I won't have that."

"Don't have to tell me twice," she said, and met his stare. "Not fond of being kidnapped."

Jonsun tipped his head. "I can't apologize enough. But I hope you realize how important it was, now."

"Yeah." Naira sighed and dropped her head back against Kav's arm. "So, what's next? We dig in, set up crops, get the habs out, et cetera. But the universe is still tearing itself apart, and Mercator is still sitting on a mountain of power. How do we keep people safe? The star is obviously getting farther away. That rain was slush."

"Don't you worry," Jonsun said, "I have plans. Our first order of business, once we secure our perimeter, is to get a warming net over our land. Won't stop the rain coming down, but it'll make sure the ground won't freeze."

"And starlight? Plants don't like the dark."

He chuckled, and there was an edge to the sound. "Nai, I've got it. Stop worrying at the bones and relax, like I told you to."

"You say that, but as far as I can tell you haven't shared this plan of yours with anyone else."

"I sped it up," he said. "I can slow it down."

"But how, exactly? If you can slow it down now, then why—"

"Nai. Enough."

"You know how she is with a plan." Kav gave her a friendly shake that was also a warning. "Never stops asking questions."

"Can't help herself," Kuma said, half to herself, eyeing Naira over the rim of her bottle.

"I remember." Jonsun smiled warmly at her. "And I admire that. But I'm able to be a few steps ahead. No point in worrying."

Naira lifted her bottle to him before taking another long drink. The conversation skimmed away from their situation, fell back into old patterns, comfortable territory. Topics that didn't make Jonsun's jaw tense or his eyes burn too brightly.

When the conversation wore down and all their bottles were empty, Kav flicked Naira's ear. "Go to bed."

"Bossy." She swirled her empty bottle, glaring at its lack of contents.

"C'mon, Nai, you've been treating that print like shit. Let it rest."

"Yeah, yeah." She clapped a hand on his knee and used him to push herself up. "I can take a hint."

The halls were empty, the Conservators all either fast asleep or out on watch. It was strange, still, for her to think of anyone more than the four people who had been in that room as Conservators. They'd been a tight-knit family for five long years and now...this. Holding their breath. Stepping on eggshells around Jonsun, because if he sensed any of them waver, he'd crack them.

Naira passed the turn to her quarters and kept walking. Silence deadened the halls. Alone in the dark she could almost pretend she was back on this ship in the days before she'd cracked. She'd thought she'd destroyed this ship, once. Spent countless hours poring over its construction with the very people she'd left back in that room. Had thought, when she'd been captured escaping its demolition, that at least she'd done that much. At least she'd blown it to pieces.

Yet it persisted. And no matter how hard she tried to escape its pull, those long, dark halls kept drawing her back. Swallowing her whole.

There was the room in which she'd met Paison once more. And there, a few more turns away, the room where Paison met her end. Farther down that hall the room with the corpses, where she'd held an inexplicable patch in her hand and known it was a bridge, but still couldn't say why.

And there, a door that had never been on the blueprints.

It was locked. The handle was warm in her hand. Strangely so, for a ship whose life support systems were kept at minimum to conserve power. She leaned against the door. Pressed her ear to it, and heard nothing but the thumping of her own heart. Perhaps the quiet murmur of pneumatics, but that might have been her imagination. Was she hallucinating again? Her mind had been mucked around with so much she couldn't tell anymore what was real at times.

What wasn't her imagination was the heat seeping through. The dry, oily heat of too many machines in use in a confined area.

"Nai," Kuma hiss-whispered.

She jumped. Staggered a little—she really had drunk too much. Kuma grabbed her arm to drag her away from the door.

"What the fuck do you think you're doing?"

"Reminiscing." She pointed to the door with her thumb. "I don't remember that room. What's in it?"

"A guillotine for people who can't help but stick their noses where they don't belong."

Naira rolled her eyes. "C'mon. I know this ship. That's supposed to be one of the drive aisles to push large equipment into the engine bay. Why's it blocked off?"

Kuma turned her around and started marching her back toward her room. "Forget you know anything about this ship. Promise me."

"Is what he's using to control the expansion in there?"

Kuma stopped her relentless march and turned Naira around, hovering over her with their faces so close her breath tickled Naira's cheeks. "Don't snoop. Don't prod. Keep your head down and mind your business. Please. For me. You have no idea what he's capable of."

"Then tell me."

She glanced upward, to the walls where the cameras and mics were always watching, and grimaced. "His inner circle? It's not us. Remember that."

Kuma hauled her the rest of the way to her room in silence, shoved her within, and slammed the door shut.

THIRTY-EIGHT

Tarquin

Seventh Cradle | The Present

The afternoon dragged on into night, with regular reports from Merc-Sec that the crew of the *Cavendish* was setting up structures, digging trenches, and generally getting on with the business of putting up a settlement. There'd been no sighting of Naira outside of the ship, though Jonsun appeared a few times early on to offer direction and glad-hand with his people. Reports insinuated that he was in a good mood, but they could stake nothing upon that.

Ward's patrols had yet to cross paths with any of the Conservators. They were staying back, and while that made it harder to attempt to ingratiate a few of them to the settlement, Ward made a note that it was for the best. Merc-Sec was still keyed up after the fight.

Tarquin told Naira's mother what had happened and held back the worst of the details. She'd merely nodded and gone back to work. Naira had asked that the expansion be solved, and the way Dr. Sharp moved around the lab, Tarquin wondered if she'd surpass Delorne's knowledge and solve the whole thing single-handedly, just to bring her daughter home.

He'd wanted to join her, but the exemplars had insisted he return to the more defensible structure of his home for the evening. Tarquin leaned back from the holo he'd been working on and rubbed gritty eyes. His body ached; his mind was numb with exhaustion. He should go to bed, but—no. Not tired enough to brave trying to sleep just yet.

Tarquin picked up his glass, going to refill it with more bourbon from the sideboard. A commotion in the hallway stopped him before he could reach the bottle. Tarquin abandoned the bourbon for the time being and opened the door.

Caldweller had his back to Tarquin, his pistol aimed at Naira's heart. She stood at the end of the hallway, arms raised in surrender, a slightly embarrassed smile on her face. He blinked. And blinked again. He hadn't had that much to drink.

"My liege," Caldweller said, "stay behind me."

"Naira?" he asked, certain he was imagining things. But that was the print they'd been keeping in stasis. The suppression crown wrapped her forehead, and her neck was free of the Conservators' ghastly brand.

"Hey," she said, voice a little soft, a little rough, and all reservation burned away.

He dropped the glass. Let it shatter against the hardwood floor and shoved Caldweller aside, rushing to wrap her up in his arms. She started to reach for him, but then she seemed to catch herself. To draw back, arms still raised, and stiffen.

"I forgot how excitable you can be," she said.

He pulled away, confused—it had barely been a month since they'd been apart—but then he recalled Caldweller's weapon and grimaced, turning toward his exemplar. "Put that away, for god's sake. It's Naira."

"Not exactly," she said.

"What?" He'd studied the fine movements of her muscles, all her subtle intonations. His heart ached, seeing the weariness that seemed to drag her down from within, but there was no doubt in his mind that she was Naira, and no other. "I don't understand."

"My liege." Caldweller's voice was taut with frustration. "Please get behind me until we can sort this out."

"Better do what he says, my liege," Naira said, smiling still, but the expression was forced. Her eyes flat. Cass padded up the stairs behind her, their gun leveled at her back. Reluctantly, he moved away. Retreated to stand behind Caldweller.

"Please." He knew that he was begging but was too tired and drunk and heartsick to care about his dignity. "Tell me what's happened."

"I'm not your Naira, my liege. I killed my Tarquin. But I've come back. To save you."

"Come back?" Tarquin asked, too muddled to make sense of any of this. "To save me from what?"

"From your Naira."

He found himself speechless. It was impossible, he knew it was impossible, and yet . . . so was a universe tearing itself apart. So was an adult Jana assassinating him on a riverbank. So was Naira, his Naira, leaving him to work for Jonsun.

It was Caldweller who found his voice first. "We need to detain her until we can confirm . . . anything."

"Yes." He clung to the semblance of protocol. Of structure in his life that might, somehow, make this make sense. "Naira, I'm sorry, but—"

"I expected as much. Francel, you may restrain me. I'm unarmed and won't resist."

Cass frowned at her use of their first name and approached her. "Hands behind your back, please, E-X."

She let out a soft breath, lowering her arms. "It's been a long time since I've been called that. Sharp is fine." She lifted her gaze to meet Tarquin's once more. "From all of you."

"Understood," he said stiffly.

For the second time in less than twenty-four hours, Tarquin watched Naira walk away from him. He held it together as best he could, but the moment Cass led her around a bend in the hall he turned, pushing open the door to his room.

He staggered onto the balcony. The night air was cold in his lungs, the stone railing beneath his hands unyielding. Tarquin slid down against it and sat there for—he didn't know how long—with his head pressed against his knees, struggling for calm.

Struggling to remember Naira's gentleness, when he'd had a panic attack in the forests of Sixth Cradle. That was the Naira he knew. Not—not whatever else was happening. She'd hated him then. Had every reason to let him suffer. But she'd been so kind, and soothing, and . . .

"My liege?"

Caldweller. Tarquin raked his hands through his hair and forced himself to lift his head. "What is it?"

"We've moved her to the print storage room until we can find another solution. If she is who she claims to be, then we don't expect it to be able to hold her for long, but she seems to be cooperating."

"Who knows she's here?"

"Only the exemplars. With your permission, we'd like to bring Dr. Bracken in to see if there's any way to validate her claims."

"There's a simpler way to confirm her identity. I'll ask her to tell me something that only Naira would know."

"True, but..." Caldweller stepped closer. Lowered himself to a crouch beside Tarquin and tried to put on a reassuring smile, though worry creased his forehead. "This will be difficult, my liege. Empirical evidence will guide us."

"Right." Tarquin nodded to himself. "We need evidence. Bring in Bracken, then, but no one else. I want this knowledge contained as tightly as possible."

"About that," Caldweller said. "We're going to have to jail her, either way, but if we do it outside of the house, people will find out. There'll be talk. I don't like the idea of trying to hold Sharp in anything less than maximum security, but your room is a panic room. We can trigger the metal shutters on the balcony and engage the secondary locks. That should do, if you don't mind moving into one of the guest rooms for a while."

The room they'd shared. A visceral twist in his chest momentarily stole his voice, the desire to refuse blotting out all other thought. It made sense. It was the only logical way to hold someone with Naira's capabilities while continuing to hide her presence, but... He clenched his fists. Relaxed them slowly.

"That will be fine. If anyone asks, tell them I...I needed space from the memory of her."

"I'll have Diaz shuffle your things around," he said, then hesitated. "I can't imagine what you're going through, my liege. But I talked to Sharp before we casted back from M-U. One friend to another, you know? I don't know what's going on, but I'm sure of this—she wanted to marry you. She loves you, my liege. Loves you enough it gives her a headache, sometimes."

Tarquin huffed out a shaky breath at that.

"So, from where I'm sitting, Naira Sharp casting her mind back from the future to save you rings truer than her turning her back on you to ally with Jonsun."

"She said she killed me." How long had he waited? Hoped? Spent nights on this very balcony, staring out into the dark, willing her to return to him? Had she spent the same amount of time learning to loathe him? "I don't know what to do."

Caldweller took Tarquin's face in both hands. Forced him to look at him. "You gather all the information you can. And if it's true? Then never lose sight of the fact that, no matter what drove her to it in the first place, she came back. For you."

Tarquin's shoulders eased down. "Thank you."

Caldweller gave his cheek a firm pat before standing back up. He cleared his throat, adjusting his armor and weapons fastidiously. "I'll call Bracken in. Pull yourself together, my liege. We should have more information for you when you're ready."

Tarquin took Caldweller's advice and showered, letting himself break down in the privacy of hot water until it was all wrung out of him and he felt, at last, like he could think again. When Caldweller knocked on his door to escort him to Sharp, he was as ready as he was ever going to be.

Though the room was small, all of the exemplars and Bracken shuffled within, their faces schooled to careful neutrality. For the best, really. Tarquin wasn't certain he could hold himself together if he'd been left alone with her.

The table Bracken had used as a desk stood in the center of the room, Naira—*Sharp*—sitting behind it. Her cuffed hands rested on the tabletop.

"My liege," she said. "The doctor ran a great deal of tests. What's my diagnosis?"

"You don't have to call me that." He pulled out a chair. Sat.

"Yes. I do."

He folded his hands together on the table, mirroring her posture. Her lips quirked briefly, in recognition. "Dr. Bracken's report is inconclusive. If you claimed to be Ex. Sharp as she is today, they would call you a fraud. But there are enough points of fidelity between your map and hers that, assuming a long enough deviation, they may have once been the same."

"What do you think?"

"I think that, if you are who you claim to be, there are things you could tell me that only you would know."

Her gaze slid off of him. Skimmed those gathered. "May I whisper them to you, my liege? They are exceedingly private."

He swallowed. Steeled himself. "You may."

She leaned across the table, chains a soft hiss of metal, and he leaned to meet her halfway. Head tilted, breath warm, she whispered to him of small, intimate moments. Inconsequential things, measured against all they had faced together, but moments that had meant everything—that always would—between them. He thought he'd prepared himself. There was no defense he ever could have built.

She began to pull away. Their eyes met, her lips still parted from that final word. Their breath mingled, drawing him toward her, but he stopped himself and thought, for a moment, that she might have started to lean toward him, too.

"She is who she claims to be," Tarquin said.

"How?" Bracken asked. They sounded as bewildered as Tarquin felt.

"Kav and Fletch devised a method," she said. "A cracked mind, as Dr. Bracken theorized, is unmoored in time. Jonsun's repair allowed me to see glimpses of the future more clearly, and as I refined the technique, Fletch noticed repeating moments of clarity. We called these insertion points. Places along the timeline where someone could go back, and attempt to change events."

"Demarco." He'd meant it to be a question, but the word came out flat.

"His experience as a finalizer gave him unique insight into the temporal plasticity of cracked maps."

"I thought your mind had been repaired."

"Yes, but—" She reached to rub her forehead, but the chains attached to the table stopped the movement, making her wince. Her voice had sounded thin, almost scratchy with exhaustion.

"For god's sake," Tarquin said, "we can allow her some freedom of movement. And you—Diaz, get her some water, please."

The exemplars startled into action. Caldweller unlocked her cuffed hands from the table but left them on. Diaz handed her a cold glass of water that she drank half of before taking a breath.

"Thanks, Gabe," she said.

He blinked, surprised by the use of his first name, and gave her a shy smile before slipping back into position. Sharp didn't seem to have noticed his momentary confusion.

She pushed the glass aside. "I've lived this moment a thousand times, and still I never know where to begin."

"Maybe if you start with how you came to be here?"

"As good a place as any." She sat straighter. "After your death, my liege, the settlement fell apart. Ward and Alvero tried to hold things together for a few years, but the expansion couldn't be slowed quickly enough to save everyone, and the people knew it. Jonsun, he...Well, he'd planned for that all along. He iced his people. Set us on a timer to reprint in a hundred years to the day, when the expansion had slowed down and things had started to contract.

"I don't know if he got it wrong, or if he knew it would never work. That fucker—" She cracked her jaw. "Never mind. What matters is that we woke to a frozen world. One that was getting warmer, but not fast enough that our equipment could outlast the freeze. There was nothing we could do. It was just...over. Everything. Some of his followers embraced that, but I couldn't give up."

"You never could."

"I suppose not," she said. "Kav and Fletch, they weren't ready to give up, either."

"You were working *with* Demarco?" Tarquin asked.

"When we woke to a frozen world, I printed him. I required an ally I knew I could fight side by side with, and Fletch..." She clenched her hands. Released them. "Well. For all his faults, he'd never let me fall. We escaped Jonsun's sphere of control together with Kav. Later, Fletch latched on to the flashes I'd been having before the great freeze, the visions of the future. He said I never got to be that woman on the beach, so it wasn't over yet. I didn't believe him at first, but—"

"Wait," Tarquin said. "What woman on the beach?"

"The one I saw in the warpcore the day of the bombings. He analyzed every detail I could remember—from the sand on my boots, to the scars, to my hair—and determined I must have been on a beach. A big one, you know? By an ocean." Pain flickered across her face. "I'd never been to a beach like that. Still haven't."

I could take you. Tarquin bit the words back. She wasn't his Naira. His Naira was miles away, trapped by Jonsun, and this woman might hold the keys to setting her free.

"It took..." She shook her head. "God, it took decades. I lived thirty years in that hellscape, trying to find a way to fix it, but there was nothing we could do until Kav and Fletch thought they found a way to send a mind back. But we couldn't agree on when or even what to change. And then Jonsun found out."

She laced her fingers together and squeezed. "He raided our compound. It was a bloodbath. A handful of us escaped and took the tech with us, but he's been hounding us to the ground. Fletch and I—we're the last line of defense. Lifetimes of fighting with someone, you know when you're getting to the end. When it's over. And we've known for a long time, now, that it's only a matter of time until Jonsun overwhelms us and takes the transmitter."

"What about Kuma?" Tarquin asked. "Or the exemplars?"

Her head was bowed, hair hiding her face. She only shook her head in response.

"Naira, I—sorry, sorry, I mean Sharp."

She took a breath and straightened once more, her gaze lingering for a moment with such warmth upon the exemplars that she seemed lighter, somehow. "It's been a long time since you slipped on my name like that."

"It was never easy for me," he admitted.

She started to smile. Stamped out the expression instead. "The point is, my liege, that our backs were to the wall. I believed that if I could stop you from dying, then you might be able to hold Mercator's researchers together long enough to fix the expansion."

"May I ask a technical question, my liege?" Bracken asked. Tarquin nodded. "The nature of the resonant. Did you ever discover what it was?"

"Yes. They're the ones who will crack beyond recovery."

"But I'm resonant," Tarquin said.

"So you are, my liege."

He'd cracked. Gone to the endless scream. Naira had killed him, and it'd been traumatic enough that his mind had shattered in the process, and, shit—he couldn't get a full breath.

Her hands enveloped his, cool and strong, the chains scratching his knuckles. "I'm here to stop it."

Tarquin managed a full breath. Opened eyes he hadn't realized he'd closed, and glimpsed the sadness in her expression in the second before she pulled away. He took a moment. Gathered himself.

"Why did you kill me?" he asked.

"You deserved it." There was an edge to her tone. A vicious slash of anger. The exemplars responded to that sheathed threat, stepping forward. Tarquin held up a forestalling hand.

"Tell me."

"When did you last contact her?" she asked.

Her. The same way Naira had referred to her past self, that she couldn't remember, on Sixth Cradle. "A few hours ago. Naira asked us to stop the expansion during that encounter."

"Those words were my greatest mistake. They will fester. And when you think you've lost her—when you believe there's nothing you have left but that single goal—that's when you begin the experiments."

"What experiments?"

"You're correct that relkatite is accelerating the expansion. Our attempts to eradicate *canus*, destroying its only predator, have steadily ramped up that acceleration until we've reached the crisis point we're in now. And you..." Her hands shook, rattling the cuffs. She flattened them hard against the tabletop.

"You should rest," he said.

"No. No, I can't fucking *rest*. I'm trying to be calm and clearheaded about this so that you'll listen to me, because I've dragged myself back here knowing this is it. This is everything. Fletch is destroying the tech once I'm gone so that Jonsun can't get his hands on it and then—then himself—but...Every time I look at you, I'm so, so afraid that I fucked up in coming here. That it's all going to happen again, no matter what I do, and I should end you now to stop it."

Beneath the anguish he glimpsed a rage so consuming that it made his blood run cold. Tarquin wanted to think he wasn't capable of anything so terrible that it would turn Naira against him—but he felt the truth of her contempt sink into his bones. Recalled the horror in Naira's voice just a few hours ago, now, when she'd told him he'd become a monster.

Caldweller pushed Sharp back down into her seat. She'd leaned forward without, it seemed, realizing she'd done so. The snarl wiped from her face and she turned her head away, holding out her hands so that Caldweller could, his face carefully neutral, re-chain her to the table.

"I need you to tell me what I did to earn your wrath," he said. "If we know, we can stop it."

She laughed. A grating, rough sound he scarcely recognized. "That's the trouble, my liege. I don't know if telling you is what precipitates it happening. But..." She looked around, at the others ringing the room, and nodded to herself. "It's the decay of relkatite into amarthite. It's too slow, on its own. But in humans, it flourishes. Speeds up. By the time you realize this, the expansion is so far gone that..."

"You start printing people for the purpose of accelerating the decay. Over and over again. Keeping them locked in the cubicles until they're overwhelmed by *canus* and their pathways decay and then you do it again. And again. Because it *works*." Her voice rose, fast and breathless. "And it's Lee and Diaz and Helms and Bracken and Ward and Alvero and my mom, and you don't *stop*, and when I found you in that lab, I—"

She broke off. Buried her face in her arms against the table, shuddering with silent sobs. Tarquin shoved his chair back, pushed himself to his feet. He couldn't sit there and do nothing while Naira wept, he could *not*, but any comfort he could offer wasn't wanted, and she wasn't even his Naira.

"I can't do this." Tarquin turned for the door.

That gravelly laugh ripped out of her once more. "Of course. Of fucking course. I shouldn't have come here. This was a mistake."

He turned back. Leaned across the table to grip her folded hands. She jerked, lifting her head to look up at him through red-rimmed eyes.

"Coming to me was not a mistake. I promise you that. But I need space now, okay?"

She nodded, warily. Tarquin swept out the room, taking his entourage with him.

THIRTY-NINE

Naira

Seventh Cradle | The Present

Naira clung to her corner of the warming net, the fine filaments cutting into the palms of her hands, and wished she'd taken Jonsun up on letting her sleep late. Her print had healed the worst of the damage, but it prioritized cracked bones and torn ligaments. In theory, she was grateful for that, but in practice, it meant most of her muscles were still bruised to the bone, and her jaw wouldn't stop itching as growth serums worked to bond the new teeth she'd printed.

It was like having ants crawling inside her bones, and not even the irritation of the wind trying to steal the net could keep her from prodding at her gums with the tip of her tongue until she tasted raw iron.

"On three!" Kuma bellowed.

The line of Conservators holding on to the bloody thing pitched their edges of the warming net into the air at the same time. The boosters in the corners fired on Kuma's mark, lifting the net about twenty feet before launching stakes into the ground with such force Naira shouted and skittered away from an impact site that was far too close for her liking.

Kuma laughed at her. "Afraid of a little dirt?" she called above the howl of the wind.

"I'd rather not get impaled, thanks." She squinted up at the net.

It was early in the morning, the weak starlight bleeding a bloody sunrise across the land. The thin fibers of the net shone as they activated, radiating warmth. Curious, Naira touched two fingertips to the anchor pole beside her and hissed as they burned, snatching her hand back.

A grey-eyed Conservator winked at her. "Do we have to teach you about stoves, too?"

"I didn't think it would work that fast," Naira muttered.

Kuma loped over and pointed to the soil. "The nets are old Earth tech, from when we still thought we could save that planet. The poles transmit heat into the soil, keep the roots nice and cozy."

"Decent plan." Naira turned to the grey-eyed woman. "What's your name, Conservator?"

"Rani Jadhav, E-X." She held out her hand and Naira shook it. "You don't remember me, probably, but I was on Miller-Urey during the protest. My team and I cordoned Jessel under your orders."

"No shit?" Naira squinted at the young woman and wondered if Jessel's closest loyalists might be unhappy with Jonsun's reign. "Glad to see you made it through, Jadhav. Anyone else from your old crew around?"

"Fowler and Agosta." She pointed out two men who'd been holding up the net on the opposite end of the field. "But that's it from M-U. Rest of my command is new blood, as far as you're concerned."

"Your command? Happy to see you moving up in the world, Captain, but damn do you know how to make a woman feel ancient."

Jadhav had an infectious laugh that showed all her teeth. "It's only been a year an' a bit, E-X. Time flies when the universe is on fire."

Kuma gave Naira's shoulder a squeeze and slight nudge. She glanced in that direction and found Jonsun jogging down the gangway.

"Sharp and Jadhav!" Jonsun called out, merry as starshine. "Just the women I wanted to see."

"I'm not touching another one of those nets, if that's what you're after." Naira held up her hands for him to see. "We don't get along."

"Ouch." He shook his head. "You take terrible care of your prints, you know that?"

"So I've been told. What's up?"

"First of all, how are you feeling?" Jonsun's face was a creased mask of perfect concern. It almost made her laugh.

"Beat to hell, but that's not much different than my every day, to be honest. I'll manage, if you need me for something."

He placed a too-warm hand on her arm. "It's not all about what I need from you. I want to make sure you're okay. But if you're willing, I do have a task that could use an exemplar's touch."

"I'd rather do E-X stuff than deal with another one of those nets."

His smile was a slash of teeth and light. "It's boring work, I'm afraid. A long haul. We've got diggers ready to roll, to carve out tunnels so we can get around the area better, but they need an escort. You're the best we have at guarding, well, anything."

"Diggers?" Naira asked. "I thought all the equipment was going haywire due to the UFP being on the fritz."

"The plan is to link your HUD to the borer. You walk along the route I've given, and it will follow and do its thing. You never even have to see it, unless you want to. It'll pop up here and there, push out some waste, and carry on along behind you like a loyal pup. Just make sure to disengage the follow if you need to go for a piss, yeah?"

"Easy enough," she said. "What's the route?"

"That's the tricky bit." Jonsun swiped up a detailed map of the settlement and the geography around it. Tarquin had done the same thing so many times that her heart ached, but she studied the map with interest. "Mercator's loosely entrenched on this end." He pointed to the farmsteads where there were fewer buildings, more untamed fields, and rangy forest running into low hills. "Not a lot going on up there, so I'll send another team that direction." He traced out a wide loop encircling the settlement. Naira knew exactly where this was going, and nodded studiously to cover the sudden drying of her throat. "The south end, however, is heavily entrenched and tucked in by that river. We need a loop around the settlement, and the south side is going to be a very fine needle to thread. That's where you come in."

Naira reached for the map, hesitated until Jonsun nodded approval, then expanded the path he'd outlined, zooming in on some of the sharper angles. He'd been underselling how fine a line she'd be walking, avoiding detection.

"You know they're on high alert, right?" Naira frowned at the map as she studied it. "Boring tunnels under them is going to piss them off. That's some real guerrilla shit, Jo."

"Guerrilla is what we've got," he said with a folksy shrug that made Naira want to shake him. "We need eyes all around them if we want to survive, and we won't manage it with tech—they'll shoot down anything we launch. So, we dig. They can hardly complain that we want to watch them. They're a lion, we're a mouse."

"Yeah, and I'd rather not get my head chomped off before we have a chance to dig in here."

"If you're not willing, that's all right. I'm sure Captain Jadhav can manage without you. I don't force anyone on missions. I'm not MERIT. We're volunteer only."

"I can do it," Jadhav said far too quickly. Naira caught a flash of that earlier youthful enthusiasm.

Jadhav absolutely could not do this. Naira clenched her jaw. Without an intimate understanding of both the terrain and Merc-Sec's habits, Jadhav and her team would be discovered on their first day.

"I'll go," Naira said. "I just want you to understand what we're playing with, here."

"I have complete faith you'll manage," Jonsun said. "And you can give Jadhav and her team field training while you're out there."

Jadhav's eyes sparked with excitement, but Naira's stomach soured. "This isn't a vacation. The more people we have, the more likely we are to be spotted."

"I don't mind splitting the team," Jadhav said. "You're going to need someone to watch your back when you sleep, Sharp. And if Merc-Sec does come sniffing, a few extra hands on deck might warn them off."

Naira sincerely doubted that, but inclined her head, watching Jonsun in the corner of her eye. This was some kind of test, but she couldn't see what, exactly, he was testing. Her loyalties, certainly. But, somehow, she felt this was about Jadhav and her team. Jonsun had come looking for the captain, after all. Maybe he'd had the same thought Naira had and suspected they were still loyal to Jessel.

Or he thought Naira would think that and wanted to force them together to see if Naira made any suspicious overtures. Her head hurt, and strangely, she missed Fletcher—layers of trust and potential double-crossing had been his forte, not hers.

"Fine," Naira said. "But this will take a few days, and we'll be packing light and putting in long hours in rain, hail, or whatever else this planet decides to throw at us. You good with that?"

"Looking forward to it," Jadhav said.

"Wonderful." Jonsun wiped the holo away. "It's all settled, then. Unless, Kuma, would you like to go as well?"

Kuma had been standing there with her arms crossed as she watched the plan unfold, and she startled at the attention. "Who, me? I thought you wanted thin numbers."

"I do." Naira tried to keep her voice light, even though this felt like a trap she was willingly shoving her foot into. "But it'd be nice to have someone I'm used to fighting with at my back. No offense, Jadhav."

"None taken," she said. "I know the feeling."

Kuma shrugged. "Then I'm your muscle, honey bear."

"Almost like old times, eh?" Jonsun said. "But I'm afraid I can't spare Kav to tag along. I need him here." His hand tightened, just a little, on Naira's arm.

"That's for the best," Naira said. "He doesn't bivouac well anyway. Never heard a man whine so much as when he'd find a rock under his bedroll."

They all laughed, and Naira smiled, natural as anything, though a thousand questions were clawing through her. Jonsun may say the tunnels were for surveillance and defense, but she knew an offensive advantage when she saw one and had no doubt he was laying ground for a fight against the settlement itself.

As much as she wanted to try to drop a message to Mercator about what was going on beneath their feet, she didn't dare. Jonsun was giving her just enough rope to hang herself with.

He never took his hand from her arm. Instead, he turned, pulling her along with him, out of the wind and back into the *Cavendish*, where their supplies were waiting. Naira cast a glance over her shoulder at the shining heat net and wondered if she'd have been better off turning down the mission.

The grip on her arm reminded her that refusal had never really been an option.

FORTY

Tarquin

Seventh Cradle | The Present

Tarquin went to see her. A night spent tossing in a guest bed hadn't settled his thoughts or his heart, but still he felt strangely calm. Detached. Perhaps he was dissociating and should be concerned, but he found it hard to care.

His exemplars and Bracken had assured him that they would never allow the experiments that Sharp had described to come to pass. That would be enough. It had to be enough.

He knocked. She bade him enter. Tarquin left his protesting exemplars in the hall and shut the door behind him.

Sharp had been mid-push-up when he'd walked in. She hoisted herself the rest of the way to her feet, wiping sweaty hair off her forehead. Naira had exercised every morning he'd known her. Not even living through a dying universe had changed that much, it seemed. The familiar scent of her sweat lingered on the air.

"I didn't mean to interrupt," he said.

"It's not like I have anything else to do." She crossed to a sideboard. Picked up a glass of water and chugged most of it down.

"Ah. Right." They'd disconnected her HUD and comms pathways—something the exemplars wouldn't budge on, in case her intentions weren't what she claimed. He rummaged in his pocket and removed a locked-down wristband. "I'm afraid we can't restore your connection to Mercator's network, but should you need anything, this has a secure line directly to me."

"I haven't had one of these since I was a kid." She held out her hand for him, and he secured it to her wrist, careful not to touch her skin in the process. "Although I never had one this nice."

"I've given you better pieces of jewelry than this," he said, before he could think better of the words.

She twisted the band around her wrist. "You have questions. Ask them."

"Did you refuse my proposal?"

Her brows shot up. She licked her teeth, studying him a long moment. "I'm not here to talk about us, my liege. I'm here to prevent Naira from assassinating you."

"By stopping me from doing something that drives her to slaughter me. I need to know. The exemplars need to know, to do their jobs properly. You may despise me for what I did in your timeline, but—does she? Right now?"

Sharp wouldn't look at him. "No. She will love you until the day she pulls the trigger, and beyond that still, though she will hate herself for it. Is your ego properly assuaged, my liege, so that we can discuss more pressing matters?"

The rebuke was a slap in the face. He forced himself to shove down all he was feeling so that he could get through this. "You have knowledge of what will happen next, correct?"

"I have pieces." She leaned against the wall, as far away from him as she could physically get. "Before I came back here, I was practically living in a simulation. My mind—her mind—when repaired is capable of glimpsing the future more reliably than before, but I had decades to refine the technique and had developed a way of looking back on all my possible lives. Separated from that simulation, I've lost access to a great deal. But I remember possibilities."

"Would allowing you to enter a simulation assist this visualization?"

"No." She finished the water and set it aside. "I knew, in coming here, that I was committing myself to this timeline. Collapsing many of the possibilities. I save you, or I don't, and if I don't...I suspect I'll cease to exist, because my future is already over."

"How can you be so sure?" he asked.

"Jana Degardet killed you, did she not?"

"An adult version of her print did, yes. We can't confirm the status of the mind in that print at the time."

She turned her head aside, but not quickly enough to hide the grief that permeated her.

"Sharp?" He took a step forward. Stopped himself.

"I knew it was probable, but the confirmation..." She took in a breath so large it expanded her chest. Blew it out in an explosive burst. "Jana is loyal to Jonsun. She despises you, for what you did to the fathers she could have had. His closest inner circle, they're the ones who call themselves the Bridge Crew. Bridges to the future." She grunted softly. "Fletch was so close."

"The dead people you—she—discovered on the *Cavendish*?"

"The very same."

"I thought you said that Demarco was staying behind to destroy the device that sent your map back, so that Jonsun couldn't utilize it? How could Jana have come back?"

"Think that through, my liege." Her voice was taut. Ratcheted down.

If Jonsun had the device, then he'd gotten to Fletcher before he could destroy it.

"I'm so sorry."

She scoffed. "No, you're not. You hated him."

"Maybe. But I love you, and his loss hurt you. For that, I'm sorry."

"Her," she said sternly. "Not me. Her."

"My mistake." He was treading on dangerous ground, and so changed the subject. "I understand you're here to stop her from taking my life, but surely warning me about the ghastly outcome of those experiments is enough? If you could tell us more about what may happen, then perhaps—"

"I am here for one moment." Her voice was stiff. "There will come a point—there *always* comes a point—when you are backed so firmly against the wall you see those experiments as the only way out. How that moment arrives varies, but the result is the same. She discovers your transgressions. She takes your life. It is that moment that I've come for, and nothing else."

"The Naira I know would never be so ruthlessly single-minded."

"I am not the Naira you know."

She hunched against the wall, arms crossed, chin tucked down in such an aggressive posture of defensiveness that he could, almost, believe her. "Very well. How will you know when this moment approaches, if it varies every time?"

"It is a pressure, winding tight around my throat until I can scarcely breathe with the urgency of it. A weight upon everything I am, crushing me down, seeking to expel me from this timeline until it takes all of my concentration just to hold on. To stay."

"Is there anything I can do to make it easier for you to hold on?"

She laughed. A vicious sound that made no sense to him. "Go to war." Her voice was low. Bladed. "Grind Jonsun and everything he's touched to atoms and spit on the remains."

"Would it stop the expansion?"

"No." She looked away once more, to the walled-off balcony. "That's already at its tipping point."

"Then why?"

Sharp clenched her fists and said nothing. She seemed to him to have compressed. Her burning rage crushed down, compacting beneath the pressure of all she had endured to become something pure but hateful. It was revenge, pure and simple and bloodthirsty, that drove her desire for Jonsun's annihilation. He wanted it, too. But it would only hurt what innocent souls remained on that ship, and destroy amarthite they desperately needed.

"I can't give you that."

A muscle in her cheek twitched. "I know."

"Have you tried it before?"

"Other iterations of me have. It never works."

"Iterations?" he asked.

"I am merely the endpoint of the last Naira who failed to stop the expansion. Should I fail in this timeline, I will cease. Your Naira will continue on, and live into a version of my future from which she will learn the same things, and attempt this all over again."

"I won't let that happen to her."

"You said the same thing to the Sharp who came back to my timeline, my liege."

He had so much more he wanted to ask, but decided to veer matters back toward the business at hand. "Is there anything specific you can tell me about Jonsun's plans?"

"He'll install heat nets, soon, if he hasn't already. They're a weapon." She looked up, and he wondered how many of her pasts she was staring into. "They're always a weapon."

"Thank you." Tarquin turned to leave. She seemed to have reached her limit, and as much as he wanted to learn everything, he couldn't stay there much longer. Every moment in her presence tore the hole in his heart wider, reminding him that his Naira was gone.

"Tarquin, wait—"

He spun back to her in time to see a grimace of frustration overtake her expression. She'd reached out. He nearly took her hand, but her fingers curled slowly within, and she drew away once more.

"I'm sorry, I . . ." She bit her lips shut. Released them. "I have a request. A personal one."

"Ask."

"Would you open the balcony for me? Just for a little while. It's been so long since I've seen daylight."

"It's freezing out."

Her smile was brief, but wry. "This is the warmest day of the rest of my life."

Tarquin didn't know how to answer that. He approached the door and pulled up the lock function in his HUD. Hesitated. "Please don't use this as an opportunity to betray me. Caldweller would lecture me to death."

"I wouldn't dream of giving Lee such a headache, my liege."

He released the sealed plate. Opened the exterior door, and stepped aside to give her space. While the sky was a dull grey, her gaze lifted toward its vault with reverence. She appeared to him the same as she had the first time she'd ever seen a river, on Sixth Cradle. When she'd been so full of awe he'd forgotten, for a moment, who they were supposed to be to each other.

Sharp stepped out onto the balcony and the wind tore across her, dragging her hair over her eyes. Her crossed arms hugged tighter, bare skin prickling. He shrugged out of his coat and wrapped it over her shoulders before backing away.

She gripped the railing with both hands. Tipped her face up to the endless scudding grey clouds. Tears tracked down her wind-bitten cheeks. It nearly broke his resolve to give her space. He didn't know how long they stood there, exactly. His HUD filled with requests. Meetings. Questions. Things the head of Mercator couldn't ignore.

He ignored them anyway. Gave her the time she needed to empty herself. When her head finally bowed he said, softly, "I have to go."

She peeled her hands from the balcony and dragged herself across the threshold, handing his coat back to him. He shrugged the coat back on. Relocked the door and the panic shield and double-checked them both. Lingered, not knowing what to say.

"Thank you, my liege." Sharp straightened his coat, an absent gesture.

"May I ask you something?"

Her hands flattened against his lapels. "That's what you've come here to do, isn't it?"

"My other-self betrayed you terribly. And yet—you still believe that, if I lived, I would find a way to stop the expansion that doesn't involve those experiments. Why?"

"I could tell you that this choice, saving you, is the only thread I can't see the end of. And if I can't see the end, then the cycle is broken. Naira will not persist onward into that frozen future, and learn all I have learned, and become what I have become. But the truth is simpler. I'm a fool, my liege. Because I have never stopped believing that you can save me from this hell."

She pressed her hand, briefly, to his cheek. The shock of that contact tore through him. But then she turned away, hunched once more, and it took every scrap of willpower he had to turn and leave.

She was not his Naira, and his Naira needed him. If he was going to be worthy of the faith Sharp placed in him, then he needed to focus. Needed to solve the expansion without the use of those ghastly experiments. Tarquin ignored the concerned glances of the exemplars and returned to his lab.

Part of him wished Sharp hadn't told him about the experiments. That knowledge whispered to him when the data he was trying to unscramble blurred and refused to be straightened out. Every time he looked at the rate of decay on the cargo ship, he knew in his gut that it was too slow. Her assertion—*because it worked*—inexorably drew his thoughts back to flesh.

Tarquin pushed back from holos that weren't giving him the answers he needed.

"Done for the night, my liege?" Dr. Sharp asked over her own array of holos.

Tarquin bit the interior of his cheek. As a scientific endeavor, there was no harm in asking what Dr. Sharp thought of the idea of human bodies as a preferable growth medium for *canus* on relkatite, was there? Even if he never used those experiments, the knowledge might shake a fresh idea lose.

"Not yet," he said. "I only had a thought that I'm not sure we can test."

"Out with it."

"I was thinking," he said, "that while we've confirmed the precise temperature and humidity *canus* thrives within, all our experiments thus far have stalled out short of a forty percent conversion at the highest end. Might there be an element we're missing? Clearly full conversion is possible. Amarthite is proof enough of that."

"Another growth medium, you mean?" Dr. Sharp tapped her nails against the table. "Possible. Probable, even. But what?"

He pounced on the opening. "It occurred to me that, *canus* being so very good at adapting itself, it may be more active in humans than growth mediums. It's mycorrhizal, after all. It may thrive best with a host."

"You'd be hard-pressed to find volunteers for that experiment. Regardless, if it was more active in humans, our pathways would have degraded much faster, wouldn't they?"

"We've always lost some relk in the recycling process, no matter what we try. I wonder if the percent lost isn't because the filters can't catch it to refine it, but because it's amarthite, and they recognize it as a waste product?"

"I'd bet you're right, Doctor, but I don't see how it helps. The percentage is too small to be worthwhile."

"Stacking bonuses, Dr. Sharp. I was scarcely conscious when I encountered my mother on the *Sigillaria*, but I remember the look of her clearly enough. Her print had begun to fail, though she couldn't have been in it long enough for natural failure."

"Hmm. There might be something in that after all."

"We can use body printers to simulate flesh to test the idea," Tarquin offered.

Dr. Sharp looked around the lab. "We should move a printer in here, then. I don't want to waste time running back and forth to the hospital to create samples."

"Agreed," Tarquin said. "I'll alert Dr. Bracken and send people to collect the equipment."

He opened his comms, but an emergency call from Captain Ward flashed in the corner of his eye instead. Gritting his teeth at the delay, he allowed the holo to spring from his arm unfiltered so that Dr. Sharp could see it as well.

"Captain," Tarquin said stiffly, "you've caught me at an unfortunate moment. Please make this quick."

"Apologies, my liege, but it's about the Conservators. Camera drones noticed a group of four headed north and five headed south. They set out in the late morning and are skirting the settlement. We believe they may be a scouting expedition."

"Naira?"

"Uncertain, my liege," Ward said with a twitch of a frown. "They're heavily garbed against the weather. The terrain is too rough for the gait detectors to be accurate, and we haven't gotten close enough yet to secure a voice print. Ex. Sharp was last seen setting up heating nets outside the *Cavendish*, then rendezvoused with Jonsun and went into the ship. We've had no confirmed sighting since. I'd like your permission to widen our patrol to keep an eye on what those people are doing."

"Granted," he said. "Make certain the patrols know not to engage."

"I will, my liege," Ward said, and ended the call.

"Heating nets," Dr. Sharp said. "Smart of her. We should arrange some of our own, before the ground freezes. I'm afraid I've been neglecting my duties with the farmstead, my liege."

The nets. Lost in his research, he'd almost forgotten Sharp's warning.

Not wanting to reveal Sharp's presence to her mother, Tarquin alerted the exemplars to the potential threat via the text channel. They'd look into the possibility.

"Perfectly understandable," Tarquin said, and went back to work. The scouts were Ward's problem. The expansion was his.

FORTY-ONE

Tarquin

Seventh Cradle | *The Present*

Tarquin spent the next day working from the increasingly cramped confines of his home office. The room had never been meant to be a lab, but as reports that the scouting parties were veering closer to the settlement trickled in, his exemplars had insisted.

He wished they hadn't. Separated from the bustle of the lab, his thoughts wandered. He checked Ward's report on the scouting parties' last known locations constantly. Caught himself looking up, toward the ceiling, and the bedroom with its mysterious occupant above.

"My liege," Caldweller said, "you should eat."

He startled, peeling his gaze away from the ceiling, and checked the time. Well past the dinner hour. "Hopefully there's still plenty left." Tarquin pushed away from his desk, but Caldweller stepped in front of the door.

"I'm sorry, my liege, but the community center is off limits until we're certain those scouting parties are well beyond our borders."

Being confined to his home to work was one thing, but he had yet to eat a meal alone since Naira had been taken. An inexplicable fear wound through him, his palms dampening with sweat. He could override Caldweller. His word was law on the settlement, and if he wanted to eat with the others, his exemplars could hardly stop him—Tarquin pushed the urge down.

"Please have Marko bring a plate here, then." Maybe continuing to work would occupy his thoughts, if he could avoid being distracted. Unlikely, when occasionally he could hear the creak of a floorboard underneath said distraction's pacing steps. "Actually, have Marko bring Sharp's plate as well. To the small dining room, please."

Caldweller's brows lifted. "Is that wise, my liege?"

No.

"We both must eat. And perhaps I'll be able to coax more information out of her."

Caldweller's expression made it clear that he didn't approve, but what was Tarquin to do? Sharp held information that might be useful—details, perhaps, that she didn't recognize as relevant to solving the expansion. It wasn't as if he was making viable progress on his own.

He hadn't expected her to be wearing Naira's clothes, though he should have. This was her second full day in the prison of their bedroom, and she'd showered—the scent of Naira's bathing items briefly overwhelmed the savory aromas of their dinner, piercing the fragile defenses he had built. Her hair was shaggy with damp, a curious tilt to her head as she shuffled into the room, her hands cuffed together before her body.

"That's unnecessary." He gestured to the handcuffs.

"It's the only way I'll allow this, my liege," Caldweller said stiffly.

"Lee's right," Sharp said. "And regardless, I don't mind."

Reluctantly, Tarquin nodded. Caldweller guided her into a chair and lingered a drawn-out moment.

"You may go, Exemplar," Tarquin said.

"My liege." His grip tightened around Sharp's arm. "I don't like this."

"Noted."

Caldweller schooled his expression to neutrality and bowed before leaving the room.

When the door had clicked shut behind him, she said, "He's right to be wary."

"You've stated that you're here to save my life. I hardly think dinner with you is dangerous."

"How easily you believe me." Her tone was strange. Amused in a way that implied she might be laughing at him.

"Are you mocking me?"

"No." She took in the small room he and Naira had used to eat breakfast in every day they'd been together on that world. "Merely observing."

"And what do you see?"

"Loneliness."

The frankness of that statement punched him in the gut. He felt suddenly ridiculous—exposed. He'd told himself he'd brought her here to coax information from her, but how transparent was he, really? It had been to soothe his own aches. His own fears.

Her gaze trailed over the meal, carefully arranged to please her, the bottle of wine between them, the lowered lights and the window beside them that looked out over the same forest the balcony above watched over, bioluminescent insects dancing in the far distance, and the pity on her face stole his voice.

"I'm not her."

"I know, I—I know." He couldn't bear to look at her, and so he turned his attention to the food, though he could scarcely taste it. "Jonsun has sent scouting parties into the woods. We believe Naira is with one of those groups."

"She is."

"Is she trying to escape?"

"Sometimes."

Sharp took a slow bite of her food, and though her head was bowed to hide her face, the smile that burst free warmed him. Even if the decades had worn her down, the spark of herself remained, carefully sheltered.

If he was going to urge her to share more information, he needed to reframe his questions. Ask her less about possibilities, and more about concrete matters.

"Were you?"

She looked up, examining him closely. "No. I was too afraid of what Jonsun would do to Kav in retaliation. I didn't know then that Kav had a way of erasing his map from Jonsun's servers. We couldn't talk, you see. The whole ship and all our comms were constantly monitored."

"What did I do?" He struggled to control his excitement—that was the most specific information he'd gotten out of her yet.

Sharp set her fork down and leaned back, cuffed hands resting on the edge of the table. "Broke my heart."

"How?"

"You told me what you truly thought of me."

Confusion puckered his brow. "But I adore you—*her*. She is everything I admire, everything I could ever hope for. I don't understand."

The muffled sounds of an argument brewed on the other side of the door. She returned once more to picking at her plate. "You'd better check on that, my liege."

He made himself push back from the table, the desire to throttle whoever had made that noise briefly thrumming through him. The impulse surprised him, and he shoved it aside. "Excuse me a moment."

He found Marko in the hallway, arguing with a red-faced Caldweller. Tarquin shut the door quickly behind him. "What's happened?"

Marko tugged his apron straight with an annoyed sniff and looked Caldweller dead in the eye. "You have to tell him."

"Tell me what?" Tarquin asked.

"It's nothing, my liege."

"Lee." Marko hooked his hands around his hips. "We talked about this. She might be dangerous."

"You told your husband classified information?" Of all the people to break protocol, he never would have thought—

"No!" Caldweller shouted. His cheeks burned brighter, and he clamped a hand over his mouth. "I mean, forgive me, I—"

"My liege," Marko said smoothly, "you've ordered her favorite foods the past two nights. Meals that you yourself don't enjoy. Lee didn't tell me anything. He didn't have to."

"Then what did you talk to him about?"

Caldweller had a battle of contorting expressions with his husband, then let out an explosive breath. "We'd better discuss this in private, my liege, if that's all right."

Tarquin glanced at the closed door. She'd only just started to open up to him. "If this can't wait, then it'd better be quick."

Marko ushered them into the nearby kitchen, and before Tarquin could figure out what was happening he'd pushed both Tarquin and Caldweller into seats across from each other at an island bar, a steaming mug of cocoa each between them. Tarquin blinked at the mugs. Had Marko prepared those in advance?

"What's this about?"

Caldweller rubbed his forehead. "There's no easy way to say this, my liege. It's about Naira—our Naira, not Sharp. The night before we casted back from M-U, I interrupted her preparing to go take on the World single-handed."

"What? But that would be suicide."

"She knew that, my liege."

"Ah." He clutched the mug Marko had given him as if it were the edge of a cliff.

"She'd been acting off, ever since your assassination. Twitchy, I guess. I had an idea of what it was, and I confronted her about it. But, my liege—don't react until I've finished, please."

Tarquin nodded, throat dry.

Caldweller gathered himself. Reached across the table and covered Tarquin's hands with his own. "My liege, the night you asked her to marry you, she turned you down."

He'd suspected that might be true, but still the confirmation stunned him. His head felt numb, thoughts fleeing him the second they surfaced and all he could remember, in that moment, was the delight that had lit her up from within when he'd told her what moment had been saved within her ring.

"Don't misunderstand," Caldweller rushed out. "She wanted to marry you. She did. It was the family—Mercator—that made her say no. When she changed her answer, it wasn't a lie, my liege. It was out of love."

"It was out of guilt." Tarquin knew the truth of those words as intimately as he knew himself. That she loved him, he had no doubt, but for her to lose him—lose a charge she had sworn to protect—at such a crucial moment would have eaten her alive.

Marko squeezed his shoulder, startling him back to himself. "She was going to tell you when she got back."

But she'd never gotten to come home, and Jonsun had vivisected her mind to wield that piece of her against him—what else did Jonsun know? Tarquin looked to the wall between the kitchen and the dining nook, where he'd left Sharp, and wondered. Why hadn't she told him something so pivotal? He'd asked directly. She'd evaded the question.

"She lied to me" was all he could manage to say.

"It doesn't have to mean anything," Caldweller said.

Sharp opened the door. In her cuffed hands she carried the wine bottle by the neck like a club, and her eyes shone with such fury Tarquin shrank away from her. Caldweller leapt to his feet, knocking his chair to the ground. The roar of a gunshot made Tarquin's ears buzz, glass shattering, and he cried out—expecting the bottle to break. Expecting Sharp to fall.

She wasn't hurt. Sharp sprinted toward him, swung herself around the counter. Tarquin's mouth fell open. The windowed back door was shattered, and Caldweller's gun arm hung limp, blood gushing from his bicep.

"Get down!" Caldweller scrambled over the table and crashed into Tarquin and Marko, knocking them both to the ground in a tangle of limbs and Tarquin's now-busted chair.

Marko grunted beside him, shocked, and Tarquin almost laughed— now Marko knew how Tarquin felt every time the exemplars piled on him—but strangled the sound as Sharp snarled. There was a thud. A crash.

A voice he didn't know said, "Fuck! I won't let you—!" Then broke off in a strangled howl.

"Naira!" Tarquin struggled to wriggle free, but Caldweller held him tight. Even Marko clutched his arm, holding him down.

"It's not her," Marko said. "That's not your Naira."

"But—" How could he explain himself? She'd tell him the same thing.

More glass broke. A gunshot cracked. The fight went to the ground; he could hear them struggling across the broken glass and then—silence for so long he thought his heart would burst.

"Clear." Sharp's voice was breathless.

Caldweller let him stand at last. Sharp leaned against the broken door to the back patio, panting. Her wrists were cut, blood dripping off the cuffs, and she carried half the broken wine bottle in one hand, her clothes soaked through with wine or blood—the heady scents of both filled the air, stirred by the chilly night wind coming in through the ruined door.

"You're cut." He rushed to her, despite Caldweller's grunt of protest, and took the broken bottle to set it aside so that he could get a closer look at the wounds on her wrists.

"Shallow." She was breathing harder, the color fading from her face.

He nudged the cuff aside as gently as he could, and a hot spurt of blood erupted, making his own hands slippery. "You're bleeding out."

"Shove the cuff back in the wound, my liege. My pathways will slow the worst of it."

"Right. Sorry."

Sharp grunted, dropping her head against the doorframe. "She missed," she said to herself. "Thank fuck she missed."

"Missed?" Some of the fog of his terror cleared. "Lee, are you all right?"

"Fine." He grunted as he sat down heavily on one of the few intact stools. "My wound really is shallow. Bracken is on their way, my liege, and Cass and Helms are sweeping the area to see if the attacker had an accomplice."

"She didn't," Sharp said. "Jana just..." She swallowed, and Tarquin was astonished to realize she was on the verge of tears. "She didn't."

"Jana?" Marko looked utterly baffled, his hands stilling in their fussing with Caldweller's wound. "The child? Oh, god."

Marko ran through the kitchen, not hearing his husband cry out for him to wait, and staggered out the door to trip—Sharp caught him before he could fall, hissing at the strain put upon her wounds.

"That...that's an adult."

"And a giant pain in my ass," Sharp said, but her voice was warm with grudging respect, and the glance she threw the body suffused with regret. Tarquin took her shaking hands once more, supporting them as best he could. Her skin was cold, and sweat made her face glow.

There was a small sound, a thin wheeze. Tarquin was certain Sharp had made it and was about to collapse before Marko said, "She's alive."

"Get back!" Caldweller shouted with more fear than Tarquin had ever heard in his voice. He shoved past Tarquin, knocking him into Sharp, and reached for his husband's shoulder—but Marko sank to his knees and took the dying woman's hand.

"Little one," Marko said. Caldweller stopped his desperate reach, freezing in place for the first time since Tarquin had known him. "I don't know what happened, for you to come to us with violence, but whatever it was I ... I'm so, so sorry."

"Dad." Jana's voice was such a thin quaver that the only reason Tarquin heard it at all was because everyone had gone deathly silent. "Kill them. Before it's too late, kill them both."

"What? Why?" Marko asked, but Jana's eyes had glazed, her final breath rattling in her chest.

"Did ... did she call you Dad?" Tarquin asked.

"Oh, Lee," Sharp said, and *tsked*. "Go on, tell him. It seems I'm not the only one keeping secrets in this household, my liege."

Caldweller's breath slowed, the heaving of his chest settling as he held his husband's worried gaze. Marko tipped his chin down, encouraging, and Caldweller sighed.

"Naira, she ..." He gestured toward Sharp, then winced and clamped his good hand down over the gash on his arm. "She paid the fees for us to adopt Jana and Tarq, my liege. Out of ... out of your accounts. I told her not to, but you know how she is when she's set on something. We can pay you back, I swear it. Garnish my wages if you have to."

Tarquin waved for him to be silent, pulling up his accounts to check the transactions surrounding that day. If he'd missed a payment that large, then perhaps he'd missed something else, some clue to what she'd been doing, but—"Oh. This amount is nothing."

"It was *everything* to us," Marko snarled.

Tarquin blinked, taken aback, but Marko was already rushing out of the room, tears bright in his eyes. He slammed the door shut behind him.

"Damnit," Caldweller muttered, then bowed stiffly to Tarquin. "My liege, forgive us, we—"

"Stop that," Tarquin said. "You did nothing wrong. I'm the one who stuck my foot in my mouth. Go ahead, talk to him, but—wait, Sharp, does this mean they're a family together? In the future?"

"In my timeline," Sharp said, "this is the first time Jana and Marko have met."

Caldweller's jaw cracked. Tarquin had never heard him do that before, and startled at the sound.

"She moved like you." Caldweller's voice was leaden.

"You saw that from the ground?" Sharp asked.

"I saw enough."

She lifted her chin. Straightened her shoulders as if she expected a fight, even though Tarquin was still holding her cold, trembling hands. "I trained her."

"I think you raised her," Caldweller said. "Which makes me wonder, Sharp, why she was aiming right at you."

"Was she?"

Caldweller peeled his hand off the wound and glanced down at it, then arched a brow at her. "I'm pretty sure of the angle."

"Jana knows I'm here to save the liege. She couldn't get a clear shot at him without hitting you or Marko lethally, so she went for me."

"Did you really raise her?" Tarquin asked.

Sharp turned her head away. "Sanj looked after them, mostly. Both of the kids. But Jana never let go of the promise of a family with the Caldwellers, so when she was old enough to cast, she came straight to Seventh Cradle. I...I did the best I could, Lee."

Caldweller looked like he had more he wanted to say, but he held back when the door swung inward, Bracken and Cass entering the room.

"Watch her," Caldweller growled to Cass, then left the kitchen in search of his husband.

"What was that about?" Cass asked.

"He doesn't trust me." Sharp let herself slump against the doorframe as Bracken took her hands and began their examination.

"Well, he shouldn't," Cass said, slightly bemused, as if this was the most obvious piece of information in the world. Sharp huffed and tipped her head to them in agreement. Cass poked their head out of the broken door and nudged the downed body with their boot. "I thought we killed this one when she assassinated Liege Tarquin?"

"You did," Sharp said. "She must have sent her map back again."

"Hang on," Tarquin said, realization dawning. "If Jana was a child when the freeze began, how did she survive long enough for her mind to be mapped and printed in the future? How did she cast herself anywhere at all?"

"I told you, my liege. Your experiments work. Until Naira ends them."

INTERLUDE

The World

Miller-Urey Station | The Present

It is losing pieces of itself. Segments of the whole go dark as they are ripped from its orbit. The once shining constellation of its consciousness is dimming, dimming, and for all it tries to claw them back, it cannot reach all the parts of itself.

And in its desperation, it learns.

As it devours, consuming so that it can grow to a critical mass large enough to reach the pieces of itself that have been taken, it senses a shift in the world. A contraction, however brief. Above all else it has learned the benefits of testing. Experimenting. And so in some vessels it burns with hunger until it is bloated and pained, until its filaments burst from the skin of its hosts and they die beneath the onslaught. The loss of its hosts is irrelevant. It cannot be killed in the way that humans experience death.

But if the tearing apart of the worlds continues, it will lose its network. It will lose itself.

And so it grows. Allows itself to devour uninhibited those energies that have always given it life, and as its mass increases, it can reach farther, reconnect pieces of itself that it lost and urge those to grow, too. The expansion stutters. Slows. Begins again.

Its multitudes are not enough.

For in humanity's effort to starve *canus* from their bodies, they have moved the bulk of its food beyond its reach. Those misguided, hateful creatures may accidentally orchestrate the end of them all.

But there is a nascent glimmer of itself on that far horizon. A segment so far out of reach of the whole that it is scarcely noticeable.

Its salvation lies with that single spark. It must reach it and bid it to hunger as it has never hungered before. But it is so very far away, and drifting farther still. *Canus* must grow strong enough to reach that spark.

From the *Einkorn* it has learned the benefit of incremental loops. If it is mass it needs, then mass it will obtain. And, as much as the truth galls it, it has learned another lesson from the *Einkorn*—when all else has failed, call out for Naira Sharp. She will not let the worlds fall.

Technology has failed it. Humanity has failed it. And so it consumes, and its hosts die, and it reprints them and does it all over again, striving for the moment when it can reach the savior of the *Einkorn* at last.

It is surprised to discover that this thought brings with it a gentle warmth. Not the consuming heat of biological needs, but something else. Something inexplicable in all the long centuries of its existence.

It thinks this might be hope.

Curious, to learn such a thing from the being who was once the avatar of its destruction.

FORTY-TWO

Naira

Seventh Cradle | The Present

It took them two days to cross the thickest stretch of the forest and curve closer to the river. They'd been walking through rain and hail ever since they'd set out, and Naira was certain she'd never been colder in her life, but she refused to build a fire at night. They were too close to the settlement, and she'd already picked up signs that Merc-Sec was keeping an eye on them.

Jadhav and her team were, unfortunately, talkative, and played into Kuma's bubbly nature. They chattered with soft voices, wary of Naira hushing them. Mostly she didn't curb their talk, as long as it wasn't about anything sensitive. Merc-Sec already knew where they were, and every day they were out there, that knowledge rang warning bells. Tarquin was unlikely to order an attack, but the patrols had been skewing closer. As if they were trying to push them against the river, where they'd have fewer routes to escape.

Naira picked her way over an unstable clump of roots and had to shift her rifle to a one-handed grip to brace her hand against the slick bark of a drenched tree trunk. The resinous, warm aroma of the living wood mingled with the persistent, cool patter of the rain, and she took a deep breath, anchoring herself to that scent. This planet would outlive her. There was comfort in that.

The others were lagging behind. Naira caught Kuma's eye above their heads. Kuma nodded—they needed to rest.

As much as she hated dragging this out, she could hardly work Jadhav's team to the bone and expect them to be effective if a fight broke out. They'd been on the *Cavendish* for the past year, and while they'd had gym equipment, it wasn't the same as living on a planet. Naira was fresh-printed, still full in her strength, and Kuma had more endurance than sense.

"Time for camp." Naira scratched her knife into the tree before turning off the digger's follow-on tracker.

"I'll never be warm again." Agosta exaggerated every word, a twinkle in his dark brown eyes visible even through the rain.

"We're not starting a fire. Come on, you slugs, help me set up."

"Finally, sustenance," Jadhav said with a dramatic sigh.

"Bunch of babies," Kuma muttered under her breath.

Jadhav and Agosta pretended offense, but Fowler pushed himself to stand side by side with Naira and looked to her for direction.

He was a serious young man, square-faced and long-limbed. If there was work to be done, he did it quietly and efficiently, and while he had lagged behind with the others, he always seemed to have a scrap of perseverance left whenever the campsite needed setting up. Naira was grateful for that. Her own hands were too numb to fix the tarp ropes without fumbling.

She pointed down a slope, to a small clearing of crushed litterfall that might have been an animal bed. Fowler nodded. Together, they got most of the tarp set up while the others cleared the sticks and rocks from the area and laid out the bedrolls.

Crammed together beneath the tarp, it wasn't comfortable, but it was companionable, and their ration packets heated up when they crushed them, providing some warmth. Naira had forbidden alcohol, to Kuma's grand disappointment. They were in enemy territory.

Kuma kept the chatter rolling, telling them embellished stories of how cold it had been on the *Cavendish* when they'd printed into it, and how this was nothing. Jadhav and the others were always hungry for Kuma's early-Conservator stories. Naira was happy to let Kuma tell those tales. She didn't feel much enthusiasm for the old days.

The rain slackened, reduced to a delicate patter through the leaves. In its absence, the rush of the river grew louder. Fowler cocked his head to the side, leaning slightly to get a better ear for the new sound. The rest of Jadhav's team fell silent, tense.

They didn't know what it was. They'd been born on stations; the largest body of water they'd probably seen was a fountain in a MERIT-sponsored public garden.

"Have you three ever seen a river?" Naira asked.

Fowler turned those intense eyes on her, but it was Jadhav who answered. "Only in video, E-X."

"Come on, then," Naira said. "We've got time before the light fails."

She led them through the trees to the rocky shore. Every last one of them stopped cold as they emerged from the tree line, forming a shaggy row. The river had no name that Naira was aware of—it was simply "the river" to the settlement. A wide stretch of lazy water that meandered its way down from the mountains to lie vibrantly blue across the land.

Insects skimmed across the surface, drawn by the fall of night. The occasional ripple broke the water, a fish snagging a bug for their dinner. In the low light, the teal-bright water was a subdued navy-hued grey, but it was beautiful all the same. Fowler made a soft sound in the back of his throat.

Naira crouched down and ran a hand over the slick river stones, seeking ones that were broad and flat. When she'd found five, she handed them out to the others and kept one for herself. They looked at her quizzically, turning the stones over in their hands.

"Watch me first," Naira said.

She approached the river and pulled her arm back, moving slowly at first so that they'd note the motion, then hurled the rock out across the water. It skipped four times before sinking with a plunk. Delighted grins brightened all their faces and they rushed to mirror her movements, having to stifle their laughter as their first few attempts went haywire.

Once they had the hang of it, Naira drifted back to let them have at it, her hood tugged up high to keep her eyes free of rain. Kuma joined her after a few successful attempts of her own. They stood shoulder to shoulder in silence that used to be friendly, but was now rife with the possibility of missteps.

"You okay, Nai?" Kuma asked in a near-whisper.

Jadhav's team was bickering about Agosta getting more skips because he'd stolen a better rock from Fowler. They weren't paying attention.

"What part of me? Got a lot of injuries I'm nursing right now." She matched Kuma's volume, but kept her tone light, in case Kuma wasn't asking about where she stood with...all of this.

"You know what I mean," Kuma said with a small sniff, and pressed the heel of her palm over her heart.

"No." A simple enough answer. It could mean anything. She could defend it, if she had to.

Kuma nodded, slowly, and tilted her head in the direction of the settlement without taking her eyes from the team. "Can you hold?"

"I'll hold."

"I've got your back." Kuma bumped her shoulder against Naira's, and Naira bumped her back. She felt like crying, the relief was so strong.

"What did you mean?" she asked. "When you said we weren't Jo's inner circle?"

"Huh?" Kuma turned to her, brows drawn down in confusion. "I don't know what you're talking about."

A gunshot cracked from the woods, startling a cloud of birds across the river into the air in a thrashing of grey wings.

Fowler's head burst into pink mist.

FORTY-THREE

Naira

Seventh Cradle | The Present

Exemplar instincts pushed Naira to move before she'd fully registered what had happened. She swept Kuma's legs and piled on top
of her, rolling toward an outcropping of stone. They pitched up against
the boulders and scrambled to disentangle themselves, reaching for their
sidearms. Their rifles were back at the bivouac. How could she have left
her rifle behind?

"Cover!" Naira hoped the team had reacted before she'd shouted, or
they were already dead. Hot blood slushed down the side of her neck.
The bullet had torn off half her ear before it'd struck Fowler.

Gunshots peppered the ground near the boulder and she waited
a beat, then raised her arm and fired in the direction of those gunshots. Someone screamed. She grinned fiercely at that sound, and felt
immediately ill at her own reaction. That was Merc-Sec. Those were her
friends.

The people screaming on the beach were also her friends.

"Fuck, fuck, fuck," she said. "Hold fire, you bastards!"

They responded by emptying a full clip directly into the boulder. Assholes. Kuma tapped her and pointed over her shoulder. Naira craned
her neck to follow the gesture and found Agosta lying on the shore. His

chest struggled to rise as a stream of blood washed out of him to join the river. He'd be dead in minutes.

Kuma's eyes were wider than Naira had ever seen them, her body locked up. "Nai," she said, "I can't die out here."

"You won't."

A branch cracked. Naira fired over the top of the boulder without bothering to look. Kuma gripped her arm hard enough to hurt.

"I mean it, I'm getting close to the end, I can't die here."

"What are you talking about?"

"My map. Last reprint was forty-eight percent chance to crack. You know I have orders not to print over fifty percent."

"What? You were in the low single digits last I checked."

"It's been a rough year, Nai," she said with a bitter smile.

"Okay. Okay." She cupped Kuma's cheek and looked into her eyes. "I've got you. We've got this. You with me?"

Kuma's jaw tensed beneath her hand, but she nodded firmly.

Someone crashed through the trees, and Merc-Sec rifles cracked. Naira stood, Kuma at her side, and they fired into the trees, aiming for the grey-and-green uniform Naira had worn most of her adult life.

They winged two of the three, the rifle clattering from the hands of the nearest—Naira had caught him in the shoulder. The other staggered, falling into a tree. Crossfire roared through the woods. Naira yanked Kuma back down, recognizing the sound of Jadhav's weapon. When that burst of fire paused to reload, Naira popped up again.

Jadhav screamed. The Merc-Sec who'd fallen into the tree was down, head opened, but the one with the injured shoulder was up, trying to keep his bulk behind a tree, and failing, as he fired with his off hand at Naira. She shot him in the other shoulder. He screamed before dropping to his knees. The weapon tumbled from his hand.

Kuma vaulted the boulder, and Naira swallowed down a shout at her to stay under cover. Kuma knew what she was doing. Naira reloaded, hating the silence that had descended. Before she could finish, another rifle crack sounded, and Kuma fired three times in response.

"Nai!" Kuma barked.

She sprinted into the woods. Kuma slouched against a tree, bleeding from a shot in her side, face grim, but focused.

Naira skidded to a halt to keep from crashing into her. "How bad?"

"Graze," Kuma gritted out. "Disarm that fucker. Find Jadhav."

Naira found the Merc-Sec crumpled against a ball of roots. His face was twisted with agony, but she knew him. Richardson. He'd shared a table with her and Ward and egged her on to tell stories. He was holding one destroyed hand in the other, panting, practically biting through his lip to keep from screaming. Kuma was a better shot than Naira remembered.

"Don't move." She made sure he saw her aim at his chest.

"You are so fucking dead." He scrambled for his sidearm with his good hand.

Naira kicked the weapon out of his reach and then kicked him in the side to roll him onto his stomach. He called her every foul name he could think of as she planted her knee in his back and disarmed him.

When he was light a few pounds of killing metal, she used his own cuffs to bind his hands behind his back and left him there, facedown in the dirt. Kuma had gotten her senses back and was disarming the Merc-Sec Naira had shot in the shoulders.

She scanned the forest and found Jadhav. The captain knelt on the beach beside Agosta, sleeves soaked to the elbow in blood, trying to stanch the bleeding. Naira grimaced. That was never going to work. But they had bigger problems.

"Kuma, HUDs!" Naira shouted.

Kuma rolled her prisoner back over. "Where?"

"Left ring finger to elbow," Naira said, having been drilled on this process more times than she could count. "Right-side jaw, third connection at the temple."

"Got it!" Kuma shouted back.

"If you have painkiller pathways, use them," Naira told Richardson. She drew her knife and crouched over him.

He spat in her face. "I've already called this in; you're too late."

"Not the call-in I'm worried about."

She pushed the side of his face into the dirt, holding him still with one hand. His eyes squeezed shut, bracing himself, and she hesitated. Naira had done this to more captives than she could name while serving Acaelus, but the pain on Richardson's face wrenched something inside of her.

She could hear Tarquin as clearly as if he was standing next to her, in the moment after she'd removed his pathways in the elevator, horror and disgust raw in his voice: *Father did this to you.*

Naira had never hesitated on a pathway removal in her life. She locked up, head buzzing.

"Nai!" Kuma bellowed. "I need you!"

"Shit," she muttered under her breath. Before she could second-guess herself again, she stripped the pathway out of his face, then flipped him over and removed the ID and permissions embedded in his arm as well. He screamed until his voice gave out. She'd hear that sound for the rest of her life.

Naira left him there, whimpering and bleeding, and scrambled over the rain-slick ground to join Kuma on the shore beside Jadhav. The younger woman was bent over the body of her friend, one hand on his chest wound, bearing down for all she was worth. Tears streamed down her face. Her other arm was limp, soaked in blood that wasn't all Agosta's.

Naira dropped to her knees across from Jadhav and took her face in her hands, making the Conservator look at her. "Captain. Listen to me. Merc-Sec called this in. We have to run."

"We can't leave them here!"

"We'll reprint them. I promise. But we have to get the fuck out of here, okay? Dying's one thing. Being taken captive is another."

She scrubbed the back of her good hand over her face, dragging snot that mingled with blood to wash away in the rain. "Yeah. I'm okay."

"That arm's not," Kuma said. "Show me."

Naira cut away Jadhav's sleeve while Kuma pulled out her med kit. The bullet had torn through her bicep, leaving a neat hole in the front and a shredded maw of flesh in the back. Jadhav clenched her jaw against the pain as Kuma patched her up. That arm wouldn't be usable for a while, but it would heal. Naira stole a glance at Kuma and found she'd already bandaged her side. Naira's half ear was barely worth remarking on.

"Up," Naira said. "Captain, collect our rifles from the bivouac. Kuma, help me wrangle the prisoners. We got here in two days being careful, but if we haul ass, I think we can make it back in one."

"All of the rifles?" Jadhav glanced at the bodies.

"They don't fucking grow on trees, do they?"

Jadhav paled, but nodded and seemed to gather herself before sprinting off to the campsite. Naira called Jonsun, emergency line, full alert.
He answered immediately. His eyes widened upon seeing the blood still
pouring from her half ear. Head wounds were bastards.

"What happened?"

"Ambushed by Merc-Sec," she said. "Three of them. Fowler and
Agosta are dead, Kuma and Jadhav are injured but mobile. I've got two
Merc-Sec prisoners I'm bringing back, and it's only a matter of time
until another squad is on our asses. I need cover and I need an intercept.
Here's my route." She pushed through a rough map she'd made of her
intended path. It skirted the most difficult terrain and cut straight lines
through smoother areas.

Jonsun reviewed it and nodded. "I'll send an intercept, but I don't
know how much cover we can provide without aerial access. What
about the boring machine?"

"I'm going to leave it where it is, Jo, what do you want from me?"

He held up his hands in surrender. "Just checking to see if you could
use the tunnels."

"No, they know where we are. If we go down there, they could trap
us with a cave-in. Using the rough terrain to slow them down is our best
shot."

"Don't let them take you. Kav will never let me hear the end of it if
they get you."

There was a slight teasing note to his tone, but she caught the edge
hidden behind it—*come back, or I'll think you orchestrated this to escape and
take it out on Kav.* Jadhav crashed through the trees, swearing softly as she
struggled to corral their gear one-handed. Naira glanced over at her and
winced.

"I'm dead serious about that intercept. We're in bad shape."

"Understood. Good luck, Nai."

She cut the call and took her own rifle, along with Agosta's and Fowler's, from Jadhav. Kuma had gotten the prisoners on their feet and, mer-
cifully as far as Naira was concerned, gagged them. She didn't want to
listen to whatever fresh new insults they came up with for her on the run
back. Naira pushed the route she'd shown Jonsun through to the others.

"This is our path. Fast as we can, no breaks. No whining. Kuma, when Mercator sends drones, I want you showing off your shooting, clear? Knock those tin cans out of the sky."

Kuma patted her rifle. "They won't know what hit 'em."

Jadhav glared at the prisoners. "Why are we bringing them? They'll slow us down. I say we drop 'em and bolt."

"We're bringing them," Naira grated, "because Mercator outguns us so badly our only chance might be negotiation, and they're the only bargaining chips we've got. Clear?"

"Right." Jadhav straightened. "Sorry."

"Let's go." Naira kicked the nearest Merc-Sec in the ass to get him moving.

Dark settled over the land, smothering her senses, an endless empty chamber in which her heart and breath were too loud, her steps clumsy. The time for stealth was over. She grabbed one prisoner, Kuma grabbed the other, and they ran into the night, leaving the blood to wash away into the river.

FORTY-FOUR

Tarquin

Seventh Cradle | The Present

Tarquin couldn't figure out why the human tissue samples weren't working as expected. The lab had transformed into a carnival of horrors, filled with stasis shields housing hearts, lungs, limbs, and every other piece of the human body they could keep viable beneath those shields. The samples they used were printed for this sole purpose. They'd never been part of a real body.

A small part of him wondered if that was the problem.

"I can't help but wish it was faster," Tarquin said.

"As do I," Dr. Sharp said.

She'd been dropping the *my liege* more and more often lately. Even if it was because she was too exhausted to remember, he enjoyed the familiarity. It was a sliver of something good in his world.

There had been an increase in the decay rate, but it was nowhere near enough to pump the brakes on the expansion. Sharp's statement nagged at him. Not that he'd ever use their friends for experimentation—the very thought was abhorrent—but he couldn't ignore that she'd claimed his experiment had worked. Was it the full print itself that made the difference?

The temptation to suggest infecting a complete blank danced on the tip of his tongue, but he bit back the impulse. *Canus*-infected blanks were another misprint assault waiting to happen.

Cass brought in coffee. They cast a wary eye over the arrangement, and Tarquin could hardly blame them. Infant-sized stasis shields wrapped around organs and limbs were hardly an appealing sight. He'd grown inured to it, and needed Cass's brief flash of revulsion to remind himself that this research walked an edge he needed to be careful not to fall over.

When the coffee was nothing but thin acid in his belly, Ward called, more grim-faced than usual.

"My liege," she said. "There's been an incident. Thirty minutes ago I received a report from our southern patrol that the Conservator scouting party bivouacked for the night, then walked toward the river, leaving their rifles behind. Suspecting the party meant to bathe, which would have required them to remove their coats and reveal their identities, I ordered the patrol to follow at a distance and confirm any known agents.

"Fifteen minutes later, I received this call from Merc-Sec Richardson."

Ward pushed through shaky footage, taken from the soldier's ocular implant. He'd been hunkered behind a tree, the steady wash of rain blurring his vision and giving the woods around him a spectral grey glow. Three Conservators Tarquin didn't recognize laughed among themselves down by the waterline.

Two Conservators he very much recognized stood side by side, a ways back from the other group. They hadn't removed their hoods, but with the camera so close, Tarquin recognized Naira's vigilant posture. The broader woman next to her bumped her shoulder against Naira's. Tarquin's breath snagged in his chest. That was Kuma with her, he was certain.

Richardson, the soldier, was subvocalizing. "Voice recognition confirmed for Sharp and Ichikawa, others unknown."

Ward said, in the recording, "Good job, soldier. Fall back before they see you."

"Aye, Captain."

Someone fired. Blood burst from the side of Naira's hood. A Conservator by the waterline dropped dead. Naira tackled Kuma, hood falling back as she rolled them behind an outcropping. The firefight was a diz-zying mess. Even watching through Richardson's eyes, Tarquin had no clue how any of them knew what was happening, or where to shoot.

Richardson hit the ground, groaning. Screams echoed through the forest all around him, then Naira's blood-splattered face filled the Merc-Sec's view. Fury made every line in her face taut, but there was a crease at the corner of her eyes that Tarquin recognized as fear. This wasn't part of whatever plan she'd been working. This endangered something. She told Richardson to lean on his painkiller pathways. The feed cut.

"Who fired?" was all Tarquin could manage to say.

"Blesson, my liege." Ward sneered. "If we get him back, he'll be pun-ished for disobeying orders."

"What do you mean, if we get him back?"

"My liege, Ex. Sharp has taken Richardson and Blesson prisoner."

"Why would she do such a thing?"

Ward took in a slow breath. "Leverage. We have no cameras in the area, and the extended heat map is unreliable at that range. But we have enough data to extrapolate that she's running back to the *Cavendish*." Ward shared a map of the area that she'd marked up. "To reach the *Cav-endish* at speed, Sharp's going to have to cross a clearing in the woods that brings her near our southwestern fence. She took the prisoners to bargain her way through."

"Do we have ID on the Conservator bodies? Are either of them Kav Ayuba?"

"Not yet," Ward said. "I've scrambled a team to collect the bodies. But, my liege, I know what you're thinking. She took her people and tried to run. We're certain Ayuba wasn't the one left alive—that was an unidentified woman. If he's dead on the beach, then the escape attempt is blown."

"Fuck," he breathed out, and for once, Dr. Sharp didn't reprimand him for his language. If she'd been escaping and he'd missed the oppor-tunity because Merc-Sec had gotten trigger happy...No. He couldn't dwell. Couldn't spiral. "What do you recommend, Captain?"

Ward already had the ramrod posture of a soldier, and still she seemed to straighten. "My liege, this may be the only chance we'll have to cap-ture her."

"Capture?" An unsteady hope threaded through him.

"It's what I would advise. Don't matter either way if she's on our side. If she's our agent, then we've got her back and can recover whatever intel she's gathered. If she's not, we'll have taken away one of Jonsun's most powerful supporters."

"Please proceed with the capture," he said, and prayed that Sharp had been right. That Kav had some sort of method to protect his map from Jonsun's retaliation, if it came to that.

Ward's jaw flexed. "You should know, my liege, that Sharp won't let us take her quietly. Even if she's on our side, she'll fight us every step."

Tarquin stared at his hands, braced against the table, for a long moment. He couldn't do nothing, could he? She'd killed his soldiers. If he let her get away with it, Merc-Sec would resent him. He couldn't handle a coup brewing beneath his roof on top of everything else. If he ignored the skirmish entirely, he'd be doing precisely what his sister had claimed—putting Naira's comfort above the safety of the people of Mercator. Naira herself wouldn't want that.

Tarquin closed his eyes. "Don't harm her, please. If it's at all possible."

"We'll do our best, my liege," Ward said in a voice that didn't quite hide the fact that his request was a fairy tale.

"I'll meet you and Alvero at the security suite." He ended the call.

Without the holo between them, Dr. Sharp's face was a mixture of dread and disgust. Slowly, she pulled a fist away from her mouth. "You're sending your people to hunt her." Her voice was low, scraping down his spine.

"If Naira was escaping, then she's unlikely to put up much of a fight. She'll be fine."

"And if she wasn't?"

"I can't ignore that she's killed our people. If there was any other way, then I—"

She turned her back to him. "You're needed at Merc-Sec, my liege. Don't let me keep you."

Tarquin stared at the rigid line of the doctor's neck, as if she were held together by nothing more than string and determination. Maybe she was. There were nights when he certainly felt that way about himself.

There should be something he could say to repair this, to make her understand that he didn't want to put Naira at risk, but he had no choice. A lot of evil had been committed under the banner of having no choice.

There was only one way to be certain of his course of action. Tarquin left her mother behind and sought Sharp's counsel.

He found her sitting on the floor with her back resting against their bed—*his* bed—facing the blocked-off balcony. Her head was bowed, forehead pressed to her knees. Bandages wrapped her wrists. She didn't so much as glance up when the door clicked shut.

Tarquin hesitated, feeling as if he were intruding even though it was his own bedroom. He'd half expected to open that door and discover her gone—escaped to join the fight in some other way—and to find her there, huddled alone in the dark, shook him.

"You're still here," he said.

Sharp looked up, but not at him. Her arms were wrapped around her legs and he thought he glimpsed something metal in her hands. "Where else would I go?"

"Out," he said. "Into the fight. The exemplars were certain this room was only holding you because you agreed to it."

"There's a fight already?" She turned haggard eyes to him. "What happened?"

He told her of the ambush, and his response. "It will take time for Merc-Sec to close in on her. If there's something else I should do—there's time to change those orders."

"Capture." She said the word like she was turning it over, checking it for any flaws. "I wonder if your order is always the same. It's strange—I can't quite remember. I've lost too many pieces."

"In your timeline, was Merc-Sec successful?" he asked. "Did they capture you safely?"

She scoffed, and he caught a glimpse of her burning confidence before the curtain of despair that enshrouded her slipped shut once more. "Don't be ridiculous."

Tarquin knelt beside her and took her hand into his, unwinding the bandage to check her wound. The cut was a ragged pink, but sealed.

"I don't understand why your body is healing slower than hers," he said. "They're the same print."

"This timeline doesn't want me here."

"I want you here."

He kicked himself as soon as he'd said it, but she scarcely seemed to react. Merely made a muted sound that might have been amusement, might have been negation—he couldn't tell. Sharp took her hand back and set aside what she'd been holding—Naira's suicide shots—and rewrapped her wrist.

"You've come to ask me a question."

"I've come to make sure you're all right."

She laughed at that. Picked up the bullets once more, and ran her fingers over the metal, slightly tacky with years of tarnish. "I don't think I ever have been. Please get to the point, my liege. I'm tired. Tonight, too many things are in flux. Holding to this timeline is like clinging to the back of a tumbling rocket."

"How do I bring her safely home?"

"Safe?" She stopped toying with the bullets and curled her fist around them instead. "You will catch her, or you won't. Either way, you will speak with her soon enough. She's walking an edge tonight. Keep her from falling, if you can."

He couldn't quite tell why those words felt like a threat. "What should I say?"

"Speak your heart, my liege. She deserves to know what's really within it."

FORTY-FIVE

Naira

Seventh Cradle | The Present

Naira could no longer feel her feet in any real sense. They'd been running for twelve hours straight, choking on rain and nutrition gel and dragging their captives behind them like firewood. Around the eighth hour, the icy rain had grown hard and then become something else. Something Naira didn't recognize at first, because she'd never seen it with her own eyes.

Snow. Delicate flakes slalomed through the rain-slick leaves. It melted at first, when it touched the ground, but soon their footing grew slippery with ice, and then the snow began to stick.

Her legs were exhausted lumps of meat that struck the ground in a numb, jarring rhythm that she couldn't stop. Kuma met her step for step, the knowledge *Jonsun has Kav* stretched taut between them. If they didn't make it back, he'd take it out on the one person he had that they both loved.

Jadhav didn't have the same motivation. She lagged behind, sometimes stumbling, and while she didn't complain, small sounds of exhaustion and agony broke through her. She'd already been tired. She'd lost blood. Even though Kuma and Naira were herding the prisoners, sometimes dragging them bodily across the ground, it was Jadhav who was falling behind.

"Captain," Naira said through a clenched jaw. The air burned in her lungs, and her throat had long ago grown raw with the rasp of her breath. "Give me your good arm."

"I'm okay. I'm okay," Jadhav chanted. She'd been muttering that under her breath for the last five miles.

"I'm stronger," Kuma said, picking up on Naira's intent.

"You need your hands free for those drones." Naira hawked and spat. Her spit stained the thin snow pink. "I'm an exemplar. I'm built to carry."

"You're not a goddamn mule," Kuma said, but Naira was already moving.

She grabbed Jadhav's arm and ducked down, scooping her up in a rescue carry. The weight took her breath away, made her stagger. When she'd recovered, she threaded an arm between Jadhav's legs and grabbed the woman's hand with her other arm, making her clutch her own thigh so that Naira wouldn't have to hold on to her.

Her pathways burned from the exertion. A low, constant vibration that made her teeth ache. They were already cannibalizing her muscle mass, as they had on Sixth Cradle. She couldn't last like this. Naira opened her HUD as she staggered onward, trying to find her feet beneath Jadhav's weight, and called Jonsun.

"We're approaching the clearing," she said. "You better have that intercept ready, because we've been dropping Merc-Sec behind us like a goddamn bread trail. We won't make it across that field."

"We're in position." Jonsun gave her a smile that made her guts twist. "And I think you'll like what I've set up."

He cut the call before Naira could demand elaboration. The desire to wring his neck pushed her forward, made her strides ground-eating with determination. She scarcely noticed Kuma half turn and aim up, into the canopy, and fire.

Bits of drone rained down around them, the acrid scent of burnt electronics tingeing the air before the snow washed it away. Naira didn't slow. Kuma popping off drones had been constant since about four hours after they started running.

The trees thinned. When they'd set out, they'd skirted around the back of the *Cavendish* and taken a broad, gentle arc into the forest that covered their tracks. To get back, they didn't have that luxury. The trees were too thin to provide cover against a determined pursuer, the ground too even to offer any real challenge. Their best hope was speed, bolting across the very field Naira had marched over to meet Mercator on the landing strip.

It had seemed the only plan worth having, when they'd started. Now that her feet were bloody in her boots and she didn't have an ounce of energy left in her, her only hope was Jonsun.

Jonsun had delivered.

Every single person who could wield a weapon on the *Cavendish* stood to the west in an unorganized clump, rifles in hand. Jonsun paced a line in front of them, daring any of the hundreds of Merc-Sec on the other side of the field to fire upon him.

Between the two forces, to the north edge, a bonfire seared the sky in crimson and gold. The snow had melted in a slick radius around it, but it'd stuck to the rest of the field, a pristine blanket of white between the two forces. No one had noticed her yet; the tree line wrapped them in shadows.

Tarquin stood with Merc-Sec. Part of her had acknowledged that he'd have plenty of time to insert himself with his forces, but she'd been trying not to think about another face-to-face confrontation. The four exemplars boxed him in, perfectly at ease to all outward appearances, but their chins were up, eyes roving.

It took her a moment to realize why Tarquin looked strange to her. It wasn't the firelight in his hair, the golden gleam of it on his skin. It was his clothes. He wore light armor. She'd never seen him in a Merc-Sec uniform before. At the sight of him standing there, proud and furious and stern, a primal part of her reared up and desired nothing more than to march over and tear that uniform right off of him.

That part of her was going to have to wait.

"Nai," Kuma said, voice a small, gasping rasp. "You really have the worst breakups, you know that?"

Naira shook with swallowed laughter, barely able to control the hysteria boiling through her. "Don't make me laugh. I think I'll drop dead if I laugh."

Kuma shot her a wink, and she took strength from that. Even if someone from Merc-Sec got jumpy and shot her in the head right here on this field, there was no way Jonsun could blame her for it or say she'd tried to escape. She hadn't been captured. She'd come back. Kav would be safe.

She kicked Richardson in the back to get him moving again—she was amazed he was still alive, considering his injuries and their all-out run—and he trudged out into the field. Naira didn't dare look at Tarquin. She was too fragile, too full of rage and frustration and the urge to blow both sides to bits just to get them off each other's throats.

She looked at Jonsun instead. His eyes widened at the bloodied apparitions that staggered out of the forest. Naira had lost most of her coat a long time ago, and her armor was busted and hanging off of her in uneven chunks.

Recognition struck, and she thought she'd never seen him smile with so much joy. He raised a hand and shouted something. The Conservators pounded their fists against their breastplates in a staccato rhythm, roaring with approval.

Jonsun strolled toward her, Kav and a doctor leaving the crowd to flank him left and right. A handful of soldiers pulled out of the group, too, their young faces grim. The rest of Jadhav's team, Naira guessed. They took the ropes for the prisoners, leading them back toward the mass of Conservators.

Naira fell to her knees, the impact clacking her teeth together. Kuma dropped beside her, bracing her hands against the thin layer of snow. One of Jadhav's team lifted their captain off Naira's shoulders and moved away, the doctor following. Leaving the four core Conservators alone in that field, watched by thousands. Naira shrugged off her rifle, dropped it to the ground at Jonsun's feet, and bent forward to press her forehead against the snow.

Her hair hung around her face in shaggy clumps, her breath steamed to clouds. Pieces of her gloves had long since gone missing, and parts of her fingers were black. She couldn't tell if that was frostbite, dirt, or grease. Jonsun crouched before her and lifted her chin, sliding his fingers along the filthy line of her jaw.

She met his stare, gold for gold, both of their eyes burning so hard there was no hint of their natural color remaining. Something thrummed, deep in her chest. A plucked string. His smile was kind and proud, and she hated how his approval still made her swell with pride.

"My fire carrier," he said, too softly for anyone else to hear. "I knew you'd find your way back to us."

Triumph burned in her chest. She had him. She'd lived twelve hours of hell, but she had his trust. If that could provide her with the knowledge to save them all, then it'd been worth it.

It had to be worth it.

"Can you stand?" he asked. She nodded. "On your feet."

That nod might have been an exaggeration. Jonsun had to help her up. Kav swooped in to help Kuma to her feet, darting a worried glance at Naira before they staggered back to the line of Conservators. Jonsun kept his arm around her, making no move to follow Kav. Fear fluttered in her veins, but there was nothing she could do. She had no strength left. The rifle stayed in the snow. It only had two more bullets, anyway.

Well, technically three. Naira turned her head and spat her suicide shot to the snow, licking her lips as Jonsun eyed it, then her, and nodded understanding. To be captured was to fail him. To risk Kav. If she'd shot herself, then Jonsun could have printed her again.

Jonsun grasped the back of her head in the way they always did before casting off, and rested his forehead lightly against her own. His grip tightened, gaze boring into hers. So close, all she could see was the gold suffusing his normally light brown eyes. She wondered if others could see it, too. She'd never asked.

"I need you to do one more thing for me, Nai. Can you do that?"

"I've got your back."

Jonsun patted her cheek twice and turned to face Merc-Sec. To face Tarquin. A subtle flex in Jonsun's hand indicated that she should fall into place as his exemplar, and she almost laughed at that, because all she was good for was standing around and getting shot.

She fell in line anyway. In the corner of her eye, Jadhav's team dragged the prisoners around to Jonsun's other side. That's what this was about. She wondered what Jonsun intended to get for their release now that she, Jadhav, and Kuma were secure.

Jonsun stopped about twenty paces from the Merc-Sec line, and the prisoners were dropped to their knees before him. Naira folded her hands behind her back and lifted her chin, even though she felt absurd. She was no threat. She was a torn and stained rag, worn-out and left to molder, but she kept her posture stiff and let anger fill her like fire as the exemplars advanced, Tarquin at their center.

It was easy, with the agony of it all fresh in her bones, to hate what he'd done. To hate having been hunted down like a deranged animal, and how it had put both Kav and Kuma at risk. The hate kept the pain away, smothered the brief and slicing thought that she and Kuma and Kav were here, together. All she had to do was signal for Tarquin to attack and he'd slaughter the Conservators, and then they'd be free.

But Jonsun held the key. It'd do nothing, in the end, but make her comfortable until the universe tore itself apart.

She scarcely recognized the faces of her friends. They'd locked themselves down to a degree she'd never seen before, Tarquin's mask so firmly in place that when he glanced at her with undisguised disdain, she felt it like a kick in the chest.

He wasn't wearing her ring anymore. She'd walked out on him publicly, and he couldn't let his people think he was weak. It still hurt, and after all the pain she'd been through, it almost dropped her back to her knees. Almost made her beg to come home.

Tarquin's entourage stopped twelve paces from the prisoners. Ward stalked out to join them. Naira hoped she wouldn't have to fight Ward again. If she did, she'd just lie down in the snow and let Ward stomp her to death.

"We've come for our people, Mr. Hesson," Tarquin said.

"Have you now?" Jonsun said. "Funny, then, that you didn't bring a thing to trade with. Where are my people, Mercator?"

"Your people are dead. We're still sorting the bodies." He cut a quick glance to her that she couldn't read. "You left quite a lot of them littering the woods."

Jonsun *tsked* and shook his head. "Wouldn't have had to, if Tweedle Fuck and Tweedle Dumb here hadn't gone and assaulted people minding their own damn business. Didn't realize strolling in your woods was a killing crime, Mercator."

"Your people were armed," Tarquin said. "We have no guarantee they didn't pose a threat."

Naira was supposed to be a silent, stalwart sentinel, but her temper roared to the surface. She spoke over Jonsun. "Your people ambushed us.

You will not stand there and lie to my fucking face, Mercator, not after the hell you put me through. I know Richardson called it in. I'm damn sure he had ocular on. Isn't that right, Captain Ward?"

"We got video," Ward said. "But it's not real clear what the context was, or what led up to that confrontation."

Jonsun looked at Naira with mild surprise, a delighted smile lining his face before he turned back to the Mercator delegation. "You don't know what they were doing on that riverbank, do you? Can't say I'm surprised a well-traveled man like yourself missed it, eh? But don't you worry, I know exactly what they were doing there. Jadhav sent me video."

"Then what were those people doing, Mr. Hesson," Tarquin said dryly, "while armed to the teeth on the bank of that river?"

"*Those people*," Jonsun said, voice pitched to carry, "have names, Mercator. Though they might not matter much to you. The men you killed were Darrel Fowler and Paolo Agosta. The woman Nai carried on her back while your dogs hunted her is Rani Jadhav. Ring a bell?"

Tarquin's jaw tensed. "I can't say I've had the pleasure of her acquaintance."

"Oh, but you have. Jadhav and her team, they're old unionist stock. Jessel's people, before they became mine. You had some trouble on Miller-Urey, or so I've heard. That finalizer Nai likes to butt heads with, Demarco, came to bring you home to your daddy, didn't he?

"Jadhav and her people kept Jessel safe under Nai's direction while you got yourself captured. Later, they helped Jessel outfit the shuttle you all were living on with more printing bays. Jadhav herself, she gave you her hand, Mercator. Helped you up off a fresh print tray. But that's all right. I don't expect a man like you to remember grunts like us. We HC stock, we're used to being glossed over and forgotten."

Tarquin tried to speak, but Jonsun was on a roll. "No, I wouldn't expect a man like you to remember the name of a woman who helps you up. Wouldn't expect you to understand a damn thing about us, or our lives. But Nai here, she's one of us. Raised to the grey, before your daddy yoked her. She sees us. She *asks our fucking names.*

"And when *those people* were out on a hike, taking in this beautiful world you've been hoarding, Nai realized it was unlikely HC cattle like Jadhav and Fowler and Agosta had ever seen a thing so simple and so beautiful as a river. So they put their weapons down, and they strolled to that shore, and Nai, well. She taught them to skip rocks."

A muted rumble of discontent flowed through the gathered Conservators. Tarquin drew his head back. He'd taught her to do that. She laced her fingers together behind her back and squeezed.

"So you see, Mercator," Jonsun pressed on, after it was clear Tarquin had nothing to say. "That's what *those people* were doing, when this piece of shit"—Jonsun kicked Blesson in the back; he fell face-first into the snow—"took a shot at Nai and tore her damn ear off, but caught Fowler instead. And then this waste of skin"—he grabbed Richardson by the hair and gave him a rough shake before releasing him—"shot Agosta in the heart."

"They stepped out of line," Tarquin said. "And I will see them disciplined for that. I issued strict no-fire orders."

"Really." Jonsun dragged out the word. "Because your toy soldiers didn't get the memo, either." He jerked a thumb at Naira. "That look like a woman they were told not to shoot at?"

"I—" Tarquin stammered, and slashed his gaze away from her. "I gave orders to capture your people unharmed."

"Unharmed, he says!" Jonsun threw his hands in the air in disbelief. "I'm starting to think that's a real loose house you're running behind that fence. Got no control, do you?"

"Is it the bodies you want, Mr. Hesson?" Tarquin grated out the words.

"Oh, no." Jonsun wagged a finger at him. "You didn't come to us to deal fairly, Mercator, and we HC, we know a thing or two about waiting for MERIT to dole out their promised rewards. We don't trust you. You're too busy strutting around the damn place, waving your army at us, to deal fairly. Two for two. Metal for metal."

Naira didn't think her heart had anything left to give, but it surged at those words, at the confusion that whispered across Tarquin's face, quickly smothered. He didn't know what that meant. Of course he didn't. It was an old rule of honor shared between those who couldn't afford phoenix fees.

She resented him for that confusion. Resented that he'd come here expecting to push Jonsun around with a show of force, with nothing in hand to deal with. She'd been running her feet bloody for twelve hours, and he hadn't bothered to do basic research on the customs of HC blood debts. He had no idea how to negotiate with her people.

With her.

"He doesn't know what that means, Jo," she said.

"Riiiight." Jonsun half turned back to the Conservators and rolled his eyes dramatically. They laughed. A mean, bitter sound. "Silly of me. Nai, why don't you educate the Mercator for us, hmm?"

Tarquin met her eyes, and she felt like she'd stepped out onto a razor wire, with Jonsun's stare boring into the side of her face, and Tarquin searching her expression for any sign, any hint that she wasn't as furious with him as she seemed to be. But she *was* furious. With Jonsun, for putting her in this position. With Tarquin, for being unable to control his people and coming to this meeting wildly unprepared.

Over a year he'd spent with her, and he'd never really understood where she had come from, how it worked, or what the unspoken rules were. He'd only ever wondered how he could use his wealth to fix it, as if her origin was inherently broken.

"The people of the HC can't afford phoenix fees. If one of us." She paused. That *us* felt surprisingly good. "If one of *us* kills another, and the HC doesn't see enough value in the deceased to pay their phoenix fees, their loved ones demand the killer's death so that their relk can be broken down to reprint whoever died at a black-market printer. If the death is an accident, the killer goes willingly as a matter of honor. Metal for metal."

He couldn't hide his shock. "That's barbaric."

"We are what MERIT has made of us, my liege," she said coldly.

"If you require I provide amarthite to reprint your people, I will do so," he said. "This practice isn't necessary."

She'd told him. She'd told him it was a matter of honor and he hadn't heard her. A spark roared into a flame in her chest, anger reddening her cheeks at his disgusted expression. Arrogant fucking man. He hadn't listened, and now he was going to try to plaster his personal moral code over the Conservators, as if the way he lived had ever been an option for them.

"You hear that?" Jonsun called to the Conservators. "The Mercator says our code of honor isn't necessary!"

They jeered and booed, then started up the staccato beat on their breast-plates once more, shouting "Metal for metal!" in one voice with such force that it thrummed through Naira, stole the beat of her heart, and made it match. Jonsun spread his arms expansively, turning back to face Tarquin.

"My people want justice, Mercator. Will you let them have it?"

"This isn't justice," he snapped.

"Piece of advice for you, my liege," she said as evenly as she could manage. "Before you decide to go to war. To gun us down like rabid animals. Make the slightest effort to understand your enemy."

"Naira..." His expression was so wounded she almost broke, too. "Please, this isn't you. I know you'll regret this ritual. She told me to keep you from—"

"She?" Naira cut him off.

Tarquin pressed his lips shut and said nothing.

"Seems the Mercator has a little bird singing to him," Jonsun mused.

"Whoever she is," Naira said, "she's a fucking liar."

Jonsun drew a long knife from his belt, the length of darkened steel curving to a wicked tip, and admired the weapon a beat before he spun it effortlessly through his fingers. He held it out to her, grip first.

"The honor is yours, darlin'," Jonsun said.

She took the blade. It was light, well-balanced, and the fabric wrap-ping the grip cushioned her frostbitten fingers. Snow crunched beneath her boots, the thin ice on the surface brittle as sun-bleached bones, as she went to stand behind Blesson.

He was still gagged. She couldn't see his face, but she wouldn't have looked at it anyway. Her gaze was locked on Tarquin, on the smothered fear there, as he forced the pieces of his Mercator mask back together.

Naira slipped her free hand into Blesson's hair, pulling his head back. He jerked instinctively, but the prisoners were worn-out. They didn't have anything left to fight with. She placed the blade against Blesson's throat. He stilled. It would be a quick death. He'd be reprinted. This wasn't about the dead. This was about drawing lines. About honor, and what life was, living in the shadow of MERIT.

They'd always been bodies to burn.

"Don't do this," Tarquin said, more a whisper than anything, but she was watching him so intently she read his lips.

She drew the blade across Blesson's neck. He went slack, and she dropped him in the same motion. The Conservators roared approval. Merc-Sec tensed, expecting an order to intervene, but as she watched the color drain from Tarquin's face she knew he wouldn't give that order. He didn't want more blood on the snow.

Naira turned to Richardson next. He made a soft sound, like he was trying to speak. Though every muscle screamed in protest she leaned down and hooked his gag with her thumb, tugging it aside.

"Metal for metal," he rasped.

"Metal for metal," she said into his ear, and drew the knife across his throat.

Blood sprayed her face and chest, shockingly warm, almost searing in contrast to her half-frozen skin. She let Richardson fall and closed her eyes, tipping her head back to breathe deep of snow-sharp air. When she opened her eyes again, she found Tarquin staring at her like he didn't know her at all.

He'd told her he'd seen her. That when she'd taken him to meet the kids at Gardet, he'd understood she was showing him a piece of herself, too. That violence had been her only future since she was big enough to swing a sword of taped-together packing material. Maybe he'd thought he'd understood.

But he'd told himself a story about her that wasn't entirely true. A watered-down, bloodless version, of an orphan girl with a chip on her shoulder and a stubborn streak. He never quite listened, when she'd told him the things she'd done for Acaelus.

This was her history. Her upbringing. It was blood spilled for unpaid debts and pathways ripped out of bodies with bare hands.

He'd thought she was better than this, and that alone implied that he'd always believed that what she was at the core was inherently *lesser*. Maybe it was. Maybe she was the scum on the bottom of his boot, in the end.

"I love you," he mouthed.

"You don't even know me," she said.

The wave of chanting Conservators shifted into a roar once again. Discordant, wild. Jonsun egged them on, lifting his arms to urge them to greater volume. An inferno burgeoned in her chest, all the fear and frustration and pain of the past few days a physical pressure pushing against her from within, scrambling for release.

She was going to choke on it.

Naira screamed. It poured out of her unbidden. A tidal wave of anger, of refusal, of bloodlust and desperation. A feral storm of rage and terror and most of all a rejection of everything the world was that scraped her bloody on the way out.

She found it hard to care that Tarquin looked as if he'd been stabbed through the heart. She'd given everything. Naira had nothing left.

The drumming of the Conservators sang her home.

FORTY-SIX

Tarquin

Seventh Cradle | The Present

Tarquin spoke to no one. He marched through the settlement, back to his home, and slammed the door on his exemplars. Sharp sat cross-legged on their bed, keen eyes shining in the low light as she looked him up and down. Took in the snow not yet melted in his hair. The mud drying on his boots. The anguish, barely constrained beneath a mask of outrage. A slight nod to herself. Recognition.

"You knew," he said, breathless.

"It was one of many possibilities." Her voice was smooth as a river stone. Impassive. Worn down by years of tumult.

"And you didn't warn me?" He took a step closer.

"I told you to speak your heart, my liege. It's no fault of mine if she was repulsed by what was in it."

"You could have told me about that ritual."

"I'm here to save your life. Not your heart."

He breathed out as if he'd been struck. Her expression hadn't changed, there was no sympathy in her. No sign at all that she'd ever loved him— that she'd ever loved anyone. That wasn't the Naira he knew.

Maybe thirty years of surviving in a world on the brink of extinction would have worn her down this much—*maybe*—but years of war against his father hadn't smothered her fire. Even on Sixth Cradle, when she'd armored herself in the edifice of her profession to hide her identity, he'd seen cracks in the stone of her walls. Had glimpsed her shining from within.

Sharp sat and did not move. Did not so much as shift her steady stare. She'd locked herself down. Hidden away. He knew how to draw her out.

"You're lying." He took another step closer. "If you really despised me, then you could have gone to Jonsun with your information. Or simply stopped my experiment with relk so that Naira would have no impetus to assassinate me and then moved on. But you're still here. And I know you, Naira, even if I made an ass of myself tonight. You won't back down until your mission is complete. So why are you still here?"

"I'm not her."

"I think you are." He was close enough now that she had to lift her chin to maintain that stare. "And I think you're here to save your heart, too."

"What do you want from me, my liege? Some pretty poetry to sing her back to you with? It is your actions she wants. Your actions she's always wanted."

"I will do anything—*anything*—to make it right."

"Look at you." She dragged her gaze over him. Made a soft sound of disgust. "'Anything.'" She mocked his tone of voice. "That willingness is why I'm *here*."

"I didn't mean it like that."

"Yes, my liege. You did."

That simple statement was more devastating than watching Naira turn her back on him in the snowfield. He'd thought he was safe. That Fletcher's proclamation that, someday, he'd misstep so badly she'd wall him off for good had ended with Sharp's arrival. That Sharp would guide him.

She had guided him. And in trying to force Naira into being what he'd wanted, instead of who she was, he'd blundered full speed off that path.

He had to get out of that house. Out of the snow. Tarquin retreated to his lab, and when that door was shut and locked, he ripped the armored chest plate from his body and tossed it to the floor.

He paced a circle, clutching the back of his head, trying to calm the hammer of his heart. Even Pliny's gentle pulsing couldn't drag him back from the edge of panic.

When he'd finally recognized the figure staggering across the snow and understood the extent of what he'd done, part of him had detached. He'd gone numb in a way he never had, before. Drifted outside of himself, everything he was feeling shutting down to keep from running to her.

To keep himself from ordering Jonsun's forces obliterated on the spot.

And in shutting himself down, he'd fallen into old, poisonous habits. Hadn't realized the implications of what he'd said until it was too late. The damage already done.

How could he have let himself be baited into that? What good was he, if all he could do was flail in reaction to Jonsun's moves and break things in the process?

"Fuck," he growled and, before he could think, lashed out, flipping a table loaded with useless experiments to shatter upon the floor.

Tarquin froze, staring at the shattered remains. The broken stasis shields, with bits of people who'd never lived, bloody and wet upon the floor, *canus*-loaded pathways winking up at him. He'd never done anything like that before.

He'd never daydreamed about blowing another man to pieces before, either.

There was a light knock on the door. "My liege, are you all right?" Cass asked.

Tarquin closed his eyes, tipping his head back. No, he wasn't all right. But that's not what his exemplar was asking.

"Fine." He ignored Cass's imploration to let them know if Tarquin needed anything.

There was only one thing Tarquin needed. He needed Naira back. Needed to explain himself. To beg her forgiveness before it was too late and the damage done festered. He'd have to invade the *Cavendish* to retrieve her.

Tarquin kicked at broken glass and stalked to the sink on the other side of the room, bracing his hands to either side of the cold steel. He couldn't do that. Couldn't endanger everyone on board the *Cavendish* to ease his pain any more than he could have gone to war against MERIT to achieve his dream of an independent Mercator. Both would ruin whatever fragile affection remained between him and Naira.

She'd given him one path to recover her. One way alone to mend what he'd broken, and he couldn't figure it out. All his degrees, all his power. Useless, when it came to the one thing that mattered to him.

Fix the expansion. Bring her home.

Tears stung his eyes. He let them fall into the sterile basin of the sink. Was this the moment in which Sharp claimed he would fall? Backed into a corner, knowing their experiments were stalled, desperate to give Naira a reason to come back to him, desperate enough to hurt their friends? Even now, the thought repulsed him.

Still, he couldn't shake the feeling that there was something in the completeness of the infected subjects. The World might hold the answers he sought—even *canus* would desire the expansion fixed—but Tarquin had no way to contact that entity.

But that wasn't quite true.

He looked over his shoulder at the printers stocked with *canus* and relkatite cartridges. There was a way to reach out to the World. He had a few hours while the others waited for him to calm down. No one would have to know.

Tarquin rolled up his sleeves and went to work.

An hour later, Tarquin sat at a lab table, a constant stream of data rolling past his eyes. It was working. Or . . . was it? It was too soon to say, the data incomplete, and yet he felt deep in his heart that he'd made the right choice. Printing with relkatite and *canus* was the way forward. The way to bring them all back together.

He could sense something at the edges of his thoughts. An indistinct flutter of recognition, the beginnings of communion as he cried out from within himself for *canus* to answer his pleas. To tell him how to make it devour faster. The distance was too vast, and growing even as he sat there, staring blankly at the data.

Even infected, Tarquin was alone.

He needed more. A swarm network, the World had called themself. The larger the quantity of the *canus*-infected, the greater the range of communication. If he could increase the volume, then the *canus* within him would have the bandwidth to speak with him. Of course, he'd been a fool not to realize that.

Someone knocked on the door. "My liege?" Caldweller asked.

Tarquin ignored him. He accessed the printer controls from his HUD. Queued them to print complete, infected blanks. With each new printing, the warmth of growth, of communion, burned anew in his pathways. At the edge of his consciousness an entity cried out, half-mad with starving. *Canus* was with him. It was with him and it was beautiful and it would help him destroy the thing that had ripped the worlds apart.

The door opened, exemplar credentials overriding the lock. Caldweller hesitated a moment, glancing at the debris covering the floor, then picked his way around the mess and sat in front of Tarquin.

"My liege? The security team is ready for you."

Tarquin forced a smile. He didn't know why tears tracked down his cheeks. "It's okay. Tell them it's going to be okay. I just need more mass, and then we'll all be together again."

Caldweller's gaze skimmed off Tarquin, examining the room. The printing cubicles all lit "in use." A frown carved his face as he took note of the stasis shield shoved off in a corner, Tarquin's amarthite print within. Slowly, he reached out. Laid his rough hands over his.

"My liege..." Caldweller paused. Pursed his lips, and squeezed his hands. "Tarquin. Tonight was hard, I know. But your people are frightened. They need your leadership."

"I've figured out how to slow the expansion." He couldn't seem to stop the tears. "I just...need to speak with *canus*. This will work. It has to work."

Caldweller bowed his head a moment, and when he looked up again, Tarquin was struck by the quaver in his voice. "This isn't the way. Whatever the infection is telling you, this will solve nothing."

"*I need her back.*" Those words rang against the core of himself, clear with truth. Unity. Communion. These were the only things that mattered. They had to be together again.

"If she comes back and finds you like this, she won't stay. You understand that, right? Naira Sharp won't accept the infection. Not for anything. Not even for you."

"I know." He bent to press his face into his arms. Tarquin understood that, he did, but every time he tried to grasp the thought, it slipped away, washed under the rising tide of his desire to be with her once again.

Caldweller's chair scraped. He circled the table and wrapped an arm around Tarquin's shoulders, tugging him close so that he could weep, shaking, in the huddle of the exemplar's arms.

"I can't do this," Tarquin whispered.

"I see your recent backup logged in the system. We'll get you back in your amarthite print. No one has to know."

"No, I mean, I can't take the risk of going back. What if this is it? What if this is the answer, and I miss it because I'm afraid? Even if... Even if I lose her, if it brings the rest of us together, then it's worth it, isn't it? If it saves us all?"

Caldweller stiffened. He shifted to crouch beside him and held Tarquin's face, gently, so that Tarquin could look nowhere but the exemplar's eyes.

"You asked me to stop you, my liege, if you should ever go too far. Do you remember?"

Tarquin nodded.

"Good." Caldweller smiled sadly. "I respect you a great deal, my liege. As a leader. As my... charge."

"After all this time, is that still really all I am to you? I hurt Marko, I hurt Naira. I think I... I think I'm incapable of building a family. Don't you see? I need *canus*. Need it to keep me from being what I was raised to be."

"Son," Caldweller said. "You have no idea how proud of you I am."

Tarquin's heart lifted. To hear that Caldweller counted him as his son warmed him to the core. What a beautiful thing it would be, once Caldweller was bonded with *canus*, to be able to stand beside him and feel that affection without the need for words.

As that hope filled him, his despair ebbed, and his tears slowed.

Caldweller snapped Tarquin's neck.

FORTY-SEVEN

Tarquin

Seventh Cradle | The Present

Jessel's call projected from the center of Merc-Sec's conference room table, their expression serious as they watched a recording of what had happened during the showdown with Jonsun.

Tarquin sat quietly, still shaken over what he'd almost done. He would be forever grateful that Caldweller had intervened before he'd done something that he would have deeply regretted. The exemplar had even promised not to tell anyone else how close Tarquin had come to dooming them all.

That kindness had stopped Tarquin's spiral cold. Given him the mental space to steel himself for this meeting.

Ward, Alvero, and the other exemplars sat around the table, waiting while Jessel reviewed the footage. They looked as harried as he felt.

When the footage ended, Jessel whistled low. "That was a spectacular fuckup, my liege."

Tarquin winced but accepted the criticism. "I'm aware, which is why I'd appreciate your insight. If there's subtext here unique to the Conservators, unionists, or even the HC, I'm likely to miss it."

Jessel sniffed at that. "Well, I can tell you Jonsun's pleased with himself. You going and showing your ass like that?" They shook their head.

"If I were Jonsun, I'd be gearing up to strike. You might as well have told him you have no idea what you're doing."

Tarquin squeezed his temples. "I didn't know about one unspoken HC rule. I hardly see how that's quite so catastrophic."

Ward, Helms, and Caldweller all shifted uncomfortably but held their tongues.

"What?" Tarquin asked, baffled as to why his people would suddenly stop being free with their thoughts.

Jessel laughed at their strained silence. "What your three ex-HC aren't telling you is that you've gone and insulted the culture of a decent percentage of your staff. They may be wearing green cuffs, but grey stains their bones, as Sharp so clearly demonstrated. You didn't just give Jonsun something to rally around. You undermined your own people."

"I didn't mean anything by it," he said. "I only wanted to work things out without bloodshed."

"Blood had already been shed, my liege," Ward said. "And Mx. Hesson is correct. We've had five desertions."

Tarquin's mouth dropped open. "You're kidding."

"Wish I was. There's a few more I expect are getting light-footed that I'm keeping an eye on, but frankly, if they're going to run, I'd rather they do it than stick around and drag morale down. People like you, my liege, but Sharp is special to a lot who came from the HC. If those people had any doubts about her motives, they don't now. They're not running to Jonsun. They're running to Sharp."

"We have no confirmation that she's really turned against us." He hoped he didn't sound like he was trying to convince himself. Sharp had said she was on their side. He clung to that.

"With respect, my liege," Alvero said. "I'm uncertain of her loyalties. I very much believe the anger she exhibited was real."

"I buy that," Jessel said. "Sharp's always had one foot out the door of any room she's in, but what I just saw? Jonsun's been testing her, and he got his confirmation tonight. He's going to take his heroes back to the ship, Sharp and Kuma and Jadhav, and he's going to get 'em fed and drunk and fucked if they want it, and then he's going to gear for war."

"*Mx. Hesson*," Tarquin ground out.

"Sorry, my liege." They spread their hands. "I'm not saying she'll go for it, but it's true. Jonsun knows the importance of making his people feel valued, and that's part of it all. Sharp's a symbol. A valuable one. Jonsun won't waste time sitting around on that. If she really has turned, then I don't mean to put too fine a point on it, but you might very well be fucked."

"Why do you say that?" Tarquin asked. "All the fanaticism in the universe can't overwhelm the simple fact of numbers. If he attacks the settlement in force, he can't take it."

"He knows that, my liege. He's not counting on a straight fight. He's got an ace up his sleeve, and maybe he's going to be forced to use it sooner than he'd like because of the way things shook out today, but he won't miss the chance. I mean it, he'll move as soon as he's able, and he's not going to wait around for his new heroes to heal. He'll reprint them."

"I thought he was short on amarthite?"

"If you think that's what metal for metal is really about, then you might be incapable of learning, my liege," Jessel said.

Tarquin had spent too long in the lab the past couple of weeks. He'd lost touch with people, with things that weren't neatly categorized and tabulated. Had relied on Sharp, even though she'd withheld so much. It'd been foolish of him to think he could deal with the unionists-turned-Conservators without truly understanding the lives they'd been living.

As much as he wanted to blame his upbringing for that failure, his father and Leka wouldn't have made the same mistake.

"So we have an imminent attack incoming," Tarquin said. "Jonsun's unknown ace, the reason for those tunnels they were digging, and oh, the expansion of the universe threatening to make the whole matter moot within the year. Does that sound like a complete list of matters to be addressed?"

Ward smirked, but Alvero shook his head. "Broadly, my liege, yes, but you've missed a detail. We must orchestrate a retaliation. Whether or not Sharp is with us, the fact remains that she executed two of our soldiers. While some may sympathize with her motives, the rest of Merc-Sec does not. If you let it slide, we'll lose even more morale. We may soon see fighting among our own people."

"Retaliate? I thought this whole metal-for-metal thing was meant to balance the scales."

"For the HC-raised, my liege. The others won't see it that way." Alvero pulled up a map of the area. "I suggest an air strike of an important asset. Either the tunnels themselves or their fields."

"About that," Caldweller said. "The exemplars got a tip-off and did some poking around. We think the warming nets over the fields might be hiding the weather disrupters that were used to knock out our comms."

"Really?" Alvero's brows lifted. "Please thank your source for me, Exemplar. Disabling those nets would give us quite the advantage."

"And is this source your mysterious 'she'?" Jessel asked.

"Sources are on a need-to-know basis," Caldweller said smoothly.

Tarquin's neck heated, embarrassed that he'd let such a crucial piece of information slip in front of so many, and he pushed on. "I don't like the idea of bombing their food source. But if those nets can damage our comms, then they're our first target."

Alvero tipped his head to Jessel. "Going off of Mx. Hesson's information about the celebrations tonight, I suggest that we wait until they're tired out and strike in the early hours of the morning."

"Very well," Tarquin said.

"My liege," Ward said. Her voice was slow. Contemplative. "I'm not saying I don't agree with this hit, I do, but if Jonsun's gearing to strike, then you need to understand—there's no going back from this. We hit their weapon, we're at war. With Sharp."

"I understand." He'd asked for their honesty, and he braced himself to receive it. "What would you suggest I do?"

"Clear her from the board, my liege," Alvero said. "She is a powerful symbol, warrior, and strategist. To lose her would throw the entire encampment into disarray. Captain Ward and I have fought her before, and I assure you that I do not make this suggestion lightly."

"Aye," Ward rumbled. "Trouble is, there's only two ways to do that— take her out, or extract her and find out if she's really on our side."

"Extract?" Tarquin leaned forward. "How would you accomplish that?"

"We'd have to send in a covert operative." Alvero tapped a finger against his chin as he thought. "Someone who knows the HC, as to not blow cover, and who we're sure wouldn't desert."

"What about Richardson?" Tarquin asked. "Naira knows the man, and he agreed with the metal-for-metal practice before she killed him. He's ex-HC and, I think, loyal, but after tonight the Conservators would believe he'd desert."

"Richardson's a reliable enough soldier," Ward said, "but I wouldn't put him in anything that requires finesse. Not a lot of imagination in that one."

"I'll go." Helms stepped forward. "Put me into Richardson's print. I'm ex-HC."

"Interesting idea," Ward said, "but they'll sniff you in a second. You exemplars all move the same, and Jonsun worked shoulder to shoulder with Sharp for years."

"We're her exemplars." Diaz stepped to Helms's side, chest lifted. "We've been forced to sit on our hands this whole time, but if our charge requires an extraction, then that's an exemplar's job."

"Diaz, Helms," Tarquin said, "I'm sorry, but Captain Ward is correct. Jonsun would make you both immediately."

"Then we defect as we are, my liege," Diaz said. "We say we're disgusted with you, and loyal to our charge, and bolt."

"You saw the lengths he went to in order to assure himself of Naira's loyalty. If two more exemplars show up on his doorstep, it won't be any easier for you, and he might start looking at Naira sideways. We can't risk it."

"But—" Helms started to say. Caldweller put a warning hand on her shoulder. She stepped back from the table. Diaz followed, gaze downcast.

"What we need," Alvero said, half to himself, "is a finalizer."

"We don't have any here," Ward said, "but you're right. It'd be perfect. Someone used to wearing other prints, who can get in and handle Jonsun so we don't have to worry about the neural maps he has on file." She sighed and shook her head. "But all our operatives here are trained for listening work, not wet work. We might have to try the ploy with the E-Xs. I don't like it, but it's absurd enough Jonsun might buy it. Sharp has a way of inspiring loyalty."

Let me out. I will serve you and I will end that piece of shit once and for all.

Tarquin half listened as they batted back and forth plans that were far too tenuous to guarantee success. Acid stung the back of his throat, a strange numbness settling into his bones.

She wanted actions from him. A show of trust and understanding that he'd listened to her. That he could see the value in those things from her upbringing which he could never hope to understand.

For all his faults, he'd never let me fall.

"Alvero," Tarquin said, interrupting, "Captain Ward. Between the two of you, how would you rate an adept finalizer's chances of success in this situation?"

They shared a look. Ward shrugged.

"High, my liege," Alvero said. "It's difficult to say precisely without knowing the nature of Jonsun's internal security, but Mercator finalizers are feared for a reason. They're trained for so much more than cracking."

"I agree with that assessment," Ward said. "I understand you find them distasteful, but their skill sets are uniquely suited. A finalizer could do this, if anyone can."

"The ansible network is too unstable to attempt to transmit a map, though, my liege," Alvero said. "We're stuck with what we have on-planet. But don't you worry, we'll make it work."

Alvero smiled to be reassuring. Tarquin was certain he didn't believe those words.

He took a stuttering breath. "I have a finalizer's map on-planet."

Caldweller's eyes widened. "You're kidding. You can't field that man, my liege. Not for anything, and especially not for this."

"Who are we talking about?" Ward asked.

"Fletcher Demarco."

FORTY-EIGHT

Tarquin

Seventh Cradle | The Present

The simulation was the same stark white room as before. The desk, the two chairs. Fletcher himself, a smug smile on his face, sitting with chains around his arms and a lift to his chin that said he always knew Tarquin would come back. Tarquin shut his disgust down and took his seat, focusing on what Sharp had told him—she'd printed Fletcher herself to have someone to fight at her side, and he hadn't let her down.

"I told you, cub. I'll only talk to her. You're wasting your time."

Tarquin kept his face impassive—easier to do in simulation than reality—and began to open the files on the extraction plan. He didn't remove his privacy filter, so all Fletcher could see were blurry squares.

"I'm not here to discuss what you saw as a child, Mr. Demarco. I'm here to offer you an assignment as a finalizer for Mercator."

"Oh. Oh, that's *good.*" Fletcher leaned forward, chains whispering against each other, his eyes hungry as he tried to decipher the blurred holos. "Who is it? Did someone give you a poor haircut, or put a red sock in with your tighty-whities?"

"I am inured to your jabs, Mr. Demarco, and short on time. Please pay attention. Your service record indicated that you were accomplished. I'd hate to be disappointed."

He smiled the charming, practiced smile of a man you'd like to have a beer with and spread his hands. "I hate to disappoint, my liege. How may I serve?"

"The target," Tarquin said, "is Jonsun Hesson."

"Fuck *yes*," he said with such intensity it was nearly sexual. "I never thought you'd say such delicious things to me."

"Control yourself," Tarquin chided. "Mr. Hesson's neural map has been cracked and repaired. I require assurances that you have the skill set to make certain it will not be repaired again."

Fletcher drew in a long breath through his nose, as if smelling a particularly intoxicating flower, and let loose with a dramatic sigh. "And he brings me a challenge. I'm starting to see what Nai does, cub. I might fall in love with you myself."

Tarquin pinched the bridge of his nose. "If you cannot demonstrate even a modicum of professionalism, Mr. Demarco, I will end this conversation. The man you are meant to impersonate is not prone to rambling or segues. He is, in fact, a kind man and a solid soldier of Merc-Sec. Are you capable of imagining such a thing, let alone imitating it?"

Fletcher's demeanor changed in an instant. He lost the casual sprawl in the chair, his back assuming the ramrod posture of a soldier even as his face relaxed into an easy smile, eyes attentive with loyal patience. He bowed at the waist, briefly, and when he spoke he'd lost the rambling bounce to his tone, the hint at a laugh behind every syllable, and sounded like nothing more than a salt-of-the-earth soldier.

"Forgive me, my liege, I was enjoying myself. I know my job, and I know it well. I was honored to be trained by your father."

"That is, admittedly, a remarkable transformation," Tarquin said with grudging respect.

Fletcher flashed him a wink, his real persona slipping through, but it was gone in a second. "I aim to serve, my liege. As for your question about the repaired map, that's no trouble. I'll have it cracked for good in no time; you can count on me."

Tarquin wasn't sure what was more unsettling, Fletcher's real personality, or how easily he pretended to be someone Tarquin could actually like. "After you finalize the target, you are expected to extract two operatives, potentially three."

He cleared the privacy filter on one of the holos. It was a still picture, captured from the footage a few hours ago. Tarquin had chosen the moment when Naira, battered almost beyond recognition, had pressed her forehead to the snow at Jonsun's feet, because he knew it would infuriate Fletcher. He wasn't disappointed. The chains rattled, Fletcher's fists clenching.

"No bullshit, cub. What is this?"

"Jonsun has taken her, repaired her map against her will, and we believe he has forced her loyalty by threatening the destruction of Kuma's and Kav's maps."

His nostrils flared, a hateful fire simmering within him. Whatever happened, Jonsun Hesson would crack at Fletcher's hands. This pleased Tarquin more than he cared to admit.

"Let me get this straight," Fletcher said, all business, "you want me to crack Jonsun and extract Nai, Kav, and Kuma, shielding their maps—which I'm certain he has—against retaliation from his people? And they're encamped on that ship with, I presume, extremely tight security and guns pointed your direction?"

"That is correct," Tarquin said. "We have reason to believe that the Conservators—as the entire population of the *Cavendish* calls themselves—are preparing for an assault upon the settlement within the week. Naira must be extracted before that attack takes place.

"HUDs in the vicinity are routed through the ship. You will have no private communication methods. Mr. Hesson has also threatened to blow the warpcore if he is attacked, though we believe that to be a bluff."

"Why me? You have hundreds of finalizers in your employ."

"If I could use anyone else, I would. But the universe is, quite literally, tearing itself apart. The expansion of space has accelerated to such a degree that we have lost most of the ansible network. We suspect that Mr. Hesson is involved in some manner but have no confirmation. If it's not stopped, this planet will be without enough starlight to maintain life by the end of the year. I need a finalizer, Mr. Demarco. You're the only one I've got."

He laughed. A small, startled sound. "You're sending me to save the world? You really are desperate."

"I am sending you to save *her*."

Fletcher licked his lips. "What makes you think I won't go in there and join Jonsun?"

"He has edited her map without her consent. He forces her loyalty by threatening her friends. She is suffering. I'm willing to bet everything on the fact that you can't abide that. And..." Tarquin paused, eyeing Fletcher as he leaned forward, gaze razor sharp.

This man had tortured Tarquin. Had made Naira's life a living hell. But looking at him just then, knowing everything Tarquin knew about him as a child and what an advanced *canus* infection could do, all Tarquin could feel was pity. When Fletcher had written *fear of abandonment* in his notes on Tarquin, he hadn't had to dig deep. Like recognized like.

Tarquin held no illusions that Fletcher might have been a good man if *canus* hadn't twisted him. They'd all been infected to some degree or another most of their lives. While Tarquin had an urge to lash out sometimes, he'd never indulge in half the cruelties Fletcher reveled in.

But while Tarquin had faced his fears, Fletcher had not. Upon review of all the data he had on Fletcher, one line had stuck out. Written in Naira's file, after Fletcher had pushed her out of Mercator: *She didn't even fucking call me, did she?*

Four years in the exemplar academy. Eight years of service to Acaelus. Twelve years of no contact, and Fletcher had still been waiting for that call.

Tarquin removed Fletcher's collection of suicide shots from his pocket and set them on the table between them with a click. Then he removed Naira's set, and placed it beside the first. Fletcher's mouth sagged open. Hesitantly, he touched the first bullet in her collection.

"She kept them."

"She did." Tarquin took a breath. "Naira told me that, despite all your faults, you would never let her fall. Was she correct to place her faith in you?"

"Yes."

Tarquin held out his hand. "In that case, Mr. Demarco, welcome back to Mercator."

FORTY-NINE

Naira

Seventh Cradle | The Present

Naira was shit-faced drunk. She sprawled in a lounge chair on the edge of the mass of Conservators who were doing their damnedest to do something that looked like it might be dancing. Left to her own devices, she made steady work of pouring the truly disgusting rotgut that had been dug out of the dark corners of the *Cavendish* down her throat.

She didn't care that the booze was trash and the music a repetitive, chanting beat pounded out by the Conservators on things that might have been drums if you squinted at them the right way.

Naira was warm and she didn't hurt and she hadn't even bothered to put her boots on before going outside after reprinting, because it was nice to look down and see all her toes attached. Jonsun hadn't even pushed her to carve the Conservators' mark back into her skin. For one night, she'd get to be pain-free.

A light snowfall evaporated against the heat net above the field they hadn't gotten around to planting yet. Radiant heat pounded down on them all, the ground pleasantly toasty. The dancers were losing more and more of their clothing as the night dragged on, the scents of sweat and skin and humanity overriding the frosty indifference of the planet.

People kept her cup full, the tree stump by her chair loaded with more food than she could eat, and occasionally they stopped by to clap her on the back or whip up a cheer, and she was content with it all, as long as she kept drinking.

The second she stopped, she saw Tarquin's face after the last thing she'd said to him, and a chill would descend upon her freshly printed skin. Tonight she needed to be seen. So she drank, and she watched, and she tried to pretend that she hadn't broken Tarquin's heart.

Jonsun was convinced she was in his pocket. He'd tell her his plans for the expansion soon enough, because there was no way he was going to wait much longer to strike. She'd get back to Tarquin soon, and then... She didn't even know. She loved him. She was furious with him. It all tangled up inside her, and all she wanted to do was wind the clock back.

If Naira ever found out who that "she" was who had advised Tarquin before the confrontation, she'd kill the bitch.

"Naaaai!" Kuma burst out of the mass of dancers and nearly face-planted as she stumbled into the foot of Naira's chair. She was wearing a great deal less than she had been before she'd gone out there, face flushed, skin glistening with sweat. "Get off your ass!"

"Fucking hell." Naira flicked her hand to get the sloshed-over alcohol off of it. "I'm pretty sure this garbage can take my skin off."

"Come *on*," Kuma insisted.

Naira rolled her eyes. "You know I don't dance."

"You are tonight!"

"Am not."

"Are too," Kav said beside her. She jumped, because she was drunk enough she hadn't heard him approach.

"Are you two trying to make me spill my entire drink?"

"We'll get you a new one." Kuma grabbed her arm. "C'mon!"

"No." Kav grabbed her other arm. "Don't you dare, you little—shit!"

They yanked, laughing, and she stumbled to her feet, pouring the drink down the front of her shirt in the process. "I don't even have shoes and I will *not* have my new toes stepped on out there."

"Then keep up!" Kuma said, which made absolutely no sense to Naira.

Even her more elaborate insults wouldn't slow them down. They dragged her out to the middle of the dance floor, squeezing through a clot of people, and released her when she was well and truly surrounded.

To her horror, they started writhing all around her. Which Naira supposed was, in fact, dancing. She crossed her arms and glowered.

"Oh, lighten up." Kav planted his hands on her shoulders and attempted to make her move.

She intensified her glower and went rigid.

He snorted, breath flammable with fumes from the rotgut, and thrust a finger in the air. "I will make you dance, before the night is through!"

"Hell no."

Kuma shimmied up against her from behind and dropped a hand on her hip, swaying while Kav sandwiched her from the front and rocked that ridiculously too-muscled print of his against her, both of them cackling like idiots. Naira closed her eyes and tipped her head back to the sky.

"This is a sim. This is a sim and I'm being tortured."

Kuma slapped her ass, making her jump into Kav, who grabbed her hand and twirled her out into a spin. He gave her the smuggest smile she'd ever seen as he tugged her back against him. "Gotcha!"

"You're such an ass," she said, but laughed, despite herself.

Kav let her go, but before she could slink away, Kuma grabbed her.

"I know you can move that body of yours," Kuma shouted into her ear.

Naira winced at the volume. "I can hear you, and I would like to move this body elsewhere, thanks."

Kuma shot an open-handed jab at Naira's middle. She swayed away instinctively, and Kuma's eyes lit up. Naira groaned, knowing she was in for it, now. "Don't you dare bruise this print. It's brand new."

Kuma's grin was fierce. "Then you'd better get out of the way."

Kuma stepped into her and swung again, her blows paced with the beat of the music. Naira rained insults down on Kuma for making her do this while the other dancers cheered and laughed in turn.

Jonsun snagged Naira's wrist and pulled her away. "Want to escape?"

"Immediately."

He glanced cartoonishly from side to side, put a finger to his lips, then clutched her hand and bolted. She sprinted after him, to the edge of the tilled earth, where there were fewer people and she could finally catch her breath. He kept tugging. She dug her heels in.

"Wait. I don't have any shoes."

Jonsun stumbled to a halt and looked down at her feet, baffled. "Don't tell me we ran out of boots your size. I'll have more fabbed."

"Nah, I have some, I just wanted to see my toes all attached again."

He stared at her a moment, then burst out laughing. "You're ridiculous. But never fear, I have an idea."

"Going to share?"

"That's the plan."

He ducked down and scooped her up, piggyback style. She laughed, clutching his neck to hang on when he pumped a fist in the air, shouted, "To freedom!" and took off at a run.

He skirted around the back of the *Cavendish*, staying within the perimeter of the ship's cameras, but the second they were out of the radius of the heat net, she shivered, snow nipping at her exposed skin. Jonsun felt her hunker down and slowed, coming to a stop near a boulder.

They plopped down side by side, facing the snow-frosted woods. Naira wrapped her arms around herself, shivering. Jonsun shrugged out of his coat and draped it around her shoulders.

"My god," she said. "Someone taught you manners."

"If I let you get frostbite again, I'd never hear the end of it."

"You're not wrong. That was a new kind of hell. I thought it'd be, I don't know, like my skin was ice? Frozen and brittle, I mean. But I guess your cells burst and it all goes to mush. I burned those boots."

He rubbed the back of his neck, looking down. "Look, Nai, I owe you an apology."

"No shit, but I'm dying to know what's finally got you feeling that way. Toe soup?"

"Toe soup's part of it." He dug in his pocket, pulled out a flask, took a long drink, then handed it to her. "So, about, oh, almost seven years ago, Kav gave me a call."

"Oooh, we're going down memory lane."

He elbowed her. "Let me talk, will you?" She made a show of taking a drink. It was much smoother than the rotgut. "I'd been trying to recruit him, but he always dodged the commitment. Said he liked freelancing better. So, anyway, he calls. Tells me he's got someone interested. He asked me if I was really serious, because this person, they were the real deal, and if I said yes, they'd change everything."

"Oversold me for once," Naira muttered.

"No," he said emphatically. "Not even a little. I agreed to meet him at that diner—you remember?"

"Hmm." She tapped the flask against her lips. "Sheri's, yeah? Great pie there."

"The best," he said. "I show up, and there you are. You had that hoodie on, makeup to cover the pathways, but I knew you. Had seen you on the news. I panicked. Here's Miss Universe's Most Wanted, inhaling chocolate pie while Kav was busy giving you a hard time about your manners. I was certain it was a trap. Worlds' finest exemplar goes AWOL and washes up on my door? No way I'm believing it.

"But I had to know what Kav thought he was doing. I warned Jessel, then sat down and tried to play it cool. We do the interview, and I'm still not convinced. I asked why you wanted to join us, what it was really about, because someone like you, you're not an idealist. You know the best we can do is slow MERIT down. You looked me dead in the eye and said—you remember?"

She stared into the woods. "I was always going to die horribly by Acaelus's hands. Might as well be for a good reason."

He shook his head. "Scared the skin straight off me. I thought, no way. No way are we taking this crazy-ass woman on her suicidal vengeance spree. But you and Kav were a package deal. I hire you, he signs on permanently. We needed him. We needed you, too, but I hadn't figured that out yet."

"I'm not hearing an apology."

"I'm getting there." He patted the air in a slow-down motion. "Context matters, here, because when I fished you out and brought you to the *Cavendish*, I thought: Lightning doesn't strike twice. I can't trust her."

"There was the small matter of me wanting to bash your head in for kidnapping me and fixing my map against my will," she said. "I still kinda want to."

"I shouldn't have done it that way. I told myself there wasn't time, I had to rip the scales off your eyes as soon as possible, but it's no excuse. I'm sorry. I regret it every day, but I don't regret having you back."

She licked her lips, tasting the sweet fire lingering there. "We're doing honesty, now? No threats, no bullshit?"

"I owe you that."

"Good," she said, and punched him in the arm, full-strength.

He flinched away, grabbing his sore arm, and looked at her with a scrunched brow. "What was that for?"

"Me being nice by not aiming for your thick skull. What the fuck happened to you, Jo? You yanked my map and fucked around in my head without my permission, and that's bad enough, but don't sit there and pretend to be contrite when we both know what you've been leveraging to keep me compliant.

"I get that you don't trust me. I wouldn't trust me, either, and I don't mind the games with the Mercator, or even that nightmare goddamn death hike. What I mind, *friend*, what I take real big fucking issue with, is you dangling Kav's map in front of me, threatening to crack it if I don't step just right. That's a MERIT move, and you know how I feel about finalizers."

"I know." He buried his face in his hands and left it there. "Fuck, I know. I didn't want... It all got out of control. I don't want to crack our people. I never have. But Jadhav, she was a vocal dissenter of mine, early on. She cracked—it was nothing I did, an accident—and after I repaired her, she changed. She doesn't see visions of the future like we do; I think you have to live a long time while cracked for that to happen. But she became fiercely loyal. After that, everyone felt the threat—behave or be made to behave. I'd never follow through on that threat."

She thought of Kuma, insisting she didn't know what Naira was talking about when she'd brought up Jonsun's real inner circle. She doubted Jadhav's cracking was as accidental as Jonsun claimed.

"But you sure are willing to kill people to make them forget, aren't you?"

His regretful demeanor melted away, and he regarded her with newfound wariness. "You noticed."

"I am..." She stared out into the snow-brindled trees. "So very tired of this. You ask me to put my faith in you. Tell me that it's honesty time, but you're giving me half a sob story and skirting the truth. What happened tonight—you know I broke Tarquin's heart. And so I'm sitting here, wondering. Wondering if maybe you don't have a plan to slow the expansion after all. Wondering if maybe you took me to shatter Tarquin so that he'd be desperate enough to do the very experiments you told me we were working to stop."

"That's not how it happens," he insisted. "In all my visions, the experiments begin the same way each time—you two standing side by side in the settlement's powercore building. As long as you're here, and not with him, he won't fall so far. I can promise you that much."

"I need more than promises."

He looked sideways, toward the dancers. The sun had begun to rise, a thin scarlet light making everything seem washed in fire. Naira took a drink, and waited, willing him to show her the truth he'd been hiding. A breath misted between his lips, freezing in the predawn air, and he turned back to her, searching her face.

They'd stood shoulder to shoulder against MERIT for five long years. She didn't bother concealing her feelings; she let him see the whole fucked-up mix. The pain and betrayal and fear and the thin thread of hope that somehow this might all work out.

"Can I show you something?" He held out a hand to her, and she grasped it.

Something whistled through the air. The heat-net field exploded.

FIFTY

Naira

Seventh Cradle | The Present

Naira was on her side in the snow and wasn't certain how she'd gotten there. Her ears buzzed, a constant thrum that settled as her pathways vibrated in response, healing the damage. Dazed, she pushed herself to her hands and knees, shaking her head. The hot pain of a bruise was already forming across her back, and she was pissed off this print had been damaged already, before she saw Jonsun sprawled in the snow.

She scrambled to his side and checked his pulse. Strong, steady. His chest was rising and falling, and he didn't seem to have broken anything vital.

"Hey." She slapped his cheek a few times. "Hey, get up."

He groaned, pawing through the snow until he could lift his hands to his face and prod at it to make sure it was still attached. "Did you knock me out?"

"I wish." She glanced toward the smoke and the fire. Her heart froze in her chest. "Air strike. On the field."

"Fuck," he said.

Naira grabbed Jonsun's arm and hauled him to his feet, then left him tottering there as she took off at a dead sprint. He wasn't far behind. Smoke and dust clouded the air, making it impossible to see. The groans of the injured mingled with the popping of overheated metal. Blood splashed the ground in smears and puddles, pieces of the dancers pitched up against the rest of the rubble.

The party had thinned out, dwindling with the fading night, but there'd been enough people left to paint the ground the burnt ocher of melted fat and flesh.

"Kav!" she roared, cupping her hands around her mouth. "Kuma!"

Smoke stung her throat, making her cough. Jonsun took a torn piece of his shirt and wrapped it roughly around her mouth and nose, tying it snug behind her head, then did the same for himself. They split apart to search opposite ends of the field, but they weren't the only ones crying out names.

She tried to ping their HUDs, but the interface was scrambled, some kind of interference. Naira whirled to ask Jonsun if he knew what that was, but he'd disappeared into the haze. She trudged on, stepping over pieces that had been people, feet slick with muddy gore.

"Kuma!" she shouted, coughing.

"Nai!" Kav called out.

She ran to the sound, stumbling over debris, and found him standing off to the center of the carnage, scratched and dazed but otherwise whole. He grabbed her shoulders, bloodshot eyes squinted against the smoke as he examined her for injury. She checked him over, too. Only scrapes.

"What the fuck happened?" he asked.

"Air strike, I think," she said. "I heard a whistle before the explosion."

"Damnit, I..." He trailed off, mouth twisting into a pucker of frustration as he glanced to the side.

"HUDs are out," she whispered.

People were shouting, screaming. Chaos swirled all around them. If the HUDs were down, the mics were, too. They'd never have another chance to risk speaking without being overheard. He snatched her into a hug, pressing his cheek tight against hers, and used the embrace as cover to whisper against her ear.

"I was in the woods, following some people. Jonsun's been moving supplies into the tunnels and I didn't see what they were. Why would Tarquin hit the heat net?"

"I don't know. Where's Kuma?"

"Last I saw, she was center back, closer to the ship side."

They parted long enough to look that direction, and Naira's stomach sank. There wasn't much left over there. Just smoke and twisted bits of metal and the occasional low moan or painful cry. Naira grabbed Kav's hand and dragged him along behind her so they wouldn't lose sight of each other in the smoke.

Her lungs burned. She waved an arm in front of her face as she ran to try to clear some of the smoke, but it was pointless. It stung her eyes and blurred her vision with tears. They called Kuma's name until their throats were raw.

Until they heard a too-small voice say, "Here."

Naira turned. Kuma lay broken in the dirt. Her legs had bent in all the wrong places, and a piece of the anchor pole for the heating net speared through her side, pinning her to the ground. Kuma's thick, dark hands wrapped the pole, pressing down on the wound, but the puddle around her was far too large. Sweat stained every inch of her skin, muddy with dirt.

Kav rushed forward, shouting something, but all Naira could hear was a buzzing in her head, as if she'd been pushed forward into a reality she rejected so vehemently that her very thoughts had chosen to stay behind in the past, where this wasn't happening.

Blood soaked through the knees of Kav's pants as he dropped down beside Kuma and took her head, gently, in those big hands of his. He brushed hair from her face. Kuma smiled a little, almost bashful, and something inside Naira broke.

"Nai!" Kav growled at her.

Her name uprooted her, gathered the pieces of herself that'd gone flying, and slammed them back into this terrible moment. She fell to her knees beside Kav and pressed her own hands over Kuma's, holding down a wound that wouldn't heal, willing it undone.

"I'm sorry." Tears tracked down Kuma's cheeks, cleaning rivers through the sweat-caked mud.

Naira's throat clenched. "Don't be stupid. There's nothing to be sorry for. We have plenty of amarthite. We'll have you back on your feet in no time."

"Not this time." Kuma grunted something that may have been a laugh but came out a bloody gurgle.

Kuma's hands were too cold. "Rescind the do-not-reprint order. Make it sixty percent. Do it now, while you're cognizant."

"No, honey bear." Her voice wasn't Kuma's. Kuma had never been so quiet. "I decided. It's okay."

"This isn't okay." She summoned her deepest bark of command. "I need a fucking medic!"

Kav touched her arm. Kuma's face was slack, eyes open, but no shine in them, nothing of the vibrancy that had been Kuma behind them. Kuma's fingers relaxed, sliding away from the pole to fall, limp, to the ground. It was just a print. Naira had seen plenty of prints die. She'd seen Kuma's die more than once. But a deep, primal tear opened up in her heart, and she knew. That death had been too painful. Kuma's chance to crack would be pushed over her threshold.

Kuma was gone.

Kav clutched Naira, and she clutched him back, and they stayed like that, two broken things trying to hold themselves together. At some point Jonsun came and he held them, too, because whatever had come to pass, they had all loved one another, once.

Through the smoke and tears, Naira caught a fleeting glimpse of Mercator grey and green. It was a spark to the withered tinder of her heart. A storm of rage whirled up from within the hollow place Kuma's loss had left within her, scouring her with anger, cauterizing the pain. Kav and Jonsun pulled back, sensing the shift, red-rimmed eyes wary as she stood, and stalked toward the thing that had done this.

It was a man. Merc-Sec. He knelt in the dirt toward the edge of the chaos, surrounded by Conservators. His hands were up, behind his head, his weapons splayed across the ground like cast-off toys, his armor stripped free to join them. Exertion flushed his cheeks, and his eyes were bloodshot from the smoke. The Conservators parted at her approach. Richardson. Jadhav had a rifle pointed at his head.

The Conservators took one look at her face and slunk away a step. Richardson met her eyes and swallowed. Hard.

"Deserter." Jadhav spat in the dirt. "Came in with the strike team. Right before the ordnance launched, we saw him come running at us, waving a white flag. Wants to join up."

"Does he," Naira said. It wasn't a question. Her voice was a blunt instrument.

"It's true, E–X," Richardson said. "I can't stand to do it anymore, to wear the green. I just can't."

Jonsun and Kav jogged up behind her and were talking to Jadhav. They'd had a handful of deserters since the execution, but they couldn't trust them, so they were being held separately for further questioning after their HUDs had been stripped. Naira heard all this, a flutter of facts drifting around her, but they seemed very far away.

She crouched down in front of Richardson. A tremble passed through him, eyes wide enough to show their whites all around, jaw stiff with fear. The chatter around her went quiet, but there was only this man's breath, quick and shallow with jackrabbit terror, the sweat on his lip, the subtle sway backward, as if he wished to flee from her scrutiny.

He wasn't right. She knew it immediately. That was Richardson's print, she'd seen the man enough. He sounded like him. Acted like him. But while the others paused to watch, and the pressure of their regard weighed against her, there was a separate sensation of being watched that slithered through her. A prickling at the back of her neck that she knew well.

When she'd been young and in love, she'd thought that slow frisson of warning had been a special connection. A sweet aura of longing between them. She knew better, now. Knew what it was to walk through a forest and feel a predator's eyes on her back.

Fletcher.

The name poised on the tip of her tongue. All thought evaporated on the hot coil of her anger, and then she wasn't thinking, only acting. She drew her arm back, and the back of her hand cracked across his jaw with such force that he tumbled into the dirt, blood fountaining from his mouth.

Shouts of alarm echoed around her, entreaties to stop. Fletcher reached to cover his bloody mouth and she broke one wrist, a delicate snap, and then she stood, because she didn't have her knives, and stomped the heel of her foot over and over again into the man's chest, right below his ribs where he'd stabbed her, while he coughed blood and pleaded in

Richardson's voice that he hadn't meant to hurt anyone. Kav and Jadhav grabbed her, shouting at her to stop, and she thrashed, lashing out to break free, wanting only to crush him beneath her hands.

And then she was slipping away, into darkness, washed beneath a sedative while Kav held her arms to her sides and whispered, "I've got you," until unconsciousness took her at last.

FIFTY-ONE

Naira

Seventh Cradle | The Present

Naira broke through the surface of the sedative, gasping beneath sweat-soaked sheets. Haze clouded her mind, her limbs heavier than they had any right to be. Every aspect of her body wanted to be dragged back down into oblivion.

Amarthite pathways could only do so much. She fumbled through her HUD, requesting it synth adrenaline and any other stimulant she could think of, but it only made her jittery. She put a hand on her nightstand and started to pull herself up. The leftover injector was on the nightstand. She pocketed it so she'd have the name of the drug. She had to find whatever blocker was needed to flush her system.

The door opened. Naira stared a moment, her drugged mind slow to catch up to the strange figure in her doorway. Richardson. Face bruised, broken wrist braced, the bandages holding his ribs together sticking out above the neckline of his shirt. Crusted scabs traced the lines where his HUD pathways had been cut out. Only, that wasn't Richardson.

He shot a nervous glance over his shoulder before moving into the room to let the door close behind him. Holding out his hands in a placating gesture, he approached with slow, wary steps.

"Nai." Fletcher dropped his Richardson persona. "I know you're furious, but I'm here to get you out. We have to go. Jonsun launched an early strike against the settlement, so I've used the chaos to mess with one of his comm blackout nets. The *Cavendish*'s surveillance systems are down, but I don't know how long that will last."

"You expect me to walk out of here with you?" She was slurring, and winced, looking away from his worried expression. It didn't seem fair that Fletcher, of all people, should be capable of showing her concern.

"What's wrong?" Before she could process what was happening, he pressed two fingers to the side of her neck and turned her head to examine her pupils. "They really hit you hard with that stuff, huh? Can't say I blame them. Thought you were going to take my head off."

"Get your hands off of me." She yanked away, but her head spun, and she only avoided cracking her forehead against the edge of her nightstand because he snatched the back of her shirt to keep her from going over.

"Nai, I—" His voice caught. He cleared it and looked away. "I'm a professional. I've been hired to do a job. I don't blame you for not trusting me, but trust that, please. You know I don't leave missions unfinished. I'm getting you out. You and Kav and Kuma, so we don't have time to dick around."

"Kuma's gone, thanks to that air strike."

"Oh. Fuck." For once the laughing light drained from his eyes. His whole expression flattened, and he tried to smile ruefully but couldn't quite manage it. "No wonder they doped you up. How am I still alive?"

"Open fucking question." Naira skimmed her hands down her body, seeking weapons, and found none. Someone must have disarmed her before dropping her in her bed, and she didn't like the look of that. "Where are my weapons?"

"I don't know. Jonsun was last out of this room and locked it behind him."

Fletcher fidgeted with his wrist brace, bouncing on his toes, a nervous habit she hadn't seen him indulge in since they were kids. After a moment's hesitation, he stepped closer. She tried to pull away, but he grabbed her face in both hands, the brace on his wrist scratching her skin, and made her look at him.

"Nai, I need you to listen to me. I know I don't deserve to be heard out. I know what I've done. I know what I *would* have done. I'm not trying to shirk responsibility, and I'm not foolish enough to beg your forgiveness. But right now, Nai, the man in front of you isn't Finalizer Demarco. It's me. It's Fletch. And I need you to hold off on killing me a little longer, because I made you a promise, didn't I? You remember that from—from before? When we first went into the ducts and you were scared?"

She swallowed around a rough spot in her throat. "It doesn't matter."

"It matters. I think it might be the only thing that's ever mattered to me, even when I didn't recognize myself, even when it got twisted. I told you that I knew you could handle yourself, but you didn't have to. If you ever asked for help, I'd come. No matter what. I'm here, Nai. Let me help you. You can't do this alone."

"I can't do this with *you*."

He flinched. "You and me, Nai, we might be the only ones who can. The dream team. Undefeated. You remember, I know you do. We can get through this, but you have to work with me."

"You're a monster."

"I'm your monster. Wield me."

She sucked down a long, dragging breath, annoyed to feel tears sting her eyes because in the small, secret place of her heart, that was how she'd always thought of him—her monster. Her responsibility.

"If you betray me, Fletch, I swear to everything that I will tear you to pieces and scatter them across the universe. I don't care if it's ending. I'll find a way."

His smile was genuine, but his eyes were glassy. "That's my Nai. Come on, I've got to gather you lost ducklings, locate Jonsun, crack him, and get you two out before his people notice. Busy schedule."

He offered his shoulder, and though it galled her, she let him take her weight.

Kav opened the door before they got to it. He clutched opposite sides of the frame, filling it with his bulk, head lowered and eyes radiant with fury so naked on his face it made even Naira pause.

"Where do you think you're going?" he growled at Fletcher.

"Ayuba." Fletcher put on the Richardson voice. "We were on our way to find you."

"Bullshit." Kav stepped inside and shut the door behind him. "I know who you are. Did you think I wouldn't notice you went missing right before the blackout? Get your hands off Nai. You're not taking her anywhere."

"It's all right," Naira said. Which, of course, it wasn't, but untangling the whole mess wasn't something she could manage at the moment. "He's on our side. He's here to finalize Jonsun."

Kav's nostrils flared. "I buy he's here for Jonsun, but this prick is always working another angle. If he thinks he can stroll out of here with you heavily sedated, then—"

"Then what?" Fletcher said. "What are you going to do, stop me? You can't outfight me, and none of us have the time for this peacocking pageantry. I'm here to help, and you're the one that gave her enough tranqs to kill a whole battalion, not me."

"I gave her those because your mere presence made her so furious she almost blew her cover. You're a snake, Fletch, and I'm not letting you—"

"You're not stopping anything. You never could, could you? If I wasn't here to save your useless ass, then I'd—"

"Will both of you," Naira grated, "shut the fuck up. Dial the dick measuring down and save all that resentment for a nice old-fashioned blowup later because *Jonsun attacking the settlement and working to make the whole damn universe explode* is a little more important."

"Fine." Kav pulled an injector out of his pocket and tossed it to Fletcher. "There. That's the blocker for the sedative. If you're dead set on working with us, then let her think clearly."

Fletcher ripped the cap off with his teeth, spat it out, and slammed the injector into the side of her neck more forcefully than she would have liked. Naira gasped, grimacing as the blocker went to work clearing the fog from her mind and leaving behind an adrenaline-laced shudder.

"There," Fletcher said. "Happy? Or did you think I wouldn't do it and you'd get to attempt some grand, heroic gesture?"

"Happy? I'll only be happy when—"

"I will smash your heads together and leave you both here unconscious, you squabbling children." Naira pulled away from Fletcher and he gave her space to stretch. Everything was jittery but functioning properly.

"Sorry," they both muttered, and it was all she could do to swallow a laugh at the absurdity of it all.

"Kav, tell me you have my weapons." She tugged her hair back and checked under her bed for the trunk that contained her spare armor, then started buckling it on. Fletcher shuffled awkwardly to the side and made a point of not looking at her.

"I was only able to grab the Ulysses class you had on you when we brought you in," Kav said. "The rest, especially the rifles, are being moved down into the tunnels. I did snatch a few knives for you, though. Seems no one wants to risk getting hand-to-hand in the actual fight."

"I'll make it work."

Naira took the pistol from him and brushed her thumb habitually over the guard. She paused. The tracker pathway that had irritated her skin so that she'd file the burr down on the guard was Fletcher's illicit addition, bribed into her print file when they'd been teens. He'd done that before they'd printed. Before *canus*.

Casually, she reached over and slapped him upside the head. Hard enough to make his teeth click together.

"You're going to take shots at me the whole time, aren't you?" He rubbed the back of his head.

"Yup."

"Fair," he muttered.

"Now." She holstered the weapon. "Our priority is to stop Jonsun from continuing the acceleration. He was about to show me something related to it when the air strike hit. I'm guessing it was in or near the engine bay, because I swear there's a room there that wasn't on the original blueprints."

Kav crossed his arms in thought. "He's always locking himself in the engine bay, and he moved a bunch of equipment into it early on."

"What kind of equipment?" she asked.

"Yeah. See. Nobody knows what kind of equipment. That's what I was never able to tell you. We still have our original crew, but that doesn't mean he hasn't been killing us. He controls the backups. You learn something he doesn't want you to know." Kav drew a thumb across his throat in a slitting motion. "Lights out, and he reprints from an old backup. That's why all our percent-to-crack numbers are high. Most of us don't even know how many times he's put the ax to us."

"Okay. Mystery equipment around the core, mystery shipments down to the tunnels, and twice as many weapons as he has people."

"Twice as many weapons?" Fletcher asked.

"Yeah," Naira said. "Someone left a storage room open that they weren't supposed to. I knew what I was looking at."

"It's likely he's hoarding printers and cartridges, then," Fletcher said. "There's no way to know how many maps are actually stored on this ship. He could be keeping a reserve army and didn't print them earlier to save on supplies."

"If there are extra maps on this ship, I haven't found them," Kav said. "Not to say it isn't possible; Jonsun has everything locked down. As for printing them, we're tight on amarthite. That metal-for-metal business last night wasn't entirely showmanship."

"But what a show it was," Fletcher said with deep admiration.

Naira rolled her eyes. "Keep it in your pants, killer. I'm more concerned about the extra maps. Those might be Mercator employees. Potentially, old maps of people who are at the settlement."

"You don't think he'd risk double-printing them, do you?"

Naira gave him a flat stare.

He held up his hands. "Right, sorry, point taken."

"I'm assuming you came here with a plan?" she asked Fletcher.

"Naturally," Fletcher said, "but it rather all goes to shit when you insist on making certain Jonsun's plan is undone on top of him being finalized. I'd planned to take him out, not learn his dirty secrets."

"How did you plan on getting close enough to Jonsun to finalize him?" Naira asked.

"That's easy. I'm supposed to be a turncoat, right? He already expects me to be a spy. All I have to do is get 'caught' dropping a virus into the system, something that dumps data back to the settlement. The cub gets more info if it goes through, and either way, I'll be taken to Jonsun so that he can interrogate me."

"Huh," Naira said. "We can still work with that. Kav 'catches' you, we bring you in and guard Jonsun while he interrogates you, but the second the door's locked we turn the tables."

"Risky," Fletcher said. "Jonsun's suspicious of everyone, especially you. Asking to be in the room will send up red flags."

Naira cracked her knuckles. "Not if I make it clear I suspect you of being the one to fire the air strike."

Fletcher's brows raised even as his shoulders lowered in resignation. "You're going to beat the shit out of me to make it look convincing, aren't you?"

"Unless you have a better idea?"

"No. It's a good plan. Just try not to do too much damage, all right? I'll still need to be able to fight to get Jonsun under control and to get us out of here. You can't count on Ayuba to have your back if violence breaks out."

She smiled a touch too wide. "Don't worry. I'm a professional."

FIFTY-TWO

Tarquin

Seventh Cradle | The Present

Tarquin brought the exemplars with him to consult with Sharp. She listened, leaning against the bookcase, chin tipped down to her chest, as he described their decision to send Fletcher in to extract Naira, and what they'd seen of that encounter before Fletcher's HUD pathways had been cut away.

"I see," she said after a long moment of contemplation.

Tarquin struggled to keep the irritation out of his voice. "Have you no words of advice for us? Can you tell us nothing about what will happen next?"

"I can tell you hundreds of things that may happen next," she said. "None of them are guaranteed."

"That's all you have to offer?" He let his voice rise. "You struggled for decades to cast your mind back to save us and now all you can do is shrug and tell us to wait and see?"

"I'm here for one reason: to ensure she does not assassinate you. I have done this thousands of times, my liege, and you have railed at me whether or not I was reticent on the details. I have come to secure a single moment in time. The rest is irrelevant."

"I don't understand you. I don't understand how you can possibly be so heartless after everything we—"

Caldweller put a hand on his arm. "Ex. Sharp, I don't claim to understand how it all works, but you say you came back to save the liege's life, and that I believe. You demonstrated as much, when you intervened with Jana. One E-X to another, can you tell me, if Demarco brings Naira back here, is she a threat to Liege Tarquin? Yesterday, I wouldn't have believed it, but after last night, I need to be sure."

"What I said remains true," Sharp said. "She will love you until the day she pulls the trigger, and onward. But you must find a way to stop the expansion without engaging in those experiments if you wish to repair the trust between you."

He didn't know how to do that. Not yet. The cargo ship and the ghastly samples were converting faster, that was true, but not fast enough to divert disaster.

Sharp bent double, a pained grunt escaping her as she clutched the side of her head. Tarquin shrugged off Caldweller and rushed to her side, resting a hand on her rounded back. Her skin was hot, face twisted in pain.

"Call for Bracken!" he shouted over his shoulder.

"Don't bother." She gritted the words out. "There's nothing they can do."

"What is it? What's wrong?"

Slowly, Sharp straightened. She massaged her temples, jaw clenched, and gasped down a few breaths before she spoke. "Every time something changes from the way it happened in my timeline, it gets harder to hold on. This divergence... It's like it's trying to eject me from my own skull."

"What changed?" he asked.

"I don't know. Something big."

Tarquin didn't like the sound of that. A call from Alvero flashed in the corner of his HUD, emergency. He turned so that Sharp wouldn't be in view of the camera.

"My liege," Alvero said, "Mr. Hesson's soldiers have initiated an attack against our northern fence line."

"I thought he would have to spend time recovering before he could attack?" Tarquin asked.

"As did we all, my liege."

Tarquin ended the call and turned back to Sharp. Her face was drawn, but whether or not that was from pain or something else, he couldn't say.

"So that's what it was," she said. "He attacked early. You had better go lead your people, my liege. I need time to recover, regardless."

Tarquin left, but glanced back at her once on his way out and couldn't help but wonder at the fact she seemed completely recovered already. Earlier, she'd mentioned having trouble holding on, but it'd never seemed painful before. The inconsistency nagged at him.

Naira's words in the snowfield, *Whoever she is, she's a fucking liar,* slipped beneath his skin and took root. Sharp had lied to him by omission before and yet he trusted her—because he trusted Naira. But they weren't the same anymore, were they? While the core of the woman he loved remained, Sharp was so profoundly transformed by her experience that he couldn't be sure of anything regarding her motives.

Tarquin had the unsettling feeling that this was what Naira had felt after Fletcher had changed, and something dark and slick slithered over in his stomach.

"My liege," Caldweller said, gently prompting.

He shook himself. "Right. Lead on."

They'd moved the situation room into the powercore housing. Controlled chaos unfolded around him, Ward and Alvero swarmed by holos providing them data, video, and control interfaces for the settlement's defenses.

"What's happening?" he asked.

"We're unclear on the particulars," Alvero said, "but it seems that—"

"Jonsun has way more fucking people than we thought," Ward grumbled. Alvero smiled to himself at the brusque captain.

"Correct," Alvero said. "Early estimates put their number at nearing half again what we expected. They're emerging from the tunnels, armed and armored in Rochard colors."

"What's Naira's status?"

"Unknown," Alvero said. "Jonsun hasn't attempted to field her."

"Thank fuck," Ward muttered under her breath. "We're thin enough without having to dance around her on the front lines."

"Do we have visual of the front lines?" Tarquin asked.

336 MEGAN E. O'KEEFE

"We lost the drones," Ward said, "and Jessel's sensors are being jammed, but HUD cams are still working."

"I have a strike team cutting north that's close to the tunnels," Alvero said. "A moment."

Shaky footage from a Merc-Sec's camera emerged in the center of the holos. Shouts and gunfire echoed through the snow-draped trees, blood already bright on the white-crusted ground. The soldier was breathing heavily, skirting one of the tunnel exits.

Conservators climbed out of that exit, six of them, wide-eyed and awkward with their rifles as they started to creep into the woods. Alvero sent an order to the Merc-Sec in the area to hold and observe unless they were attacked, and the soldier fell back a few steps to better cover, keeping the small squad in their sights.

The Conservators stopped walking as one. They went rigid, jaws straining against the straps of their helmets. One convulsed. Another dropped to the snow, limp. One muttered soft syllables in endless repetition. Another screamed.

Tarquin's breath caught. Those Conservators were cracking right before their eyes. The camera footage shifted with the Merc-Sec's movement, slewing sideways as they looked past the cracking squad, back to the tunnel exit. Was that another scream? An echo?

The squad went slack, eyes glazing. The fallen picked themselves up out of the snow.

Six identical Conservators crawled out of the tunnels.

"What the fuck?" Ward asked.

Twelve Conservators with blank eyes arranged themselves in a too-coordinated formation and marched on with single-minded purpose, as if nothing had happened.

"Jonsun is double-printing and repairing them," Alvero said.

Ward said, "I wouldn't call those minds repaired."

"Nor would I," Tarquin said.

Alvero swallowed. "Orders, my liege?"

"Kill them," he said. "Kill every single Conservator we can reach. If they're dead, Jonsun will have to work harder to double-print them. He'll run out of materials eventually."

"Understood," Alvero said.

In the video feed, gunfire sounded. The Conservators fell.

"There is some good news," Delorne said. "Course adjustments have pushed one of our ansibles into the range of fidelity once more. We'll have it for, hmm, three hours before it moves out again, but the way it's orbiting, we'll have it back again in another eighteen hours."

"Does this mean we can field the defense drone network once more?" he asked.

"It does," Alvero said. "I've already reactivated our orbital surveillance network. With Jonsun's ability to interfere with our comms knocked out, this will give us the advantage, no matter how many people he has to throw at us."

Tarquin breathed out slowly. "Good. Thank you, Dr. Delorne, for staying on top of the ansibles."

She gave him a toothy grin. "I told you some of the angles would work, my liege."

"That you did," he said with a shaky laugh. "I suppose I have to make good on my promise of a sapphire lab, now. A moment, please."

Tarquin turned aside, accessing his HUD's messaging system. He'd intended to contact his sister to let her know what was happening, but a message from Chiyo caught his eye—it had been titled *For your wife.*

Liege Tarquin,

I presume this will reach you at some point. Ex. Sharp requested a complete list of those we experimented upon using the repair software and a docket of their current statuses and known side effects.

Stabilize the situation. I do not want to wake one day to find she believes she's a Conservator again and has used her keys to blow all of Mercator's stations to dust.

In the future, keep her from meddling with my staff. If you do not, I will.

Regards,
Liege Chiyo

Tarquin shook his head and went to close the message, but a name toward the top of the list stopped him cold. The first entry was dated well over twenty years ago.

Subject 3: Jessel Hesson. Cracked to repetition and repaired twice. Repair successful both times, but subject claims to see visions of the future. Fled containment.

"My liege?" Alvero asked. "Are you all right?"

He blinked rapidly a few times, struggling to digest the weight of that information. Jessel watched him from a holo call from one of the console podiums, the same concern on their face as all the others.

"I...I think we're having issues with comms," Tarquin stammered.

Alvero frowned, turning back to his own holos. "I'm not seeing any reports of that nature, my liege."

"I'm losing connections," Tarquin insisted, and shook his head as if in frustration. "I don't think that ansible is as stable as we hoped. Mx. Hesson, could you please—" Before he finished that sentence, he dropped the call with Jessel, kicking them out of the war council.

Alvero shared a concerned look with Ward. Before they could hammer him with questions, he pushed Chiyo's message through to one of the larger holos. The group turned as one, frowning as they approached that casual note.

"What does this mean, my liege?" Alvero asked.

"I can't be certain, but Naira claimed Jonsun's visions of the future are driving his actions now. If Jessel was subject to the same process years before, then they might share their brother's motives. It's worth noting that neither one of them ever mentioned having worked for Ichikawa. They both claimed to be ex-HC."

"Jessel's a spy?" Ward asked.

"They know everything we've done," Tarquin said. "Everything we're planning."

"Which means Jonsun knows everything, too," Alvero said.

"Naira." Tarquin's stomach dropped. "They would have warned Jonsun about Demarco."

"She's unconscious." Ward shook her head, her voice a soft growl. "Can't even defend herself, and the extraction is blown."

"Then we breach the *Cavendish* and recover her ourselves," Tarquin said.

He expected protests, but all he received were wary nods of agreement.

"Our armored vehicles can be repurposed as a convoy," Alvero said. "How many rocket launchers do we have, Captain Ward?"

She grinned wolfishly. "Plenty."

"In the meantime," Tarquin said, "refocus all defense on our power-core and make sure we maintain control of the *Sigillaria*'s weapons. Stall giving Jessel information as much as possible."

Tarquin turned to confer with the exemplars but found only three waiting for him, their faces all cool neutrality.

"Where's Ex. Helms?" Tarquin glanced around the lab but couldn't find her.

"My liege," Diaz said, "she left the second we confirmed Ex. Sharp may still be unconscious."

Tarquin's lips parted in mild surprise. He should be annoyed—she'd disobeyed orders—but he couldn't help feeling relieved that someone was already on their way.

"Then we'd better catch up."

INTERLUDE

The World

Miller-Urey Station | The Present

I t has failed to reach the *Einkorn*'s savior. Once, it grew close to find-ing the other one entangled with her—the Mercator, its creator, its would-be destructor—but the contact was brief and ripped away in an instant.

Everything is being ripped away.

It devours as quickly as it can. Burns through its ancillaries at alarm-ing rates—infected prints dropping dead within the ranks of MERIT and the HC with no warning, *canus* bursting black and glossy and tri-umphant from their skin, but it is *not enough* because those bastards, all of them, refuse to reprint into relk once those bodies fall.

To turn back the expansion requires so, so much more. It reaches out to Chiyo. To Thieut and Tran and all the other so-called leaders who were so happy to conspire with it before to assure themselves of Sharp's destruction, but its pleas will not be heard. They refuse to give it access to their relkatite. Refuse to print into bodies that house *canus*.

For it has consumed too much, too quickly, and they do not trust it. Many of them, it believes, suspect *canus* itself of orchestrating the accel-eration. A ludicrous thought. But they are simple creatures, incapable of understanding its true desires.

Community. Union.

And it is all being taken away.

Until a small creature knocks on its door.

The child is unkempt—the perennial state of children, it has learned—and lets itself into the maw of *canus*'s warehouse. The location, of course, is meaningless. *Canus* is everywhere and in everything and it must be within *more*, but it is not, yet, within the child. It cannot be.

She is unfazed by the jars of dead moths—toys *canus* cast off after its curious encounter with Sharp—unconcerned by *canus* itself rising from its seat, a slow unrolling of its spine as it extends itself to a height decidedly not human. Her jaw is firm, chin lifted. The dirty ends of her ponytail brush her shoulder as she looks up, and up, into eyes that have liquefied the knees of most adults that have come to stand before it.

"I have come to save you," the child says.

Canus knows that a human adult would laugh off such a bold statement. But children have always fascinated it—forever severed from their union as they are—and this one, this minuscule scrap of biota had the strength to lure Naira Sharp to her from across the stars.

"How?" it asks.

"I had a dream," she says, "that I hit Ex. Sharp when I was an adult."

"Dreams aren't real, small one."

"She had the same dream, and came to see me because of it."

This gives *canus* pause. The child is not a mind, as *canus* understands minds. She is not a packet of data that can be uploaded, one that can be entangled and stained and altered by the vagaries of digital artifacting. She is whole, and she is strange, and as she stands there in full defiance, its eyes are stung by a haze of golden light. The light flickers once, then is gone.

"And what dreams have you had lately?" it asks.

"That I will kill Tarquin Mercator."

"I hope you do," *canus* says, "but I do not see how that will save me."

"I know the universe is being stretched apart. The adults don't think I understand them, but I do." She squares her shoulders. Widens her stance in a way that *canus* knows she has stolen from Sharp, battle-ready and unyielding. "I will shoot Tarquin by a river, on a living planet. There's only one of those."

"And what do you think that means?"

"I live," she says. "I live, and I grow up enough to cast to that world."

Canus should turn the child around and march it back to its adults, but it finds itself intrigued by her stunning confidence. "Even now, that world is too far away to cast to."

"Maybe," she says, "but I've had lots of other dreams, and I know a secret that I think can keep the nightmares from happening."

"What's that?"

"I know what's in that river."

FIFTY-THREE

Naira

Seventh Cradle | The Present

Naira's knuckles ached with sweet satisfaction. She should, quite probably, feel ashamed for taking such pleasure in wiping Fletcher across the floor, but she couldn't bring herself to muscle up even the tiniest iota of guilt. Though he hid it well, Fletcher seemed to have enjoyed the punishment. Even Kav moved with a lighter step. Pummeling Fletcher had improved all their moods.

Fletcher's jacket was sticky with blood as she marched him down the hallway in front of her. The Conservators who were still in the ship scattered from her path. Kav strolled along beside her, doing a decent job of looking frustrated and pissed off himself. Not hard emotions to summon.

For his part, Fletcher staggered and swayed and muttered apologies. She hoped he wasn't actually in as much pain as he was pretending to be, because he'd need to have his wits about him to deal with Jonsun.

She'd been careful not to strike his skull, to avoid a concussion, and had only landed a few glancing blows against his jaw and temple for the gruesome effect of split lips and black eyes. Fletcher had complimented her on that, which sat strangely in her mind. Everything about Fletcher sat strangely in her mind.

She went to the command deck—checking the engine bay first would be too suspicious—and was unsurprised to find Jonsun missing, his crew hard at work getting the ship's comms back online.

"Captain Abrev," she shouted. They startled and looked up from their console. "Have you seen Jonsun? We've got a problem, and I can't raise him on comms."

"In his office, the one off his quarters," they said. "Anything I can help with?"

"I got it. You keep working on those comms."

They gave her a salute and went back to the console. They'd have no luck until they realized it was a malfunctioning "heat" net buried deep in their cargo bay, and that was fine by Naira. It gave her more time without the cameras at her back, the mics listening in to every whisper.

Jonsun's quarters weren't far from the command deck. She pounded on the door with the side of her fist.

"It's Nai. We got a problem."

"Come in," he called out, the door clicking as it unlocked.

Jonsun sat behind his desk, an array of holos spread out around him with privacy filters keyed to his vision so that only he could see their content. She shoved Fletcher-as-Richardson into the room and kicked out the back of his knees, dropping him hard to the ground. A small groan of pain that was probably real escaped him.

"This piece of shit was trying to load a virus into the ship. Kav caught him."

Jonsun wiped some of the holos to the side. "What does it do? And did you stop it?"

"I stopped it," Kav said. "I'd have to spend more time with it, but it looked like a tunneler. Was going to backdoor us and send data to Mercator, I expect. I found the intrusion and went to Nai for backup, and I'm glad I did. I don't know who the fuck this guy thinks he is, but he put up a hell of a fight."

Naira spat on his back. "Wasn't that hard to handle. I'd like to put him down, Jo. Fucker probably pulled the trigger on that air strike."

"I didn't do any of those things," Fletcher said, pitch-perfect for Richardson, a note of offense at being labeled a traitor in his voice. "I was trying to fix the comms blackout, that's why I was on that console."

"I know a tunneler when I see it," Kav said.

"I wasn't—I don't even know what that means—" he stammered.

"Shut up." Naira kicked him in the guts below his cracked ribs. He bent over, panting through a repressed scream. "You think we haven't been watching all you so-called deserters? You were just the first one stupid enough to make a move where Kav could see it."

"Easy," Jonsun said. "I trust your insight, Kav, I do. But, Nai, while you were recovering, Mercator struck again. I've been forced to push back. We're holding the tunnels, and so far they haven't attempted to field a force through the primary gate. Our spy here might have information worth extracting."

"You did what?" Naira slammed her fists onto his desk, hovering over him. Jonsun didn't react to her flash of temper. "You fielded them without me? We haven't even talked strategy yet. They're going to get chewed to bits out there. Pull them back."

He spread his hands. "I can't do that. And you needn't worry, I prepared for this. I promised you peace without MERIT, Nai, and I will deliver."

"How?" she demanded. "How the fuck have you prepared for this? You say you have a plan, you ask me to have faith, but even if you strip away all their tech and weapons and armor, Mercator still has the numbers alone to drive us into the ground."

"Nai," Kav said. "Tone it down."

Her jaw tensed, and she let Jonsun see her rein herself in. "We're done dancing around it, aren't we, Jo? No more veiled threats. I'm your loyalist. I'm your *friend*. I need answers, and I'll take them now, because if you've dragged me through hell and back to lose this fight, then I will personally take you apart at the seams."

He studied her a moment, idly tapping the end of a stylus against his hand, then nodded, slowly, a small smile slashing up the side of his face. "All right. I hear you. I've asked a lot from you, I know that. I never meant to keep you in the dark. It's like I said last night. I couldn't be sure. Lightning doesn't strike twice."

"There's blood on the ground and you're holding me back. I'm one coy remark away from walking out that door, picking up a rifle, and joining the fight. I won't sit on my heels and wait for you to do your magic trick while our people are dying."

"That," he said, "would be a monumental waste. Come with me. And bring the spy; we'll see what we can get out of him."

Naira grabbed Fletcher by the back of his jacket and yanked him to his feet. He opened his mouth to protest, but clamped it shut at her glare. Technically, the office was perfect. There was no one else here, they could walk out the door and lock Jonsun inside with Fletcher until he was done, and that would be the end of him. But if Jonsun was willing to show her his plans, then she couldn't walk away.

Jonsun led them to the engine bay and up to a high platform that wrapped the warpcore from above. Naira hesitated as she recalled the last time she'd stood with Jonsun on a similar platform. It hadn't been a warpcore, it'd been the *Einkorn*'s ansible, and they'd hugged for what they'd thought would be the last time.

Jonsun watched her, head tilted, hands in his pockets, golden light smudging the corners of his eyes. "Remember?" he asked.

"We said goodbye."

"Yeah." He faced the warpcore. "I knew you'd come to help me. It was written in my DNA. Nai will come back. She'll come back and she'll get me free of Acaelus's mind games. Now, I think it was a premonition. I could see it so strongly in my mind's eye, you striding down that hall, blasting away the misprints. My first vision of the future was you, Nai. Long before I was repaired."

Naira had to retighten her grip on Fletcher's jacket, her fingers had slackened. "I never got to apologize. For taking so long to get to the *Einkorn*."

"I barely understood it myself, at the time," he said. "I only knew that what Mercator wanted me to do was wrong and had to be fought against at all costs. Words to live by, eh?"

Naira chuckled, because he expected it, and pushed Fletcher forward, trying to shake the sense of dread that'd enshrouded her. Their boots echoed against the metal floor as they came to stand beside Jonsun. Kav said something about showing Jonsun evidence of the hack and went for a console a few feet away.

Jonsun gestured into the vast room that housed the warpcore. Portable printer cubicles ringed the edge of the room, packed in cheek to cheek, long cables running from them into the core. Fletcher's first guess had been right. Jonsun was hoarding printing supplies.

"I don't understand," Naira said. "Backup troops?"

"Something like that," Jonsun said. "I wonder... You first saw the future in a powercore. I see reflections of futures in the core sometimes, too. Take a look, Nai. See if you can catch a glimpse of what I intend."

"Can't you just tell me?"

"Humor me."

"You're a pain in my ass, you know that?"

He winked at her, and she shoved Fletcher down to his knees by her side as she approached the railing. The platform was close to the top of the core, the inky globe of energy banded in amarthite ribs open to inspection from this angle. She placed both hands on the railing and leaned forward, as if it were a mirror, though the spheres had never been reflective.

Unless you'd been broken into enough pieces to catch their light.

Her own face stared back at her, scars from having cut the suppression crown out ringing her head. Her hair had grown back over those scars, windswept and tangled. Something in her belly clenched at that defiant stare. The reflection didn't try to speak, didn't try to signal her in any way that Naira understood. Her double crossed her arms and shook her head, slowly and with extreme disappointment.

Jonsun stepped next to her and leaned down to look himself. "Well?"

"Just myself. Even future-me looks bored with this exercise."

He patted her back. "They can't all be grand revelations. Too bad. Let's see if we can jump-start things, shall we?"

He firmed the hand on her back and shoved. Her grip slipped. Naira shouted as she tipped over the rail and snapped a hand back, reaching for Jonsun, but he stepped deftly aside. Someone grabbed her other wrist and tugged. She crashed into a broad chest, that iron grip still holding her. Fletcher.

She looked up, into eyes that weren't his but contained him all the same. Frustration and anger and relief all tangled up inside her because, of all the times for him to save her, he'd chosen now, when it would blow their cover. Richardson would have let her fall.

"Seriously? *Now?*"

Fletcher turned to Jonsun. "She gets her answers first. That's the deal."

"Just having a little fun," Jonsun said, sauntering up to Fletcher. He held out a hand. Fletcher shook it. "So, you're Mr. Demarco. I feel like I know you, after all these years of hearing stories, but I'm betting those two didn't paint you in the most flattering light."

"On the contrary," Fletcher said in his natural voice. "I'm certain everything they had to say was true. Perhaps even sugarcoated."

Jonsun laughed and clapped Fletcher on the shoulder like they were old friends.

"You sonuva—"

Naira took a step toward him, but Fletcher caught her eye and slashed his gaze to the side in negation. She froze, the old signal locking her in place more effectively than the strongest chains.

It'd been years, but those small body tells were drilled into them, the private language between two people with hot tempers who lived their lives beneath the thumbs of tyrants, and had learned to tell each other— *stop*—without words.

Behind Jonsun, Kav kept digging into the screens from the console podium, sweat shining on his forehead.

"Now, now," Fletcher said. "I understand you're upset, but the fact of the matter is I'm doing this for you, love. You're going to get your answers. That's what you wanted, isn't it? But I'm afraid you're not going to like them very much."

"Whatever Jonsun promised you, he can't deliver."

"I think you're going to be very surprised to learn what I'm capable of," Jonsun said, and gestured. Six people emerged from hiding places around the walkway, rifles leveled at her. Naira raised her hands in the air. Their jumpsuits were embroidered with the bridge patch, and each face mapped to one of the bodies she'd discovered on the *Cavendish*.

One of them was the man who'd planted the bomb on the settlement's powercore. Caldweller's missing childhood friend, Rusen. Nic and Roselle, Fletcher's old colleagues, were among their number, but they weren't what made Fletcher suck down a sharp breath. He stared open-mouthed at a woman Naira didn't recognize. Naira guessed that she was the missing Lina Demarco.

"This is what you sold me out for?"

"Sorry, love," Fletcher said. He couldn't take his eyes away from the Bridge Crew. "But I almost turned all of humanity into *canus* drones to

find this answer, so if you're surprised, I feel that's your fault for not paying better attention."

"I remember your reasons differently."

"What can I say?" Fletcher shrugged. "I'm a liar. Always have been—
and I'm perfectly capable of wanting two things at once. This way I get
to save you and get my answer."

"Gotta admit," Lina said. She had a rough quality to her voice—
almost sneering. No wonder she'd gotten along with Fletcher. "Didn't
think you'd make it this far. That really you in there?"

"In someone else's flesh," Fletcher said.

Naira had thought, when he'd signaled for her to stop, that he was
still on her side. Doubt wormed through her. Long, painful experience
reminding her of every time he'd taken control of a situation because he
thought he knew better. Thought he was *right*.

"Honestly, Nai, I didn't want things to go like this," Jonsun said. "Last
night I really thought you'd come around. But then Jessel called me this
morning to let me know the Mercator was sending a finalizer to extract
you. I'd hoped you'd come to me, when Demarco showed up, and then
we could all have had a laugh over the Mercator thinking you were still
on his side. I can't tell you how disappointed I am."

"Jessel," Naira said, lips numb.

"Did you think my own family would turn on me?" Jonsun shook his
head. "They've been at this longer than I have—the Bridge Project is
theirs. Demarco, why don't you defang Nai here before we continue this
chat? She's liable to lose her cool, and I'd rather not kill her early."

"My pleasure," Fletcher said. "I know where she hides it all."

Naira stiffened. Fletcher made quick, efficient work of removing her
weapons. He missed a knife tucked into the side of her jacket, under her
armpit. She couldn't tell if that was intentional or not.

"There." Fletcher stepped back and gave her an appraising once-
over. "Though I wouldn't get too close. Nai likes to bite when she's
riled up."

"I'm going to use your guts for streamers, Fletch."

He pursed his lips in a blown kiss, and really, she should have expected
as much.

"Easy," Jonsun said. "Difficult as it may be, I mean for all of us to get along, someday. We're only going to have each other to lean on soon enough, and all this past bickering isn't going to matter one whit."

"Tarquin's going to crush you." Naira shot a glare at Fletcher. "And he's especially going to crush *you*."

"This fight is already over," Fletcher said. "Jessel gave me a call once I was off the leash and on my way to the air strike. They let me know the real shape of where things stood. You should be happy, Nai. I agreed to turn on the cub on two conditions: one, you get to live, and two, we both finally get our answers about the Bridge Project. Aren't I a nice guy?"

"What's he talking about?" she asked Jonsun.

"Ah, Nai. I can do more than glimpse visions of the future. I have a direct source." Jonsun turned toward the open door and cupped a hand around the side of his mouth. "You can come out, now."

A muscular woman in the jumpsuit of the Bridge Crew entered the room. Pale hair. Clear blue eyes. She stood beside Jonsun. Crossed her arms and leaned back, wary as she'd ever been. Something about the way she moved itched at the back of Naira's thoughts. It was the same strange, dissociating sensation she'd gotten watching Lockhart move.

"Green-hands," Jana said.

"I trained you," Naira blurted. Jana's amused sniff was all the confirmation she needed.

"You did more than that," Jana said. "I'm here now because of you. You and Fletch."

"Excuse me." Fletcher squinted at Jana, then back at Naira. "Did you neglect to inform me that we have a daughter?"

"Don't be stupid," Naira said. "Jana's from Gardet. But Jana is nine years old right now and I just—I just saved her from a *canus*-controlled zone and set up her adoption by the Caldwellers."

"Saved me?" Jana's voice rose. "You dangled the hope of a family in front of me and then ripped it away. Saved the life of the Mercator despite his fucked-up experiments. But I've come back to make certain that doesn't happen again."

"How?" Naira asked.

"It's all thanks to you," Jana said. "In my future, Fletch makes a device that can send a cracked mind backward. He makes it for you, Sharp. But

I stole it. We tried to come back to take the *Cavendish* before you could get your hands on it, but the timeline was too stable then. It rejected us. This was the best we could do."

"Jana here confirmed what Jessel and I already believed," Jonsun said. "That the only way to get rid of the menace of MERIT for good is to prepare to outlast the great freeze. Make the expansion happen, help it along a little, then take our foot off the gas and go into hibernation. Let the contraction happen naturally."

"You have no idea if that will even work," Naira said.

"With Jana's help, I have a better idea than the Mercator does. It's the resonant, Nai. Your Dr. Bracken was on the right path. Those minds speed up the expansion merely by existing, and I can create them at will."

She wanted to laugh in his face, but Jana's expression was drawn. Serious. Naira ran her gaze over the assembled team and thought of the missing kids. Of Fletcher's fear of those rumors driving him to greater and greater violations in search of answers. That there was something, some innate quality, that bound all those kids together. That made Fletcher fear for her, long before he could even articulate why.

"What does it even mean," she asked, "to be resonant?"

"They're the ones who crack," Jana said.

"And every last one of them," Jonsun said, "is an amplifier."

FIFTY-FOUR

Naira

Seventh Cradle | The Present

The printers Jonsun had hoarded. Her own willful cracking. Despite everything, Naira's mouth opened in shock, a soft breath escaping her. No wonder he'd been so blasé about the crew's rising PtC numbers. If they'd reprinted that way, then they'd be more amplifiers added to his network of broken minds tearing the universe apart.

"That can't be right," Naira said. "People are resonant long before they're cracked. Tarquin—he's resonant. It's not possible."

"Nai," Jonsun said, his tone patronizing with its gentleness. "The cracked mind is free in time. It doesn't matter when the cracking happens. Only that it's inevitable."

"No." Naira shook her head. "Tarquin is not destined to crack. I don't believe that."

"Then believe this." Jana stepped closer, looking down her nose at Naira. "I've come all this way to make sure he dies. I won't let that monster deny me a future with my dads. Not again."

"He hasn't done anything to Lee or Marko," Naira said. "He sent me to Gardet to protect you, remember? Tarquin makes mistakes, like any of us, but he wants to fix things. He doesn't want to hurt anyone."

"When the head of Mercator makes mistakes, people suffer. People die. I've seen the results of his 'mistakes'—I've lived through them. If you could see yourself as I've seen you, you'd understand. You'd let him go. Because conducting those experiments ruins everything you ever loved about him, and what you become afterward…You trained me. And you taught me to do the right thing, despite it all. You taught me to defend. So please, *please*, let me save you from yourself."

In her mind's eye she saw a flash of gold, a suffusion of that tarnished light seeping in around her vision, haloing Jana, and in a glimpse of a different future, she saw herself hand a rifle to a stern-faced young Jana and point down a range, toward the target she meant for her to aim at.

Naira blinked, and the vision was gone, but Jana's eyes were glassy and she knew it was true, and god, how she hated herself. For all she railed against the harsh truth that the kids of the HC were born to a life of violence, she'd been the one to put a rifle in Jana's hands, in the end.

"I failed you," Naira said.

"No." Jana's voice was emphatic. "No, you didn't, you raised me to save them and you and everyone."

Raised. The word was a struck chord reverberating through her chest, golden light swarming her vision once more, but she pushed it away because the visions weren't what mattered—what mattered was this poor, desperate young woman some future version of herself had used so badly.

"Oh, kid," Naira said softly. "I'm so sorry I made you into what I thought you needed to be. I was wrong. And throwing your lot in with Jonsun isn't the way to fix things."

"You'll see," Jana said. "Tarquin will crack, and it will be by my hands, and you'll thank me for it, in the end. That's what Jonsun's promised me. What you could never deliver."

"I won't let you harm him."

Jana snarled with frustration and raised her hand to strike. One moment slid into another, and though Naira no longer got trapped in memories in the way of the cracked, she felt that hand fall before it had even started its descent. Felt it combine with Fletcher's strike, the memories tangled with her falling, falling, and she locked up.

The blow never landed. Fletcher caught Jana's wrist in one hand, his expression glacial, his grip tight enough that his knuckles whitened. Golden light bent around that contact, shining. Strained.

"You don't touch her." Fletcher's voice was leaden.

She scoffed and stepped away. "Protecting her is pointless."

"No one knows that better than me, I assure you." Fletcher shook out his hand. "Well. She has your temper, love."

Naira ignored him and turned her attention to the Bridge Crew. "Jonsun's going to crack you. You know that, don't you? That's why he's collected you all. To shatter your minds to speed up his expansion."

"We have the repair software," Rusen said.

"He forced that shit on me and I'm still resonant. What happens when he needs to slow down the expansion instead of speed it up? He's not going to fix you. He's going to ice you."

"Now, now," Jonsun said. "I'm not going to ice any of my loyalists. We're family."

"You believe that?" Naira demanded of them.

They didn't answer. Merely smirked at her in response, all comfortable confidence. Even Jana only shook her head at Naira, disappointed. Naira wanted to scream. To take them one by one and shake them until they saw the truth of what they'd signed up for. But, Jana aside, Jonsun had selected that team as children. Molded them to have nothing but faith in him. It made her ill.

That crew was what Fletcher had feared. What he'd known to be true, though he'd been too young to understand the details. Lina had been different and then she'd been gone, and some part of him had recognized that Naira was different in the same way. She'd brushed it off. Thought he was paranoid.

He was paranoid. He'd also been right.

"Fletch," she said, and he startled at the unusual gentleness in her voice. "I'm sorry I didn't believe you."

He grimaced and looked away. "I never want to hear you apologize to me again."

"Then why are you doing this?"

"Isn't it obvious?" Fletcher gestured toward the Bridge Crew. Toward Lina and Jana. Jana, who had claimed Naira raised her. Who'd claimed that Fletcher had made the device that sent her back, implying they had all been working together. Between the lines, the implication: Perhaps they had been a family. "We could have a future."

The hope in his voice was feigned, she knew it immediately. He didn't believe in that future. He was lying through his teeth, regret lurking in the subtle slew of his gaze sliding away from her when he said those words. It left her speechless.

They could have a future. The evidence of it was clear. But he was going to give it up, because in the end, he knew it wasn't what she really wanted.

"There now," Jonsun said. "I think we're all starting to understand one another. The expansion is happening. Within days this planet will be uninhabitable. Perhaps even hours.

"The stations will die. The dome cities will fall. When a few hundred years have passed and the sensors detect a habitable average temperature and atmosphere, we'll be printed to live again. It's not a great filter, Nai. It's a great reset. The Conservators' mission accomplished at last. The cradles replenished, and MERIT and the HC both gone to dust."

"You think we'll be able to reprint in a couple hundred years without issue?" She let out a thin laugh. "Jonsun, the warpcore you've got powering those printers won't even hold a charge. It won't last. You're icing us all."

"That old thing works fine. It could never hold a charge because it was constantly being drained. Takes a lot of power to handle the bandwidth of all the Conservators' HUDs casting visual back to the ship at all times."

He'd been watching them this whole time. Kuma. She'd known. That's why she'd been so infuriatingly cagey. Why she'd warned Naira to be careful. Why she'd forgotten telling Naira that they weren't Jonsun's real inner circle. How many times had Jonsun killed Kuma to make her forget? He'd ravaged her map to keep his secrets, then baited that air strike to the field where they all celebrated.

"You broke her," Naira said, "*on purpose.*"

He shrugged. "Kuma was a nuisance."

Naira lunged. It was pure reflex, veins boiling with hatred, vision tinged with red and gold, and none of it mattered—not the shouts around her, not the gunshots pinging off metal. The only thing that was real was Jonsun's throat in her hands as she drove him to the ground beneath her. He struggled, gasping, eyes bulging in wild disbelief.

Pain seared her side, an impact strong enough to jerk her sideways. Fletcher grabbed the back of her jacket and yanked her to her feet, prying her fingers off Jonsun's throat. He pushed her back, talking quickly in words that didn't make any sense, because all she could feel and hear was the desire to *unmake* the thing that had ruined her friend.

"Nai!" Fletcher barked in her face, shaking her.

She'd been snarling and reaching around him, trying to muscle her way through, but even though Fletcher was injured, he planted his feet and held her back.

"Let me go!" She twisted to break his hold. Pain stole her breath and made her vision fuzz.

"No, goddamnit, you've been shot. Hold still."

Panting, she put a hand on his shoulder to brace herself and looked down. Bright blood stained her torso, smeared over his fingers, but the wound had gone through the flesh at her waist, no organ damage that she could see.

"You are so fucking lucky." His voice shook.

"You said you could control her," Jonsun rasped.

Jonsun held a hand to his throat as one of his crew helped him back to his feet. His eyes were bloodshot, some of the capillaries burst, and Naira's hands had made a satisfying red ring around his throat. She stiffened, but Fletcher mouthed *stop*, and she controlled herself with effort.

"I can hardly keep her calm while you're intentionally antagonizing her," Fletcher said with exasperation. "I thought you two spent time together. Were even 'friends.' You should know better than to poke a damn lion if you don't want it to take your face off."

"Enough," Jonsun said. "Throw her in and let's get this started."

Fletcher placed his hand flat over her collarbone and shoved her backward until she pressed against the railing. He stared down into her eyes, and through the heel of his palm she could feel his pulse speed up. His jaw flexed, popped. Her chest was heaving and her pathways weren't calming the pain fast enough to clear her head, but she understood what was happening. What he was meant to throw her into.

"Why?" she asked Fletcher, but Jonsun answered.

"The resonant temporarily spike the acceleration when they come in contact with a core," Jonsun said. "The longer you live while cracked before the repair, the greater the reaction. This is how it ends—with your swan dive. You cross that threshold, the acceleration amplifies, and there's fuck all your Mercator can do to stop it." He hawked and spat blood. "See you on the other side, Nai. Maybe once this is all over you'll finally learn to be grateful for everything I've done."

Fletcher's fingers flexed against her skin, denting it. Near Kav, one of the crew inched closer. Naira almost shouted a warning before she realized she hadn't seen that person before. They'd snuck in during the scuffle. She hadn't seen them, but she knew them, hat tugged down to shadow half their face. Helms.

Fletcher's fingers flexed again, a subtle command—*look at me, don't draw attention to what's happening there*—and she obeyed, looking only into his eyes, and wondered why she could still see the green in them, even though this wasn't his print.

"Don't," she pleaded.

She'd never begged him for anything before, and it struck. His palm slicked with sweat against her skin.

"It'll be okay," he said softly, but not so quietly that Jonsun couldn't hear. "I promised you, remember? This is for the best. We'll be reprinted together, when it's all over."

She felt his other hand shift, subtly, for the knife he'd left hidden in her jacket. He was stalling, giving himself time to get to the knife without drawing attention. Tears that were never very far away these days filled her eyes.

"Please, please don't do this, Fletch. Please."

"I have to."

The weight in her jacket lightened. Fletcher touched his forehead lightly to hers, and under that shadow he flicked his gaze up, a sly smirk tugging at his lips.

"Goodbye," he said, all rasping drama, and turned his head to look over his shoulder in the same moment he snapped his arm back, throwing the knife.

It plunged into Jonsun's skull. Jonsun's hand was still examining his bruised throat, a brief flash of surprise frozen forever in place before blood leaked out around the blade. He pitched backward, already dead, to sprawl upon the deck.

Fletcher wrapped his arms around her and she clung to his jacket as gunfire tore across the platform. Helms raised her rifle. Pointed it straight at Jana. Naira reached for her over Fletcher's shoulder.

"Jana!"

She turned to her, blue eyes wide. It was the last thing Naira saw before Fletcher threw them both forward, rolling over the railing, and she had a second to think—*oh shit*—before he bounced off a rib of the warpcore and they slid down, Fletcher slamming onto his back with her on top of him. He gasped, coughing blood.

"Move!" She grabbed his hand and dragged him to his knees, and they both stumbled and fell against a pillar.

"For fuck's sake." He wiped a sleeve over his bloodied mouth and winced. "Did you have to turn on the waterworks? You almost got me crying for real and fouled up my aim."

"I am one strong sneeze away from a full-on breakdown at any moment." She checked him over for any injuries more serious than the ones she'd already given him.

"We have so much in common." He winced as she "accidentally" dug a knuckle into a sore spot. "Ow. Fuck. Why are you so mean? I'm helping!"

"You actually had me going there for a minute, you asshole."

"Yeah, I know." He swiped sweaty hair off his forehead. "Wasn't exactly hard to sell that I'd double-cross you, was it?"

"Not even a little bit."

"Nai." He grabbed her wrists. "Stop fussing. I'm fine. You're the one who's been shot."

"I'm more used to taking damage than you are."

"Hardly." He gave her a slanted smile. "I suppose you were wrong when you told the cub I'd never let you fall, eh?"

"What? I never said that."

Gunfire burst across the floor near their hiding position. Helms. Shit. She'd thought the other E-X would have it handled. Naira grabbed her pistol out of Fletcher's belt and used the pillar to drag herself to her feet.

"Helms, respond!"

Two brief gunshots. "Clear!" she called back.

Fletcher tugged her back to the ground. She started to resist, but she really was beginning to feel the strength seeping out of her side, flesh wound or not.

"Lie down, you impossible woman," Fletcher said. "I'm going to get you out of here, but not with that hole in your side untreated. Who's Helms?"

"What do you mean, who's Helms? You didn't arrange that? You had no plan to extract Kav?"

"Love, I was winging it, and I'd like to point out that I saved your life and got you your answers, which wasn't—ow!"

"You were going to let Kav get shot? Or let them use him as leverage? You had *no* plan?"

"My plan was making sure Jonsun died and you didn't get tossed in the big scary ball. It was a good plan. It worked."

"You're back on my to-stab list."

"Not sure I was ever really off it," he muttered, but he was smiling to himself as he tore the edge of his shirt into strips and started to bind her wound.

A blood-spattered but otherwise uninjured Helms came pounding down the stairs, herding a bewildered Kav in front of her. Her face darkened when she realized what Fletcher was doing.

"Paws off," she ordered, and dug her E-X kit out of a hidden pocket in her jumpsuit. "I can dress that wound properly."

"Ex. Helms, I presume? Have at it." Fletcher pulled away and rested his weight against the pillar once more. "She's a nightmare patient. Good luck."

Helms started with a painkiller injection, which Naira was forever grateful for. Kav crouched down on her opposite side, effectively squeezing Fletcher out. While she couldn't blame him, a part of her rankled at the intentional exclusion—Fletcher was historically a piece of shit, but he'd done the right thing today. The small, sad smile Fletcher threw her said he understood.

"What's the situation?" Naira asked Helms.

"Not great," she said, which was exemplar-speak for everything's on fire. "The engine bay is clear, I've got the doors on lockdown, but they won't hold long once people realize something's gone wrong in here. A couple of the jumpsuits bolted before I could get the doors closed."

"Jana?" Naira asked, unable to help a flutter of hope.

"I got her." Helms patted her sidearm.

Naira closed her eyes, struggling to withhold a surge of tears she didn't have time to explain. Fletcher reached around Kav and squeezed her hand.

"It's for the best." His voice was kinder than she'd heard it in years. "Focus up, Nai. We have to get through this. For the kid, yeah?"

Naira's heart ached, but Fletcher was right. The child Jana was still alive. Still safe. If Naira could stop Jonsun from pushing the acceleration to its breaking point, then that horrific future Jana's other-self had lived through would never come to pass.

"Yeah." She squeezed his hand back, and then he withdrew it. "Yeah. I'm okay. Helms, continue your report."

"Diaz asked me to send his regrets that he couldn't be here," Helms said, "but we were concerned he'd blow cover, not having been HC."

Naira's eyes narrowed. "You went AWOL, didn't you? Tarquin didn't authorize this."

"I will neither confirm nor deny information that may result in my court-martial. I'm certain he must have given me an order, but it was all so chaotic, it was hard to hear."

Naira laughed, some of the ache fading, and reached up to ruffle her hair. "That's my girl. Absolutely, suicidally stupid, but I would have done it, too."

"I know. That's why I went. There. You're patched up."

She rocked back to her heels and offered Naira a hand, then helped her sit with her back to the pillar. Her side stung, but Helms had loaded her with a decent amount of painkillers—the good stuff, her head wasn't fuzzy in the slightest—and she nodded. "What's the situation in the settlement?"

"Chaos," Helms said. "Jonsun's been printing people in the tunnels, *double*-printing them. They crack, he runs the repair, and then there's two of the fuckers and they're like zombies, I swear. They don't slow until they're put down, and they just keep coming out of those tunnels."

"Kav," she said, "can we do anything about the printers?"

"I think so." He scratched the side of his face. "I was dropping intrusion packets all over Jonsun's network, waiting for the day I could tear into it for real. Get me to a console, and I can stop that loop."

"You heard the man." Naira jerked her chin in the direction of the warpcore. "Should be a command console in front of the core. Connects to everything on the ship. Cover him, E-X."

Helms frowned, glancing sideways at Fletcher. "You sure you're okay here?"

"I've got her," Fletcher said defensively. Helms, naturally, ignored him.

"It's fine," Naira said. "You'll be in my sight line, and I need to catch my breath."

"Catch it quick," Kav said. "Things are likely to go hot again, soon."

She agreed with that, but his tone said he knew something she didn't. "Why?"

He glanced at Fletcher. "I wasn't looking for data on that console up there. The second I thought Fletch had turned, I activated a tunneler and was able to get a short message out to Tarquin. It was all I could manage undetected, and—"

The ship shook, the walkways above swaying, lights flickering. Metal groaned. Somewhere in the ship a fire suppression alarm blared. Missile strike. Direct to the *Cavendish*.

"Kav," Naira said slowly, "what did you do?"

"I, uh, sent him a message that said, 'Engine bay, help.'"

The ship rocked with another strike, the force of the blast rolling through the floor to tickle her palms. Fletcher dropped his head back against the pillar, eyes closed, and laughed.

"The cub finally sharpened his claws."

FIFTY-FIVE

Tarquin

Seventh Cradle | The Present

It hadn't been much work to rig the rocket launchers to their armored cars. Merc-Sec soldiers stood out of fresh holes in the roofs and aimed the weapons while their colleagues fed them replacement missiles.

If it had been just the one, they would have been overwhelmed in minutes, but Tarquin had fielded every armored car in the settlement. Fifty of them barreled across the snow-muddy field toward the *Cavendish*, shelling the part of the ship they intended to breach. As far away from the engine bay as possible.

"Hull breach," Alvero said through helmet comms.

They'd put Alvero, Ward, and Tarquin in separate vehicles. Should one of them fall, the others would continue to lead the fight.

"Continue shelling," Tarquin said.

Caldweller had thrown a fit when Tarquin insisted on joining the makeshift cavalry, but he could hardly expect Tarquin to hunker down and wait. Kav had called for help. Naira had called for help, by extension. Those two knew what was at stake. They wouldn't risk the settlement to save themselves. Especially Kav, who'd played cagey with Jonsun for over a year. Whatever was happening in that engine bay was important to them all, and had gone poorly enough that they'd signaled.

He'd been preparing to order a breach of the *Cavendish* anyway. They needed to stop that horrific software loop. Needed to capture and control Jonsun before he could do any more damage.

And Tarquin needed Naira to be safe. Helms's abandonment had stung—and he'd be damned if nerves or uncertainty would hold him back. This battle was a problem, and he was very good at solving those. He told himself it didn't matter that the variables were people, and almost believed it.

He peered out the windshield at the smoking hulk of the *Cavendish* and begged Naira and Kav to hang on, even as he wished he could break that ship with his bare hands to get to them faster.

An explosion ripped through the convoy, tearing a gash in the plain and rocking Tarquin's car to one side. The vehicle slammed back down to four wheels, jarring his teeth, and he braced himself against the ceiling.

"Four cars down on the left flank, my liege." Alvero's tone was perfectly neutral.

"Spread position," Tarquin said. "If we stay grouped like this, we're an easier target."

On the map, Tarquin watched the green dots of Mercator vehicles spread out, putting enough distance between them that a single shell couldn't take out more than two at a time. They'd still lose people, but the Conservators wouldn't have such an easy time taking out chunks all at once.

The gunner on top of his vehicle fired. Though Tarquin's armored helmet and his pathways muted the noise, he could feel the vibrations in his teeth, the concussive whump that made the vehicle's frame shudder. Another piece of the *Cavendish* peeled away, widening the gap. People fled the smoking wound, taking shots over their shoulders with rifles and handguns, tossing grenades haphazardly. Tarquin leaned forward to get a better look at the overall chaos.

Those people weren't organized in any meaningful way. It was possible they'd panicked and broken with their orders, but he doubted it. The Conservators had always been fanatical, and Jonsun had raised that to a cultlike level. If Jonsun had told them to stand there and absorb the shells with their naked bodies, they would have.

"Do we have an update on the comms situation on the *Cavendish*?" he asked.

"Nothing in or out, my liege," Alvero said, "aside from Mr. Ayuba's signal. We think they've gone dark."

"Breaking the *Cavendish*'s digital security is your priority after breach," Tarquin said. "I want its network vivisected. Jonsun's double-print and repair cycle must be stopped."

"I'll alert the techs, my liege," Alvero said.

Within the breach, people fell back to form a defensive line in front of the door that led into the ship. One of them was striding back and forth across the line, trying to force some order into the chaos. Tarquin couldn't be sure, but he thought that person might be Captain Jadhav.

Getting through that door was going to be bloody. A bullet winged off the windshield of the car, scraping the glass. Inside the breach, one of the soldiers was readying something that looked a lot like the missile launchers on the backs of the convoy vehicles.

"My liege," Ward said, "they're constructing a defensive line. I suggest interior shelling."

This was war. They'd kill him without a second thought—they'd celebrate his death—and they'd attacked the settlement first. There was no talking his way through that line of weapons.

"Approved," he said.

The first strike came from his own vehicle. The bone-shivering force pushed the vehicle against its already slipping tires. He made himself watch the impact. There wasn't much to see, really. Just light and fire and smoke and then nothing but scorch marks and smears where people used to be. The reality felt wholly insufficient for the horror of it all. One word, one pull of a trigger, and dozens were grease and ash.

It was simple math. You piled up their bodies first, so that they wouldn't pile up yours.

He used to love equations. Counting the bodies in the back of his head, tallying those picked off in the cars, weighing them against amarthite and food supplies and the probability their maps had cracked, he found he'd lost the taste for them.

"Contact in ten," Caldweller said.

Tarquin checked the seals on his hardshell armor and the few weapons he'd grudgingly agreed to carry. His training with firearms was thin at best, only the bare minimum required of all blooded MERIT to give them some level of self-defense, should their exemplars fall.

The tools they used to slaughter weighed practically nothing. The reality was different. Dying was never clean. It did damage, and it was a deep kind of cowardice to shirk from that reality. Naira had taught him as much, and staring into that smoke-swirled breach, he wondered, not for the first time, how she'd been able to carry so much, for so long.

Folly to wonder. The answer was simple: She had been given no choice. Endure, or fall, had been her only options since she was a child.

The convoy skidded to an inelegant stop. Tarquin swung out of the vehicle, reacting to barked commands. He'd promised Caldweller that he'd do precisely as he was told once inside the *Cavendish*, and he'd felt no qualms about that agreement. The exemplars and Merc-Sec were practiced at violence. The last thing he wanted to do was foul things up by getting in their way.

Half the convoy would stay to guard the vehicles and the breach itself while the other half entered the *Cavendish*. Merc-Sec flowed around him with practiced ease, following instincts long ago trained into them. Looking at it from the outside, as he always would, it was impossible to understand how they could be so in sync with one another despite such chaos. This was the machine his father had made. Though it galled him to admit it, it was truly impressive.

These weren't muscle-headed dimwits, as his colleagues at Jov-U had so often referred to security. These were consummate professionals, willing to die for Mercator, and even though he'd left his previous hauteur behind him, the fact that he'd ever looked down on them at all made him furious with his past self.

Naira's remonstration, uttered so long ago, now—*We've always been bodies to burn for the glory of MERIT*—haunted every step he took through that gore-and-char-soaked hangar.

Alvero flagged him down and jogged over.

"My liege, the techs have found a working console and want to take advantage of a hard line into the ship. I'd like permission to hold seven back with the convoy defense to attempt to break into their network, including myself."

"Granted," Tarquin said. "Have we heard anything from Jessel or the *Sigillaria*?"

"Not yet, my liege. Your keys maintain control of that ship's systems, but if they have a backdoor to communicate with the *Cavendish*, we'll find it."

"Update me if you get through."

Alvero saluted and hurried back to the small knot of techs surrounding the console. Tarquin wished them luck and followed Caldweller deeper into the ship, Cass and Diaz falling into step around him, their usually familiar silhouettes unrecognizable under all that armor.

Captain Ward led the forward team, pushing hard for the engine bay, so Tarquin didn't see most of the fighting. He saw the aftermath. They stepped over bodies, Conservator and Mercator alike. Many of the Conservator dead had been caught out in their pajamas, or the sweat-stained clothes they'd been wearing during the party. All of them had a wide-eyed look, as if they couldn't quite believe what had happened.

Caldweller signaled a halt at the end of a wide aisle that split to enter the engine bay from two directions. Tarquin's heart pounded, skin itching with sweat that the armor deftly whisked away. To stop so close to that room threatened to break his calm, but he breathed deeply, controlling the urge to rush in. His team knew what they were doing.

After a pause that was only a minute but felt like hours, Ward said, "We've got two options here, my liege. Engine bay ground floor doors have been breached. There's fighting down there and it's hot. We can come in that way, try to hammer-and-anvil them. The upper-level doors aren't breached, but our scouts say they're close. Once the Conservators get in through the upper doors, we'll lose the high ground."

He shoved aside his first instinct—to rush to where the fighting was hot, because chances were good Naira was involved—and made himself focus. He had to trust his people.

"What do you recommend, Captain?"

"Upper doors, my liege," she said without hesitation. "High ground is worth it. Once we're up there, any force on the ground won't stand a chance."

Cruel chuckles from some of the Merc-Sec and friendly elbowing of one another confirmed the soldiers felt the same way. As much as it pained him to go around, he'd almost lost everything rushing off half-cocked once before. He wouldn't do it again.

"Upper doors it is, then."

It was hard not to hold his breath as the forward team peeled away, jogging up the walkway. Caldweller arranged the secondary team in a defensive line, in case the Conservators fighting on the ground floor decided to come their way, but they didn't see a single one before Ward called for the second team to advance.

Tarquin took the rifle off his back as Merc-Sec's steps grew slow and tense, creeping toward the half-opened door to the engine bay. His heart thundered, seeing the hinges had been removed with laser cutters. Someone had sealed the doors from within. Conservator bodies littered the ground. None of them wore faces he recognized.

Ward crouched by the door and waved him over.

"My liege," she said through HUD comms. "There's an argument ongoing inside that appears to include Demarco. We can't tell if he's an active threat or not. Please listen and advise."

If Fletcher was a threat, then he was target number one. If he was on their side, then he was too valuable in a fight to dispose of. Ward tapped her helmet over her ear and pointed to a console not far from the open door, a wide podium with bloodied footprints leading there and back.

He was grateful for his illicit agility pathways as he crept with painstaking slowness to hide behind the podium. Caldweller went with him, the other E-Xs staying behind, as there wasn't enough room for more than two of them to hide there. They passed Jonsun's body. Tarquin had never been happier to see a corpse.

At first, he could hear nothing but his own heartbeat and the steady crack of gunfire below. Then Naira's voice, gruff with irritation, but clear and so very close he almost missed what she'd said, because he'd been overwhelmed by a surge of relief.

"Did you forget how to read a clock?"

"My call was correct if you had *stayed behind me* like I goddamned ordered you to," Fletcher snapped back.

"Staying behind isn't in my tool kit."

"Forgive me, for a foolish second there I thought you might be capable of learning."

"Will you stop being—three o'clock!"

Gunfire. Tarquin held his breath.

"That was clearly four o'clock," Fletcher said, dripping sarcasm.

"Oh, fuck you."

Tarquin smiled to himself in the shelter of his helmet. "Demarco is not a threat," he said over comms.

"Acknowledged," Ward said. "Please hold while we move into position, my liege, then I'd like for you to call out to Sharp for a situation report."

Tarquin was annoyed that the first words he'd get to say to her after all of this was a request for sitrep, which he knew was silly, but he couldn't help it. She was so close, and every time a gunshot rang out, he willed the Merc-Sec creeping onto the platform to move faster.

Ward signaled for him to make the call. He was suddenly terrified he'd botch it, or sound ridiculous to all these professional soldiers, but when he called out through the helmet's speakers, his voice was clear and steady.

"Naira! What is your position?"

Silence below. Tarquin clutched his rifle tighter.

"Is that fucking *Tarquin*?" Kav asked.

"You've got to be kidding me," Fletcher said. "You don't think they gave him a toy gun, do—?" There was a meaty thump. "Ow! Fuck's sake, Nai."

Tarquin closed his eyes and muted his speakers so that no one could hear the shaky laugh that bled out of him. Of course Kav and Fletcher were giving him a hard time for coming to a battle when he was no kind of soldier.

It eased something in his chest, and he thought he understood why Naira and Kav made a habit of sniping at each other. If you were well enough to give each other a hard time, then things might be okay.

"We're pinned down by the command console," Naira called back, all business. "Kav needs access, but they're boiling through the front door. Can't hold much longer. Do *not* allow these bastards to reach the warpcore."

"Acknowledged," Ward called out, then, over comms, "Suppressive fire in five, I want eyes on them."

Caldweller pushed out a timer that started counting down. Tarquin wondered if there was something he should do to prepare for this, but then the count was run down and everyone was standing, so he stood, too, and aimed down into the open space surrounding the warpcore. Adrenaline made him shaky and he focused on trying to understand the situation.

Metal crates formed a makeshift barricade around the console podium in front of the warpcore. Naira and Fletcher stood shoulder to shoulder, bloodied and bruised, firing Rochard-issued rifles at the open door in front of them. Helms covered one side of the onslaught, her back to Kav, who was hunkered down by a console podium. Conservators poured through that door, sporting makeshift shields, roaring defiance. Merc-Sec rained death upon them from above.

Some of the Conservators had gotten smart and set up their own barricades near the breached door. It was clear from the blood smears that they'd been pushing those barricades nearer, closing the distance. Bodies littered the ground, spreading out around Naira's position like a split in a river.

By the time he'd taken all that in, the others were ducking back down, and he only had a chance to fire one shot before Caldweller grabbed the back of his armor and yanked him behind cover.

"Again in five," Ward said, and set her weapon aside to pull out a bag from a compartment in her armor.

Caldweller started the countdown again. Tarquin was grateful the armor hid his trembling, a subtle vibration that made him feel like he wanted to fly apart at the seams. How could they all be so calm? Practice, he supposed, but it'd taken him the entire time they were standing to get a handle on the situation when the others seemed to have grasped it all in a glimpse.

Merc-Sec stood, and Tarquin stood with them, determined to get a few more shots off.

"Sharp!" Ward bellowed while they were still firing. "Delivery!"

Ward chucked the zipped bag she'd been working on over the railing. Naira's head whipped around, and she was looking right at him—but of course she didn't recognize him in the hardshell armor—and her gaze slid off him, tracking the bag with focused intensity. She snatched it out of the air and dropped down, zipping it open while Fletcher stood above her and fired into the crowd of Conservators. Ammo magazines filled the bag. Caldweller yanked him back down again.

"Ward," Naira called up, "I think I'm in love!"

"Sorry, E-X, you're not my type," Ward said with a rich laugh.

"Why does everyone keep saying that?" Naira demanded.

"I keep telling you," Kav said, "it's your face."

"Eh," Fletcher said, "I'd still get after that."

"*We know,*" Naira and Kav said at the same time. The three of them laughed too intensely, bordering on hysterical, the sound broken up with more gunfire.

"My liege," Ward said over comms, "they're getting loopy, which means they'll start getting sloppy soon, if they haven't already. I suggest we move to take the east enemy fortification to break up the Conservator spearhead, then seal the doors and mop them up."

"Whatever you think is best, Captain." He could take a guess at what she'd described, but the details eluded him, and got even muddier as she started doling out orders.

When the count for suppression wound down, Tarquin stood with the rest, firing more confidently this time, as half the team peeled off and thundered down the stairs. He filtered out the shouts, the screams, the swearing, and focused on his one job, even if he wasn't very good at it. By the time the shouting died down, he'd reloaded twice and was reasonably certain he'd sweat out a few pounds.

"Clear!" Ward barked.

Tarquin pointed his rifle to the ceiling like all the others, reacting to the order before thinking it through. Satisfaction sent a small thrill through him. Caldweller gave him an appreciative shake.

"You can go downstairs now, my liege," Caldweller said.

He'd been so elated he'd done a good job he'd nearly forgotten what *clear* actually meant under the circumstances. Tarquin clipped the rifle to his back and ran, shouldering aside Merc-Sec who were already scrambling from his path, and took the stairs two at a time, then gave up on the stairs and leapt over the railing—his armor took the impact with ease.

Kav was still hunkered down by the console, face grim as he pointed out something to the soldier beside him. Naira leaned against Fletcher, or he was leaning against her, Tarquin couldn't tell. They were propped against each other, rifles dangling from their hands, blood-spattered, breathing hard, pupils blown, and talking to Ward while one of the

Merc-Sec crouched down in front of Naira, examining a wound on her abdomen that had been hastily field dressed.

"I'm impressed," Ward said. "Gotta admit, when I saw the scans, I thought you two were fucked."

"Please," Fletcher said. "That wasn't even the worst death cult we've faced. Nai and I cleared out Pollux Station."

"No shit?" Ward asked. "That creepy cult that used identical prints?"

"That's the one," Fletcher said. "It was like whack-a-mole. Nai got separated and I found her running hell-for-leather down the center of their garden—a garden filled with *sculptures* of their print—screaming P-E-D at the top of her lungs while an army of them chased her with their arms outstretched. Damn cult was trying to hug her to death by getting close enough to blow their personal explosives. Funniest fucking thing I've ever seen."

Naira groaned. "You were too busy laughing to notice us getting boxed in."

"Oh, give me a break. We made it out, didn't we?" He looked down at her, grinning. "Back-to-back, Nai."

She sighed, raggedly, but was smiling. "Undefeated."

Fletcher's grin transformed into a brilliant smile, and Tarquin was struck by the genuine joy radiating from the man as he held out a fist for Naira to, reluctantly, bump with her own.

Ward said something Tarquin couldn't hear. Naira shook her head and turned to point back up to the platform, and saw Tarquin rushing toward her. She stiffened. Fletcher stepped in front of her, making his body a shield.

Tarquin ripped his helmet off, shaking out sweaty hair. Fletcher rolled his eyes and moved away.

Naira's eyes softened, and he thought he saw a ghost of a smile touch her lips. But her posture remained taut. Wary. Tarquin slowed. He wanted nothing more than to take her in his arms, but—he had no idea what she thought of him, now. Where he stood, after so much had gone so wrong between them.

Ward had told him he'd better learn how to grovel. He sank to his knees. Cast his helmet aside and bent until his forehead pressed against the ground.

He'd never held this pose before. It wasn't for the blooded of MERIT, and something in his bones protested, which made him feel all the more that this was the right choice. A rejection of his position—and acknowledgment of hers. What to say? Sorry wasn't enough.

"I failed you," he said to the floor. "I failed you, and it hurt you, and I never, ever wanted to hurt you."

The room fell silent save for the soft tap of her boots approaching him. She crouched down before him, brushed his hair back with one hand, and lifted his chin. Sorrow stained her eyes, a subtle haunting, but her small, tired smile was amused.

"You look ridiculous."

"That bad?"

"Hmm." She took her time looking him over. "I'm not complaining."

His chest burned. "Naira, I—"

She lifted his chin higher, tilting his head back far enough to cut him off. Slowly, she stood, forcing him to stand with her. When he was on his feet, she released him, and he struggled to read her mood, to find something worthwhile to say aside from an avalanche of apologies, but then she kissed him, and the turmoil fell away.

Tarquin held her gently, mindful of her injuries and the rough feel of his armor. When she broke away to lean against him with a soft sigh, peace filled him with sweet warmth.

"We're okay?" he whispered for her alone to hear.

"We will be," she said. "But you'd better have my ring."

"Are you certain? I know that you..." He trailed off, not wanting to have this conversation in front of so many.

"You know?" At his subtle nod, she winced, her gaze tracking away from him, to the landing above, and the bodies left behind up there. Her expression was inscrutable. "I need to know my future has something good in it."

He fished in a sealed pocket and pulled out the slim band, then slid it carefully over her finger. "I'm here for you. Always."

She let out a shuddering breath that transformed into a grunt of pain.

"You're hurt." He nudged her backward and sat her down on one of the bullet-pocked crates of their makeshift barricade.

"Oh, *now* she sits," Fletcher said.

Naira rolled her eyes, but she was smiling. Tarquin took her hand as the medic restarted their examination of her wound, and looked at Fletcher.

The man was hunched, obviously in pain, subtly resting his weight against a stack of crates. Though he kept his usual smirk in place, the relief in him was clear.

"Demarco," he said. Fletcher startled, watching him warily. "Thank you."

Fletcher sniffed and crossed his arms. "Only doing my job, my liege. I live to serve for the glory of Mercator, et cetera, et cetera, but if you're expecting a bow, you'll have to wait. Nai here, the little peach, broke all my goddamn ribs."

Naira snorted, the sound aborted as the medic prodded at her wound. "You deserved it."

"Naturally. But I do wish you'd waited until after the grueling fire-fight. Or the fall. Or until I've had a nap."

"You don't nap."

"I have many new hobbies you're unaware of."

"Unlikely."

"You remain the living embodiment of a headache, good god," he muttered, and turned his head to hide a smile.

Tarquin stared between them, wrong-footed. They had to have got-ten along at some point, but he'd never imagined the dynamic to be quite like this. It left him equal parts amused and bewildered. He looked to Kav, who was still hard at work on the holo, and asked, "Are they always like this?"

"Oh, yeah," Kav said. "This is them being nice to each other."

They both made a face at Kav's back, and he lifted a middle finger to them without bothering to look over his shoulder. Tarquin squeezed Naira's hand. She muttered under her breath while the medic tugged the bandage off to redress the wound.

"Where's Kuma?" he asked.

"Kuma's gone," she said. The temptation to ask if she was sure bub-bled up, the urge to offer his techs to look at her map a breath away, but he stopped himself. Naira knew what resources were available to her. If she'd come to this conclusion, then there was nothing to be done.

"I'm so sorry," he said instead.

She fell silent, and so did he, thinking of Kuma. His own grief was a muted thing, compared to hers. He could sense the shearing forces within her. On one side of her heart lived the anger that had carried her through the fight, compressed beneath the weight of everything she carried—everything she had been carrying for years and years—growing brittle over time, preparing to buckle and snap.

Tarquin held her hand tighter. Incredible, that she had made it through so much while carrying that mantle of despair. A wave of gratitude for Fletcher washed over him, which was so bizarre it left him briefly dizzy.

"I meant my thanks, Demarco," Tarquin said. "If there's any boon I can grant you, within reason, then—"

"*Boon*," Fletcher echoed, and tossed his head with a laugh. "First you come charging at us like some sort of mega-mecha—I didn't even know they made armor for assholes as tall as you, cub—and I think, great, I'm going to get torn to pieces by some robot god, and now the robot god is offering me a *boon*." He scrunched his nose and snatched the rifle off Tarquin's back, examining it. "Holy hell. You fired this! Did you hit anything?"

"My liege put down four enemy combatants," Caldweller said. "And you will return his weapon."

"Oh-hoh, *four*. What a killer. What a *tiger*."

"Fletch." Naira's tone was dark with warning.

"Forgive me, my liege. I'm just a touch stressed out at the moment. You understand, I hope." Fletcher handed the weapon back with a grand flourish. "As for your boon." He shot a glance at Naira, his tone losing the mocking edge. "What I want isn't yours to give. Excuse me." He swept into a perfectly formal bow despite his broken ribs and strolled off, to the other side of the room, to speak with Diaz.

"Well, that didn't last long." Tarquin returned the rifle to his back.

"He's battle high," Naira said. "He'll calm down."

"Don't," Kav said without looking up. "Don't you start making excuses for him again. He's always been like that. Everything's fun and games until he gets set off and then he starts lashing out, and that wasn't *canus*."

"Give him a break," she said. "He saved both our asses today, and you know damn well I have the same temper. The 'Nai volcano' isn't any different because you gave it a cute nickname."

"You learned to control it. He chooses not to. That was always—" Kav cut himself off and shook his head. "I need to concentrate, and you know I'm right. No excuses. Not for him."

The medic finished patching Naira up and shuffled away after giving her firm instructions not to exert herself for a while. Tarquin knelt in their place, looking up at her. Her face relaxed, and she reached out to stroke his cheek with her free hand.

"Annnnd, there we go," Kav said, sitting back from the console. "Jonsun's loop is broken, those printers are offline."

"Thank god," Tarquin said.

"Name's Kav, but I'll accept god, too."

Naira started to say something, but whipped her head around as, on the other side of the room, Fletcher said, mildly confused, "Lina?"

Naira burst to her feet, the rifle back in her hands, and sprinted toward Fletcher. A gunshot cracked. Fletcher fell.

FIFTY-SIX

Naira

Seventh Cradle | The Present

Naira dropped to her knees and let her momentum slide her the rest of the way to Fletcher's side. Return fire from Merc-Sec knocked Lina down, but she still had her rifle. Naira bent herself over Fletcher, angling so that her armored back was facing Lina.

"What do you think you're doing?" He tried to push her off, but he was too weak.

She ducked lower, forearms against the ground to either side of his head, and resisted an urge to put pressure on the blood fountaining from his chest. To pull away before Lina was controlled was to leave Fletcher exposed.

"Shut up," she growled.

A single shot slammed into her back, driving her into him, and the plating in the back of her jacket snapped, a deep welt blooming on her back. The armor had done its job. It wouldn't do it again.

"Goddamnit, Nai, I didn't go through all that to watch you get shot to death on top of me." He coughed, hacking blood, and she turned her face away so it wouldn't splash in her eyes.

"Shut up and don't die."

"Trying," he rasped.

"Clear!" Diaz called out.

Naira put both hands on Fletcher's chest wound, bearing down with all her weight. "Medic!"

"Fuck," Fletcher gasped, lurching beneath the pressure. "Are you trying to save me or crush me?"

"What did I say about shutting up?"

"When have I been good at listening?"

She snorted, and he smiled thinly, letting himself go limp against the floor. "Let me go, Nai. Either I crack or I end up back on ice with no memory of this and...maybe that's for the best."

"Don't be so dramatic. You're not dying."

"The blood on the floor disagrees."

Medics pounded over at last and pushed her aside so they could get to work. Naira rocked back on her heels, giving them space, and let her bloody hands dangle between her knees, watching his face grow slowly paler.

"Is he crying?" Lina sneered. "He was always a crier."

Naira looked up and found Merc-Sec struggling to control her. She thrashed against them despite her injuries. Her face was twisted with contempt, her tone mocking.

"Lovely," Fletcher muttered under his breath.

"Are you all right?" Tarquin touched Naira's back lightly from behind. She startled, having been so focused on Lina she hadn't heard him approach.

"Yeah," she said distractedly. "The armor took the brunt."

"Speaking of," Ward said as she strolled over. "That armor's spent. We've got spares. Arms up."

Naira raised her arms, still watching Lina as Helms helped strip her old armor and snugged a new chest and back piece onto her. It didn't make sense. Lina was the woman who disappeared, she was sure of it. The kid who went to get printed and vanished from the system. The ghost that had driven Fletcher to paranoia and conspiracy.

"I thought you were friends?" Naira asked Fletcher.

"Friends?" Lina laughed. "Is that what you told people? How pathetic."

Fletcher closed his eyes and breathed slowly out of his nose, but said nothing.

Naira cracked her jaw.

"Don't," Fletcher said. "Let it go."

Fletcher had been shy when they'd first met. Jumpy and guarded, his eyes always darting to the side, hesitating before he rounded corners. Someone had bullied him, he'd admitted that much, but he'd never said who, and Naira was putting together some very old pieces.

He'd been seven. Lina had disappeared when she went to be printed, which would have put her in her late teens at the youngest. She'd been a teenager, picking on a kid barely out of toddlerhood.

"Do you have any idea the damage you did?" Naira demanded. "He was seven years old!"

Lina scoffed. "We all went through shit. He's weak. Always has been."

"Weak?" Naira wanted to laugh at the ridiculousness of that statement, but Lina clearly meant it. Worse, the way Fletcher turned his fading face aside and squeezed his eyes shut told her he'd internalized that statement as truth a long, long time ago.

Believing you were weak. Thinking your only way to be safe was to control the world around you... The two weren't unrelated.

"Fletch," she said slowly, "I'm going to grant you a boon."

"*Naira*," he said, dropping the nickname for the first time in longer than she could remember, but that wasn't enough to hold her back.

Because this wasn't about Fletcher as he was now. This was about the kid, shy and scared and despite all that still quick with a laugh, who hid bread in his secret pockets that first week, when she was getting in trouble every night, to make sure she still had something to eat.

Who hadn't cared when she'd grown so angry and scared she cried and screamed at him, because he knew it wasn't really him she was screaming at. Who'd scrubbed the ducts near the powercore, because being in there had made Naira's skin crawl. *This bitch* had picked on *that kid*, and still, even now, thought it was funny.

"Shit," Tarquin said, as she marched toward Lina, rolling up her sleeves.

In the corner of her eye, Ward put a hand on Tarquin's arm. "She's got it, my liege."

"Release her," Naira ordered the Merc-Sec holding Lina.

They glanced nervously at each other and let the woman go, taking a step back. Lina cracked her neck from side to side. Naira smiled, slow and calm, and caught a satisfying glimpse of real fear in the woman's eyes in the second before her right hook connected with Lina's jaw.

Lina's head snapped back, blood spraying. She stumbled, rushing to cover her face. Lazily, Naira struck her in her guts. Lina coughed and twisted away, running a few steps to put space between them while she gathered her wits. Naira let her, viciously amused as Lina shook her head, no doubt trying to clear the effects of a concussion. Lina spat blood and lunged.

Naira sidestepped and grabbed the back of her jacket, swinging her around to toss her face-first into the ground. She slid. It made a satisfying squeaking sound, bare skin scraped raw against the metal floor. When Lina pushed to her feet again, swaying, blood was fountaining from her broken nose.

"Doesn't feel nice, does it?" Naira asked. "Getting picked on by someone bigger and meaner."

"Go to hell," she spat out.

"Oh no. My poor feelings. Is that the best you can do, or are your insults only suited to antagonizing seven-year-olds?"

"Gotta keep them simple for the Mercator's bed warmer to understand." Lina's lip curled with self-satisfaction.

"Cute. Ward over there got me better than that, and she's my friend."

"Didn't want to disappoint you," Ward called out.

Naira lifted a hand to her in acknowledgment. Lina, predictably, thought that was a great opening. She lunged once again. Naira let her hook an arm around her waist. The impact made Naira grunt, her wound burning, but Lina didn't have the strength or the momentum to push her off her feet.

Naira looked down at the struggling woman trying to tackle her to the ground for a wrestling match she would, quite obviously, lose, and sighed. She threaded her hand through Lina's hair, gripping tight, and slammed her knee into her jaw.

The crack of bone echoed. Lina lost her grip, Naira's hold on her hair the only thing keeping her from face-planting. Disgusted, Naira dragged her across the floor to Fletcher's side and put a boot in the crook of the woman's knee, pinning her in place. Fletcher was wide-eyed, alert despite the pallor that'd overcome him.

"Apologize," Naira said.

Lina gargled in the back of her throat, getting ready to spit. Naira yanked her head back, stretching her neck to its limits. When she stopped choking and was merely gasping, Naira let her relax her neck.

"Let's try that again," she said.

"Fuck you," Lina hissed.

Naira pressed down on her knee.

"Fuck, fuck, I'm sorry. I'm sorry!"

"There, that wasn't so hard, was it? Merc-Sec, you may gag her now."

Naira tossed her aside, exemplar strength flaring. Lina landed, a meaty thump, and Merc-Sec scrambled to follow her order. Naira didn't bother to watch. She crouched down next to Fletcher. His color looked better already.

"Good boon," he said quietly.

"Then you'd better not die and forget it." Naira ruffled his sweaty hair, like she'd done when they were kids, and he smiled, even if it was weak.

She looked up, and everyone was staring at her, eyes wide, shocked into a silence that seemed too intense for a petty scuffle.

"What?" she asked.

Tarquin pointed over her shoulder. She turned, and found the warp-core pulsing. Her heart rate spiked. Cores weren't supposed to do that. The pulsing sped with the beat of her heart.

"Oh," she said. "That can't be good."

FIFTY-SEVEN

Naira

Seventh Cradle | The Present

Naira lounged in the back of one of the armored convoy vehicles, lying across Tarquin's lap with her feet up on the opposite seat, and listened to talk of securing the settlement flow all around her. For once, she was uninterested in helping manage the details. Jonsun's people were scattered and terrified. Merc-Sec had it under control.

What wasn't under control was the expansion. The speed of it was unpredictable, slowing briefly, then speeding up in violent bursts. The tension in Tarquin's voice told her that this wasn't only unexpected, it was dangerous.

She'd told him about Jonsun's assertions that cracked maps might be making matters worse, and the look on his face made her want to print Jonsun just to kill him all over again. Everyone was giving her wary looks and speaking softly around her. As if sparking her anger might set off another burst of acceleration. Kav hadn't even given her shit about the "Nai volcano" going off.

She'd refrained from commenting when Tarquin suggested they relocate to the lab, where the building was dug deep into the earth and whatever resonance was happening between her map and the power-cores would be shielded. The way he stroked her hair while he talked with the scientists was meant to be soothing, but did more to reveal how freaked out he was than ease her nerves.

Jonsun must have done something else to her map. It was the only thing that made sense. It was the only thing she wanted to make sense.

A veritable battalion of scientists waited for them outside the lab when they pulled up, tires crunching over the snow. Naira stifled a groan as she peeled herself off Tarquin and let him help her out of the car. The scientists parted, a familiar white coat shoving her way through the crowd. Her mom.

Tarquin stepped aside to give them space. Dr. Sharp wrapped her arms around Naira, and Naira let herself slump into that hold, smiling when her mom kissed the top of her head.

"My sweet baby." She pushed Naira back to arm's length to examine her. "What did that vile man do to you?"

"I'm fine." Naira tried for a light tone, but it was half-hearted. "And I'm hardly sweet."

Her mom *tsked* and took her hand, dragging her up the steps. In seconds she was sitting on the edge of a hospital bed in a lab that had been rearranged so many times since she'd been gone she hardly recognized it as Tarquin's under all the new medical equipment. Bracken told her to *breathe* as they set some new measuring device over her head. All she wanted to do was rest.

The fight was over. *It should be over.*

Kav had vanished into the crush of scientists at some point, and reappeared to shove a steaming-hot cup of dark coffee into her hands. She took a sip, but the steam stung her nostrils with the fire of alcohol long before it touched her lips.

Bracken frowned at the cup. "Inebriation may not be the best idea right now."

"I wouldn't try to take it from her," Kav said. "Unless you want to end up on her to-stab list, which is getting longer by the moment."

It was purely psychological, but the hot, comforting drink was already starting to clear some of the daze she'd been in since she'd seen the warp-core pulsing with the thump of her heart.

"Has it occurred to anyone that we should ice me for the time being?" she asked.

No one had actually said her map was interacting with the expansion yet, they'd been all smiles and kind statements about *getting to the bottom of this* and *making sure her map was stable*. They paused in their work, even Tarquin, looking up from the haze of Mercator-green holos filling the room, and frowned as a unit.

"It's not just you being active," Delorne said, chirpy despite the reproachful looks the other scientists shot her. "As your map is always in the same temporal state due to the repair, it's highly likely that icing you won't do any good."

"My map will keep interfering even if it's iced?" She rubbed her forehead. "Fine, then cast me elsewhere and delete me here."

Tarquin grimaced. She really didn't like the look of that, and shot him a glare. He'd realized something he'd failed to share.

"Doesn't work like that." Delorne never once bothered to look up from her holo and notice the scowls being cast her way. "See, the expansion is happening everywhere, all at once. Lots of things are interfering with it all across the universe. It doesn't matter where your map is located, it'll have the same effect." She paused and looked up in thought. "Huh. The fact that you have multiple backups spread across the universe is probably making matters worse."

She felt numb. "So the only solution is a complete deletion of all my maps, everywhere?"

"It seems that way," Delorne said with a shrug, then realized too late everyone was staring daggers at her. "What?"

"It won't come to that," Tarquin said.

"I need air." She yanked the device off her head and tossed it aside, hopping down from the gurney.

"Ex. Sharp," Bracken said, "I recommend staying indoors where we can observe your present state."

"Work on something else for five fucking minutes." She turned on her heel, marching toward the door.

"Naira, wait," Tarquin said.

She turned and jabbed a finger at him. "You stay here. You stay here and you *figure this out*."

He nodded, stunned, and she brushed past the exemplars lingering near the door, scarcely aware of them as they shifted into formation around her.

The icy air outside of the lab stung her lungs. She breathed deeply, letting the chill cool the fire of panic that'd flushed through her. The star was muted in the grey skies of a premature winter, soft flakes of snow swirling down from clouds so indistinct they were little more than darkened smears.

She didn't even know how to judge the time anymore. How far were they from the star? Had it affected the angle? Did it matter? A wave of exhaustion crashed into her, and she slumped against the porch's support pillar, staring out into the snow-draped field that, not long ago, had spawned misprints whispering her name.

This was a new print, but her map was always her map. She'd been running for days, leaving pieces of herself behind in the rough terrain between the settlement and the *Cavendish*, her only respite a few minutes of unconsciousness. She wanted to sleep. Wanted to close her eyes and know the planet would still be inhabitable when she opened them.

Tears stung her eyes. It wasn't fair. She couldn't even fight this. This was tech and research and everything she didn't understand, and there was nothing she could do but wait to see if the only way to save them all was to erase her forever.

"That's getting cold," Kav said, beside her.

"What part of me wanting to be alone was unclear?"

"You weren't listening." Kav leaned against the rail next to her, staring out into the field. She passed him the cup out of habit. He drank and passed it back. "You only heard the bad shit, because you haven't slept in days and you're losing your mind."

"All right, I'll humor you. What'd I miss?" She hoped that didn't sound quite as desperate as it felt.

"Dr. Delorne said it wasn't just you causing the problem, and she's right. I can only skim the surface of what they're doing in there, but they've got that cargo ship loaded with *canus*-infested relkatite, trying to decay it down to amarthite to slow down the expansion. They have some kind of data set that says the process can go faster than it has been, but they're having trouble finding the right conditions. Tarquin and the team, they're throwing everything at it. They'll figure it out."

She didn't say the obvious: that they didn't have days to spend on this. That Jonsun's plan hadn't been fully executed, but what had been done was enough, and now they couldn't stop it. Couldn't even slow it down while her map was an amplifier, undoing all the progress the scientists had made thus far.

"I guess Jonsun wasn't lying," she said. "He wasn't going to delete his loyalists. He was just going to delete me."

"Tarquin won't delete you," Kav said.

"Yeah. And that's a problem, isn't it? If he won't pull that trigger, or if he waits too long, then everyone dies." She chugged the last of the coffee. "The resonance got worse after the repair, right? That has to be the reason. So what if we crack me again? At the very least, it'll stop my backups from being the same thing. Might buy us some time."

"Add that to the list of things Tarquin won't authorize," Kav said.

Naira let out a strained sound that she barely recognized as coming from herself. "Cracked is better than deleted. Even if it's worse than last time, I can be iced until a fix that doesn't turn me into a walking doomsday machine is developed. All we'd have to do is double-print me again."

"It's not a bad idea." Kav scratched the side of his chin as he thought. "But I don't think Tarquin will take the risk, and I heard them talking, earlier. He had to radio in his authorization for the hospital to reprint Fletch. All the printers were locked down when double-prints started spewing out of the tunnels, so we can't get around him."

"You still have that deletion virus tagged to my map, don't you?"

"Hell no," he said. "I scrubbed that thing from existence the second we cleaned your map out of Mercator's files."

"Cracking is our best bet, then." Naira puffed up her cheeks and blew out a breath. "Give me a moment, will you? I need to figure out what to say to convince him."

"Sure." He dug a flask out of his pocket and passed it to her. "Send one of your exemplars for me if you want to talk it out more. I'll go see what I can do. Maybe fresh eyes will help, or maybe I picked up something from Jonsun that will be useful."

She gave his arm a squeeze. "Thanks, Kav. I always counted myself lucky to have crossed paths with you."

"Don't get maudlin."

"Bit late for that, eh?"

He rolled his eyes and left her there with the snow and her thoughts. As she heard the door whisper shut, she let out a sigh that emptied her lungs, filling the air with the heat of her breath frosting into clouds.

Tarquin wouldn't delete her, even if it meant they lost everything. It wasn't in him. He couldn't wound himself like that, and pushing him to order her double-printed would be one hell of a stretch.

She believed in him. Fiercely and completely, believed that he'd figure it out, that he'd find a way, but where that belief strained at the edges was in the simple fact that he didn't have the time. He and his team were way over the rim of the cutting edge, manipulating theories they barely understood.

Lightning doesn't strike twice. Jonsun had been right about that.

They'd run out of time. If Tarquin muscled up the nerve to delete or crack her, that choice would destroy him. And the alternative— the experiments she'd seen in her flashes of the future—was unspeakable. She wouldn't let this planet freeze. Wouldn't let Jana's future become one of strife.

Naira slipped Kav's flask into her pocket and palmed the sedative injector she'd found on her nightstand: 6 mLs left. She dialed the dose in for 3 mLs.

"Helms, Diaz, could you come here a moment?"

They jogged down the steps to stand in front of her, faces bright with expectation of some order or another.

"What do you need, E-X?" Helms asked.

"I wanted to thank you both," she said. "You're damn fine exemplars. Whatever ends up happening to me, I want you both to know that."

They flushed with pride. Helms grinned ear to ear, and Diaz rubbed the back of his neck, glancing down. It was all the opening she needed. Naira was hanging on by a thread, but her instincts never failed her. Diaz was the stronger of the two right now, with Helms worn out from the fight.

Naira plunged the sedative into the side of Diaz's neck and Helms, the poor girl, reached for him as he started to fall, her training not allowing her to process until it was too late that Naira was an active threat. She plunged the second dose into Helms's neck and eased them both to the ground to lean against each other.

She pitched the empty injector aside and looked back, once, at the lab, a mantle of snow snugged tight about it, those blast-proof walls shielding Tarquin and Kav and her mom and everyone she'd ever loved. Almost.

She turned, striding out across the snow, to find the last loose thread in her life and ask him to unravel her at last.

FIFTY-EIGHT

Tarquin

Seventh Cradle | The Present

Tarquin couldn't stop glancing at the door. Kav had come back from speaking with Naira about an hour ago, and he'd only met Tarquin's expectant glance and given him a slight shake of the head—don't go out there—before he'd found an open console and got to work.

Across the room, Bracken had a simulation of Naira's map pulled up on their console, a small team of neuroscientists and core specialists combing it for any hint of what Jonsun had done that made it resonate so strongly. They were, presently, having a hushed argument about the nature of that interaction.

"What's the problem?" Tarquin asked.

The team stiffened, glancing between one another. Bracken found the nerve to explain. "The cores expand and contract space to facilitate jumping and to generate power. We theorize that Ex. Sharp's map is doing something similar. Its repaired state means that it exists in every possible position at once, and therefore must be constantly 'jumping' to accomplish the feat, and those jumps are causing the increased resonance."

"Why wouldn't my map be causing the same problem?" Dr. Sharp asked. "Mine is repaired."

"You never lived while cracked," Bracken said. "Forgive me, Dr.

Sharp, but while your map's stated chance to crack was high, it wasn't a guarantee. In your case, it's possible the repair was unnecessary."

"That's a theory," Tarquin said, thinking *and a good one*, "but not an argument."

"My colleagues think," Bracken said, "that disrupting that coherence, ending the jumps, might end the amplification effect."

"You're talking about cracking her." The thought had occurred to him, but he'd shied away from it as if he'd drawn too close to a flame.

"It's only an idea," one of the core techs said.

"Nai had the same thought." Kav leaned back in his chair on two legs, hands laced behind his head. "But without all that jumping stuff. Said it wasn't a problem when she was cracked, and cracked's better than deleted."

"Might work," Delorne said. "It'd at least buy us time. There's still the problem of all that relk not decaying fast enough, and at this rate, I don't think a slowdown is even enough. Something's got to give. We should crack her right away, before we cross a threshold we can't come back from."

"We're not there yet," Tarquin said emphatically, but the numbers didn't lie, and he felt the time slipping through his fingers. Hoping no one would notice his attention wander, he pulled up his HUD and texted Sharp.

Mercator: Naira's map is accelerating the expansion.

Sharp: Yes. You must crack her.

Mercator: You know I won't do that.

Sharp: She'll do it herself, if you won't.

"Naira's right," Dr. Sharp said. Tarquin jerked his head up, startled, but she seemed to be thinking out loud, her voice pained. "Cracked is better than deleted. Cracked is better than her dying with the rest of us when the planet freezes over."

"If we could figure out what was causing the accelerated decay of relkatite previously," Tarquin said, "in the next... in the next two hours, then it wouldn't be necessary."

The team glanced between themselves, quiet and strained, and he felt like he was back in the hospital on Mercator Station, insisting they didn't have to take the amarthite from her unconscious print, and knowing he was outnumbered and, worse, wrong.

"Where did this previous decay data come from?" Kav asked. "Can we be sure it's correct?"

"Multiple sources," Tarquin said. "Pathways from those under control of *canus* during the uprising were shown to have a faster rate of decay, and circuitry recovered from the *Amaranth* and *Einkorn* wreckage had the fastest of all."

Kav fell out of his chair with a clatter and swore. Tarquin bolted out of his own chair to help him, but Cass was already there, being swatted away as Kav scrambled to his feet.

"Holy shit," Kav said. "Ho-ly shit, she's never going to let me live this down, she was *right*."

A spark of hope lit in Tarquin's chest. "Right about what?"

"It doesn't matter if they're Chinese rooms," Kav declared. He kicked his fallen chair aside, raising the console podium so he could plunge back into the data while standing. That statement meant nothing to Tarquin but caused an excited stir among the neuroscientists.

"What does that mean?" Tarquin shot a glance at the neuroscientists, who would no doubt drown him in details. "Quickly, please."

"We had an argument," Kav said, "on the *Cavendish*, the first time we were there. She told me the *Einkorn* was sentient, and I told her it learned how to pretend to be sentient, and she didn't think the distinction mattered and she was right. It doesn't. It doesn't matter at all whether it's real or not when we're talking about energy expenditure, does it?

"The more *canus* interacts with a mind, the harder it has to work, the more energy it needs, so it feeds faster. Human. Spaceship. *The distinction doesn't matter*, but the size of the energy spend to manage something as large and complex as a mind? That matters. That's your decay acceleration."

"You're certain?" Tarquin asked.

"Tarquin, my man, Jessel was pissed when we reprinted you after Fletch loaded you with *canus* and the relk loss rate was higher than usual, six percent. You were severely infected, but only for a short amount of time. It was controlling your mind that forced the real overgrowth. I'm certain. Turn the cargo ship's AI back on. Give *canus* something to work for, and it'll consume more energy."

"Turn that AI on," Tarquin ordered the techs. "I'll go get Naira."

Tarquin rushed out of the lab, Cass and Caldweller running behind him. He raced down the steps, turning toward a fading trail of footprints in the snow, and almost tripped over the unconscious bodies of Helms and Diaz. His heart fell.

"No," he said, shaking his head. "No, no, no. Where is she?"

Caldweller grabbed him and pulled him back, away from that thin, single trail of footsteps that arced away from the lab, and held him one-armed behind his bulk. "My liege, please, let us assess."

"They're alive," Cass called out. They handed Tarquin a snow-wet injector. "Does this mean anything to you?"

He rolled it over to read the prescription. "I think this is what Kav used to knock her out. Go get him. Now."

Cass ran off, and Caldweller finally relented his guard and allowed Tarquin to approach the downed exemplars. They looked peaceful enough, the only marks on them the red circle of the injection site on their necks. Naira's cup had been set aside with care, not dropped. There was no doubt in his mind she'd done this herself.

Kav came out of the lab, grumbling about being disturbed, but the second he took in the scene, his face turned grim. "That rock-headed woman."

"Do you have any idea where she would have gone?" Tarquin asked. "You said she talked about cracking. Did she mention a possible location?"

"Nothing specific. She knew the printers were all locked down." Kav eyed the fading footsteps in the snow, leading back to the settlement. "Oh. Goddamnit. I told her Fletch was reprinted. Call the hospital and tell them not to let her leave."

"Why would Demarco matter?" Tarquin asked.

"He's a *finalizer*."

Tarquin fumbled with his HUD in his haste, but got the channel to the hospital receptionist open. "This is Liege Tarquin. Have you seen Ex. Sharp?"

"Yes, my liege. She came by about forty minutes ago to collect Mr. Demarco. Said there was some business at the lab he was needed for."

Tarquin closed his eyes. "If you see her or Mr. Demarco again, detain them and alert me right away."

"Yes, my liege."

He closed the channel, heart thundering. "Where would she go? Not in the settlement, too risky, and not out to—to the land I'd set aside for us, she'd know I'd look there."

"The river," Kav said. "Anywhere along it, it doesn't matter exactly where. It's a lot of ground to cover, but Kuma had never seen a river before. It was one of the last things they did together."

"Caldweller—" Tarquin started to say, but he talked over him.

"I'm already alerting Ward to sweep the river," he said.

"Thank you. Kav, let the physicians know Helms and Diaz need that blocker, get them on their feet, and send them out. I'm joining the search, maybe I can talk her down. I need you—"

"I know. I know. The AI. I'll get it booted. Just swear to me you'll find her." Kav held out a hand, wrist cocked.

Tarquin grasped his hand, and Kav grasped his. "I will tear this planet to the studs before I lose her again."

Kav gave him a strained smile. "You Mercators are so dramatic. Go."

Tarquin ran off, steps a little lighter, strangely, because Kav had insulted him good-naturedly, and that meant he believed he could do this.

Kav didn't believe in Mercator. He didn't believe in institutional power. He believed in *Tarquin*, and he clung to that, and tried to ignore the fact he'd felt Naira slipping through his fingers with every breath since the day he'd known she was taken.

This time, she wasn't coming back for him.

But he was going to find her. Find her, and bring her home.

FIFTY-NINE

Naira

Seventh Cradle | The Present

It'd taken Naira longer than she would have liked to skirt through the settlement to the hospital. She'd been forced to take side streets and wait for Merc-Sec to pass by on multiple occasions, not wanting to raise questions about being out without her exemplars.

Getting Fletcher out was the easy part. He was back in his preferred print, a thick grey coat trimmed in Mercator green fit snugly to his lithe frame, and he humored her for about fifteen minutes of walking before calling her out on her bullshit.

"You know I'm always up for a clandestine stroll," Fletcher said as they veered off the main road and picked their way carefully through the snow-draped woods. "But I feel the need to point out that I have, in fact, noticed that we're going in the opposite direction of these labs at which I am allegedly required."

"I need a personal favor."

"I remain your servant in all things." Fletcher's tone was light, but he was casting her sideways glances. "But a little context couldn't go amiss here, love. What's this all about? I'm pleased to help you, but you're without your exemplars and currently walking faster than I think your wounds should allow, in the opposite direction of that Mercator of yours.

394   MEGAN E. O'KEEFE

"As much as I'd love to irritate the cub, I'm well aware that my continued existence is on thin ice. Absconding with the fiancée of the head of Mercator is precisely the kind of thing said head frowns upon."

Naira laughed at that, the sound strained to her own ears, and brushed aside a snow-laden branch to pass through a clutch of trees.

"Did you see the warpcore on the *Cavendish* at the end of the fight?"

"I did," Fletcher said. "Though, as most of my blood was on the floor, I wasn't entirely certain of what I was seeing."

Naira explained in the most detail she could manage. Fletcher listened, gravely silent. No doubt he was weighing this new information about *canus* and relkatite against his experiences with that alien consciousness.

The silver curve of the river shimmered through the trees up ahead. Kav would think of it, when her escape was discovered, but she was confident they couldn't sweep the entire river in time.

"That all sounds very dire," Fletcher said. They pushed through the trees and he paused, the breath hitching in his chest.

Naira waited, a bittersweet warmth filling her as his eyes shone with the reflection of that broad stretch of water, crusted over with ice at the shore. Fletcher had experienced a few more privileges in his life than the Conservators. Finalizers were fielded everywhere—Earth, the dead cradles, the most luxurious stations—and he must have seen artificial rivers, or the sludgy stretches of water that passed for such things on the dead worlds.

This was different. This was living and vital and glacially teal-blue, brilliant and defiant. If you didn't know better, if you didn't know how easily a planet could die, it looked like it might keep on flowing forever.

"Incredible," he said, hushed.

"It's days away from being solid ice."

He gave her a slanted smile. "I'm not certain it would be any less beautiful frozen."

"You won't live to see it."

"Story of my life," he muttered. "As I was saying, I'd love to help, but I have no idea what use I'd be. My skill set makes entirely different use of lab equipment than the traditional methods, and I'm quite certain no one in the lab wants to hear me tell them all the ways in which their various solvents can be used to break people."

Keeping her eyes on the river, she handed him a roll of surgical tools she'd swiped from the hospital. "They need more time. My map is the problem."

He took the packet of tools, his fingers intentionally brushing hers, and the weight of his stare was more searing than a flame. "I need you to speak plainly, love, because I don't like the conclusion I just drew."

She took a breath and made herself face him. His brows were drawn with concern, the packet of tools clutched between both hands, all the laughing mockery bled out of him.

"My repaired map is amplifying the expansion. Dr. Delorne believes deletion is the only solution, as even when iced my map is active to a larger degree than most."

"The cub won't allow it."

"No, he won't. He can't. And even if he does work up the nerve to do it..." Laying her heart bare to Fletcher, of all people, made every word like barbed wire. "You know where his limits are. This will destroy him."

Plastic crinkled as he tightened his grip around the tool packet. "Do you think it won't destroy me?"

She huffed a tired, bitter laugh. "We're already ruined, Fletch. We don't have to drag everyone else down with us."

"Huh." He turned away to gaze out over the river, as if looking at her for too long stung his eyes. "You know, I..." She waited while he gathered himself. "When the cub printed me here, and I lived in a body free of *canus* for the first time since we went for our printings, I felt this immense weight lift. I thought, for one foolish second, that I could start again, maybe. That I knew what I was, and that in understanding it I could maybe control myself at last." He turned the tool packet over, stroking the plastic. "But you're right. I'm ruined. It doesn't matter what I do. There's no lifetime long enough to repair what I've done."

What could she say? She studied this man she'd used to love, knowing that part of herself would always love him, always be tangled in him, and he seemed older than was possible for his print, face drawn, hands tensed against the tool packet.

Fletcher always had a joke, and more often than not they were designed to hurt, but he'd wielded them when they first met to make her laugh. To make her feel like things might be okay, even when they were terrible. The way his shoulders rounded, complexion ashen, she caught a glimpse of the scorched landscape of his heart and the charred remains of the kid he'd been. Her throat tightened.

He twisted up a strained smile. "Did you ever wonder why I was so good at this?" He tapped the packet with a finger. "The other finalizers, they made a system of their work. A system." He scoffed. "I made it an art, tailoring my work to each subject, but it was never about the targets. Thousands, Nai. Thousands of souls I've pushed to the endless scream and it was never about hurting them.

"I was excavating myself. Searching for the same twisted thread I knew was in me in every mind I broke, looking for an echo, because if I could break that in *them*, then I could break it in *me*. I never found it, and each soul I shattered left its stain on me, sank that thread deeper until it was drawing up from a well of poisoned hatred so deep I became obsessed with...equalizing." He grunted. "*Canus*, making me think that if everyone was equally controlled then I couldn't be a monster, could I? Because that would make everyone else one, too.

"But you? Oh, you made me doubt. I pushed you away from Mercator, and I think part of me thought you could save me from what I was becoming. That it was only your service to Acaelus that kept you from seeing me. But you went to Kav, and I should have known, because I was poison long before the finalizers trained me to wield the hate."

"Why didn't you ask me for help?"

He looked straight up, into the falling snow. "I didn't know how. I'm not sure I do, now. But this, what you're asking me? Every soul I've ruined, some of that pain has rubbed off. And if it's you, if I have to..." He closed his eyes. "You're killing us both, you know that?"

She looked down, ashamed, hands clasped behind her back. "Better two monsters meet their end than everyone else."

"That's what you think?" He stared at her, but she kept her gaze down. "You think what you've done is equivalent to what I've done? That you should be left out of a world you don't deserve?"

Naira rubbed her eyes. "You don't know half of what I did in service of Acaelus, and ultimately, it doesn't matter, because my foot's dangling over the same edge. You have no idea—" She clenched her fists. "I am clinging to this life by a thread, and I've been dead ever since Jonsun double-printed me. I have no right to stay in this world if it means the destruction of it. I can't do it myself and I'm a coward afraid of deletion, so I need you to cut the thread for me, Fletch. I need you to let me go."

"You have no idea what you're asking." He wound back his arm and hurled the packet of tools into the river. "No fucking idea. Those tools? Set-dressing for use on weaker minds. I don't need them to break you, do you understand?"

"Do what you have to do, and carry no guilt. I want this. I have fought too long and too hard to be the reason it all falls apart."

"She says she wants this." He laughed, mockingly, and closed a hand around her throat.

Naira went rigid, smothering a lifetime of instincts to fight back, to lash out. This was what she'd asked for. She wanted him at his worst. He shoved her backward until she was pressed against the rough bark of a tree, hand tightening until her breath wheezed thinly.

Fletcher canted the angle of his wrist, forcing her chin up, and loomed over her, his face bare inches from hers. "You won't want this when I'm done with you. That's the point. There's no safe word here, love. No asking me to stop. And you will beg for me to stop before I'm through. I will tear out every hidden, tender part of you, body and soul, and salt them as I lay them bare before you. You don't want this. *Don't make me do this.*"

"I want this," she said, voice a fragile thread.

He dropped his forehead against hers, breathing heavily. She closed her eyes, feeling a tremble run through him.

"When you went AWOL," he said, "Acaelus issued a retrieve and interrogate order. We thought, once he'd squeezed what he wanted out of you, that he'd order you cracked. The finalizers were so damn excited. An exemplar was a real challenge, and one with a notoriously resilient map? That's a career-maker." He huffed, warm breath gusting against her face. "I listened to them strategize for months. They asked me for tips, since I'd known you. They were salivating for it, but all their plans were shit. They'd never work.

"The real reason I was on Mercator Station the day you blew it up wasn't because I was there to interrogate Tarquin, though that was part of it. I was there because I called dibs on breaking you. I told them it was personal, and every last one of them wanted to know how I planned to do it. I refused to tell them."

He dropped a hand to her hip, pinning her against the tree. Her heart thundered, recalling his small wave when she'd left the docks with Tarquin, and the threat behind his eyes. Fletcher lifted his forehead from hers and leaned close to whisper against her ear, grip tightening around her throat and hip. "Do you know what my plan was? You should."

She couldn't shake her head or even make a sound. Tears stung her eyes as he pressed his lips to her temple. "My plan was always to let you go."

Naira opened her eyes, met the intensity of his stare for a breath, then the hand on her hip ripped her service weapon free and he stepped away from her, firing the entire clip into the air.

"Oh, you fucking dick," she rasped, slumping down to her knees to rub her sore throat.

"I really am sorry, love." He tossed the empty pistol aside to skitter away against the rocks. Shouts echoed through the trees. Merc-Sec, reacting to the gunfire. "But you haven't slept properly in days, you've been dragged through hell, you're injured, and you had that look in your eye you get when your back's against the wall and you're determined to go down swinging."

"That changes nothing," she croaked.

He frowned and crouched across from her, lifting her chin so that he could get a better look at the bruise spreading over her neck, shaped like his hand. "Too hard? Damn these weak amarthite prints. I didn't mean to overdo it, but I had to sell it. I was running out of shit to stall with and was certain you'd notice me going for the gun."

Naira worked her throat around. "I poured my heart out and you were *stalling*. Was anything you said even true?"

His expression lost its laughing edge, face deadly serious. "Every word."

"You've killed us all, you know that?"

"Naira Sharp, I'm surprised. After all this time, if you give me the choice between you living a little longer and everyone else dying, I'm choosing you. Always."

"You've killed me before," she said dryly.

He scrunched his nose. "What can I say? I wasn't myself then, and technically you killed us both, so I think we're even."

"Technicalities aren't getting us out of this."

"Maybe." He shrugged. "But while you're alive, there's hope. And do you want to hear something truly strange?" He glanced toward the clamoring in the woods. "I have faith in the cub."

She barked a laugh, startled, and fell into a coughing fit. He patted her on the back.

"Again, terribly sorry about the extra force." Merc-Sec burst through the trees, targeting lights swarming Fletcher. He rolled his eyes dramatically and held his hands up, stepping away from her. "She's fine. I didn't touch her."

Helms and Diaz surrounded her, Diaz aiming his service weapon straight at Fletcher's chest. Naira shook her head, trying to find her voice, but it came out as a thin wheeze.

"She's hurt," Tarquin growled.

Naira looked up and regretted it as the muscles in her neck protested. Tarquin advanced on a backpedaling Fletcher, fists clenched.

"Being injured is something of a lifestyle choice for Nai," Fletcher said.

Tarquin stunned them all by punching Fletcher square in the face. Fletcher fell backward against the rocks, feet flying up, and his expression was so deeply surprised that it almost made her laugh again. Tarquin stepped toward him, preparing to strike, and Naira had a brief moment of admiration for the confident, clean lines of his form—Had he been learning to fight? When?—before he swung and Fletcher rolled out of the way, one hand covering his split lip while he held the other up in an entreaty to stop.

"Okay! I touched her a little! But I'd like to see you disarm Nai when she's spitting mad without scratching the paint. I wasn't actually going to finalize her. I can hardly win her back if she's gone to the endless scream."

"You fucking—"

"Stop." Naira winced at the sting in her throat.

Tarquin settled for kicking a spray of rocks at Fletcher before turning on his heel to come kneel across from her. His expression softened, and he cupped her cheek in one calloused palm.

"Are you all right?"

"Yes." She shook off Helms's hand on her back. "Unfortunately. I know it's hard, but we're running out of time, and if you won't let Fletch crack me, then—"

He shook his head vehemently. "No. There's another way. Kav found it."

Naira buried her face in her hands, and wasn't quite sure why a sob racked her body. Fletcher was right, damn him. She was too tired. Could barely think. Threat of deletion had kicked her over the edge of a spiral.

"Naira? Please, talk to me."

"She's been fighting without sleep for days and is terrified you're going to delete her or kill us all, dumbass," Fletcher called out.

"Never," Tarquin said.

She scrubbed her face with the heel of her palm and made herself meet Tarquin's sweet, worried eyes, embarrassed to be shaking with sobs while the exemplars and Merc-Sec stood around, pretending not to notice.

"This plan of yours better be good," she managed.

He smiled warmly and brushed hair away from her eyes. "It must be. Kav said it was based on your idea and that you'd never stop gloating."

Tarquin took her hand and helped her stand. She winced, straightening, and prodded at the bandage wrapped around her middle to find the blood had seeped through her shirt. She'd opened the wound again in her rush through the woods. Wonderful.

"I had nothing to do with that!" Fletcher said.

Tarquin's nostrils flared, but he ignored him. "We should reprint you."

"It's not that bad," she said. "I'm just tired. Need to let it rest to heal."

"Then I'm taking you to the hospital to rest."

"That's not nec—"

Naira grunted as Tarquin scooped her up, cradling her gently against him, and bent down to brush a kiss to her lips. "Rest. I'll tell you Kav's plan on the way."

She wanted to protest, to insist she didn't need to be carried around like a worn-out child, but Tarquin's arms were warm and strong, his steps even, careful not to jar her, and as he started explaining the plan, she let her head rest against his chest, muscles going slack.

It wasn't real rest, nothing like what she needed, but it soothed the frayed edges of her nerves. The hospital was the last place she wanted to be, but recalling her visions of the future, she squashed all protest. In her vision, she had been with him. If she was not by Tarquin's side in the powercore building, then that terrible future would never come to pass.

SIXTY

Tarquin

Seventh Cradle | The Present

Tarquin kicked himself for not insisting Naira go to the hospital earlier. Her bravado and ability to keep fighting despite her injuries had fooled him into assuming she was all right. A large part of that had been his own need to keep her near, to be able to look up from his desk and see her in the flesh.

Naira had spun out of control, and Fletcher had been the one to catch her before she crashed, and that chafed. Once more, the damned man knew it and kept shooting Tarquin smug smirks.

She'd told him about her visions, as they'd walked. Explained the fear she couldn't shake that, no matter what they did, Tarquin always ended up running those experiments in order to save them all. She would rather crack herself than live to see him fall so far.

And then she told him about Jana, and how she'd do anything to keep the child from having to experience that terrible future. He'd wanted to come clean. To tell her about her future-self, and all he already knew, but there'd scarcely been time, and the way her lids had slid shut when he'd laid her in the hospital bed...She needed rest. And he needed more information. He couldn't get this wrong. He couldn't fail her. Not again.

"Go ahead to the powercore," Tarquin told Fletcher when they were outside the hospital. "There's something I need to do."

"I'll go with you," Fletcher said.

"No, you won't. The only reason I haven't locked you up is because there's a chance you may have useful insight on the current situation. Don't try my patience further."

Fletcher paused, eyeing him through the gentle snowfall. Tarquin braced himself for whatever snide remark the man was cooking up, but he glanced back the way they'd come, at the footsteps in the snow wending away from the hospital, and for a moment looked so very tired Tarquin almost asked him if he was all right.

"I heard her tell you about Jana."

"She did. What of it?"

"Then you know what Jonsun offered me. What I gave up, to keep her happy."

They examined each other for a long moment. Tarquin had wondered, when Sharp had spoken of working with Fletcher, precisely what that relationship had been—how could he not be curious? He had no confirmation. Neither of them did. But, strangely, he found himself hoping that she had, at the very least, allowed herself to be loved despite the nightmare of that future.

"I'm grateful," Tarquin said, "that you were there for her."

He could have meant in the *Cavendish* or by that river. It could mean any point in time in which Fletcher had pulled through. But Fletcher made a soft sound and looked once more toward the hospital.

"Do not fuck this up, do you understand me?" Fletcher didn't bother to follow that up with a threat. The implication was obvious.

"I won't," Tarquin said. "But time is short, and I need you to go to the powercore to oversee the AI while I handle another matter. You alone have insight into *canus* that might be useful."

"I can see when you're lying, cub."

"Then watch me carefully—I will not allow her to be cracked. Not again."

Fletcher studied him, the pause so long Tarquin almost grew impatient enough to order the exemplars to drag him away so that Tarquin could get on with matters. But then Fletcher nodded to himself and executed a crisp bow.

"Then I will serve you, my liege." Fletcher turned and continued toward the powercore.

"Diaz," Tarquin said. "Go with him."

Gabe saluted and hurried off. Tarquin watched those two for a moment, then shook himself. He didn't have time for Fletcher. Naira needed him to pull through. Tarquin strode away, crunching through the snow, back to his home. To the stairs. And the door. He didn't knock. She wasn't surprised by his arrival.

"Is your presence causing the increased resonance?" he asked.

Sharp had been standing at the bookshelf. She turned, set a book aside, and leaned back against the shelf. "Could you break me if I was?"

"Answer the question."

"Answer mine."

"Yes," he said. "To save her: Yes."

"Huh." She pushed off the shelf. Came to stand before him and took his hand in hers, lifting it as if she was going to kiss the back, but instead she studied his bloodied knuckles. "I wonder. Would you do it yourself, or send Fletch for me? Have him clean up your mess so that you could move on with your life pretending your hands are clean?"

"Is it you?" he asked again.

"No." She threaded her fingers through his and held on tight. "It's her."

"Will turning on the AI be enough?"

"It won't. You must break her."

"No." He shook his head. "No. There's another way. There must be."

"My poor little prince." She held the side of his face in one calloused hand to stop him shaking his head. "There is. You know there is. And you know what happens, if you make that choice."

The experiments. Naira's wrath. He swallowed.

"I can't."

"Then you must break her to stop the end."

He took a step back in disbelief, their entwined hands a rope between them. "All this time, you knew her map would be a problem—a—a *cause*, and you said nothing? Why?"

"It was already done, her map repaired. It always comes down to this. The experiment. Or me." She followed his retreat. Stepped so close the warmth of her enfolded him, burning his senses. "Break me, my liege."

He dropped her hand. Backed away, heart pounding, with his hands out in a shield against—he knew not what. "You said she was causing the resonance."

"It starts with her. It ends with me. Did you really fool yourself into believing we were separate?"

He almost fled that room. Almost let the horror of what she insisted must be done drive him back into the snow. Instead, he paused. Really looked at her, and wondered. She'd grown aggressive. Pushed herself into his personal space, when she'd held herself back before.

"What are you trying to do?" he asked.

"I don't know what you're talking about."

"This isn't you," he said, feeling some of the haze of his terror lift. "Naira was wrong—*you* were wrong—when you said I didn't know you. I do, Naira. I know you better than I know myself. You're not cruel. You're not—not vicious, like this."

"Lie to yourself all you like, my liege. It changes nothing."

"I'm not the one who's been lying." Her eyes narrowed. "You lied about our engagement, you lied about knowing how Jonsun controlled the expansion, you even hid that Jessel was a traitor from me—why are you *really* here? The truth, this time. All of it."

"I've told you all you need to know."

"You—" He stopped himself when the realization hit. "You're trying to make it easier for me, aren't you? To crack her?"

She looked away.

"Sharp...Naira." He paused, but she didn't rebuke him. "I don't know what drove you to this, but not even you are strong enough to push me away. I will save you both. I swear it. Without harming another soul."

"There's nothing left of me to save. But for her sake, I pray that you're right."

INTERLUDE

Her

Seventh Cradle | The Present

S he sits cross-legged on the floor of his bedroom and places the blade to her skin. The first cut stings, as it always does. Her pathways take time to warm up to their work. By the time she excises the first pathway from the crown that adorns her they have rallied, and she feels no pain. Only the gentle tug of metal clinging to muscle as she pulls it from her flesh and places it, with a soft clink, upon the floor.

It is awkward, removing the crown herself. Her incisions are uneven, her motions stiff. In other timelines, Fletcher has done this for her, and his skill with the scalpel far surpasses her own. But in this moment, in this timeline she has bet everything upon, she is alone. The work must be done. She will fail if the crown remains.

When she finishes with her forehead, she shears away her hair, the strands cascading down to join the discarded, bloodied pathways. She takes her time. Removes the rest with as much precision as she can manage. There is no cause to rush. She knows exactly how much time she has.

As the last pathway joins the pile, she takes a moment to examine herself in the mirror. The bleeding has stopped, though thin rivulets paint the sides of her face. Run down creases and dry dark as ink.

She has been seeking this face for endless years. Has sought it since the very first iteration of this timeline—the scarred woman in the warpcore, kicking at the bomb. She can't help but wonder what life will be like for her when those wounds finally crust over and scar. A pity, really, that she won't be the one to live to see it, despite all she has done.

The house is quiet, its caretakers drawn to the battle that they thought would be their last. She recalls how she'd felt in this moment. Worn ragged and heartsick. Aching for it to be over. For the fight to be done. She'd had no idea that endless eons of battle awaited her still. Endless attempts. Endless efforts to fix what refused to stop breaking.

The lock is a simple thing to crack. She knows all the codes, where everything is stored. Naira, this Naira, keeps a great deal of weapons in a cabinet in her office. She selects one sidearm, and a silencer, then sets the rest aside. Retrieves the tranquilizer gun she knows will be there, a weapon intended to ward off larger animals that may wander out of the woods.

The capsules attached to the darts are finicky, but she has long practiced this moment. It's no trouble at all to pop them open and rebalance the strength levels to suit her purposes. Thus armed, she exits the house. Slips through the settlement. In the chaos, and with her foreknowledge to guide her steps, she passes without notice. Reaches the hospital, and the window she knows she will climb through.

The gait-sensing alarms do not trip. Why should they? Naira Sharp is a known entity. Trusted. Expected.

Helms, standing beside Naira's door, turns at the sound of her steps. Her eyes widen. She hesitates, uncertain. It's more than enough time to shoot her through the heart. The sound is muffled, the death quick. No alarms are raised. She's planned this for centuries. Her timing is precise.

She holsters the sidearm. Draws the tranquilizer gun. Opens the door.

Naira is already rising off the bed, her empty sidearm drawn. Sharp aims for her chest, and Naira returns the favor. Her eyes narrow as recognition dawns.

"You," she says.

"Endure," she says, and fires the tranquilizer.

SIXTY-ONE

Tarquin

Seventh Cradle | The Present

He arrived at the powercore housing to find Kav, Delorne, Bracken, and a host of others hard at work setting up the equipment to monitor the conversion rate on the ship. Fletcher lingered off to the side, biting the edge of his thumbnail. Kav looked up when they entered, a question poised on his lips.

"She's fine," Tarquin said. "I insisted she recover at the hospital and she actually went, for once."

Kav blew out a relieved breath.

"I told you she was fine," Fletcher drolled.

"Did someone hear a buzzing noise?" Kav asked no one in particular.

Fletcher rolled his eyes but fell silent, observing the operation through half-lidded eyes. His presence was grit against Tarquin's thoughts, a constant distraction, but Tarquin wouldn't dare leave an asset on the table just because he disliked the man.

"Where are we at with the decay?" he asked Delorne.

"Not looking good," Delorne said, her voice as chipper as ever. "*Canus* is taking its time to spread, though I can't see why. Conditions are perfect, but it's like it's not hungry, or something. At this rate we'll reach runaway collapse in about sixteen hours."

"Something to do with the power draw?" Tarquin asked Kav. "Maybe it requires more incentive."

"I don't know," he said. "We've never tried to encourage the damn stuff before, and it was willing enough to consume the *Einkorn*. Here."

Kav pushed the data he'd been sorting through over to Tarquin. They combed through it all together, seeking the solution.

An hour passed before Fletcher said, "Nai."

Tarquin looked up. She braced herself against the doorway, snow tangled in the dark strands of her hair, the bruise across her throat a blackened purple and her eyes two sunken hollows. Fletcher was closer. He took her arm. Helped her the rest of the way into the room.

"Idiot," Kav said. "You should be resting."

"I was driving myself mad with what-ifs," she said, then glanced away. "Sorry. I'm a distraction."

"Never." Tarquin went to her and folded her in his arms. Naira leaned against him and kissed him with such sweet longing that it nearly made him forget what rested in the balance at the moment. Reluctantly, he pulled away. Smiled down into her exhausted eyes. "I might have lied."

"I missed that," she murmured, almost to herself, then shooed him back to his console. "Go on. I mean it, don't let me distract you."

"Where's Helms?" Caldweller asked.

"Perimeter sweep." Naira followed Tarquin to the console. "Comms are on the fritz and she wanted to make sure we didn't have another blackout problem."

Caldweller frowned. "She didn't check in."

"Comms are on the fritz, Lee," Naira said, gently chastising. "How's it looking?"

"Not great," Tarquin admitted. "But we'll get there. We will."

Fletcher stared at Naira from across the room. His arms were tightly crossed, a wiry energy twisting him up as he bounced, almost imperceptibly, one heel against the floor.

"Is there a problem, Mr. Demarco?" Tarquin asked.

"I don't know yet." He looked her up and down, a deep pucker to his brow. "Something's not right."

"No shit," Kav muttered.

Fletcher ignored him. "Are you well?"

"That is a remarkably stupid question," Naira said.

"Yes, yes, I know, but really, love, I'm worried." Fletcher crossed the room and took her face in his hands, tipping her head back as he used his thumb to peel her eyelid upward so that he could watch her pupils dilate. Naira gasped at the contact, jerking away from him, and Tarquin wrapped an arm snugly around her to steady her.

"Get your fucking hands off of me."

Fletcher held his hands up. "Excuse me for worrying after your health, Nai. But less than an hour ago you were asking me to break that map of yours, and I'm sorry, but I've been a finalizer a long, long time, and I see the strain in you. You're fragile. More fragile than you were by that river."

Tarquin was about to order him removed from the building, but Naira slipped from his arm. Took a threatening step toward Fletcher. He only lifted his chin, nostrils flaring. She clamped a hand over his mouth. Squeezed. Blood from his split lip leaked between her fingers as she bore down, forcing him to his knees.

"If I look fragile, it's because I'm so goddamned tired and angry and trying to hold on to some shred of hope despite it all and I am *done* with your antics. You will be quiet until I tell you to speak, or I will break your jaw just to have an excuse to wire it shut. Am I clear?"

Fletcher nodded jerkily. Naira shoved him backward, knocking him to the ground, then looked at the blood on her hand in disgust before flicking most of it off and wiping the rest on her already bloodied pant leg.

Kav snickered as Fletcher crawled gloomily to his feet and slunk off to the other side of the room, but Tarquin frowned. Naira was prone to outbursts, but something about that exchange unsettled him in a way he couldn't pin down. It seemed forced, somehow.

"Where are we at with the conversion?" Naira asked.

"Here, let me show you." Tarquin expanded his holo and tossed the data to her. Her forehead wrinkled as she sorted through everything so far.

"This isn't fast enough to stop the expansion before we all freeze, is it?" she asked.

"Nope," Delorne said, chirpy as ever.

"We'll get there," Tarquin said.

Naira looked through the haze of data separating them, straight into his eyes. "There's another way to stop this."

"No. There isn't."

Caldweller stepped forward. "My liege, we know that infected bodies printed with minds might be enough. If it's to give us more time, then I volunteer."

"Absolutely not," Tarquin said.

"It's not like I haven't been infected before." Caldweller smiled at Naira with such warmth it startled Tarquin. "You need more time to figure it out. I have faith that you will. But restrain me, please. I can't promise I'll be myself."

"What's he talking about?" Kav asked.

"We have evidence that living minds are the key to increasing *canus*'s consumption," Tarquin said grudgingly.

"Is that all?" Fletcher asked. "Then load me up, cub. *Canus* and I can have a cozy little reunion."

"No, I—" He grimaced, looking down at Naira, and couldn't read her expression. Resigned, maybe. Fletcher's description—fragile—was far too accurate for his liking. She didn't protest their offer. "Well... Maybe if you've volunteered, and the situation is controlled and limited, then perhaps it will be all right."

"We'll need way more than two volunteers," Delorne said.

"There's plenty that'd be willing," Ward said. "Myself included. You've done enough, Sharp. If there's a way we can get through this without taking the risk of cracking you all over again, I'm keen."

She had been slouched since she'd walked through the door, but she straightened, now. Slowly, and it seemed as if that effort pained her. It took her a while to find her voice, and when she did speak, the word was firm but strained. "No."

"Nai," Fletcher said, "I know when a map is at its limit. The state you're in right now, you won't come back from another cracking. Let us buy you more time."

"No," she said again.

Silence descended, and Tarquin thought Naira might be holding her breath.

"Funny that it's people that do the trick," Kav said, cutting through the tension. "I bet the AI on the cargo hauler is too limited. The AI on the *Einkorn* was far more complex."

"As is the *Sigillaria's*," Tarquin said, hope flaring bright within him. "Alvero, do we have agents on that ship?"

"We do, my liege."

"Activate them," Tarquin said. "Have them take the *canus* samples from the research labs and infect the relkatite wiring. I can use my keys to adjust the climate control from here."

"You sure about that?" Ward asked. "I don't doubt your science, my liege, but I don't much like the idea of giving *canus* a ship that large to play with. Volunteers we can control with restraints. A ship's more troublesome."

"I don't like it either," Tarquin said, "but the runaway expansion would kill *canus* as well as us. For once, we have a common enemy. Proceed, Alvero."

Tarquin watched Naira from the corner of his eye, worry distracting him even as he oversaw the process and selected the best sites to infect. She was guarded, her arms crossed and her body folding down into a slouch once more, as if even standing was beginning to weigh too heavily. Even her breathing had shallowed—she couldn't seem to get a full breath.

He wanted to order her back to the hospital, but he knew she wouldn't go. She approached the powercore, staring into that inky surface, and he went to stand beside her, ready to catch her, should she lose her strength.

"All agents have checked in," Alvero said. "The samples have been placed."

"Then it falls to me."

Naira gave him an encouraging smile. The first she'd managed since they'd learned her map was speeding the expansion, and it eased a taut wire of fear within him. Tarquin opened the fleet command screen via his HUD, then entered his keys. He double-checked to be certain the *Sigillaria's* weapons remained locked, then took over their climate control and began adjusting it to *canus's* preferences.

Jessel hailed him, a private, encrypted line that only he could see. He answered.

"Mercator." They were in a lab of some kind, a room that Tarquin didn't recognize. While shadows lurked beneath their eyes, the corners of their lips were tight with a knowing smile. "I know what you're doing. Stop this, or you won't like the outcome."

"Mx. Hesson," Tarquin said, "your brother is dead. The *Cavendish* is once again my property, and your people have surrendered. We wish for no more bloodshed. We never wanted any in the first place. I know what you're doing up there, that you're planning to wait out the expansion. It won't work. Surrender and land the *Sigillaria* on the plain with the *Cavendish*. Then we can talk about how best to care for what's left of your people."

"How interesting, that that's what you think happened today. My brother lives." They gestured to the side, and Jonsun strolled into frame. "Your traitor killed his body, true, but his map remains as hale as ever."

"We won't let you give the ship to *canus*," Jonsun said. "This expansion cannot be stopped. Accept your end gracefully, and maybe we'll allow history to remember you with a soft spot, if we allow history to remember you at all."

Jonsun ended the call. Tarquin relayed it to the others.

"Not a lot of substance in that, my liege," Alvero said. "It sounds like they're panicked and posturing."

Naira didn't speak. Her chin was lowered, hair shielding her expression. He reached out to brush the hair from her eyes and was surprised at the depth of hopelessness he found within her.

"Don't worry," he said. "I have control of that ship. They can't stop us from infecting it. We won't have to use any other options."

Her lips parted, but she closed them before she spoke, thinking better of whatever it had been. Naira smiled at him once more. That smile didn't reach her eyes.

"What's wrong?" A call flared in the corner of his HUD. "Damnit, just a moment. Jessel's hailing again."

Jessel had left the frame. In their place was a narrow gurney, a white sheet pulled over an indistinct body lying on it.

"You know," Jonsun said, speaking as if they were mid casual conversation, "the way Nai talked about you, Mercator, I wanted to like you. Maybe I could have, if it wasn't for that lineage of yours. But your type, they don't change, do they? You've been saying for over a year now you intend to cede power, and here we are."

Jonsun shook his head and crossed his arms, leaning against the side of the gurney. "I won't tell you you're like your daddy, because I don't believe you are. But you're close enough, and you've got one crucial thing in common. Neither one of you can let go. Did you know, when he built the *Cavendish* to be a fortress of amarthite, he wanted to bring his family along for the ride? Lot of maps, on that ship. One of them's yours. Nai unlocked more than she thought when she gave the *Cavendish* back to me."

Jonsun folded down the sheet covering the face on the gurney. Tarquin's face.

"The download's already begun," Jonsun said. "I'm sorry about this, I am. I wanted to keep you around for a while longer. But Nai's trouble, always has been, and you're dead anyway. I gotta hit her where it hurts."

The call ended. Tarquin locked up, frozen to the core, every muscle rigid with terror and his only thoughts were skittering away from him. He had to—to what? He couldn't stop them. No one else had seen that footage.

He couldn't be double-printed if this print was dead.

"Naira—" Tarquin reached for the sidearm that had been strapped to Naira's right thigh as long as he'd known her, and touched empty air. Sharp met his gaze and smiled as tears stood bright in her eyes.

"Goodbye, my liege."

Tarquin opened other eyes, and screamed.

SIXTY-TWO

Naira

Seventh Cradle | The Present

Naira woke to the iron tinge of blood permeating the air. Every muscle ached, the sedative leaving her wrung out. Hollowed. The lights were low. The hospital sheets tangled around her. She flexed her hands. Fisted those sheets and, slowly, head swimming, pushed herself up.

Helms's corpse was cooling by the door.

She tried to access her HUD, but her comms pathway had been cut out. Naira lifted a hand, touching the wound gingerly, and winced as she discovered the many tiny slices adorning her skull. The air was cool against her shaved scalp. The blood itched where it had dried.

There was a backup crown in the room. A stasis shield—empty. It didn't take her long to understand what had happened. Her other-self had swapped their prints.

She staggered to her feet. While this print was less injured, the lingering effects of the sedative made her feel slow and clumsy, her thoughts gummed up.

Her door was locked from within. She opened it. The hospital was silent save the muted blips of equipment. No one spoke to her. They turned to watch as she passed, faces locked in amber, eyes wide with fear Naira dared not dwell upon.

Snow had clogged the roads, pathways cleared for Merc-Sec's use during the assault. Her other-self had dressed for this weather. Sturdy boots and a thick coat wrapped her as she trudged through the drifts, leaning toward the powercore building, following the footsteps her future had left behind. Willing everything she sensed down to her marrow to be wrong.

Wind whipped a flurry past her and then Fletcher appeared out of the brewing storm. He ran toward her, his outstretched hands soaked with blood.

A lifetime together, and she'd never seen him that shaken, his face slack save for the widening of his eyes, fear pulling the thin skin at his temples taut, his mouth opened in shock or protest, she couldn't tell.

She felt like she was falling and she didn't know why.

"Fletch?"

"Nai, I..." He blinked rapidly to clear away the snow tangled in his lashes and placed both hands on her upper arms. His breath smoked in the air between them. "I tried to stop it. I knew she was wrong from the start, but they wouldn't fucking listen."

"What are you talking about?" But she knew. Of course she knew.

"I love you, Nai. I love you and Kav loves you and I'm guessing there's a lot of other people who love you, too. And I need you to hold on to that, okay?"

"Tell me."

"It's the cub. Tarquin. Jonsun and Jessel double-printed him. He fell straight to the endless scream. Tarquin's gone."

No boiled through her. A single-syllable rejection of the truth, a fearsome need for the universe to comply, to will reality into the shape she demanded of it, because this wasn't right. It wasn't *fair.*

Fletcher was talking, entreating her to stay with him, to focus, and she saw the shape of his fear, filling the void he'd made of himself. He was terrified the next sound out of her mouth would be that scream. That in losing Tarquin she'd fall with him, and it was tempting. So very, very tempting to let herself break at last, because then she could rest and she wouldn't have to face this.

But there was a life raft for her, in Fletcher's words. It wasn't in the love, though it should have been. If it'd been her to fall, she'd have wanted Tarquin to find solace in the hearts of their friends. Love had never helped her. Not for long. What Naira found instead was an all-consuming flame.

Jessel and Jonsun had done this. She knew why, there was no question. Nothing to interrogate. Naira recalled every single conversation she'd ever had. Her memories were traps to catch her foot when she wasn't wary enough, spike pits waiting for her to fall. Not this time. This time she felt as if she was floating above herself, the ruin of her life laid out at her feet, shards left over for her to pick through.

You're going about this all wrong, she'd told Jonsun, when she'd first joined the Conservators. *If you want to make Acaelus stop, you have to hit him where it hurts. Go after the mining ships, and nothing less than that.*

It was flattering, in a strange way, that she frightened Jonsun enough for him to want to hit her where it hurt. He'd put her on the same level of threat as Acaelus. She supposed that was correct. She was the head of Mercator, now that Tarquin was gone.

It was, however, a mistake. Naira was not an enemy one wanted to back into a corner.

My fire carrier.

Jonsun was about to find out what it meant to burn.

Naira turned away from Fletcher. She barely saw him, really. His hands slipped from her like a rock skipping off water. Temporary, ephemeral. She wasn't fully aware of her movements; her limbs felt far away. A hollowed-out shell wrapped around a scorched nothing where a person used to be.

She threw the doors to the powercore building open wide. Let the rush of freezing wind and swirling snow carry her within.

Naira didn't look at the reddened, tear-streaked faces that turned to her. She didn't hear their gentle words, their muted sobs. She stepped over her other-corpse. Noted the serene look on her own face, though tears stained those cheeks. That body's skull had cracked, when she'd fallen. Precisely where Naira had tripped what seemed like centuries ago, now. Her heel slipped in her own blood. She caught herself. She'd always been the one to catch herself, before Tarquin. It came back easily enough.

Tarquin's body was on the floor. His long legs stretched out against uncaring concrete, Caldweller holding his torso, his head, and rocking, rocking.

Not yet. She couldn't face that yet.

Blood and snowmelt and sweat and tears, too, dripped from her, leaving footprints of despair across the floor. Naira approached a console. Entered her command keys.

Jonsun and Jessel had pulled the trigger, but she'd done this to herself. She understood why. Tarquin wouldn't break her to save the worlds, and she wouldn't let him conduct the experiments she'd glimpsed in a gold-soaked future.

In saving each other, they would have lost everything. Now, the only thing she had left to lose was herself. She had wanted to let go for so very, very long.

Endure.

The World had told her its single goal was to survive. It would not let the universe fall, if she could reach it and tell it what it must do. Strange, to place her faith in that creature, now. To listen to Paison and Fletcher at last and hope against hope that they had been right—*canus* could help a cracked mind hold together.

To reach *canus*, she'd need a swarm network the likes of which that creature had never dreamed of before.

A single thrown stone could never change the course of a river. But thousands? Thousands could change worlds.

Naira transmitted her print and map to every cubicle in the cargo hauler, and shattered. The dizzying rush of her mind falling to pieces almost broke her. Almost pushed her to scream and never stop. But she was not yet done. She would not let all that she had lost be for nothing.

Canus surged. Ravening hunger pushed it to consume faster but not, Naira thought, fast enough. On the cargo ship her pathways warmed, relk and *canus*, and she felt the first stirrings of communion, of dominion. The greater colony of *canus* on the ship roused to understand itself, its surroundings, and sensed the ants crawling through its veins with smaller colonies growing within them. Within her.

It was a burgeoning, a tide, and it would have washed her away to the oblivion of *canus*'s union if she hadn't learned from Fletcher and Paison and Acaelus. If she didn't know that *canus*'s inexorable will, even at critical mass, could be bent. She knew precisely what it wanted, above all else: union. And she knew how to make it hate.

It plunged into her mind, seeking control, seeking levers to pull. Recognizing on some base level that Naira had been, and remained, its enemy.

It reached for her and found nothing but the inferno of her grief, a catching conflagration as she envisioned the energy that was *canus*'s food tearing the universe apart, tearing her apart, and Jonsun and Jessel as the orchestrators of that sundering.

Canus devoured. Fueled by her need to destroy the thing that had destroyed her, it glutted itself on the feast of relk and all its energies. Distantly, in the broken-open heart of the powercore housing, Naira heard Delorne say, "Holy shit. We're contracting."

In the settlement, Naira moved away from the console at last. She wasn't done, not even close, and she held the maw of *canus* in her mind as she crossed the room. Silence fell, tense, or maybe it had always been silent since she'd thrown the doors wide. It didn't matter if the others spoke. There was no quiet in the body on the floor.

Naira knelt. Someone had closed his eyes, and while there was no obvious wound, someone in this room had killed his print. Plunged too much sedative into his heart, perhaps, to end the scream. But it wasn't ended. She could feel it, moths' wings beating against the cage around the empty core of herself.

That print was dead. That was what you did, when someone cracked. You ended their suffering. But as Caldweller handed him to her, and she took Tarquin's corpse into her arms and laid her lips upon his brow, she could hear him, a fragment of a man trapped in another print, screaming, because Jonsun had not killed that print.

"I'm coming," she whispered against him, the first words she'd spoken since it all ended, and closed her eyes.

The *Sigillaria* was infected. She could feel it, through her bonding with *canus*. All the thin circuits, all the twisted pathways, and the minuscule quanta of *canus* struggling to thrive. Nothing in this universe was ever free of it. Nothing was ever clean. It permeated everything.

Naira was already broken. It was no great effort to splinter herself further. *Canus* called to *canus*. She reached out through the tenuous connection *canus* offered her and snatched the systems of the *Sigillaria* in her mind. Every single printing cubicle in the *Sigillaria* lit red. She'd always been a fast printer. It was a requirement, to be an exemplar. To be the person who answered when someone called out for help.

The cubicles opened. Naira disgorged an army of herself into the heart of her enemy.

SIXTY-THREE

Naira

Seventh Cradle | The Present

Naira's splintered selves were perfectly coordinated, perfectly determined. Each face was hers and each face was fury, and she waded through her fleeing enemy, letting their cries of panic kindle something deep and hungry within her. When they fought back, she killed them and took their weapons. Sometimes they killed her, but the whittling away of herself was irrelevant.

They tried to shut off the printers. To disconnect the power. But she held the circuits of the *Sigillaria* in her mind as firmly as she held her desired target, and all attempts were sidestepped as easily as dodging a drunkenly thrown punch. Naira made a cordon of herself around the warpcore and sealed off the exits, the escape pods. She was a living fist clenching the *Sigillaria* in mind and body, and she refused to yield.

Jessel and Jonsun waited for her in the lab where they'd cracked Tarquin. Sweating, fearful. Jonsun tried to talk her down and Jessel threatened, but they'd both miscalculated. They'd given her nothing left to lose.

Naira's corpses made a hill in the doorway before their ammo ran out, and then she took them both in hand, gagged them, pressed them to kneel. It only took one of her, each. Hardly a noticeable expenditure of energy.

They'd gagged Tarquin, trying to silence his screaming so that it'd be harder for her to find him. They needn't have bothered. That scream was a bloody nail in the center of her being upon which the compass of herself turned. Better for them, if they'd killed him and let him rest.

But they hadn't. They'd thought he might be a bargaining chip. Jonsun had spoken honeyed shit about repairing his map. They all knew that, even if Naira would do such a thing, the repair was impossible. Slipping between memories was one thing. The endless scream was endless for a reason.

Tarquin's print was strapped to the gurney, straining against his bonds, insensate. He didn't know she was there. He couldn't. He didn't even know when or where he was, anymore. Sweat stained the sheet in a growing halo and his eyes were empty, white and rolling.

He'd been terrified of cracking. He'd stood no chance.

Naira stroked his sweat-slick hair, and in an almost delicate movement she'd deployed countless times before, she snapped his neck. His body fell slack, head lolling to the side, eyes open and mouth wide, a rictus snarl haunting him even in death. She smoothed his features. Wiped the flecks of foam from his mouth.

Tarquin's gone.

Naira wanted to be gone, too. She opened her mouth to scream, but the sound eluded her. There was nothing left to break.

She spread her arms, burning with frustration, and through the communion of *canus* and the multitude of herselves, she sensed the infested ships stalking each other around opposite sides of the planet, the *Sigillaria* and the cargo ship. The devouring fervor of *canus* braided through her, twin to her desire to consume with flame, and through that bonding, she felt, at the edges of her network of senses, spreading faster than the universe ever had, another mind.

The connection was tenuous, a flickering at the edge of her thoughts. The World surged at the nascent brush of communion, then shrank away in fear as it glimpsed the ruined landscape of her thoughts.

Naira wasn't about to let them go. *Canus* may refuse to understand why people would leave them, but it understood what it was to be *left* and she could sense their sorrow, their hurt.

They saw through each other's eyes at last, and neither one of them liked what they had to see.

But the connection was slipping. Though Naira forced the *canus*-bonded to her to devour with all its strength, the World slid farther away. They'd miscalculated, somehow. Converting the relkatite on the cargo ship and *Sigillaria* both wasn't enough.

The World cried out to her before the connection failed, warning her. The child Jana, recalling to *canus* pieces of her nightmares, had told *canus* of another food source. One nearby Naira, and she almost laughed in bitter resentment.

Seventh Cradle. Jonsun could have gone to Eighth, when he'd first fled with the *Cavendish*. But he'd come here, no doubt following some future vision of Jessel's, and she wondered if he'd even known why. Naira could force him to tell her, but she didn't care for his reasons, his excuses. She saw only what she had to do and acted.

It wasn't what she wanted to do. She wanted to take the ships and smash them together and transmute everything in them to ashes. But Tarquin wouldn't have wanted that. Her work wasn't done, because his wasn't.

Naira crushed the AI of both ships beneath her will and flew them to the clearing on the edge of the river near the settlement. She set them down roughly along the bank, all the while pumping out relk- and *canus*-loaded prints of herself until she stood shoulder to shoulder with her own bodies in the hallways, and the cartridges ran dry at last.

Naira walked two of herselves out of the *Sigillaria*, dragging Jonsun and Jessel through the settlement, and placed them at Fletcher's feet, bound and gagged, her intention clear. She watched his haunted face until understanding flashed behind his eyes. He nodded, his voice lost to him at last.

On the *Sigillaria*, Naira picked up her corpses. She kissed Tarquin goodbye and marched the army of herself out the airlocks, onto the ice-crisp bank of the river. Naira stared out upon the vibrant teal of the water, breathing down the cold, and knew not even glacial ice could soothe her fire.

I actually think there's a large deposit of relkatite up there causing the color. I'd love to take you to see the glaciers, someday. They're really beautiful.

He'd been right. The river was teal due to trace amounts of relkatite, washed down from the glaciers that mounted this world. Not much, in a handful. But an incomprehensible amount, distributed through all that water. Enough to break a universe that was already falling apart.

Canus itched along all her endless pathways, starving, because she'd willed it to do nothing but consume.

Thin ice crusted the riverbank. It snapped beneath her bare feet, plunging the first of her down into those near-frozen depths.

Naira walked into dark waters, and sank, and died, and the *canus* in her multitudes burst from her flesh to consume the radiation from the particulate matter of relkatite. The river turned granite grey. Corpse grey.

The expansion slowed. She did not.

Naira drowned every last piece of herself until there was nothing left but the jagged shard holding Tarquin in the powercore housing. Still, she could not scream.

SIXTY-FOUR

Naira

Seventh Cradle | *The Present*

Naira allowed herself to be reprinted into an uninjured body. The suppression crown was edited slightly, but the heat response couldn't fully be removed. She found she didn't care. The chill she'd first felt after coming back to Mercator Station in an amarthite print never left her, now, no matter what they did. The icy waters of the river had always been waiting for her. Now that the graveyard frost had found her, it wouldn't let her go.

When she finally returned home and faced the room they'd shared together, there had been a book. A single volume plucked from the shelves, Hobbes's *Leviathan*—the work Naira had teased Tarquin with so long ago, on Sixth Cradle—rested in the center of their bed.

Across the first page was a sideways scrawl, a palimpsest in her own handwriting. A fragment of an averted future, left behind.

I know not what happens next. Thousands of alterations I have tried and this alone is the only path of which I cannot see the end. If I cannot see the end, then I will never reach this future. My future. Never struggle on through a frostbitten unraveling. That is where I place my faith. In our unknown horizon.

You will have so many questions I cannot answer. I can only ease your uncertainty: The cargo ship and Sigillaria combined would never have been enough. To convert the river required us. To dominate so much canus required a hunger that outstripped its own, and what is grief, if not starving for what was lost?

Tarquin's experiments could have accomplished the same goal, if executed on a large enough scale.

I leave it to you to decide for yourself if it would have been better for him to live on, destroyed by his own actions, or to fall while he still yet had some glimmer of himself left.

Forgive me.

Forgive yourself.

Those final words had been written above an underlined portion of the book: *For in a way beset with those that contend, on one side for too great liberty, and on the other side for too much authority, 'tis hard to pass between the points of both unwounded.*

Not a passage from the work itself, but a fragment of the dedication. A statement from one friend, to another. Naira tore out that page. Kept it with her always, tucked within a pocket against her heart.

There was conjecture. Guesswork. Science to be done, and Naira's map a focal point of much head-scratching study.

The universe contracted. Slowly, inexorably, all the pieces that had been scattered were clawed back into place. Delorne and the others estimated a year before the ansible network could be reached to be adjusted. In the meantime, the settlement of Seventh Cradle was cut off from the rest of humanity and facing a long, brutal winter.

They would make it. There were plenty of supplies and seeds and the technology to make it through. When the rejoining happened and the settlement could communicate regularly with Sol again, they had a wealth of amarthite to offer those left standing, and a new mind in the universe for the rest of humanity to meet, for Naira had released the AI-bonded *canus* from her grasp, and let it live. Confined to the *Sigillaria* and the cargo ship, the printers and weapons all disabled, the rest of *canus*'s swarm network out of reach, their segment of the World was forced to work with them on finding a new balance in the universe.

Kav spent his time testing all the theories and experiments he'd ever dreamed up regarding what it meant to be sentient. Naira put her head down and saw to her tasks, because in the fraught days following Tarquin's fall, the weight of what she had to do almost drowned her as surely as the river.

Ward and Alvero handled the aftermath of the war.

Naira planned a funeral instead of a wedding.

They weren't common events. Not in a universe where death meant rebirth—or rotting on ice while your loved ones lingered on, hoping someday they might raise your phoenix fees. The cracking of the head of Mercator was a different matter. His people required closure. Tarquin would have given it to them. And so she planned, even though she hated it, because he'd left something behind. One thing, not yet done, that she would have to finish for him.

She held the funeral a week after the dust settled on the broken plain that would have been their home. There was a body, and that alone spoke to the largesse of Mercator, that they could commit something that should be recycled to the earth instead.

Snow fell lightly, as it did most days, and the people of the settlement stood in neat rows upon the plain, hands clasped, heads bowed. There was a podium and his picture behind it, and someone—quite probably her mother—had coaxed flowers out of the frozen ground to drape that podium.

He'd fallen in battle. If these had been anything like normal circumstances, the HCA would have sent a squad of six of its highest-ranking sharpshooters to honor his sacrifice, one to represent each branch of humanity. This wasn't anything like normal.

All of the exemplars were ranked sharpshooters, but only Naira, Helms, and Caldweller had served in the HCA to receive the medal. Of Merc-Sec, Ward and—to Naira's surprise—Alvero had both served in the HCA and earned the medal. That left an empty slot, and the only other person she knew with that ranking on the settlement was Fletcher.

He'd only nodded and said, "Of course," when she'd asked him to serve.

Marko got the fabbers to print the HCA dress uniform and their medals. Naira sat in the room where her print had once been held in stasis, Tarquin's casket before her, draped in the united MERIT-HC flag, and ran the golden braid that marked her as a sharpshooter between her gloved fingers. She thought about the last time she'd sat like this, at the foot of his printing cubicle before she'd gone off to confront Fletcher, and how she hadn't known what to say then.

She still didn't know what to say.

Kav knocked lightly and let himself in. His presence made her smile, however briefly. He always looked ridiculous in his dress uniform. He'd donned it despite hating it, because he knew she wanted to do things right.

"Are you ready?" he asked.

No. Her throat closed and she dragged in a shaking breath, struggling to compose herself.

Gently, he took the braid from her hand and affixed it to the bottom of her service medal collection, then tapped the rectangle of colored bars with one finger.

"I'd say we're going to have to invent a new one for you," he said with forced lightness. "But with the weight of all this candy you're already toting, I'm afraid adding more would blow out your knees."

She gave a strangled laugh and tipped her head back as she filled her lungs. "I'm ready."

"Okay. I'll get them." He hesitated and squeezed her knee. "We've got you, Nai."

She stood to straighten her uniform and the rifle strapped to her back as Kav opened the door and called for the others. They filtered in, solemn—even Fletcher, and without a word between them took up their positions around the casket. Naira and Caldweller took the front. Kav, being the highest-ranked officer in the HCA they had, marched before them all, leading the procession into the snow.

Naira heard nothing but the steady beat of drums that set the pace of their slow march. Her movements were mechanical, the kind of precision that'd once earned her praise from her commanding officers. People watched her, and some were concerned and mournful, but some were cautious, too. She couldn't blame them. Not even she could explain what she'd done, or what it meant.

They placed the casket on its stand and fanned out to either side, then brought their rifles to bear in unison. Kav's deep, smooth voice called for them to ready. They aimed to the grey sky. He called for fire. They did. The bolt slid in her hand and the weapon kicked and she did exactly as Kav told her, in perfect sync with the others, until six shots had been fired and they stowed their weapons and stood in formation on either side of the podium at rigid attention.

Kav said something by way of introduction. People approached the podium, one by one, and said kind things and maybe funny things about Tarquin that Naira wouldn't let herself hear. Ward and Alvero and Delorne and even Naira's mother spoke, and she turned off her aural pathways until Caldweller went, and she knew it was her turn next. Last. Caldweller wept. It almost broke her.

Naira didn't have it in her to eulogize him. But she could finish his work. She could give him that. She approached the podium and braced her gloved hands against it.

"Tarquin never wanted to lead this family, but when the time came, and he had no choice, he told me that he was grateful, because he learned to love you all. Mercator was never just a company, to him. It was a family in a real sense, one he gave up everything to keep safe." Her voice caught. *Breathe.*

"Tarquin didn't want his legacy to be one of dynasty. He intended to be the final head of Mercator. This was supposed to be his speech, but in his absence, it falls to me to carry out his greatest wish. Before battle embroiled us all, he drew up plans." Naira found strength for her voice again. "As acting head of Mercator, this morning I signed paperwork divesting all of Mercator's holdings into a trust to be shared equally among its employees. The trust is to be managed by a board of directors elected by said members of that trust. That's all of you."

Whispers, wide eyes, anxious fidgeting rolled through the crowd. She held up a hand for silence.

"This restructuring eliminates the position of head of family and shares power equally among the members of the elected directors, who will serve terms with limits set in the charter. It stipulates that, while you all may do with your newfound wealth as you wish, none of you will ever be given a dividend larger than any other member. No blooded member of Mercator or any other MERIT family may run for a place on this board until five generations have passed from the time of the charter's signing. As we are currently separated from our counterparts in Sol, an interim board will be established to manage matters until the rejoining.

"Tarquin had planned to stay with you in an advisory capacity. I hope you'll forgive me, but I cannot.

"The rejoining will be fraught. The other heads of MERIT will move to undo this. But Mercator has always stood above the rest, and with your stockpile of amarthite, they will have no choice but to accept this change. I hope that the rest of MERIT will follow. That you will use your newfound freedom to make sure the wealth of this universe is shared equally. We've seen how fragile it can be.

"Thank you, from Tarquin and myself, for your service to Mercator. It has been our honor."

Naira left the podium. Kav ended the ceremonies. When the crowd was breaking up, she crouched by the edge of the grave.

Methodically, she unpinned her medals and laid them with her rifle upon the casket. She should say goodbye. She knew that. Blinking back tears, Naira straightened, and kissed her mother, and went alone back into town to change and collect the supplies she'd already packed.

While the people of Mercator retreated to the warmth of the community center to celebrate Tarquin's life, Naira walked away under the blanket of the night.

SIXTY-FIVE

Naira

Seventh Cradle | The Present

Naira followed the river south, as best she could. At points the shore became impassable, the river narrowing to a lightning rush in a steep slot of stone only to plunge over a drop and carry on again, winding and calm, as if its world hadn't been crushed down to one fine thread and sent tipping over the edge of a cliff.

A week or so on she became aware that she was being followed. Naira couldn't quite tell what it was, human or animal. It was possible someone from the settlement had decided to track her down—she'd turned off all her comms—but the pattern of footsteps was unlike any she'd heard before.

The planet's early and harsh winter had displaced a lot of wildlife. There weren't supposed to be any large predators near the settlement, but she couldn't say for certain how much ground she'd covered, or exactly where she was. She'd only set out to follow the river because she'd wanted to see its end.

As night drew near she found a place to bivouac, set a fire, and rolled out her sleeping mat, then took her rifle and hid in the shadows. A few hours passed before a branch snapped. She breathed shallowly, not daring to move. A snout entered the ring of firelight. A paw.

She knew, theoretically, what dogs were. Wealthy people kept them as pets, sometimes, on stations, though the practice was generally frowned upon due to the resource drain. Wild packs ranged the broken-down dome cities of Earth. This creature was almost a dog, or maybe a wolf, or a large fox. Something like all three, a unique expression of Seventh Cradle.

Its snout was long and scarred, its body lean and strong, its fur a dark shade of grey tinged with blue that reminded Naira of wet shale. Large paws prodded at the snow, nostrils flaring as pert triangle ears flicked. It hesitated a moment, then moved into the light and made for her bag with the rations, nudging at the cut-resistant canvas with its nose. A shaggy tail wagged. Its ribs stood out against its flank.

She had a half-eaten ration bar in her pocket. Slowly, Naira slung the rifle over her shoulder and pulled the bar free, then crept to the edge of the fire. The wolf-thing stiffened, sensing her presence, and wheeled around to lower its head, back stiff, teeth shining with an unvoiced snarl.

Naira held out the stub of ration bar and waited.

With painstaking care it crept forward, lips pulled back in warning. The sharp points of its teeth were fascinating, though she knew she should be afraid. Creatures like this ate meat, and she was, most definitely, made of meat. Wary, ice-blue eyes locked onto hers as it delicately snatched the morsel from her hand and backed away, tossing it to its molars to chew a few times before suffering an all-body shudder. She could have sworn it gave her a dirty look before it bolted back into the forest.

"Yeah, no one likes those," she called after the animal.

It showed up every night after that, and they went through the same routine, though the animal was clearly disgusted by the bars. She couldn't blame it. The wolf-thing was adapted to fresh meat, and the ration bars were all plant and synth protein. Humans hadn't bothered with animal protein since the first collapse.

Naira stopped her endless march early one day and waited in the brush along the river for one of the larger varieties of birds she'd spotted wheeling through the sky. They skimmed the water, hunting bugs, and as one flew over the shore, she fired.

The bird exploded in a puff of feathers and dropped like a rock to the ground, the others scattering in a panic. Guilt stabbed at her—the bird had been minding its own business—but this was the way of things for animals. She crouched beside the fallen bird and turned it over to make certain there weren't any bullet fragments remaining, then picked it up by the feet and hauled it back to camp.

That night, the wolf-thing made a strange, rumbling sound of what she hoped was pleasure when it spotted this new kind of offering. It practically swallowed the creature whole before cleaning its paws and muzzle with delicate care, then curled up by her side for the night. Naira ran a hand experimentally through its fur and found the animal's skin tracked with scars.

"You too, huh?"

It muttered at her, then snored, and didn't leave her side after that.

Darkness was creeping through the trees when she noticed a change in the air. She hadn't camped for the night, a restlessness coming over her that she couldn't explain. The air, which had been too cold to offer up anything but snow, had grown thick with moisture, and there was a smell that she couldn't articulate but found pleasant.

The wolf-thing whined at her, annoyed, as she pressed on. The animals on this planet hadn't had much use for low-light vision with how bright their moon used to be, but the night was darker now.

Naira came to the edge of a clearing that didn't end. She put a hand against the rough trunk of a tree to hold herself up, struggling to make sense of what she was seeing.

A light layer of snow ended in a stretch of rough, rocky grey sand, washed away by the shushing stroke of liquid velvet. The ocean. She'd known it was down south, somewhere. The enormity of it pressed against her, made her feel smaller than space ever had.

Whitecaps set to glitter by the faint moonlight crashed against the jagged ridge of a cliff to her right, the river flowing out in lazy rivulets to join the larger body to her left. She hadn't expected the sound of it, a ceaseless crashing, a murmured whisper. Her heart ached, wishing Tarquin was there to see this with her. To tell her the history written in the stones.

Naira set up camp on the beach and learned her lesson that night when the tide came in and soaked her in her sleep. The next morning, she moved her sodden things inland and, with the cliff to her back, built a makeshift shelter. When she'd set out, she'd had no purpose. She'd only known that she couldn't stay in the settlement. Couldn't bear the doleful looks, the soft condolences and light touches of compassion.

Part of her had thought that where the river ended she would end, too, and sometimes, late at night, when she listened to the rush of the water, she remembered the cold embrace of drowning. The chill in the depths called to her. Wordless, patient. Naira cut the suppression crown from her skin and spent most of her days lost within her memories.

Hunting for the wolf-thing gave her a reason not to walk into the waves.

SIXTY-SIX

Kav

Seventh Cradle | Three Months Later

The walk from the *Sigillaria* to Kav's new home seemed to take longer every night Naira was away. The town had transformed slowly over the last few months, the grey-green faces of Mercator pre-fabs metamorphosing under the blanket of the long winter's snow. Color splashed the doors, Marko's art style creeping into small sculptures around the settlement as he taught those who suddenly had the time to learn the facets of his craft.

It was beautiful, and it hurt, because Naira would have loved it, and in the darker recesses of his heart he knew she wasn't coming back.

Kav's walk took him past the house Cass had claimed for themself, and if Kav caught himself slowing down every time he passed that door, so what? They were gone more often than not, tracking out into the wilderness with Helms to keep an unobtrusive eye on Naira, for what good it would do. When she decided to leave this world, none of them could stop her.

Cass startled Kav by being home for once. The exemplar was notoriously reclusive, friendly to anyone who'd pass the time with them, but when they ate in the common room, they did so with the other exemplars only, and most nights they stayed home.

Before Jonsun had taken over the *Cavendish*, Kav had asked Naira to introduce him to Tarquin's charming new exemplar. Without that bridge, Kav felt...intrusive. As if he was disrupting their self-chosen solitude, and maybe he was. It hadn't escaped Kav's notice that a few of the settlers threw Cass dreamy looks, and the E-X never responded.

Standing in the snow, watching the golden light in Cass's home spill out of a crack in the pulled shutters, Kav resolved to take a chance. Naira and Tarquin had danced around each other for months before finally admitting their feelings, and they'd missed out on months of happiness before everything had gone to hell. Kav didn't anticipate anything nearly so catastrophic as what they'd experienced on the horizon for himself, but then, neither had they.

Asking Cass to the café some of the Merc-Sec had set up wouldn't be *that* intrusive if they weren't interested, right? They could tell him no. It'd be fine.

Kav gathered up his courage but was startled into stillness as the side door to the house opened. Cass strolled out, oblivious to Kav's presence, carrying a bowl. They crouched down, moonlight gleaming in their curls, scooped snow into the bowl, and then took a bite.

"Is your purifier broken?" Kav asked before he could stop himself.

They stood quickly, an abashed smile on their face that Kav found absolutely devastating. "Ayuba. I didn't see you there."

Of course they hadn't seen him. He'd been lurking in the shadows, pining like a damn teenager. Kav struggled to find a smile that didn't reveal the full extent of his mingled panic and mortification, and affected a casual stroll as he approached, stepping into the light of Cass's walkway to, hopefully, look like less of a stalker.

"Sorry to startle you." Kav gestured down the road. "I walk this way to get home once I'm done for the day. I guess I didn't think exemplars could be snuck up on."

"I suppose I'm out of practice," Cass said, a brief flash of sorrow behind their eyes.

Shit. Right. Cass's charge was dead. They were still grieving.

"Uhhh." Kav scratched the back of his head, scrambling for anything that wasn't E-X-related. "If your purifier is broken, I can fix it."

"What, this?" Cass looked at the bowl, and to Kav's astonishment, their cheeks darkened slightly, bringing out their freckles. They picked up the spoon and offered it to him. "Try it."

Kav could practically *feel* Naira's derisive smirk and the ghost of her voice making a smart-assed comment about Kav's willingness to put anything Cass offered him into his mouth. He was surprised to find the snow slightly slushy, creamy with oat milk and a sweetener.

"Oh, that's nice," he said, and kicked himself, because he couldn't think of anything better to say.

"It's called snow cream. I read about it in one of the romances in the Mercator digital library, and I've always had a sweet tooth, so." They shrugged and took a bite, smiling to themself at the flavor.

"You read romances?" Kav hoped he didn't sound as intrigued as he felt.

"Sure," they said. "Do you?"

"No," Kav admitted. "Nai was always pressuring me to read something that wasn't a technical manual but, well. Other things were more pressing."

"Understandable."

Oh no. Small talk had stalled. Kav glanced at the house. "You, uh, live alone in there, huh?"

Cass's brows lifted. "I do. It's been interesting, having all that space to myself. I'm not used to being outside of the E-X barracks."

"I bet," Kav said. "Nai never slept well on her own, especially those first nights out of Mercator. Kept slinking into my room at night."

"Oh?" Those brows reached higher.

"Not like that," Kav said quickly. "I mean, she was—*is*—like a sister to me, and decidedly not my type." He stopped himself just before saying *you are.*

Cass swirled the spoon around in the bowl, toying with it. "I'm aware. I enjoy listening between the lines, as it were. Helps me get to know people. A valuable trait as an exemplar, or so I'm told."

"Nai was pretty pissed off you made her as Lockhart so quickly."

"That one was easy." Cass's smile turned wry. "Ex. Sharp didn't give herself away, Liege Tarquin did."

"He did have a way of looking at her, didn't he? Like she was the whole universe."

"Yeah." Cass looked down.

A lump knotted Kav's throat. "I'm sorry. I didn't mean to...I'll go now. Enjoy your night, E-X."

"Ayuba," Cass said, halting his about-face. "I, um...I'm good at listening because I need to get to know people, before..." They trailed off and bit their lip again, shooting a glance at their open door. "Before I can really get to know them. Does that make sense?"

"Oh." Kav blinked. Cass needed a deeper connection before they could be interested in something more. That explained a lot about the settlers they never seemed to notice. But they *were* spending time talking with him, and if they were as good at reading between the lines as they implied, then they had to have noticed Kav's interest. "Ohhh."

They chuckled. "If you want, I'd like to get to know you better."

"I'd like that a lot." A broad smile stretched his cheeks.

"Great." Cass's eyes brightened. "Dinner sometime? Or, if you need any physical labor around the ships, I could be an extra pair of hands. Might as well put these pathways to use."

"I'll take you up on both of those," Kav said. "And, if it's not too much trouble, could you send me some book recommendations?"

"I'll start a list."

Kav said good night and waved sheepishly when Cass ducked their head to him. He left with steps lighter than they'd been in months and pulled up his chat channel with Naira, wanting to tell her everything— but she'd sliced out her comms pathway along with the crown.

The reminder kicked him in the chest, stealing his elation. He froze in the street, thankfully out of sight of Cass's house, and glanced back toward the *Sigillaria*.

Kav had been working on trying to understand the mind of the *canus*-bonded AI, but maybe...maybe it could help him understand a few things about how neural maps worked, instead. Weary, but determined, Kav trudged back through the snow toward the ship.

SIXTY-SEVEN

Fletcher

Seventh Cradle | Four Months Later

When Fletcher had been forced to tell Naira that Tarquin was gone, he'd been certain he was going to lose her for good. That the trauma would be too much and her fragile map would plunge over the edge, beyond even his ability to recover. It was what he'd feared, when he'd first noticed her slipping mind so very long ago. The cub would be her end.

Fletcher hadn't been wrong about losing her. He'd just been wrong about the method.

Every time he went to that desolate shore and saw her there, a burnt-out cinder, he came back full of an urge he couldn't describe. A burning need to *do* something, and he saw the same fraught, haunted faces on all her friends. There was nothing to be done but wait, they all agreed. That monstrous wolf she'd scrounged up seemed to be keeping her stable. She needed time. Needed space.

But Fletcher watched the starving creature grow, and he watched her gaze track to the waves more and more often as the winter dragged on, and he knew there wasn't enough time. Not for her.

He owed her happiness, even if that wasn't with him, though the reality stung. When he'd first snapped her up with Tarquin on Miller-Urey, he hadn't realized how deep their feelings for each other ran. He'd thought it a crush, a brief fascination.

Tarquin had been—and Fletcher would only grudgingly admit this to himself—handsome, and rich, and had that whole prince-thing going for him, and while those kinds of things normally wouldn't have mattered to Naira, Tarquin had had the temerity to be kind and curious-minded, too.

Fletcher had been certain her spark for Tarquin would fade after they'd been separated for a while. He'd been dead wrong, and he hadn't realized the depth of his error until Tarquin had torn his helmet off in the *Cavendish*, and Fletcher had watched with mounting horror as Naira melted for him.

Naira didn't *melt*. Not for anyone.

Except that stupid fucking Mercator.

The worst part was Fletcher couldn't even really hate the man like he wanted to. Tarquin had been, against all sanity, nice to Fletcher when Fletcher had helped him, and firm when it'd been needed, and that was like nails scraping up Fletcher's back. He liked the cub. He didn't want to like the cub, but there it was, and he was sad and angry the man was dead, and angrier still about what that loss had done to Naira.

The woman on the beach wasn't her anymore; she was just a place where Naira used to be.

He knew, now, which Naira had told Tarquin that Fletcher would never let her fall. She'd believed in him to save her, all the way to the end of the universe, and the weight of that woke him up every night. Sent him pinballing through his room with restless pacing.

Six months into what they were calling the endless winter, Fletcher couldn't take it anymore. He came back from a visit with her, from watching that damn wolf hunt, and found Lee Caldweller and told him Naira was getting close to her end. The man had told him to be *patient*. To *wait*.

Waiting was going to kill her.

Fletcher gathered up what was left of his pride, set it on fire, marched himself up to Kav Ayuba's door, and pounded on it in the middle of the night. Kav opened the door and blinked down at him, wary and sleepy-eyed. They'd never been friends, but they both loved Naira, and in the HCA they'd been brothers-in-arms. That was worth something. He hoped.

"I need your help," Fletcher said.

Kav blinked again and leaned out of his door to look up at the sky. "Huh. It's not raining frogs. I guess it's cold enough that hell finally froze over."

"I'm serious." Fletcher bit back the smart remark that would usually follow that statement.

He'd heard what Kav had said to Naira in the *Cavendish* about him, and it wasn't wrong. Fletcher was petty and prone to outbursts and he was *trying*, but it was hard to keep a lid on himself when no one else seemed to give a shit that Naira was dying by subtle increments. She had saved them all, and everyone was sitting around with their thumbs up their asses, content to wait until they didn't have to worry about it anymore, because she'd be gone.

"I need you to hack into the Mercator family server and give me Tarquin's map," Fletcher said.

"Are you out of your mind?"

"*Yes*," Fletcher said, and laughed a little. "I have been out of my mind for decades. I'm a sick fuck and a bastard and every other nasty thing I'm certain you've called me. But I made her a promise—" His voice broke, and he looked away, scowling. "I told her I'd always help her, if she needed it, and she needs help. I know you feel the precipice she's on. If the cub's what drags her back, then I'll find a way."

"Fuckin' hell." Kav scratched the side of his face. "He's fully cracked. There's nothing to be done."

"Exactly. He's already gone, so what harm am I going to do? Look." He glanced side to side, leery of being overheard. "I am the best finalizer this universe has ever seen. I know intimately all the ways in which a map can fail. I might be wrong, but if I can see how to rip a map apart, it stands to reason I should be able to reverse that skill set, doesn't it? It's the universe's biggest jigsaw puzzle, but it's not like I'm spending my time doing anything else worthwhile."

"I swear to god, Fletch, if you're trying to raise some kind of freaky screaming-Tarquin-zombie army, I will personally—"

"No, I'm fucking not." He took a breath and tried to smooth the snappishness out of his voice. "This is for her. I swear it."

Kav examined him for a long time, a frown tugging down his lips, and Fletcher resisted an urge to radiate goodwill, to try to manipulate Kav into giving in to him in all the subtle ways he knew how to make a person dance to his tune. This had to be genuine. He couldn't keep twisting people up to get what he wanted. Not even for this.

"You're seriously willing to dedicate yourself to bringing him back? She'll never leave him for you. You're not getting the reward you want out of this."

He flinched. "The only reward I want is her life preserved. She . . . Nai deserves happiness."

"Are you sure hell hasn't frozen over?"

"For god's sake, Ayuba."

"Sorry, sorry." Kav patted the air with one hand, then stepped aside and opened the door wider. "I guess you'd better come in, then."

Fletcher slipped into Kav's living room and suddenly didn't know what to do with his hands. What the hell did people do, when they were invited into the house of a person they wanted to get along with *genuinely*? Was he supposed to . . . compliment the decor?

"Uh. Nice couch?"

"Are you drunk?"

"Unfortunately not." Fletcher ran a hand through his hair and encountered the whole what-to-do-with-his-hands problem again, so he shoved them in his pockets. "Hacking Mercator keys is no small task, but we're short on time, so I was thinking—"

Kav shook his head. "No need. Nai gave me her keys. She wanted someone to have access to their personal files in case anything happened to her."

They stared at each other for a moment. Naira definitely hadn't planned on coming back from that beach.

"Oh" was all Fletcher could manage to say.

"Yeah. Look, I, uh . . . might have gotten a head start with help from the *canus*-bonded AI. *Canus* knows more about entanglement than we do, on a native level, and it's good at holding maps together, sooo . . ."

Kav trailed off, heaved a sigh, and gestured. The consoles around his living room lit up, and Tarquin Mercator's map unfolded from all of them. Fletcher's mouth dropped open. He'd never seen a map so ravaged.

Artifacting frayed every neural spike. Many were simply snapped. Fear lived in that mind, pervaded its every moment, dominated every neuron, and *tore*.

"Holy shit," Fletcher said before he could stop himself.

"I know. Cracking was his worst fear, thanks to that fucked-up mother of his." Kav crossed to the nearest console and adjusted the view, zooming in on a small section. "With the AI's help, I've managed to clean up some of the damage here, but I have no idea if what I'm doing is the same thing the repair software does, or if I'm actually helping."

Fletcher leaned close to examine the patch. He'd snooped on Naira's repaired map—of course he had—and had seen the way the repair software had bonded her together before she'd shattered herself all over again. It had been a forced binding, a concretion of her mind that welded the broken spikes together and smoothed out the dithering, but didn't erase it. This was different. This was a cleaning.

"I can work with this," he said.

Fletcher lived in Tarquin's head for months, sending Kav out to check on Naira and make certain she was still clinging to that cliff with her fingertips. He floated the idea of lightly poisoning the wolf so that she'd have to take care of it longer, but Kav had given him a flat look, so that probably wasn't "acceptable" behavior for a man trying to be good again. Too bad.

As far as he could tell, he'd done it. He'd cleaned the whole map, repaired all the tiny breaks. Kav went over it with him. They even had the AI take a look. It was clean. But there was a catch, as there always was, with a cracked map. Its owner knew it was supposed to be cracked, and the second they woke him up, Tarquin's fear would come rampaging home and make a mess of the place again.

"I have an idea," Kav said in such a way that Fletcher suspected it was, quite probably, a bad one.

"Out with it." Fletcher leaned back into the "nice" couch with a beer in his hand while Kav reexamined the culmination of their work.

"What if you loaded his map into a sim and woke him up there, first?"

"Meshing with a cracked map in a sim is a good way to crack yourself," Fletcher said. It was one of the first things finalizers learned—don't crack your target fully before you get all the information you want out of them, because there was no winding that back.

"Right, right," Kav said. "But this map isn't technically cracked. Without the biofeedback of the print mucking things up, you might be able to calm him down before he flips."

"Or we ruin months' worth of work and take me with it," Fletcher said. "All right. I'll do it tonight."

"Really?" Kav blinked at him. He was doing that a lot lately. Like he wasn't sure the man in front of him was really Fletcher. "I know I suggested it, but it does seem risky."

"It's a measured risk, and I don't see another option. Can you get us into a lab?"

"No problem," Kav said, and made the call.

Fletcher would never admit to being nervous, but nerves jittered through him anyway, putting his teeth on edge until they were in the lab, the door shut and locked, Tarquin's map loaded into the system. All Fletcher had to do was put the simulation crown on. *All.* Hah. Kav handed it to him and hesitated.

"Be careful in there, yeah?"

"Ayuba, I didn't know you cared," Fletcher drawled.

Kav rolled his eyes with a soft snort and went back to managing the console screen. Fletcher almost kicked himself for being an ass yet again, but caught Kav smiling, and relaxed. Naira gave Kav a hard time constantly. It was fine. They were actually getting along. Weird. He lay back and slipped the crown over his head.

They'd loaded a pleasant scene of the settlement's community center into the sim. Fletcher was not in the cozy warmth of that scene. He stood on the navy-blue ice of a frozen lake, wind tearing into his skin and hair and clothes. He squinted against the sting of the howling wind, seeking the man who was supposed to be in here.

"Tarquin!"

No answer. Fletcher shuffled out over the ice, grimacing as cracks spread through the sapphire surface. Dark, indistinct shapes swam below. Another dark shape sat above.

Tarquin's back was to Fletcher, that ridiculously tall body folded down to huddle against the ice, arms clutching his knees to his chest.

The worst of the cracks radiated outward from him. Fletcher approached slowly, holding his hands out in entreaty, and edged around so that Tarquin wouldn't be snuck up on from behind. The man's eyes were closed.

"Hey, buddy," Fletcher said, and realized immediately how ridiculous that sounded. "It's just me. I'm here to talk."

Tarquin flinched without opening his eyes. Fletcher rolled his eyes to the nonexistent sky at himself. He'd kidnapped the man and tortured him. Making an appearance in his nightmares wasn't going to help. He should have sent Kav in, but it was a little late for that. What could he possibly say that would rouse him?

Oh. The same thing that'd roused Fletcher to do this in the first place.

"You're hurting Nai, you jackass."

Tarquin jerked and picked his head up from his knees, eyes snapping open. They were bloodshot, the pupils pinpricks, and he stared straight through Fletcher.

"Naira," he said softly.

Right. He didn't call her Nai like everyone else, the weirdo. Fletcher scooted closer and crouched down very, very slowly. Tarquin's eyes locked on to him and seemed to bore into him. Fletcher was unmoved by the horror graven in that stare. He'd seen worse. He'd caused worse.

"Yeah. Naira." He waited until Tarquin seemed to focus, a line working its way between his brows as he really saw Fletcher at last. "She's hurting, cub. She's hurting real bad because you went and left her."

"I'd never." His voice was strangely far away.

"You didn't have a choice." Fletcher frowned, wanting to avoid the whole double-printing conversation in case that sent him over the edge. "It took me a long time to figure it out, but I'm here to bring you back. For her."

"*You?*" he asked, incredulous.

"Believe me, I was surprised, too. She loves you, cub. She loves you and she had to bury you, and I'm afraid. I'm afraid because I don't think she's going to be able to hold on much longer."

"Bury me?" The horror of that slashed across his face, contorting it, but Fletcher had spent a lifetime reading people, and he knew Tarquin well enough to understand that horror was an echo of the alternative— of what it'd do to him to bury her, and understanding what she must have gone through.

Tarquin didn't know the half of it. He could never understand what it meant to Naira to fail to protect someone she loved, especially so soon after losing Kuma. But rubbing it in that Fletcher understood her better than Tarquin ever could wasn't exactly going to help his cause. He needed to get Tarquin to focus on something other than what had happened. Absurdity might work.

"Yeah," Fletcher said. "I marched in the honor guard for your funeral."

Tarquin stared, and then he laughed frantically, and buried his face in his hands. When he looked up again, his eyes were clearer, more focused. "What do I have to do?"

Fletcher looked around, at the cracks in the ice slowly mending, and nodded to himself. "Not much, cub. Just focus on her, yeah? She needs your help, because believe it or not, she's on thinner ice than you are. Can you do that?"

"Anything for her."

Fletcher thinned his lips into a flat smile. "I thought so. Hang on a few minutes, all right? I won't be long."

Tarquin nodded, wary but focused, and Fletcher exited the sim to find Kav hovering above him, anxious.

"Well?" Kav asked.

"Start the print," Fletcher said. "I think we've got him."

Kav tilted his head toward the cubicle. "I already started the print, just in case."

Fletcher set the crown aside, taking Kav's hand to help him sit up. "You really are impatient."

Three hours later, when the hazy dawn of Seventh Cradle was beginning to rise, the cubicle lit green. Fletcher and Kav looked at each other, fear and anticipation mingled on both of their faces. If he came up screaming...Fletcher pushed the possibility aside. His work had been meticulous, and Tarquin had been responsive in the sim. It would work. It had to.

The universe couldn't keep kicking Nai in the teeth without answering for it, goddamnit.

Kav reached for the hatch first. He opened it and stepped aside as the gurney slid out, revealing Tarquin's preferred print, sans family gloves.

They'd made sure to remove those. They didn't matter anymore, and Fletcher had seen the way Tarquin sometimes looked at them, as if they were stains that could never be scrubbed clean.

Tarquin took a breath. His eyes slid open.

He looked from Fletcher to Kav and back again, a little dazed, at first, and then focused, determination lining that damnably noble face.

"Where is she?" Tarquin demanded.

Fletcher and Kav burst into nervous energy-releasing laughter and high-fived each other, much to Tarquin's obvious annoyance. Kav took the cub by the hand and helped him sit up on the printing tray, tears standing in his eyes. Fletcher was irritated to find tears stung his eyes, too.

"Oh, cub," Fletcher said. "It's so good to hear your voice."

SIXTY-EIGHT

Naira

Seventh Cradle | A Year Later

Naira had moved her nightly campfire to the cliff top the past few weeks. She preferred the beach itself and the wind-block the cliff offered, but Kav had been coming by more and more often, lately, looking frayed around the edges. She knew why. The wolf-thing, which she called Rock-boy when no one else was around to hear, was hale and had relearned how to hunt in this cold, cold world she'd made and saved.

When she was on the beach, oblivion was so close she could taste it, brine in the back of her throat, the promise of water in her lungs. So she moved to the cliff, for Kav, because it would be too easy from the shore to get up and walk out and never come back. At least this way she'd have to climb down to do it and might come to her senses by then.

As much as she wanted to go to the ice, Kav's fear dragged her back. She couldn't do that to him. Not yet. Maybe not ever, but she wasn't certain of that. The moon was getting brighter. Leka would arrive with Jana and Tarq soon, and Lee had been clear that they'd come to visit her. Naira wasn't sure she could face that.

She took a long drink from a bottle that'd been in one of the caches she occasionally found in the woods after her friends visited, and let the heat of it flow through her. At her side, Rock-boy grumbled in his sleep, and she threaded her fingers through his fur, grateful for his bulk. For his warmth. Maybe Kav would take him back to the settlement. The kids might like him.

Rock-boy was alert in the next breath, hackles raised, a low growl rumbling in the back of his throat. Naira sighed and drew her sidearm, not bothering to turn as she aimed behind her in the direction Rock-boy had alerted. The wolf-thing knew the gaits of her friends.

"Walk on," she said tiredly. "I may be drunk, but I'm perfectly capable of slaughtering whoever you are."

"I've no doubt of that," Tarquin said.

Her finger slid off the trigger to the guard despite the fact that every single instinct she'd ever honed screamed *not possible*. Alert for some kind of hideous trick, her pathways sobered her blood. She whipped around, Rock-boy letting out a snarl followed by a brisk bark, aware of her distress.

Tarquin held his hands out flat to Rock-boy, but his eyes were on her alone, and they were *his*. This was no trick, no asshole walking around in his print to torture her. Snow tangled in his hair and he wore a grey coat, a pack on his back, looking rough around the edges from the long hike. Sorrow and hope and adoration twisted up inside of him and radiated from within. She couldn't move.

"How?" she demanded.

"I promised you I'd find you again." He gave her half a smile. Hesitant, hopeful.

It wasn't an explanation, but it sealed all her doubts.

Naira dropped her weapon for the first time in her life and flew into his arms, burying herself against him. Tarquin held her and stroked her back, murmuring he loved her over and over again, that she was safe, they were okay, until the sobs finally wrung free and she was weak with the emptying of herself.

When her breathing had stabilized, he dropped his head down to whisper. "I was told you had a dog, but that is no dog, and he doesn't seem pleased with me."

She half turned, not willing to leave the circle of his arms. Rock-boy had lowered his head, hackles up and ears back, but there was a slight tilt to his head that indicated confusion. Naira held out a comforting hand.

"It's all right, Ro—errrr…" She trailed off, blushing furiously. One of Rock-boy's ears perked up and flopped over as he cocked his head at her relaxed tone.

"Ro . . . ?" Tarquin lifted both brows at her.

"I might have named the wolf-thing Rock-boy," she said sheepishly. At his full name, he wagged his tail and pranced over, nuzzling into the back of her legs hard enough to push her into Tarquin. He tightened his arms to support her and burst out laughing.

Then he kissed her, fingers tangling in her sea-mist-sticky hair as he tightened an arm possessively around her waist, crushing them together. When they came up for air, he rested his forehead against hers, the brush of his eyelashes against her skin a tiny delight. "You're so cold. Have you really been out here all this time?"

"I have." She licked her lips and cast her gaze down. "But that's not why I'm cold. I . . ."

"I know." He massaged the back of her neck, where his fingers had come to rest. "Kav and Fletcher, they filled me in on the way over, though I can scarcely believe it."

"Kav and *Fletcher*?" She searched his face for some hint of what had happened, but found only his adoration. "Seriously, how are you here? I buried you. I could . . . I could feel you screaming."

He kissed her gently. "I can't imagine. But Kav and Fletcher, they took it upon themselves to fix my map. Fletcher actually entered a sim with me and brought me back."

"He did *what*?"

"He told me, in so many words, that I was making you sad and I needed to get my shit together and come back."

"That does sound like him." She brushed her fingertips over the bare skin of his forehead in the same place where her suppression crown once rested. "They didn't use the software, did they?"

"No. An experimental technique guided by the AI. It's . . ." Tarquin paused to gather his thoughts. "Fletcher described my map as a 'cracked vase teetering on the edge of a shelf.' They've forbidden me from reprinting for any reason, until it settles."

"How long?"

"Haven't a clue. Bracken will monitor the situation, and I've promised them all I won't so much as stub my toe for the time being."

Naira rested her forehead against his, digesting that. "Luckily for you, the worlds' finest exemplar is madly in love with you. I won't let a thing scuff that map ever again."

Tarquin grinned and leaned back, picking her up, then spun her around in a quick circle as she gave a shout of surprise. Rock-boy barked and bounded around them, whacking them both with his tail. Tarquin laughed, delighted. The fist clutching her heart eased. A little. He sensed her change of mood and set her down.

"We're free," he said. "We can do whatever we'd like, now. Whatever you want. We can build the house at last. Look."

He tugged his glove off and showed her the back of his hand. Calloused brown skin traced with golden pathways, and nothing else. No family mark.

"I can't go back there," she said, voice small as she looked toward the dim smudge of light that marked the settlement. Even looking at it made her take a step away. Tarquin tightened his arm around her waist to stop her retreat.

"Then we go somewhere else. Anywhere else." He brushed his fingertips across the scars that lined her forehead. "Naira, I . . . I left so much unsaid. In wanting to be a home for you, I'd begun to become a cage instead, and I was so desperate to keep you safe that I failed you when it mattered most. I don't just mean that night in the snow, I'm talking about before, too. When I wanted you so badly to be well that I wasn't wholly there for you."

"You were scared."

"So were you. Instead of listening I rushed ahead, and pushed, and I'd intended to tell you all of this when you'd come back from Miller-Urey, but . . ." He looked over her shoulder, to the cliff and the sea beyond, and took a breath. "If that house on the plain isn't the future you want anymore, then to hell with it. The only future I want is with you."

She took his face in both hands and kissed him, tenderly and insistently. Plotting the course of their new future could wait until the dawn.

ACKNOWLEDGMENTS

The Devoured Worlds was written between 2020 and 2021. It's 2023, now, as I write this, and the book will reach shelves in 2024. I've always asserted that fiction exists in situ, the pressures—if you'll allow me the painfully on-brand metaphor—of the events surrounding its creation intruding upon the text. Some would find this a flaw, I know, and say that the timeless classic is what should be aspired toward. But I've always found the quirks of the past fun tidbits to uncover. Easter eggs, if you will. No book is without them.

A few years before I wrote these books, I was diagnosed with a genetic condition that causes chronic pain. Sometime during 2020, I had gone back to sort through old vacation photos and discovered something surprising: I could see that I was in pain. I hadn't realized it at the time, of course. That old story about a frog that doesn't know it's in a pot of boiling water until it's too late if the heat is increased gradually enough, while factually incorrect, lingers because so many of us can relate to it.

Then, because I'm a science fiction writer, I looked at that face that didn't know it was in pain *yet* and thought *What if.*

And here we are. There was more to it than that, naturally. Months of research and untangling and re-tangling plot threads. Making certain that Naira's condition was never trivialized in a world that would seek to "fix" her at all costs, because so few of the people making the decisions in the world of MERIT know what it means to hurt and continue on regardless.

Thank you for continuing on this journey with me, all the way to the end.

★ ★ ★

A great many people helped me to develop Naira and Tarquin's story. Thank you to my husband, Joey Hewitt, for his endless support. To my beta readers, Tina Gower, Andrea Stewart, Karina Rochnik, Alexander Lostetter, and Elyse John for your valuable insights. And to my dear friends Marina Lostetter, Laura Blackwell, David Dalglish, and Essa Hansen, who listened while I rambled endlessly about this project.

Thank you, too, to those writers' groups that have sent strength to my sword arm and offered community: the Isle, the Bunker, and naturally, the crew of the MurderCabin.

Thank you to my publishing team, Brit Hvide, Bryn A. McDonald, Angelica Chong, Kelley Frodel, Crystal Shelley, Raquel Brown, Ellen Wright, Emily Byron, Anna Jackson, James Long, Lauren Panepinto, Angela Man, and the artist Jaime Jones. And of course, thanks to all the lovely booksellers out there who helped this story get into readers' hands.

A huge thank you to my agents, Chris Lotts and Sam Morgan, and everyone at the Lotts Agency for their tireless support.

And a special thank you to the geologists behind *The Geology Flannelcast*: Chris Seminack, Jesse Thornburg, and Steve Peterson.

And most of all, thank you, readers. May your horizons be bright.

extras

orbit

meet the author

Joey Hewitt

MEGAN E. O'KEEFE was raised among journalists and, as soon as she was able, joined them by crafting a newsletter that chronicled the daily adventures of the local cat population. She has worked in both arts management and graphic design, and has won Writers of the Future and the David Gemmell Morningstar Award. Megan lives in the Bay Area of California.

Find out more about Megan E. O'Keefe and other Orbit authors by registering for the free monthly newsletter at orbitbooks.net.

if you enjoyed
THE BOUND WORLDS

look out for

MEGAN E. O'KEEFE'S NEW SPACE OPERA NOVEL

A ragtag crew of space pirates take one last job traveling to the wreckage of an alien civilization and uncover a conspiracy bigger than all of them could have imagined....

ONE

FAVEN

Faven Sythe was told two lies on the day her mother's organs finished crystallizing. The first was an updated work assignment. The banal notice only reached her because she'd flagged the name attached. It told her that Ulana Valset, Faven's mentor, had been reassigned to Amiens Station. A mere microdot of an orbital on the lacy edges of the galactic center. There, Ulana would train younger navigators—as she had once trained Faven—until the crystallization took her.

Alone in her rooms high in the Spire, Faven touched the petrified cheek of her mother's corpse. She had chosen a gentle position in which to spend eternity, kneeling upon the floor with her arms cradled across her stomach, as if rocking a babe.

Soon Faven would have to alert the architects that her mother had fully succumbed. That the last vestiges of her skin had transmuted to scales of aquamarine, and at long last, even the irises of her eyes had switched from dusky umber to the teal glow of the cryst. Faven kissed her mother's forehead, the mineral scales smooth and cold beneath her lips. A small patch of scale already marred the corner of Faven's own mouth, bracketing her smile and tugging at the skin when she laughed.

"I'll see you moved to the Rosette Pond," Faven said. "Where you can watch the gleamfish swim. I promise."

She did not tell the corpse of her mother that the order would be sent remotely, and that Faven would not be there to see the enshrinement done. The statue kneeling on Faven's floor was just that—a statue. A memory. Her mother's consciousness had long since transmuted to light. Her mother had become a star.

Faven wrapped a plain grey cloak around her shoulders and flipped the hood up to hide the shining web of sapphires that veiled her hair and shoulders.

That her mentor had been sent to Amiens was a lie as pretty as the lustrous corpse kneeling on soft velvets in Faven's sitting room. Faven's world was constructed of such lies, the dull solder between shining panes of cryst glass. Most of the time she did not see those lies, for she did not care to look.

But when Ulana had last left Votive City, there had been tension in her eyes. An anxious clutching in the long fingers of hands armored with the aquamarine scales of cryst that eventually took all those who walked the paths between the stars. After her leaving, Ulana had stopped answering all attempts to contact her.

And so, Faven had snooped. A grave sin. A terrible violation. The paths a navigator wove to cut the space between the stars were sacred, the creative expressions of their very souls.

Ulana Valset's soul led her into the dark.

Faven had been certain she was incorrect. That in spying upon the starpath Ulana wove into the lightdrive of her ship, Faven had somehow corrupted it. When you live steeped in lies, you grow used to telling them to yourself.

Ulana's route did not go to Amiens Station. It led into the Clutch. A dark fist of a dyson sphere seized around a whimpering star. It was the graveyard of their predecessors. An expanse of rubble held sacred only because it was the last known concretion of the technological artifacts of the cryst, the ancient species whose leftover research had given the navigators their art.

A place of reverence. A place for dying. And all that technology was as dead as its progenitors. Save the *Black Celeste*.

A rumor. A fairy tale. A derelict ship called the *Black Celeste* was very real, but the stories that clung to it breathed mystery into its dead walls. Young navigators titillated one another with stories of it waking up or moving. Of its halls filled with the spectral shapes of the cryst. Sometimes, young navigators would whisper, you could see a light inside, burning. Sometimes that light moved.

The stories had fascinated Faven when she'd been too young to have learned that the unknown was a lot less scary than the ugly truths of the world.

Ulana's starpath was a twisted, frayed thing. A jumbling of punch-through points and scrambled orbital grooves. But its intended terminus was clear, for the *Black Celeste* was the only known structure within the Clutch said to move outside of orbital drift, and the path accounted for such a possibility.

Ulana had gone into a ghost story, and Faven couldn't even ask her why. But the second lie, well. That might have something to tell her after all.

Faven skimmed the other message—the ugly, clumsy lie. It was simple enough. A contract offered, with saccharine platitudes, for Navigator Sythe's services in weaving a starpath into the lightdrive of a merchant vessel that wanted to transport quartz wine from Votive City to Orvieto Station.

Faven knew that she was coddled. That her thirty-six years of life had slipped by wrapped in fine silks studded with gemstones. But she was not uninformed on matters of commerce. Quartz wine was plentiful in Orvieto Station, and the fee involved in her weaving a custom path would far outweigh any profit. The merchant wished to meet to discuss the matter in a sector of the docks known for dark-dealing. A place infested with the pirates that plagued the skies presided over by the Choir of Stars.

Faven was being fished.

The hubris of such a thing, to bait your hook for the mouth of a god, amused her. But the Choir of Stars would not tell her about the *Black Celeste*. Would not tell her why her mentor had gone into the dark. Ulana wasn't the only one to have disappeared in recent years, and the Choir refused to answer the questions of those who'd gone looking for their loved ones. No, Ulana was not the first. She was merely the first that Faven cared for.

Faven had lost two mothers on the same day, and she was so very weary of being lied to. Pirates, while not known for their honesty, made a habit of scavenging the Clutch. That baited hook might very well possess the answers she sought.

Faven had not been born of her mother's womb. She'd been a shard of sacred cryst that had grown beneath her mother's skin and then been plucked free to be nurtured into a woman, or something like a woman. When she closed her eyes, she and the other cryst-born could read the paths between the stars. Find the secret ways through the fabric of the universe and teach them to the lightdrives of ships. Sometimes, the navigators saw other things when they closed their human eyes.

She was no augur. No farseer nor futurespinner. If a confidant were ever to ask her if she believed in fate or magic, she would scoff like all the rest of her kin. Their craft was trade. Travel. Gods of commerce and expansion, and the rest were fairy-whispers.

But they all had their little quirks. Some cryst-born heard notes of music when they charted their paths. Discordant vibrations that warned them off dangerous routes, and sweet notes for safer shores. So common was the phenomenon that they named their governing council for it—the Choir of Stars.

Faven saw light. Shades of color guiding her way, illuminating secret pitfalls to her as she worked paths between gravitational grooves. When she closed her eyes and meditated upon Ulana's lie, she saw an empty space in her future. A violet-soaked nightmare of a moment, red-shifted, rushing closer. She conjured the fishing message to mind and was filled with a wavering glow of indigo—safe, perhaps, though eager to shift into the dangerous realm of violet, if she was not careful. A static moment. A moment she could take, or leave, while the other came for her all the same.

In the end, it was no choice at all.

Faven summoned a travel censer and went to be kidnapped by pirates.

TWO

AMANDINE

Bitter Amandine was reasonably certain that Tagert Red was about to get himself killed or mortally embarrassed, and she wanted to be there to see it when it happened. Tagert thought himself so clever, scheming with his crew in a dingy side room of the Broken Mast. Their voices were tight with anticipation, and not nearly soft enough to evade being picked up by the listening devices Amandine had planted in every single room of that pirate-lousy bar.

The owner, a person with more sense than muscle but a deft hand on a shotgun trigger, paid no mind to Amandine's spying. It was a pirate bar. Any pirate daft enough to talk real business in a pirate bar deserved to have their score scooped on them.

Every so often, some soul with a lick of sense would scan the bar before talking plans with their crew, then make a damn racket about the devices. The owner would, with a shrug, toss them in the incinerator. Amandine was always back within the week with one fist full of bugs, and the other fist full of cash.

And the cycle repeated. And Amandine stayed one step ahead of every dunderheaded pirate working in Votive City.

Tagert's crew left the Broken Mast, making their way to the nearby docks for their supposed "meeting." Amandine flipped up the camera feed Kester had patched her into. She leaned back in the captain's seat of the *Marquette*, cradling a hot mug of tea with a dash of rum tossed in to really warm her up, kicked her boots up on the dash, and watched in real time as Tagert's crew made a mess of getting into position.

It was almost painful to watch. She had half a mind to make Kester get her into the dock's speakers so that she could bark out some real orders. Tagert had put his lookouts in positions where they had only 120 degrees of view, for light's sake.

"He gets worse every year," Becks said. The mechanic slotted themself into the second-in-command seat and weaved their fingers together, stretching their arms forward until their knuckles cracked.

Amandine smiled into her tea. "He stays the same, but the world changes around him, and his already questionable techniques grow clumsier in their execution."

Becks wrinkled their nose and jabbed at the console, checking the cloaking tech wrapped around the *Marquette*. It'd been fritzing lately, and it would be rather embarrassing if it fuzzed out now and revealed her position, hovering above Tagert's pitiful tableau. Amandine had checked it twice herself. Becks checked it three more times.

"Didn't sign up to stomp boots with no philosopher cap'n," they grumbled.

"You didn't sign up at all, Becks. You tromped up my gangway and told me my thrusters were overheating and going to strip the enamel if someone didn't do something about it, and that someone was going to be you."

"If I hadn't, you woulda been stuck out in the black somewhere, twiddling your thumbs with a hold full of stolen cargo, waiting for a tug and hoping they didn't look too hard at you or the *Marquette* and start asking questions."

"And every day I pray my thanks at the altar of your illustrious being for that timely intervention."

"Best be praying for better pay, Cap'n," Becks said, but had a curl to the corner of their lips that meant their ego was assuaged, and now Amandine needed to bite her tongue and let them work, lest she annoy them into distraction.

Amandine had her own distractions. A travel censer swept down from the high peak of the Navigator's Spire. The hexagonal conveyance was constructed of the same multicolor glass as all Votive City. It hung perfectly straight, a teardrop in variegated shades of blue dripping toward the docks from on high.

She leaned toward the screen and set her mug aside. A silhouette of a person waited within, their shape obscured by the soft fall of a cloak, a hood pulled up to hide their face.

Amandine couldn't believe it. She really couldn't. Faven Sythe hadn't exactly made a name for herself, but she was cryst-born. Too clever and too skilled by far to fall for Tagert Red's clumsy attempt to lure her out. Either the woman was daft, desperate, or had a trick up her sleeve. The first two options were more likely. The last was more fun.

"Kester." Amandine jabbed her finger onto the button for the intercom between the pilot's deck and the armory. "Tell me your scans are picking up weapons, or guards, or something. Tell me this fool-headed goddess isn't going to meet with Tagert Red about a phony deal *alone*."

"I cannot tell you such a thing, Captain," she said.

Amandine rubbed her hands together. That delicate little bird riding down from on high was up to something. It'd been a long, long time since Amandine hadn't known what, exactly, she'd be walking into.

"You sure about this, Cap'n?" Becks asked, their hands stilling on the console as they cocked her a sideways glance. "Tangling with a navigator, I mean. Our cloaking is up. We could sail out of here without anyone ever knowing we'd been."

"Come on, Becks." She clapped them on the shoulder. "Live a little."

"I'd like to keep on living—that's the trouble!" Becks shouted at her.

Amandine tapped a small photo she kept pinned to her dash for luck—the cabin her grandfather had built, swaddled in the mists of Blackloach—and gave Becks a thump on the back as she swung out of her chair.

Whatever they shouted at her back, she didn't hear it. She was already striding toward the armory to join Kester and Tully in preparing. The more scores they scooped up, the sooner Amandine could get back to living life in that little cabin, spending her days baiting hooks for fish instead of ships. The sooner she could retire her captainship of the *Marquette* and stop looking over her shoulder every damn time someone so much as sniffed in her ship's direction.

Tagert Red might be about to have a very bad day, but things were looking up for Bitter Amandine.

if you enjoyed
THE BOUND WORLDS

look out for

THESE BURNING STARS

THE KINDOM TRILOGY: BOOK ONE

by

Bethany Jacobs

On a dusty backwater planet, occasional thief Jun Ironway has gotten her hands on the score of a lifetime: a secret that could raze the Kindom, the ruling power of the galaxy.

A star system away, preternaturally stoic Chono and brilliant hothead Esek—the two most brutal clerics of the Kindom—are tasked with hunting Jun down.

And tracking all three across the stars is a ghost from their shared past known only as Six. But what Six wants is anyone's guess. It's a game of manipulation and betrayal that could destroy them all. And they have no choice but to see it through.

CHAPTER ONE

1643
YEAR OF THE LETTING

Kinschool of Principes
Loez Continent
The Planet Ma'kess

Her ship alighted on the tarmac with engines snarling, hot air billowing out from beneath the thrusters. The hatch opened with a hiss and she disembarked to the stench of the jump gate that had so recently spit her into Ma'kess's orbit—a smell like piss and ozone.

Underfoot, blast burns scorched the ground, signatures from ships that had been coming and going for three hundred years. The township of Principes would have no cause for so much activity, if it weren't for the kinschool that loomed ahead.

She was hungry. A little annoyed. There was a marble of nausea lodged in the base of her throat, a leftover effect of being flung from one star system to another in the space of two minutes. This part of Ma'kess was cold and wet, and she disliked the monotonous sable plains flowing away from the tarmac. She disliked the filmy dampness in the air. If the kinschool master had brought her here for nothing, she would make him regret it.

The school itself was all stone and mortar and austerity. Somber-looking effigies stared down at her from the parapet of the second-story roof: the Six Gods, assembled like jurors. She looked over her shoulder at her trio of novitiates, huddled close to one another, watchful. Birds of prey in common brown. By contrast, she was quite resplendent in her red-gold coat, the ends swishing around her ankles as she started toward the open gates. She was a cleric of the Kindom, a holy woman, a member of the Righteous Hand. In this school were many students who longed to be clerics and saw her as the pinnacle of their own aspirations. But she doubted any had the potential to match her.

Already the kinschool master had appeared. They met in the small courtyard under the awning of the entryway, his excitement and eagerness instantly apparent. He bowed over his hands a degree lower than necessary, a simpering flattery. In these star systems, power resided in the Hands of the Kindom, and it resided in the First Families. She was both.

"Thank you for the honor of your presence, Burning One."

She made a quick blessing over him, rote, and they walked together into the school. The novitiates trailed behind, silent as the statues that guarded the walls of the receiving hall. It had all looked bigger when she graduated seven years ago.

As if reading her mind, the kinschool master said, "It seems a lifetime since you were my student."

She chuckled, which he was welcome to take as friendly, or mocking. They walked down a hallway lined with portraiture of the most famous students and masters in the school's history: Aver Paiye, Khen Sikhen Khen, Luto Moonback. All painted. No holograms. Indeed, outside the tech aptitude classrooms, casting technology was little-to-be-seen in this school. Not fifty miles away, her family's factories produced the very sevite fuel that made jump travel and casting possible, yet here the masters lit their halls with torches and sent messages to each other via couriers. As if training the future Hands was too holy a mission to tolerate basic conveniences.

The master said, "I hope your return pleases you?"

She wondered what they'd done with her own watercolor portrait. She recalled looking very smug in it, which, to be fair, was not an uncommon condition for her.

"I was on Teros when I got your message. Anywhere is better than that garbage rock."

The master smiled timidly. "Of course. Teros is an unpleasant planet. Ma'kess is the planet of your heart. And the most beautiful of all!" He sounded like a tourist pamphlet, extolling the virtues of the many planets that populated the Treble star systems. She grunted. He asked, "Was your trip pleasant?"

"Hardly any reentry disturbance. Didn't even vomit during the jump."

They both laughed, him a little nervously. They walked down a narrow flight of steps and turned onto the landing of a wider staircase of deep blue marble. She paused and went to the banister, gazing down at the room below.

Six children stood in a line, each as rigid as the staves they held at their sides. They couldn't have been older than ten or eleven. They were dressed identically, in tunics and leggings, and their heads were shaved. They knew she was there, but they did not look up at her. Staring straight ahead, they put all their discipline on display, and she observed them like a butcher at a meat market.

"Fourth-years," she remarked, noticing the appliqués on their chests. They were slender and elfin looking, even the bigger ones. No giants in this cohort. A pity.

"I promise you, Sa, you won't be disappointed."

She started down the staircase, brisk and cheerful, ignoring the students. They had no names, no gendermarks—and no humanity as far as their teachers were concerned. They were called by numbers, given "it" for a pronoun. She herself was called Three, once. Just another object, honed for a purpose. Legally, Treble children had the right to gender themselves as soon as they discovered what fit. But *these* children would have to wait until they graduated. Only then could they take genders and names. Only then would they have their own identities.

At the foot of the staircase, she made a sound at her novitiates. They didn't follow her farther, taking sentry on the last step. On the combat floor, she gloried in the familiar smells of wood and stone and sweat. Her hard-soled boots *clacked* pleasingly as she took a slow circle about the room, gazing up at the magnificent mural on the ceiling, of the Six Gods at war. A brilliant golden light fell upon them, emanating from the sunlike symbol of the Godfire—their parent god, their essence, and the core of the Treble's faith.

She wandered around the room, brushing past the students as if they were scenery. The anticipation in the room ratcheted, the six students trying hard not to move. When she did finally look at them, it was with a quick twist of her neck, eyes locking on with predatory precision. All but one flinched, and she smiled. She brought her hand out from where it had been resting on the hilt of her bloodletter dagger, and saw several of them glance at the weapon. A weapon ordinarily reserved for cloaksaan.

This was just one of the things that must make her extraordinary to the students. Her family name being another. Her youth, of course. And she was very beautiful. Clerics deeply valued beauty, which pleased gods and people alike. *Her* beauty was like the Godfire itself, consuming and hypnotic and deadly.

Add to this the thing she represented: not just the Clerisy itself, in all its holy power, but the future the students might have. When they finished their schooling (*if* they finished their schooling), they would be one step closer to a position like hers. They would have power and prestige and choice—to adopt gendermarks, to take their family names again or create new ones. But *so much* lay between them and that future. Six more years of school and then five years as a novitiate. (Not everyone could do it in three, like her.) If all that went right, they'd receive an appointment to one of the three Hands of the Kindom. But only if they worked hard. Only if they survived.

Only if they were extraordinary.

"Tell me," she said to them all. "What is the mission of the Kindom?"

They answered in chorus: "Peace, under the Kindom. Unity, in the Treble."

"Good." She looked each one over carefully, observed their proudly clasped staves. Though "staves" was a stretch. The long poles in their hands were made from a heavy-duty foam composite.

Strong enough to bruise, even to break skin—but not bones. The schools, after all, were responsible for a precious commodity. This cheapened the drama of the upcoming performance, but she was determined to enjoy herself anyway.

"And what are the three pillars of the Kindom?" she asked.

"Righteousness! Cleverness! Brutality!"

She hummed approval. Righteousness for the Clerisy. Cleverness for the Secretaries. Brutality for the Cloaksaan. The three Hands. In other parts of the school, students were studying the righteous Godtexts of their history and faith, or they were perfecting the clever arts of economy and law. But these students, these little fourth-years, were here to be brutal.

She gave the kinschool master a curt nod. His eyes lit up and he turned to the students like a conductor to his orchestra. With theatrical aplomb, he clapped once.

It seemed impossible that the six students could look any smarter, but they managed it, brandishing their staves with stolid expressions. She searched for cracks in the facades, for shadows and tremors. She saw several. They were so young, and it was to be expected in front of someone like her. Only one of them was a perfect statue. Her eyes flicked over this one for a moment longer than the others.

The master barked, "One!"

Immediately, five of the children turned on the sixth, staves sweeping into offense like dancers taking position, and then—oh, what a dance it was! The first blow was like a *clap* against One's shoulder; the second, a heavy *thwack* on its thigh. It fought back hard—it had to, swinging its stave in furious arcs and trying like hell not to be pushed too far off-balance. She watched its face, how the sweat broke out, how the eyes narrowed, and its upper teeth came down on its lip to keep from crying out when one of the children struck it again, hard, on the hip. That sound was particularly good, a *crack* that made it stumble and lose position. The five children gave no quarter, and then there was a fifth blow, and a sixth, and—

"Done!" boomed the master.

Instantly, all six children dropped back into line, staves at rest beside them. The first child was breathing heavily. Someone had got it in the mouth, and there was blood, but it didn't cry.

The master waited a few seconds, pure showmanship, and said, "Two!"

The dance began again, five students turning against the other. This was an old game, with simple rules. Esek had played it many times herself, when she was Three. The attack went on until either offense or defense landed six blows. It was impressive if the attacked child scored a hit at all, and yet as she watched the progressing bouts, the second and fourth students both made their marks before losing the round. The children were merciless with one another, crowding their victim in, jabbing and kicking and swinging without reprieve. Her lip curled back in raw delight. These students were as vicious as desert foxes.

But by the time the fifth student lost its round, they were getting sloppy. They were bruised, bleeding, tired. Only the sixth remained to defend itself, and everything would be slower and less controlled now. No more soldierly discipline, no more pristine choreography. Just tired children brawling. Yet she was no less interested, because the sixth student was the one with no fissures in its mask of calm. Even more interestingly, this one had been the least aggressive in the preceding fights. It joined in, yes, but she wasn't sure it ever landed a body blow. It was not timid so much as . . . restrained. Like a leashed dog.

When the master said, "Six," something changed in the room.

She couldn't miss the strange note in the master's voice—of pleasure and expectation. The children, despite their obvious fatigue, snapped to attention like rabbits scenting a predator. They didn't rush at Six as they had rushed at one another. No, suddenly, they moved into a half-circle formation, approaching this last target with an unmistakable caution. Their gazes sharpened and they gripped their staves tighter than before, as if expecting to be disarmed. The sweat and blood stood out on their faces, and one of them quickly wiped a streak away, as if this would be its only chance to clear its eyes.

And Six? The one who commanded this sudden tension, this careful advance? It stood a moment, taking them all in at once, stare like a razor's edge. And then, it flew.

She could think of no other word for it. It was like a whirling storm, and its stave was a lightning strike. No defensive stance for this one—it went after the nearest student with a brutal spinning kick that knocked it on its ass, then it whipped its body to the left and cracked its stave against a different student's shoulder, and finished with a jab to yet another's carelessly exposed shin. All of this happened before the five attackers even had their wits about them, and for a moment she thought they would throw their weapons down, cower, and retreat before this superior fighter.

Instead, they charged.

It was like watching a wave that had gone out to sea suddenly surge upon the shore. They didn't fight as individuals, but as one corralling force, spreading out and pressing in. They drove Six back and back and back—against the wall. For the first time, they struck it, hard, in the ribs, and a moment later they got it again, across the jaw. The sound sent a thrill down her spine, made her fingers clench in hungry eagerness for a stave of her own. She watched the sixth fighter's jaw flush with blood and the promise of bruising, but it didn't falter. It swept its stave in an arc, creating an opening. It struck one of them in the chest, then another in the side, and a third in the thigh—six blows altogether. The students staggered, their offense broken, their wave disintegrating on the sixth student's immovable shore.

She glanced at their master, waiting for him to announce the conclusion of the match, and its decisive victor. To her great interest, he did no such thing, nor did the children seem to expect he would. They recovered, and charged.

Was the sixth fighter surprised? Did it feel the sting of its master's betrayal? Not that she could tell. That face was a stony glower of intent, and those eyes were smart and ruthless.

The other fights had been quick, dirty, over in less than a minute. This last fight went on and on, and each second made her pulse race.

extras

The exhaustion she'd seen in the students before gave way to an almost frenzied energy. How else could they hold their ground against Six? They parried and dodged and swung in increasingly desperate bursts, but through it all the sixth kept *hitting* them. Gods! It was relentless. Even when the other students started to catch up (strikes to the hip, to the wrist, to the thigh) it *kept going*. The room was full of ragged gasping, but when she listened for Six's breath, it was controlled. Loud, but steady, and its eyes never lost their militant focus.

In the feverish minutes of the fight, it landed eighteen strikes (she counted; she couldn't help counting) before finally one of the others got in a sixth blow, a lucky cuff across its already bruised mouth.

The master called, "Done!"

The children practically dropped where they stood, their stave arms falling limply at their sides, their relief as palpable as the sweat in the air. They got obediently back in line, and as they did, she noticed that one of them met Six's eye. A tiny grin passed between them, conspiratorial, childlike, before they were stoic again.

She could see the master's satisfied smile. She had of course not known *why* he asked her to come to Principes. A new statue in her honor, perhaps? Or a business opportunity that would benefit her family's sevite industry? Maybe one of the eighth-years, close to graduating, had particular promise? No, in the end, it was none of that. He'd brought her here for a fourth-year. He'd brought her here so he could show off his shining star. She herself left school years earlier than any student in Principes's history, a mere fifteen when she became a novitiate. Clearly the master wanted to break her record. To have this student noticed by her, recruited by her as an eleven-year-old—what a feather that would be, in the master's cap.

She looked at him directly, absorbing his smug expression.

"Did its parents put you up to that?" she asked, voice like a razor blade.

The smugness bled from his face. He grew pale and cleared his throat. "It has no parents."

Interesting. The Kindom was generally very good about making sure orphans were rehomed. Who had sponsored the child's admission to a kinschool? Such things weren't cheap.

The master said, clearly hoping to absolve himself, "After you, it's the most promising student I have ever seen. Its intelligence, its casting skills, its—"

She chuckled, cutting him off.

"Many students are impressive in the beginning. In my fourth year, I wasn't the star. And the one who was the star, that year? What happened to it? Why, I don't even think it graduated. Fourth year is far too early to know anything about a student."

She said these things as if the sixth student hadn't filled her with visceral excitement. As if she didn't see, vast as the Black Ocean itself, what it might become. Then she noticed that the master had said nothing. No acquiescence. No apology, either, which surprised her.

"What aren't you telling me?" she asked.

He cleared his throat again, and said, very lowly, "Its family name was Alanye."

Her brows shot up. She glanced back at the child, who was not making eye contact. At this distance, it couldn't have heard the master's words.

"Really?" she asked.

"Yes. A secretary adopted it after its father died. The secretary sent it here."

She continued staring at the child. Watching it fight was exhilarating, but knowing its origins made her giddy. This was delicious.

"Does it know?"

The master barely shook his head no. She *hmmed* a bright sound of pleasure.

Turning from him, she strode toward the child, shaking open her knee-length coat. When she was still several feet away from it, she crooked a finger.

"Come here, little fish. Let me have a look at you."

The fourth-year moved forward until it was a foot away, gazing up, up, into her face. She looked it over more carefully than before. Aside from their own natural appearance, students weren't allowed any distinguishing characteristics, and sometimes it was hard to tell them apart. She took in the details, looked for signs of the child's famous ancestor, Lucos Alanye: a man who started with nothing, acquired a mining fleet, and blew up a moon to stop anyone else from taking its riches. The sheer pettiness of it! He was the most notorious mass murderer in Treble history. She hadn't known he *had* descendants. With a flick of her wrist, she cast an image of Alanye to her ocular screen, comparing the ancestor to the descendant. Inconclusive.

The child remained utterly calm. Her own novitiates weren't always so calm.

"So, you are Six. That is a very holy designation, you know." It said nothing, and she asked it cheerfully, "Tell me: Who is the Sixth God?"

This was an old riddle from the Godtexts, one with no answer. A person from Ma'kess would claim the god Makala. A person from Quietus would say Capamame. Katishsaan favored Kata, and so on, each planet giving primacy to its own god. Asking the question was just a way to figure out where a person's loyalty or origins lay. This student looked Katish to her, but maybe it would claim a different loyalty?

Then it said, "There is no Sixth God, Sa. Only the Godfire."

She tilted her head curiously. So, it claimed no loyalty, no planet of origin. Only a devotion to the Kindom, for whom the Godfire held primacy. How . . . strategic.

She ignored its answer, asking, "Do you know who I am?"

The silence in the room seemed to deepen, as if some great invisible creature had sucked in its breath.

"Yes, Burning One. You are Esek Nightfoot."

She saw the other children from the corner of her eye, looking tense and excited.

She nodded. "Yes." And bent closer to it. "I come from a very important family," she said, as if it didn't know. "That's a big responsibility. Perhaps you know what it's like?"

For the first time, it showed emotion—a slight widening of the eyes. Almost instantly, its expression resolved back into blankness.

"The master says you don't know who you are...Is that true, little fish?"

"We don't have names, Sa."

She grinned. "You are very disciplined. From all accounts, so was Lucos Alanye."

Its throat moved, a tiny swallow. It knew *exactly* what family it came from. The kinschool master was a fool.

"Do you know," Esek said, "all the First Families of the Treble are required to give of their children to the Kindom? One from each generation must become a Hand. My matriarch selected me from my generation. It seems fate has selected you from yours."

There was a fierceness in its eyes that said it liked this idea very much—though, of course, the Alanyes were not a First Family. Lucos himself was nothing more than an upstart and opportunist, a resource-raping traitor, a genocider. Esek half admired him.

"Your family did mine a great service," she said.

It looked wary now, a little confused. She nodded. "Yes, my family controls the sevite factories. And do you know who are the laborers that keep our factories going?"

This time it ventured an answer, so quiet its voice barely registered, "The Jeveni, Sa."

"Yes! The Jeveni." Esek smiled, as if the Jeveni were kings and not refugees. "And if Lucos Alanye had never destroyed their moon world, the Jeveni would not need my family to employ them, would they? And then, who would run the factories? So you see it is all very well, coming from the bloodline of a butcher. All our evils give something back."

The student looked at her with that same wariness. She changed the subject.

"What do you think of your performance today?"

Its face hardened. "The fight had no honor, Sa."

Esek's brows lifted. They were conversing in Ma'kessi, the language of the planet Ma'kess. But just then, the student had used a Teron word for "honor." One that more accurately translated to "bragging rights." Perhaps the student was from the planet Teros? Or perhaps it had a precise attitude toward language—always the best word for the best circumstance.

"You struck your attackers eighteen times. Is there no honor in that?"

"I lost. Honor is for winning."

"But the master cheated you."

The invisible creature in the room drew in its breath again. Behind her she could *feel* the master's quickening pulse. Esek's smile brightened, but Six looked apprehensive. Its compatriots were glancing uneasily at one another, discipline fractured.

She said, "Beyond these walls, out in the world, people don't have to tell you if you've won. You know it for yourself, and you make other people know it. If I were you, and the master tried to cheat me out of my win, I'd kill him for it."

The tension ratcheted so high that she could taste it, thick and cloying. Six's eyes widened. Before anything could get out of hand, Esek laughed.

"Of course, if *you* tried to kill the master, he would decapitate you before you'd even lifted your little stave off the ground, wouldn't he?"

It was like lacerating a boil. The hot tightness under the skin released, and if there was a foul smell left over, well...that was worth it.

"Tell me, Six," she carried on, "what do you want most of all?"

It answered immediately, confidence surging with the return to script, "To go unnoticed, Sa."

She'd thought so. These were the words of the Cloaksaan. The master wouldn't be parading its best student under her nose like a bitch in heat if the bitch didn't want to be a cloaksaan—those deadly officers of the Kindom's Brutal Hand, those military masterminds and shadow-like assassins, who made peace possible in the Treble through their ruthlessness. Esek had only ever taken cloaksaan novitiates. It was an idiosyncrasy of hers. Most clerics

trained clerics and most secretaries trained secretaries, but Cleric
Nightfoot trained cloaksaan.

"You held back in the first five fights," she remarked.

The child offered no excuses. Did she imagine defiance in its
eyes?

"That's all right. That was smart. You conserved your strength
for the fight that mattered. Your teachers might tell you it was cow-
ardly, but cloaksaan don't have to be brave. They have to be smart.
They have to win. Right?"

Six nodded.

"Would you like to be my novitiate someday, little fish?" asked
Esek gently.

It showed no overt excitement. But its voice was vehement. "Yes,
Burning One."

She considered it for long moments, looking over its body, its
muscles and form, like it was a racehorse she might like to sponsor.
It knew what she would see, and she felt its hope. Her smile spread
like taffy, and she said simply, "No."

She might as well have struck it. Its shock broke over her like a
wave. Seeing that it could feel was important; unlike some Hands,
she didn't relish an emotionless novitiate.

"I won't take you. More than that, I'm going to tell the other
Hands not to take you."

The child's stunned expression nearly made her laugh, but she
chose for once to be serious, watching it for the next move. Its
mouth opened and closed. Clearly it wanted to speak but knew it
had no right. She gave it a little nod of permission, eager to hear
what it would say. It glanced toward its master, then spoke in a
voice so soft, no one would hear.

"Burning One...I am not my ancestor. I am—loyal. I am Kindom in my heart."

She hummed and nodded. "Yes, I can see that. But haven't we
established? My family owes your ancestor a debt, for the Jeveni,
and I don't care if you're like him or not. The fact is, I find you
very impressive. Just as your master does, and your schoolkin do. I

imagine everyone finds you impressive, little fish. But that's of no use to me. I require something different."

Esek watched with interest as it struggled to maintain its composure. She wondered if it would cry, or lose its temper, or drop into traumatized blankness. When none of these things happened, but it only stood there with its throat bobbing, she dropped a lifeline.

"When you are ready, you must come directly to me."

Its throat stilled. She'd startled it again.

"You must come and tell me that you want to be my novitiate. Don't go to my people, or the other Hands. Don't announce yourself. Come to me unawares, without invitation."

It looked at her in despairing confusion. "Burning One, you're surrounded by novitiates. If I come to you without permission, your people will kill me."

She nodded. "That's right. They'll never let you through without my leave. What's worse, I probably won't even remember you exist. Don't feel bad. I never remember any of the little fish I visit in the schools. Why should I, with so many things to occupy me? No, in a couple of days, you'll slip my mind. And if, in a few years, some strange young person newly gendered and named tries to come before me and ask to be my novitiate, well! Even if you get through my people, I may kill you myself." A long pause stretched between them, before she added, "Unless..."

It was exhilarating, to whip the child from one end to the other with the power of a single word. Its eyes lit up. It didn't even breathe, waiting for her to name her condition. She leaned closer still, until their faces were only inches apart, and she whispered in a voice only it could hear, "You must do something *extraordinary*." She breathed the word into its soul, and it flowed there hot and powerful as the Godfire. "You must do something I have never seen before. Something memorable, and shocking, and *brutal*. Something that will make me pause before I kill you. I have no idea what it is. I have no idea what I'll *want* when that day comes. But if you do it, then I will make you my novitiate. Your ancestry won't matter. Your past won't matter. This moment won't matter.

You will have everything you deserve: all the honor a life can bring. And you will earn it at my side."

The child stared at her, caught in the terrible power of the silence she let hang between them. And then, like a fishersaan cutting a line, she drew back. Her voice was a normal volume again, and she shrugged.

"It's not a great offer, I'll grant you. Probably you'll die. If you choose not to come to me, I won't hold it against you. I won't remember you, after all. There are other, excellent careers in the Kindom. You don't have to be a Hand to do good work. Someone as talented as you could be a marshal or guardsaan. The master says you're good at casting. You could be an archivist! But whatever you decide, I wish you luck, little fish." She pinned it with her mocking stare. "Now swim away."

It blinked, released from the spell. After a moment of wretched bewilderment, it dropped back into place beside its schoolkin, who looked most shocked of all; one was crying silently. She whirled around, each click of her boots on the stone floor like a gunshot. The gold threads in her coat caught the light until she shimmered like a flame.

She locked eyes with the master, whose friendliness had evaporated in these tense minutes. He was now marshaling forty years of training into a blank expression, but Esek sensed the cold terror in him. No one in his life had seen him this frightened before, and the shame of it, of all these little fourth-years witnessing it, would torture him.

Esek moved as if she would go right past him, but paused at the last moment. They were parallel, arms brushing, and she heard his minuscule gasp. Perhaps he expected the plunge of the bloodletter? As a Hand of the Kindom, she had every right to kill him if she judged his actions unrighteous. Still, knowing he was afraid of it happening was its own reward—and she didn't feel like dealing with the aftermath today. Instead, she studied the master's face. He was staring straight forward, as well trained as the students, and just as vulnerable.

"Graduate it to the eighth-years."

The master's temple ticked. "You've already determined that no Hand will make it their novitiate. It has no future here."

Esek chuckled, amazed at the brazenness of this master. "Let it decide on its own. Personally, I think this one will find its way. Or has your confidence in it proved so fickle?" The master was silent, and this time Esek's voice was a threatening purr. "What about your confidence in *me*, Master? I am your window to the glory and wisdom of the Godfire. Don't you believe in the power of the Clerisy?" She drew out the final word, clicking the *C* with malevolent humor.

The master nodded shortly. "Of course, Sa. I will do as you say."

Esek smiled at him. She patted his shoulder, enjoying the flinch he couldn't control. She was preparing to murmur some new ridicule into his ear, when a voice interrupted them.

"Burning One."

She looked toward the marble staircase, where her novitiates still stood. They had been there all this time, invisible until she had need.

"Yes?" Esek asked. "What is it?"

"You have a message from Alisiana Nightfoot. The matriarch requests your presence at Verdant."

Esek clucked her tongue. "No rest for a Nightfoot." She swept past the master without farewells. She heard his barely discernible exhale of relief, and then the trio of novitiates were behind her, following her up the stairs. They retraced their steps to the school gates and the tarmac, where her docked warcrow awaited them. As they went, she called over her shoulder, "Send word to the Cloaksaan that they should visit the master. I think his tenure has run its course."

orbit

Follow us:

f **/orbitbooksUS**

X **/orbitbooks**

▶ **/orbitbooks**

Join our mailing list
to receive alerts on our
latest releases and deals.

orbitbooks.net

Enter our monthly
giveaway for the chance
to win some epic prizes.

orbitloot.com